Black Abbey

Black Abbey

MAY CROMMELIN

(AUTHOR OF ‘ORANGE LILY’, etc.)

Introduction, notes and glossary by Philip Robinson

PUBLISHED BY THE ULSTER-SCOTS ACADEMY PRESS FOR THE
ULSTER-SCOTS LANGUAGE SOCIETY

Black Abbey by Maria Henrietta De la Cherois (May) Crommelin was first published in London in 1882. This edition has been edited with introduction, notes and glossary by Philip Robinson.

ISBN 978-1-8384549-6-8

CONTENTS

INTRODUCTION

Maria Henrietta Delacherois-Crommelin (1849-1930) was known as 'May' Crommelin, and was born on the 30th August 1849, the second daughter of Samuel Arthur Hill Delacherois-Crommelin of Carrowdore Castle (1817-85). She was the author of over 50 books, short stories, and magazine articles, and became widely known as a travel writer as well as a novelist. May Crommelin continued to live, at least part of the year, in Carrowdore Castle until the 1880s when, after her father died in 1885, she took up semi-permanent residence in London. Her 1930 gravestone in England records "MARIA HENRIETTA F.R.G.S. AUTHORESS second daughter of S. de la Cherois CROMMELIN of Carrowdore Castle, Co. Down Ireland".

The first book by May Crommelin was published anonymously in 1874 when she was only 24 years of age. *Queenie. A novel* was a 3-volume romance, as was her second novel *My Love She's But a Lassie*, published in 1875. These were set in Canada, England, and Ireland, but without much local reference or description, and largely restricted to high society. Her next three books had an unmistakably Ulster backdrop: *A Jewel of a Girl*, (1877), based around Cushendun and north Antrim; *Orange Lily*, (1879), set in the area of Carrowdore in the Ards Peninsula of east Down, and *Black Abbey* (1882), located at Greyabbey, near Carrowdore.

Black Abbey is Greyabbey

Although there is an adjacent townland to Greyabbey that is indeed called "Blackabbey", this novel is unquestionably set in and around the village of Greyabbey. It was a characteristic of May Crommelin's Ulster novels that she used an adjacent place-name as a fictional substitute for the otherwise obvious setting of the real place. In *A Jewel of a Girl* (1877), set in Cushendun, county Antrim, the name of 'Red Bay' is used (and is referred to as such in *Black Abbey* and *Orange Lily* too). In *Orange Lily* (1879) May Crommelin's home village is renamed "Ballyboly" (the townland of Ballyboley lies between Carrowdore and Greyabbey), and it is in *Orange Lily* that May Crommelin anticipates her sequel, and first calls Greyabbey by its new 'fictional' name: "*One day in the following week there was some talk up at the farm about a wedding to be held on the morrow in the village of Blackabbey, about a mile away.*"

The medieval Cistercian monastery of Greyabbey was established in 1193 and both it and the village which grew up beside it on the shore of Strangford Lough have, since the 17th century, been contained within the (Scots Plantation) estate of the Montgomery family. About two miles distant, mid-way between Greyabbey and Ballywalter, is the site of the 'real' Blackabbey, but with no visible remains of any old buildings. A Benedictine priory was founded there in 1204 as the priory of St. Andrew of the Ards, although it was better known as the Black Abbey or the Black Priory.

In May Crommelin's *Black Abbey*, the "De Burgo" landlord's house of "Black Abbey" had within its wooded demesne "old chapel ruins" build by the "Black Abbey Monks" 700 years previously that (in the late 19th century) "*lay most picturesquely in a small hollow, wooded all around, and amid which slid quietly the brook that laughed through the portions of wall still remained, however: one pierced with a fine chapel window; another, in which a low arched doorway, with zigzag carved edging, faintly bore witness to the chapel's hey-day of fresh-built fairness seven hundred long years ago.*"

When *Black Abbey* was published in 1882, the ruins of the Greyabbey monastery did indeed lie within the private grounds of Rosemount (Greyabbey) House.

May Crommelin's Dutch Calvinist and French Huguenot roots

In May Crommelin's *Orange Lily*, the strength of the Williamite sympathies of the author for the Orange dimension of local folk-culture is perhaps surprising, coming, as it does, from a 'gentry' perspective. Similarly, a broadly sympathetic understanding of the radical Presbyterian 'dissenter' tradition of the local Ulster-Scots tenantry is perhaps even more so, given her family's long-standing Anglican church association. But Maria Delacherois-Crommelin's family background did not have the usual Anglo-Irish credentials. In fact, both the Delacherois and the Crommelin sides of her ancestry were French Huguenot Calvinists in origin.

In the late 17th century, Louis Crommelin, from whom May was descended, was living in Holland as leading member of the French Huguenot refugee colony there. In common with the Duke of Schomberg and most of the other Huguenots in the Netherlands, he had pledged support to Prince William of Orange in the religious wars in Europe leading up to the Glorious Revolution of 1688 in England and the 1690 Battle of the Boyne in Ireland. After the events of 1688-1691, Louis Crommelin received a personal invitation and a royal grant from King William III to lead a Huguenot colony of 70 French-speaking families, including two of Louis' brothers, three sisters and some cousins, in establishing the linen industry on the Dutch model in Lisburn in 1698. Over 1000 looms and 'Dutch' spinning wheels were imported from Holland. In consideration of Louis Crommelin having spent £10,000 on the venture, William III also conferred a pension of £200 a year on Louis' son.

In the winter of 1689/90 a French pastor, Jean Dubourdieu, had acted as chaplain to the Huguenot regiments in the Lisburn area, and by 1711 the Huguenot colony had grown to 120 familes with its own French-speaking pastor and church. Despite the Huguenots being originally Calvinists, they conformed to the established Church of Ireland right from the start in response to their royal patronage. Many of the early Crommelins are buried in Lisburn Cathedral, including May Crommelin's ancestor Louis Crommelin.

But May's full surname was Delacherois-Crommelin, and she was equally descended from another first-generation member of the Williamite Huguenot colony at Lisburn—Nicholas De la Cherois. Daniel De la Cherois, a brother of Nicholas, arrived in Lisburn in 1699 after having married Marie Angelique Crommelin (a cousin of Louis Crommelin) in London. Nicholas had also married before coming, in his case Mary Crommelin, a sister of Louis. Nicholas and Mary's grandson Samuel De la Cherois then adopted the composite name Delacherois-Crommelin in accordance with the conditions of the will of his cousin, Nicholas Crommelin of Lisburn. Both Nicholas senior and his brother Daniel De la Cherois fought at the Battle of the Boyne in 1690.

In 1689 King William III had formed two regiments of French Huguenots which he brought to England from Holland. In the first of these, Nicholas De la Cherois (May's great, great, great-grandfather) was appointed major, his brother Daniel De la Cherois a captain, and yet another brother, Bourjonval De la Cherois, a lieutenant. They all landed in Ireland at Groomsport in 1689, and accompanied King William from Carrickfergus on his march south to face King James in 1690. Major Nicholas De la Cherois distinguished himself at the Battle of the Boyne. Afterwards, with only a small band of men, he made 1,500 of King James's men lay down their arms, and was presented with a large reward of 1,500 crowns for this action. Bourjonval De la Cherois was killed at Dungannon by rebels in the aftermath of the battle, and Daniel De la Cherois was rewarded for his actions by being appointed governor of Pondieberry in the East Indies.

INTRODUCTION

In the Public Record Office of Northern Ireland is an unpublished manuscript: "Louis Crommelin, His life. His Ancestors, His People, His Descendents" written by "Miss May Crommelin, of Carrowdore Castle". It contains not only a full account of the family connections with William of Orange, but also an unabridged and detailed aaccount of the atrocities suffered by her Protestant Huguenot ancestors in France. But this knowledge of her Huguenot identity was not simply the result of geneological research into 'family history' on May's part, but deeply ingrained in the family psyche.

"Bridget Colbert", the young heroine of *A Jewel of a Girl* (1877) acts as a fictional outlet for May Crommelin to express her Dutch Huguenot pride. In the novel, Bridget discovers, in the library of her Cushendun home, a leather-bound manuscript book written in French called "The Colbert Chronicles" which is clearly her own Crommelin family's history tracing the movement of the Huguenot family from France to Holland with every gory detail of slaughtered infants and other genocidal persecutions described in the novel. These family stories were collected not only at home in Carrowdore Castle, but also in the Netherlands where she spend many holidays with her Dutch Crommelin relations. The dedication of *A Jewel of a Girl* is:

> *"To, Hermann Crommelin and his children, in memory of pleasant days spent at Oud Berkenroede, this story is dedicated by their Irish Cousin, the Writer. September. 1877"*

At a later point in the story of *A Jewel of a Girl*, Bridget travels to the Netherlands with her aunt "Ina Colbert" and stays with her Dutch Huguenot "Colbert" cousins! While there (at "Weide Zigt" near Haarlem) they all set out on a Sunday morning for church – the "French Protestant One." The description of the strict Calvinist service resonates so closely with the Scots Presbyterian forms of the day in Ulster that we can understand why the theme of Ulster-Scots Presbyterianism practice (rather than doctrine) was so properly understood by the author when it came to making this a dominant theme of the novel *Black Abbey*:

> *"The ancient church stood round the corner of a narrow, cobble-paved street. Through the old doors, over uneven stone flooring, the womankind passed up the plain building to their cane chairs; while the men sat around the walls in pews, rather like open whitewashed ward-robes, with their hat-pegs behind them, and desks in front, adorned with copper candle-sticks, above which their very few heads appeared like Jacks-in-the-box. The whitewashed walls; narrow windows, hung with green curtains; the organ, that, like many a human being, had grown hoarse and querulous-voiced with age; the sombre pulpit (a mighty wooden two-decker, wherein the clerk commanded below, and the pasteur nearer the ceiling, beneath his sounding-board)—all gave an impression of severe simplicity. … The service began. A canticle was given out, which all, still sitting, sang. The singing was not beautiful, and was inexpressibly slow; but the whole breath of each singer was honestly given; and the good intentions therewith mingled may have—who knows?—fused the discordancy into true sweetness as the words rose upwards beyond hearing of mere human ears. Then entered the stout pasteur, in his black gown, ascended his pulpit, and looking down upon his brethren and sisters, gently invited them to "prier Dieu," and gave an extempore prayer. After this, they sang one psalm of fine old Clement Marot, that did one's heart good—such a one as persecuted Huguenots chanted in caves, or among lonely vineyards, in secret meetings … ".*

The Ulster-Scots Presbyterian ethos of the *Black Abbey* commonality

In *Orange Lily*, May Crommelin's 'prequel' to this story, the author displayed (and recorded for posterity) a convincing insight into the vernacular voice of the *'Scotch-speaking descendants of*

Scotch-bred colonists' in the Carrowdore / Greyabbey area. The quantity of Ulster-Scots linguistic content is perhaps greater in *Orange Lily* than in *Black Abbey*, but as the glossary at the end of this book will confirm, this does not apply to the quality or authenticity. The reason is simple. There is a difference between the two novels in the frequency of appearance of Ulster-Scots speaking characters, always limited (correctly) to the commonality – the tenant farmers, workers, and other individuals below the social status of the gentrified 'big house' and the 'educated' Presbyterian manse which takes centre stage in *Black Abbey.*

Black Abbey opens with "Rev. Joseph Cosby", the kindly old Presbyterian minister of "Black Abbey" Presbyterian Church, bringing home to the manse his orphaned grand-daughter "Bella". The novel unfolds a story of Bella's childhood interaction with the "De Burgo" children in the landlord's house – a story that develops into adult relationships fraught with social, cultural and even intellectual tensions between the 'Established Church' family and the Presbyterian one. Indeed, the manse household is soon enlarged by the arrival of a nephew of the old minister, "Luke Cosby", who in due course becomes the new 'young minister' of Black Abbey.

In terms of social status, the superior attitude of the De Burgos towards their overwhelmingly Presbyterian underlings often manifested in their attitude towards the Cosbys:

> *"Dear old Luke!' he added, 'what a good fellow he used to be! What a pity he is only a Presbyterian minister!*
>
> *... the world is big and crowded; and I am afraid, among my circle of acquaintance, no Presbyterian minister little short of the fame of Moses would be likely to be known*
>
> *... It was sad that she herself was only a Presbyterian minister's granddaughter; but still, gentlemen would not mind that."*

"Bella", the Presbyterian minister's granddaughter, had to be 'renamed' by the patronising De Burgo children if she wanted to play with them, as her name sounded too common. So "Bella" becomes "Bonnibel" (Scots: *bonny belle*).

Greyabbey's Presbyterian 'troubles', and their manifestation in the *Black Abbey* story

Throughout the 18th and 19th centuries, the population of Greyabbey Parish was over 70% Presbyterian (with about 20% Episcopalian Church of Ireland and 10% Roman Catholic and 'other'). The rural part of the district was even more 'Presbyterian' – actually over 90%, but this marked a contrast with the residents of the village of Greyabbey. The largest denomination there was Church of Ireland (about 50%), and with the Presbyterians only making up about 30% of those living in the town or on the Greyabbey (Rosemount) House estate, virtually the entire rural class of tenant farmers, small-holders and farm labourers in the surrounding countryside was Presbyterian.

In May Crommelin's neighbouring home district of Carrowdore there was a very similar religious demographic. Her own household at Carrowdore Castle and a significant number of the Carrowdore villagers adhered to the Episcopalian Church, but the surrounding rural district was again overwhelmingly Presbyterian.

But the Presbyterians of this part of the Ards Peninsula were, in reality, very far from being a monolithic religious block. The longest 'internal' controversy within the denomination across Ulster during the 18th century was between liberal 'New Light' ministers and congregations on the one hand, and the generally conservative 'Old Light' ministers and congregations on the other. Their actual differences were complex, with each side often grossly misrepresenting the 'errors' of the other. When the majority attempted to enforce orthodoxy by compelling all Presbyterian ministers and elders to 'subscribe' to the Westminster Confession of Faith on ordination, open warfare was declared, and two separate Presbyterian denominations began disputing ownership of Meeting Houses and appointments of ministers. The 'New Light' faction were generally a minority across Ulster but their break-away 'Non-Subscribing Presbyterian' group became a separate denomination as the 'Remonstrant Synod of Ulster' in the 1820s.

As an Episcopalian, May Crommelin's understanding of these Calvinistic disputes among her Ulster-Scots neighbours in the surrounding population might seem surprising. But although her family had been Espicopalian since her Dutch Huguenot ancestors arrived in Ulster with the Williamite army in the 1690s, this was due to their absolute loyalty to King William III and the Established Church that he became the Head of. The former Prince of Orange had, of course, been a Calvinist member of the Dutch Reformed Church and May Crommelin's visits to her own Dutch cousins had aroused great interest in her own French-speaking 'Calvinist' and Huguenot roots.

If the Presbyterians of the Carrowdore area were largely orthodox and 'Old Light' Calvinists, the opposite was the case in Greyabbey. Probably the best known Presbyterian minister of Greyabbey was Rev. James Porter who was hanged by Lord Londonderry in 1798 for suspected involvement with the United Irish insurrection. In theological terms, he was overtly 'New Light' and took the Arminian stance in opposition to strict Calvinism. Significantly, the Arminians took their name from Jacobus Arminius (1560-1609), a Dutch theological student and minister of the Dutch Reformed Church who opposed the strict Calvinist teaching on Predestination. After his death some of his followers gave support to his views by signing the

Remonstrance in 1610. In 1629, however, the works of Arminius were published for the first time, and by 1630 the Remonstrant Brotherhood had achieved legal toleration. It was finally recognized officially in the Netherlands in 1795. When the Ulster Presbyterian 'New Lights' formed their own denomination in 1830, they called their Synod the 'Remonstrant Synod of Ulster', and the small number of Presbyterian church buildings they then controlled were called 'Remonstrant Meeting Houses'. Clearly these Dutch Reformed Church connections struck a chord with May Crommelin, and she recognised a tradition that she could strongly relate to intellectually, historically and culturally, if not necessarily in terms of religious doctrine. To create a plausible fictional context to explore this theme, there could have been no better setting than "Black Abbey".

In 1830 the "Greyabbey Affair" occupied pages of newspaper space, as an unholy precedent-setting battle took place between the Remonstrants and the Orthodox Presbyterians for the possession of the pulpit and the Meeting House at Greyabbey. The sitting 'New Light' minister, Rev James Watson (with almost universal support from his congregation), had 'joined with' the Remonstrant Synod. The reaction of the Presbyterian Synod was to declare that if one or two members of any breakaway congregation wanted to remain 'orthodox', they could apply to the Bangor Presbytery for a replacement orthodox minister. This was done by a handful of 'Old Light' members and they obtained the Greyabbey landlord's approval for the transfer of the Greyabbey Meeting House to them and had a replacement minister approved by Wm. Montgomery, Esq. With the real prospect of public disorder on Sunday morning and two rival ministers attempting to occupy the pulpit, Mr Montgomery (as Magistrate as well as Landlord), declared in favour of the Orthodox party, and had the Meeting House Door nailed shut and placed an armed guard there.

On the arrival of the 'old minister' Rev. John Watson, Mr Montgomery had Watson arrested and marched off under armed escort to Carrowdore Castle! This was 20 years before May was born, but nonetheless an event deeply impressed in her mind. However, Mr Crommelin of Carrowdore Castle had no intention of getting involved. The *Belfast Guardian* carried this report:

> *"The Rev. John Watson was again arrested Sunday last, on order of Wm. Montgomery, Esq. Rosemount, J.P., on his way to the Meeting house, at the Cross-roads, under the idea that his presence there would tend to excite riot. After his arrest, he was transmitted to Carrowdore Castle, the residence of D. Crommelin, Esq. J.P. Here Mr. Watson refused to give bail, when requested to do by Mr. Crommelin, who, after sometime, declined interfering further in the matter. Mr. Watson was then brought to Mr. Montgomery's at Rosemount, and having there also refused to give bail, he was liberated, after having been some hours detained in custody."*

In *Black Abbey*, the kindly old minister "Rev. Joseph Cosby" is probably based on the badly-abused Rev. John Watson of the 1830s, but "Rev. Luke Cosby" (the new young minister and nephew of Joseph Cosby) was even more likely based on Watson's successor in the 1860s, William Hall. It was Rev William Hall who was minister in Greyabbey's Meeting House during the time May Crommelin lived in Carrowdore. He was a charismatic preacher and innovator whose career closely echoed that of "Luke Cosby", including a lecture tour in America to raise funds to rebuild the Meeting House.

The outcome of the 'Greyabbey Affair' of 1830 was a very public apology from Mr Montgomery of Rosemount House to the Remonstrants – declaring not only that they were the legal possessors of the Meeting House, but also that he himself (although not a Presbyterian) was in agreement with them doctrinally.

The following letter from William Montgomery, Esq. of Rosemount, to the Rev. H. Montgomery, appeared in the *Northern Whig* of 4 March 1830, and it castigated those of the orthodox minority that had 'deceived' him:

GREYABBEY AFFAIR

"SIR—I have to thank you for transmitting to me the copy of the Minutes of the General Synod, held at Cookstown, in 1828; which I shall, as you request, return on the earliest occasion. Should I see Mr. Alexander Montgomery, as I expect, tomorrow, I shall give both it, and also the book of 1829, to his charge. These documents, and your very civil communication, have completely opened my eyes to the deceits that have been practised upon me. No man, unless his errors be intentional, can, or might to be ashamed of acknowledging them; and, I am free to admit, that the representations which had been made to me, from a quarter, and in a manner that I could hardly discredit, gave me a most false impression of the conduct and proceedings of the Remonstrants in this parish. I now feel myself called upon to give you the most ample assurance, that those erroneous impressions are completely erased from my mind, at the same time, hoping, that you may be induced to accept the apology which I now, with perfect sincerity, offer, for having ever entertained them. That my motives should have been misapprehended by you, is most natural, as certainly appearances were strongly against me. I am little known beyond my own private circle; my pursuits have been such as not to place me before the public; nor am I at all ambitious of that distinction; but those who are acquainted with my disposition well know, that of all men I am the last who would even listen to a suggestion which I thought could, in the slightest manner, infringe on the liberty of the subject, much less exercise my authority, as a Magistrate, with an oppressive intention, or to promote party views. — In the conversation I had last week with you, I mentioned, that it was farthest from my intention, at any time,

to interfere with religious disputes; or, in this instance, to take any part, as was imagined, with the Synod. This statement I now give to you under my hand, confirmed by the assurance, that I am about to have the sometime promised lease of this Meeting-house drawn up, to be granted in trust for the Congregation of the Remonstrant Presbytery of Bangor. I have attentively examined the Overtures and Protest; I have compared them with the Westminster Form of Presbyterian Church Government; and am sure, it must be evident to the weakest understanding, that the Overtures are in direct contravention of their Code. I shall only add, that so perfectly am I convinced of their being subversive of the liberties of Presbyterianism, that were I a member of your Church, while I declare myself a Trinitarian in faith, though certainly not according to the doctrine of the Westminster Confession, I should most assuredly be a zealous Remonstrant. I trust that you will permit me to subscribe myself now, and for the future, my dear Sir, with esteem, your sincerely obliged,

WM. MONTGOMERY.

P. S. — I beg you will consider yourself at full liberty to make whatever use of this letter you please,

Greyabbey, 26th February, 1830."

This letter from William Montgomery of Rosemount House, J P and landlord of Greyabbey, was addressed to the formidable leader of the Remonstrant cause in Ulster, the Rev Dr Henry Montgomery. As an ex-Moderator of the General Presbyterian Synod of Ulster, Dr Montgomery became the unrivalled champion of the New Light Presbyterians' refusal to 'subscribe' to the Westminster Confession of Faith, just as Dr Henry Cooke was the celebrated champion of the 'subscribers' or orthodox party. It was largely due to Dr Montgomery that a share of Presbyterian Church property and of the Regium Donum were preserved to his section of the church. Finally ousted, the minority orthodox members of the Greyabbey congregation were granted a plot of land by Mr Montgomery on the Strangford Lough shore to build a church that was known as the "Old Light Meeting House" (later Trinity Presbyterian Church on a different site). But this grouping or property gets no mention in *Black Abbey*.

The historical reality of Wm. Montgomery's liberal and tolerant support for the Greyabbey Presbyterians stands in contrast to the portrayal of the semi-absentee landlord "Mr De Burgo" by May Crommelin in *Black Abbey* as a snobbish tyrant. Indeed, the author had also caricatured the landlord and head of the Carrowdore Castle household in much the same light in *Orange Lily*, a fictional commentary clearly not based on her own family experience.

But it is the representation of the Presbyterian ministers in *Black Abbey* that make this book an exceptional commentary on the religious complexities of life in an Ulster-Scots community, warts and all. The two main protagonists in this regard are both Presbyterian ministers: Mr McCloy from 'a neighbouring parish' who is so rude, pompous and intolerant as to make his Old Light views a personification of darkness itself; and Luke Cosby, nephew of the manse and the 'young minister' (once the story and its characters mature).

The debates in the Black Abbey manse between the 'liberal', urbane, intelligent and loveable New Light minister of Black Abbey (Luke Cosby) and the visiting Old Light 'neighbouring' minister with all the opposite qualities (Rev. McCoy) often focused on the late 19th century controversy of introducing instrumental music, hymns and choirs into Presbyterian 'Meeting Houses' – which in Scotland and Ulster had previously (since Calvin and Knox's day in the 16th century) exclusively practised unaccompanied 'psalmody' from the Scottish Psalter. In the mainstream Presbyterian churches this controversy didn't really manifest until after the 1880s. However in the Non-Subscribing Presbyterian church in Greyabbey, the minister (Rev. William Hall) was using a harmonium (played by his daughter) and hymns, as early as the 1860s. Rev. William Hall indeed also answers the description of "Luke Crosby" in many other ways, including undertaking a fund-raising lecture tour of America about 1864.

In the novel, Luke Cosby dreads the very arrival of Mr McCoy at the Black Abbey manse:

> *"'Verily! he is my arch-enemy,' groaned poor Luke, looking round the parlour as if it would be his horsehair-and-mahogany furnished torture-chamber for the next two hours. 'He is always hoping to prove me unorthodox from some careless word I may let slip, and watches my lips like a terrier at a rat-hole. But I will disappoint him. … I will put a watch upon the door of my mouth to-day. It would grieve poor Uncle Joe too much to have some of my opinions declared sins to him; although he is placidly aware that they are different from his own in some matters not necessary to salvation.'*
>
> *Their talk abruptly ended as the visitor, who was short and full-paunched, made his entrance with the sort of triumphal air often assumed by persons of his proportions. Soon the dinner began. Mr. McCoy, it is but truth to say, resembled a pig a good deal in his outline of head, expression of gaze, and manner of supping his mutton broth. His hands and nails, too, were dirty. What a contrast with Mr. Cosby …"*

When Mr McCoy couldn't follow the thread of Luke Cosby's discourse, he resorted to rudeness:

> *"Luke had somehow got to speaking of the doctrine of evolution to Nannie, in the strong hearty voice that was to her an encourage-*

> *ment in the mind-battles, to the old man a comforting assurance of orthodoxy—and that, to both, by its sound. Should evolution come to be held scientifically true, Luke would not shrink, he said (and the theory was then new!) from holding it as therefore theologically so—not inconsistent with the original act of creation; the revelation of such aeons-long-enduring a plan and purpose in God's continuous action upon the universe as was to him a thought of immeasurable grandeur—Mr. McCoy now broke in, with a humorous side-nod at Nannie, 'I haven't understood one word of all you've been favouring us with for the last half-hour, young man, he, he! nor, I'll venture to say, did others. 'Deed, I'm thinking ye've maybe blinded yourself with your own dust'"*

But the recurring issue (both historically and in May Crommelin's narrative) was the question of whether instrumental music was lawful or not in worship, and inextricably linked to that, the singing of hymns rather than psalms:

> *"Nannie now tried, in her turn, to keep the guest from leading the conversation, and addressing Luke, innocently said, 'It is a pity there is no harmonium here, you are so fond of music; and the Fräulein has sent me some grand stirring German airs this morning, which Luther would certainly have set hymns to, and not, as he said, left to the devil'*
>
> *She caught with surprise a look of sorrowful reproach from Mr. Cosby's mild face. But the stranger, patting his body, and then leaning back and stretching himself with a satisfied air as if assured he had laid in sufficient munition at dinner, said with a leer of aggressive insolence, as it seemed to Nannie's dainty discernment, 'It's to be hoped he'll keep his love of it to himself; and not be piping to his sheep in public worship, like too many false shepherds amongst us these days.'*
>
> *'And why not in public worship?' cried Luke, who, like a war-horse scenting the fray, could no longer restrain himself, but rushed to battle.*
>
> *The burning question, whether instrumental music was lawful*

or not in the Presbyterian form of worship, had begun between two opposing champions.

'He is too combative, that boy of mine; too combative!' murmured the poor old minister to Nannie in a mild agony, longing to pour oil on the troubled waters, but only it seemed, when he tried to intervene, pouring it on flames.

Mr. McCoy was rash enough at first to dare upon arguing out the matter, perhaps not rightly knowing how redoubtable was his opponent, nor that Luke was already considered one of the keenest in debate, as well as most eminent of scholars in his sect. His opponent was soon fairly overborne by the simoom-blast of that burning eloquence, which also silenced good Mr. Cosby into wondering admiration, and enchanted Nannie. But as soon as the storm was over, the asinine foe raised drooping ears and tried to show by a sarcastic bray that he was 'of the same opinion still.'

'Our young friend is apparently fond of musical boxes—he, he! He's of the rising generation you see, Miss White, and they like their play-toys.'

'Well,' said Nannie, whom he had addressed apparently as one of those 'silly women' alluded to by St. Paul, and merely wishing to let him know she had a mind of her own, 'it has always seemed to me that as St. John saw harps in heaven, it cannot be wrong for us to have music in our houses of God on earth.'

'It's no business of ours what the angels choose to do,' stuttered Mr. McCoy, getting into a rage; 'what we want is scriptural precedent for all we're to do; ay, that's it—ay! that's it. Did Paul travel with a barrel-organ?' (fuming and snorting). 'And, pray, where is it mentioned that fine ladies screeched like opera-singers in the sanctuary, as—as they do I'm told in your church?'

The eyes of both the other ministers were upon the fair and honoured guest; but she, though so wise and well-read in their eyes, made foolish answer with kindling grey eyes: 'When Miriam played and sang upon her timbrel before the Lord—'

'That will do. That will do. I thought you knew little about it,' interrupted Mr. McCoy, holding up an offensively obtrusive outspread palm in vast apparent pity of her ignorance. The two other

> *ministers looked inclined to smile, though respectfully grieved for their discomfited spokeswoman.*
>
> *'All that dancing and piping has no place nor divine sanction in the New Testament economy, young lady, having passed away with the beggarly elements of the ceremonial law.'"*

There can be no mistaking the author's position on these same issues. Indeed, it is hard to believe that she wasn't re-telling the substance of debates she had been involved in herself. But here we have another example of May Crommelin's unique contribution – a detailed and authentic record of the complexities of the Ulster-Scot's mind set in the 19th century.

PART I

'Mein Kind, wir waren Kinder,
Zwei Kinder, klein und froh;
Wir krochen ins Hühnerhäuschen,
Versteckten uns unter das Stroh.

'Wir krähten wie die Hähne,
Und kamen Leute vorbei —
"Kikereküh!" sie glaubten,
Es ware Hahnengeschrei,'

Heine.

'Play on, play on; I am with you there,
In the midst of your merry ring;
I can feel the thrill of the daring jump.
And the rush of the breathless swing.
I hide with you in the fragrant hay,
And I whoop the smother'd call,
And my feet slip up on the seedy floor,
And I care not for the fall.'

Willis.

CHAPTER 1

'ALL THE FIELDS ARE TIED UP FAST WITH HEDGES, NOSEGAY-LIKE'

ONE balmy spring evening, some thirty years ago, a shabby gig crawled homewards along the shore of a lough, of which the salt waters, after leaving the Irish Sea, twisted inland among low hills so tortuously as almost to separate a fair-size extent of country from the mainland.

In the gig sat only a stout, short, Presbyterian minister, and a little child.

Away westwards, in the heart of the dear, green island, the sun was sinking behind a range of shadowy violet hills with such crimson trailing glory, that half the sky over-head, and the wet, wide sands and gleaming shallows here on earth below, were rosy likewise. The lough was glorified this night; though at most low tides its surface was a bare, ugly sight.

On the other side of the road, the peninsula* itself showed an open, treeless country; all dimples and swells and rises, mapped out by ragged hawthorn hedges into innumerable thriftily tilled small fields, over which the salt breezes, from broad sea in front and narrower lough behind, blew ever fresh, imparting a sense of cleanliness as it were in their breath, that seemed to brace one morally as well as physically. Many a stranger praised that fine air, which seemed to have formed and nurtured the shrewd, hard-working, practical character of the folk of that north country. But foreign or sickly natures often pined there for softer airs and more southern landscapes; for warmth and colour,

* Ards Peninsula, County Down

and some of that beauty of nature which Black Abbey people thought of as no necessity, but a luxury.

On this evening, however, the clean prosaic country looks its best; for it is a May twilight, and all its network of hedges is snowy, and the whole air fragrant with hawthorn.

The little minister, sitting bolt upright, sniffed first the faint, sweet flower-scents from the one side, and soon after the salt odours of decaying, or tide-bare, sea-weeds from the shore, with perfectly equal pleasure.

'Sure, now, such a grand year for the hawthorn—that's your own flower, dearie!—never was,' he said cheerfully to the child. 'Truly, "the earth is the Lord's and the fulness thereof." … Ay! dear, ay! "The sea is His, and He made it; and His hands prepared the dry land" … Indeed, indeed! the lines have fallen unto me in pleasant places! I don't suppose, now, there is a pleasanter place to live in than Black Abbey* in the world.' (He looked about him with the most utter childlike contentment. He would have thought the same, most likely, had he been born in the Bog of Allen, or brought up in the Black Country.)

A broad-faced little man he was, dressed in a suit of rusty black and a limp white tie, which suggested truly that he had neither wife nor daughter to scold or coax him into tidiness. In person, one must own, he was podgy, while his features were, at first sight, far too rubicund to be reverend; but there was a guilelessness, an utter trusting innocence of expression about them, that made one think irresistibly of a middle-aged, ugly cherub, And few could look Joseph Cosby, the Presbyterian minister from Black Abbey, in the face without feeling comforted with a world that had, after all, produced so good a soul; one that was, at his age, still so transparent, so hopeful, and as

* Black Abbey = Greyabbey. The author also used this pseudonym for Greyabbey in *Orange Lily* (1879)

innocently, easily mirthful, as a babe that will laugh at anything but another's woe.

As he drove, he had fondly put one arm round the little girl in deep black at his side, so that one hand only was free to hold the reins. But that mattered little; for the old wall-eyed horse, fresh from reminiscences of the plough, 'dandered'* along at his own good will, and would have gone no faster had his master used the whip (which he had not the heart to do), or known how to drive—(which he didn't).

'Hup, hup! Tchk, tchk!' clacked the minister contentedly. 'Bella, dear! isn't this a nice drive?'

'You go very slow, grandpapa,' said Six-years-old with vast disapproval, as, in spite of all the noises that her reverend relative was making with his tongue, the beast of burden quietly stopped a moment to snatch a mouthful of grass.

'Are you warm, my wee birdie?'

'Yes, of course; if I wasn't, I'd tell you,' said the child, with admirable frankness and decision, and a sort of contemptuous wonder at her grandfather's ignorance of childhood's ways, since he thought she could be so silly as not to ask for whatever she wanted.

'Well, my pet,' he went on, suppressing a chuckle of amusement, but beaming with satisfaction at her air of intelligence, 'look now at the blue mountains—the Morne Mountains—away there. That big one is Slieve Donard.'†

'Big! I don't think it's very big,' said the little one with a dubious air; for, being unable to judge of distances, it looked to her mind like a haycock, that she and her doll could easily jump upon.

---

* dandered = ambled

† The Mourne Mountains and Slieve Donard are seen clearly from the lough-shore at Greyabbey

Her grandfather laughed.

'Ah! but then you come from America, dearie, where everything is larger than here—except little girls. Still old Ireland is—Hi! Oh, my! *Please* take care. Whoa, whoa … O dear, dear! … *Wynd!!*'

These last half-terrified, wholly pitiable ejaculations were called forth by a sudden and alarming incident. Their old horse, being off-horse in the plough, was obstinately hugging the hedge on the right-hand side, when a farmer, exercising a colt bare-backed, in the cool of the evening, came round a corner screened by hawthorn. They seemed, to the helpless old minister, to get all mixed up with the gig; while he himself pulled wildly at the wrong rein in his nervousness, blocking up the road thereby, and making the young horse plunge.

At last matters got righted, and the farmer pulled up beside the gig.

'I'm feared you're not good, yet, at the driving, Mr. Cosby. Haw! haw! haw!' said he, with a deep laugh; as if things in this life seldom tickled his humour very much, but that the sight of his minister holding a pair of reins really *did*. But as the latter blushed to his very ears, while sounding his tongue in penitence against the roof of his mouth, the farmer went on in lusty reassurance. 'Well! well!—you'll be on your way home from Derry? I heard tell you were gone up there.'

'Yes, indeed. To fetch back my poor grandchild here.' And the good man gave a big, significant sigh.

'Ay, ay! Just so. … I *did* hear tell that your daughter, Mistress Hawthorn, had left a wee girl behind her, when she died out in America,' replied the farmer, with the averted glance, though matter-of-fact voice, that, in his class, betokens sympathy.

'Isn't she the very picture of her mother?' fondly went on the minister: regret for his loss, with delighted thankfulness in the possession of this living treasure, being curiously blended together as he regarded little Bella.

'Well, indeed, yes!—but a heap purtier. This one is a very bonny wee lass.'

The child bridled with pleasure at the compliment, young though she was. Certainly she was pretty; very pretty. A rosy-cheeked little maid, with brilliant brown eyes, and masses of waving brown chestnut hair, which now she shook back over her shoulders most engagingly. The most open face, the most charming air of assurance, that everybody in the world must love her and be delighted to obey her, had this poor minister's little grandchild in the shabby gig.

'Well, good evening to you, Mr. Muckle. We must be moving. Hup, hup! Tchk, *Wynd!* This last plough-man's ejaculation was hurled with indignation and reproach at the head of the old horse, who would not do more than just drag one leg after the other as slowly as was compatible with moving at all; though his master shouted, shook the reins, and tried therewith to beat him. But Dobbin whisked his ancient tail over the said reins, and tucked them down tight (a feat which the minister's habit of letting them dangle quite loose had taught him to execute), then crawled on with malicious triumph in his wicked old eye. Up jumped Bella, seized her grandfather's cotton umbrella in her little arms, and before he could utter a word, was banging the trickster's ribs soundly. Away started Dobbin in an alarmed trot, while Mr. Cosby, divided between dismay and delight, tried to restrain the final blows, but looked round laughing for applause at the farmer.

'Yon's a pair!—yon's a pair!' nodded Muckle to himself, with some queer-sounding explosions of a mirth that was called forth so rarely, he did not quite know how to express it; and a kindly pity at how the good minister was 'put upon' and deceived by man and even beasts. 'That very wean* can take more care

* wean = child

of herself,' was his final reflection, as the good man rode on, grinning and dangling his legs.

Meanwhile, the gig, leaving the lough, was making its way through dreary reclaimed bog-lands towards the coast of the Irish Sea. The after-glow had faded from the sky; the twilight deepened; white mist-blankets hung suspended over the surface of the damp low ground. Only for the all-pervading sweetness of spring, the view around would have been utterly displeasing to any one less contented than the good minister; but—with his little grandchild leaning her head against him, wrapped in his shawl, encircled by his arm and fast asleep—the worthy man was happy.

When the child re-opened her eyes, the country had changed. There were richer, bigger fields around; ashes in the hedgerows; and in front dark masses of wood enclosed by a park wall, their grandly swelling curves against the sky broken in the centre by the straight lines of chimneys belonging to what seemed a noble house among the trees. The lodge, with its arched gateway*, faced the road; beyond was utter leafy darkness, save for a little door of twilight that the strained eyesight could just discover at what seemed the far end of a long wooded drive.

'Oh, where does that go to, grandpapa?' asked the child eagerly, sitting up again.

'That is Black Abbey, dearie; and it belongs to Mr. De Burgo—who is older than I am, though you wouldn't think it.' (This last, *sotto voce*.)

'Are there any little children there?' went on Bella, who, like other children, cared only to hear of her kind

'(Now, how did she guess that, I wonder?) … Yes, my pet, three of them; without fathers or mothers either; just like you.

* The author's home at Carrowdore Castle had a lodge with arched gateway.

… Ah! dear, dear, it's queer to think of. … One little boy and two girls, dear.'

'I'm very glad,' thoughtfully replied the small damsel, still gazing with wide innocent eyes at those chimneys, 'because then I should like to marry that little boy, and live in that nice house.'

The grandfather was quite tickled with merriment, though for worlds he would not have hurt his little child's feelings, or those of any child, by showing he laughed at it.

'Oh! the sense; oh! the worldly wisdom of the babe,' he thought, giggling to himself like an aged child, with unexpected returns of his risible affection. … 'But the innocence, too! thinking the children up at Black Abbey just the same as herself. Ah! well, well, the little ones are no respecters of persons; many a good lesson they teach us, sinful and worldly that we are!'

'I would like to play with those little children, granda'. May I play with those children?' continued Bella, whose perseverance in sticking to an idea argued, if well directed, great things for her future.

'You'll have me to play with, birdie; and the dog and cat; and Luke—your cousin Luke,' replied the poor minister, a little grieved to find this little six-year-old creature would have wishes he could not gratify.

'Why is Luke my cousin?' persisted the child, who was in a mood to take nothing for granted till she had got her supper; though what doting grandfather could resent the gross disbelief of a cherub burying a sleepy curly head against one's shoulder?

'His papa was my step-brother, dearie, and very dear to me. And now Luke comes often to stay with me, and is like my own son, as you are my own wee granddaughter,' said the good man, fondly. 'Is she very tired? … Cheer up … We're almost home—almost home.'

They had meanwhile skirted a great corner of the demesne, always beside the park wall and under the deep shadow of woods. Now, in the open twilight country lay a shadowy, white-washed village; and further away a broad grey line against the paler grey horizon, whence came a fresher breeze, whispering of the sea.

And now the minister looked with a broad friendly smile at two fields, no better than those around, with as ragged hedges—but his own. Then a clump of ash-trees and brushwood; a tiny marsh, in which the sweet pale-lilac lady's-smocks stood up delicately here and there; next an orchard; a privet hedge topping a little white-washed wall. A wicket-gate and straight gravelled path led, through a modest garden plot, to a neat small farmhouse, witha 'hall door' opening onto the garden, a window on either side and four lesser ones above; the walls as snowy with whitewash as the outbuilding beyond; and all pleasantly set in the green of a few elms and elders. Beyond the garden was the yard gate on the road-side also; where stood in the twilight a lanky, shabbily-dressed lad of seventeen, with a gun on his shoulder, eagerly awaiting the gig.

'Well, uncle Joe! How are you?' he hallooed in a gay, pleasant young voice, while they were still far off.

'Well, my boy, *both* well—' shouted back the minister, as fond as he could, adding reverently in a more ordinary voice—'for which God be praised.'

'Sit up Bella, dearie,' he went on, as the gig turned in at the gate and stopped. 'I do declare the poor innocent is fast asleep.'

'Give her to me, Uncle Joe. I'll put down the gun,' said young Luke, holding out his arms to receive the dormouse that only curled herself round sleepily at the change, and put down her head on the lad's shoulder.

He felt a pleased sense of strength and of bestowing protection as this young helpless creature that had been sent from the other side of the world nestled to him, so warm and soft. He had no sister, and had often wished for such a little one.

And so Bella was carried over the threshold of her future home, into the snug small manse-kitchen that was redolent of tea and the frying of eggs and bacon.

CHAPTER 2

THREE LITTLE THIEVES

'MIND you come back in time for your lessons with the schoolmaster,' shrieked, in her native tongue, a German governess standing on the Black Abbey doorsteps on sunny afternoon.

'Ja, ja!'—'Oui, oui!'—'Yes!' shouted back in three different childish keys from far back down the drive, where the owners of the voices were in hot flight. The last yell came from a chubby, handsome boy who had far outstripped the lesser girls behind him; and who now, with his head thrown back and his arms braced tight, was swelling with pride at felling himself the fleetest, though biggest and eldest.

Away through the shrubberies they scampered, till, when out of sight of the house, the leader halted, waved his arm like a general, gazed about anxiously like a scout, and then ran in an opposite direction at apparently unutterable risk, selecting the most inconvenient of ways. He jumped ditches and fell on his nose; scratched himself in hedges, despising gates close by; finally made a hot, triumphant rush through the intricacies of a coppice, where he believed only himself and his accomplices behind could have threaded their way, ending in a great snowberry thicket wherein outlaws of his size were easily hidden. Beyond this was a grassy nook fronting a reedy mere, and almost hidden in the brushwood. Here he lay down panting; and the little girls, who had copied his every previous action with difficulty but devotion, did likewise, still more breathless. After a few moments, the leader found his voice again, and spake jeeringly:

'*I* answered her in English. She can't make me talk her lingo, as she does you.'

'Now, that's just like you. Hector, and it's not fair when you know we *have to!* burst out his sister Aileen, a sweet little gipsy, black-haired and blue-eyed, who got into a passion every alternate half-hour of her life, and was all love and penitence during the intervening ones.

'Yes,' chimed in the other and smallest girl, with a sense of touching upon a burning question which lent a curious earnestness and gravity to her words, 'it's all very well for you, 'cause you're a boy; and boys are let do everything that's nice. But your grandpapa says gurls must do what they're told—and we didn't want to be girls.' And the little speaker, who was a ward of old Mr. De Burgo, heaved a big, big sigh.

'I'd much rather have been a boy,' cried Aileen nobly; and not without reason.

Hector felt a pleasant inward swelling of complacent superiority; but perceiving, from their wounded air, that a rebellion was brewing in his natural female subjects, who could not always be reconciled to their inferiority, he thought it best to be soothing.

'Oh well, of course, I'd rather be a man,' said he, with big-voiced, kindly patronage. 'Still, it's very nice for you two to be girls; and it's wrong, I'm sure, to grumble. Every-body can't have the best, you know; and if there were no elder sons, what would become of the properties?'

An awed silence followed. The children could not imagine what evil would not have happened to Black Abbey if 'the heir,' as little Hector loved to hear himself called, had been born to petticoats.

'And now—to business!' cried the leader cheerfully.

'What shall we play at to-day? Speak you first; then I'll give my vote.'

This meant that his might differ from theirs—but would probably be decisive.

'Let's have a funeral, and bury you, Moonyface, because the digging would tire you,' cried Aileen, with kind consideration.

Poor little Nan, or Moonyface, faintly demurred.

'No, I have a better plan. But first beware—is any enemy near?' interrupted Hector, as captain of this desperate band of outlaws.

All looked cautiously around their den, where they believed no human foot had ever trod before themselves. None of their enemies—'big people'—were in sight.

'All safe,' pronounced Hector. Then, slapping his leg with a martial air, and curling a ferocious lip, he whispered his scheme in a tone that almost curdled the blood, while four round eyes dilated in eager awe.

'We are very badly treated. They have given us no brown sugar for ever so long! … We must steal some!'

Nannie gasped; Aileen shrieked with excitement.

'But how, Hector—how?'

'That's why, don't you see, that I have solemnly called you to consult,' retorted the captain testily; but added, with recovered grandiloquence: 'At least, I've begun our plot, for She thinks we're off in the chapel wood—but here we are.' (*She* was a dark allusion to the governess.)

It was then agreed that first the haylofts above the stables must be gained; this retreat having a fine outlook upon the house-foes.

'We'll go as red Indians—single file,' ordered Hector. 'I take the post of danger in front. Moonyface, keep behind me and look out well. T. B., you are not as afraid as she is—to the rear-guard.'

'It's very fine saying you've got worst,' muttered Aileen, alias Tomboy or T. B., in great disdain. 'It's far safer to be only looking ahead, with Nannie behind you to keep all safe there. But if you were always afraid somebody would be grabbing you behind, see if you wouldn't get the cold shivers down your back, *like I do!*

This remark being treated with lofty silence, they began their march; crawling like tortoises through most of a wet grass meadow, and spoiling future hay; making desperate rushes, and having hair-breadth escapes from being seen by the labourers as they neared the farm-yard; though no one would have heeded them. At last they gained the pleasant haven of the great byre, and sprang into a chaff-loft off it.

Here, choking, sinking, and 'lolloping along,' as Hector called it, they managed to squeeze through a tiny trap meant only to let the chaff through from the threshing-house, which they had now gained. This spot had the charm of being locked; but, without resting, they raised a rickety ladder and climbed to a series of old lofts overhead; some so dangerous that none else knew all their holes or would have ventured across them. At last, they gained the wished-for one, so full of hay that they could scarcely crawl through the top of the door. There they lay down panting after their terrible fatigues. It was to them an enchanting spot. Some of the windows were roughly shuttered, making a gloom delightful for burrowing in the up-heaped hay.

But others were open, giving passage to broad beams of sunlight in which the motes danced thick, whilst the swallows dashed in and out, building their nests against the old rafters overhead.

Hector peeped cautiously out.

Below lay the old-fashioned courtyard; opposite was the back of Black Abbey House, sunny, irregular, and solitary. Down there, was only an old coachman to be seen sauntering down an inclined path to the servants' door; up here were twilight, hay-heaps and desperate robbers.

'He's off to his tea, regular as the clock,' whispered Hector. 'No time to be lost now. Nannie, you must go.'

'Oh, not me, please!' implored that unhappy youngest brigand, of only five years of age.

'Of course, it must be you,' retorted Hector. 'Wouldn't they 'spect *me* in a minute, if they met me? I'm a marked man' (with a sigh), 'and Aileen always blunders. But you've got such an innocent baby face, you're just meant for a spy.'

Now the oath of allegiance to their captain had been taken with such solemn rites by his band (even to pricking their thumbs, and sucking reluctantly some drops of their own blood), that moderate tortures would hardly have made poor Moonyface disobey. So, in misery, she climbed down a ladder to the stables below—the despicably ordinary entrance to their fortress.

One minute passed—three, five. The watchers above began to tremble for their unhappy companion. Then a small figure, carrying a parcel as big as itself, was seen tottering up the incline from the servants' door, and—actually!!—put it down on the ground to rest herself. Out rushed the others swiftly—silently crossed the yard, and, dragging both Moonyface and parcel back to safety, pushed both, with heaves and struggles, up the ladder.

In the loft, Hector tore away some hay, disclosing a dark tunnel by the wall, into which all crept, while he again stuffed the entrance. Then, groping forward for three yards, they came to a round nest, completely covered by the superincumbent hay, but lit by a delightful window.

'A whole stone!!' said Hector, first breaking silence.

'Well, there's nothing like frightened people for doing things. My! *I* wouldn't have done it, not for a purse of gold. And won't we just catch it, if it's found out. … Girls, they'll hang us!'

Nannie burst into tears.

'I'd only have taken some handfuls,' chimed in Aileen.

'Oh! there'll be an awful whullabaloo!*'

Nan sobbed louder.

'Well, it's done now, and at all events we'll never betray you,' said Hector, with a consoling thump. 'They daren't really kill us, you know; so don't cry, old girl, but have some sugar. T. B., hoke† out the bread and butter.'

Thus elegantly adjured, Aileen disinterred a former candle-box containing a hoard of eatables, remarking, as she did so, 'The mice have been at it. '

'Never mind. They're clean animals,' said Hector, who, with prospective smacks of enjoyment, was liberally dispensing chubby fistfuls of sugar. 'And there's another dollop for you,' he continued, giving Nannie a second help, and affectionately putting his arm round her. 'Now, tell us all about it'

Nan, whose small soul was all devoted to Hector, dutifully obeyed.

'The back door was open; and cook's key was in her store-closet, so I turned it wis bos hands,' she explained. 'And I heard the clink-clink of tea-cups in the servants' hall, and something in my chest went jumping up and down. An' I was awfully 'fraid. And I seed this big parcel in front of me, with a wee hole snipped to peep in at the sugar. An' I was too frightened to wait; so I took it and ran, but it was so heavy! And then I near fell up the little path; and then you came.'

'Have some more,' said the captain, with his mouth full. For some time they ate sugar with stolid industry, feeling this a sort of duty, after the risks they had run to procure the delight.

Then Aileen observed, with a rather disgusted air, 'I think the sugar has grown nasty.' There seemed a tacit understanding on this point: so it was stuffed into the candle-box, and a council

* whullabaloo = widespread rumour

† hoke = dig, grub

of war held. A fresh hiding-place, away from their guilty booty, seemed now an immediate necessity.

'Let us get into the loft above the big archway,' suggested little Nan. 'We can pulley ourselves up, like the men do the oat-sacks.'

The others stared, amazed at the boldness of the idea; for poor Nannie's secret terror of being hanged, or sent to prison, had made her fairly desperate. But no sooner said than done.

The great archway—under which no carriages drove since Black Abbey was deserted, save for these children—was in a square tower, ending in a belfry that crowned the woods around, and was a landmark to the country*. The pulley-ropes Nan spoke of hung down from a trap-door dizzily high overhead. They had been used that morning, and carelessly left.

Hector, astride of a wooden support fastened to them, was soon pulled above; he then dragged up the little girls, whose arms ached, and whose courage almost oozed away at the sensation, nearly as horrible to Nannie as being hanged. But they had gained the oat-granary, only other-wise accessible through several store-rooms kept locked by the steward. They were indeed safe. A long time they played, till Hector, growing weary, teased the little girls, and they whimpered. At which, like a disgusted male, he gazed out of the windows; and at last gave an excited yell.

'There's the master—going away—going from the house. He's shaking his stick; he's in such a rage!'

'No lessons to-night—glorious!' shrieked Aileen, rushing to see the National schoolmaster, who taught them daily for an hour, disappearing far below. But the captain was dumb; and then slowly uttered, with a tragic gesture, 'It must be hours past lesson-time, and we'll all get whipped. ... And how are they ever to find us? — *We can't get down!*'

A horrible, round-eyed silence followed.

---

* Answers the description of the arched lodge of Carrowdore castle

It was too true!

A high wooden breastwork surrounded the trap-door. Stretch their arms as they would, none of the little ones could reach down to open the trap-lids that had swung up so easily; and the ropes dangled just out of grasp, though Hector's efforts to get at them made him exhausted. Then, they all sat down in silence.

'They'll never think of looking for us here; not for days and days perhaps. Then they'll find us, like the lady in the oak chest,' said Hector lugubriously; then, dismayed at the howl of anguish that broke from the little girls, he hastily ordered, with reassumed courage, 'Shout—shout loud!

A childish shriek for help in this awful need rang through the old walls, startling the pigeons that bred in the belfry—again, again!—but no answering sound of succour came, though they listened breathless. Then, hoping to break the lock, all three pulled with might and main at the door, grasping each other round the waist in line. But the only result was that Hector's hands slipped off the handle; and he tumbling back, they all fell in a heap on the floor.

'Oh! it's all up with us now,' said Hector resignedly, with the calm of a man who, having done his best to save his followers' lives, now exhorts them to face death firmly. 'Girls, you'd better say your prayers.'

'Do you think it's for stealing the sugar? 'cause then we'll go to hell;' asked little Nan, with a scream of utter mental anguish she could no longer smother.

'*We* didn't steal it,' gravely returned the brother and sister, looking at her, appalled at the prospect of poor Moonie's damnation, yet feeling a sense of satisfaction that themselves had still a good chance of heaven. Little Nan sank into a pile of oats, and leant her head against a post, feeling very sick. 'To go into drefful flames—and without Hector and Ailie, too—and they had eaten *more* sugar!'

'We'll help you to pray,' said both her companions with great pity, but self-relief. So, scrambling on their knees, the trio put themselves in intensely devout attitudes. But all the victim could utter, was, 'Oh, dear Lord, I'm awfully sorry zat I stole that nasty old sugar—but *please* let us out; for Rebecca'll cry so dreadfully if she can't find me to-night; and so will cook and the coachman' At this hitherto uncontemplated aspect of affairs—grief for the loss these kind friends would sustain, added to that most touching of all our woes, pity of ourselves—the loving little hearts brimmed over, and they all gave a simultaneous howl.

'What will grandpapa do without me?' sighed Hector.

'He's so cruel, he'll be glad to get rid of *us*,' sobbed Aileen.

'Girls! I feel the starving beginning inside me,' went on Hector in a sepulchral voice; it was just his usual supper-time; and, at that, all remains of fortitude left him, and he bellowed, whilst Aileen's grief became sympathisingly heart-rending. Only Nannie pulled her short bib over her head and wept behind that in silence; feeling such an unutterable, small sinner that she dared not even relieve herself by more noise.

Then the granary-door burst open, and the heads of the grinning steward and Rebecca, the fat old nurse, appeared in the aperture; the latter, first agonised lest her charges had broken some bones, as was highly likely, then amused in the revulsion of feeling.

'We thought no one would ever hear us shouting,' explained Hector, with a rather shame-faced air, his weeping having promptly subsided.

'Not hear ye, man alive!—we might have heard you at the village. It was like the roaring of a young bull,' replied the steward unfeelingly.

But Rebecca was carrying Nan, her especial nursling, indoors, exclaiming fondly, 'My white dove, my poor lamb; was she crying all by herself, under her bib?'

And Rebecca's pity went so far, that she insisted to the governess that none of the children must be punished for missing their lessons, after such a terrible fright. While, as to the sugar, that unprincipled old woman and her accomplice the cook certainly never reported its loss, when that was discovered. For Mr. De Burgo, the children's grandfather, had come home on a flying visit, then. 'And that old Herod would be only too glad of the chance to take the poor infants' lives,' quoth the nurse.

'Och! the forlorn orphants!* Well; it's little enough of sweetness *he* gives them,' assented the cook, who had just as unflattering an opinion of her master's character, and who rather rejoiced at his being in any way despoiled.

---

* orphant = orphan

CHAPTER 3

THE OLD HOUSE IN THE WOODS; AND ITS INMATES

Black Abbey seemed in the children's minds a huge, magnificent, and awe-inspiringly ancient mansion. It was indeed a fine old house, mantled in parts with masses of beautiful unclipped ivy, that tenanted screech-owls and bats; the former being no doubt answerable for the popular tradition that ghosts of monks or nuns* (which, no one well knew, so some said 'both together!') from the ruins in the Chapel wood, haunted the place. Certainly, want of paper and paint made the house seem 'capable of them,' as Rebecca had to own, when denying the flattering accusation: but it was a solid old house, and so pleasant still, despite neglect, that no wonder the children loved and innocently admired it. The door in the middle of the old house frowned, with its carved head-piece of the grim De Burgo arms, down on handsome though aged horse-shoe steps, and a lichened dry fountain on the gravelled terrace.

Two wings projected on either side of the house; and all was crowned with quaint gables and steeply-pitched roofs on which the pigeons were evermore strutting. Beyond the grey terrace balustrade the ground sloped down in a steep lawn to the rich emerald meadow, through which a weedy stream slid; while further was a peep of the Chapel ruins embosomed in trees; and last of all, a peep of brilliantly blue sea framed in the green setting of the woods.

---

* monks and nuns … 'together'. There is a 'nun's well' beside the ruins of Grey Abbey, and earlier tradition relates to such an illicit practice.

As for the life led here of Mr. De Burgo's orphaned grandchildren and ward, one morning's description is the same as that of a thousand mornings they thus spent; saving Hector, who, after a while, went to school. When the breakfast gong sounded, there would be a wild rush of glee from the school-room, where the children had been learning with hungry impatience after the horrible ordeal of dressing. In the oak hall, the four old servants were all standing in a solemn row, loving to keep up the respectability of the house of De Burgo by a decent show at prayer-time. Little Hector, who liked acting master during his grandfather's absences (very long, but not long enough in the household opinion!), would scramble into a great arm-chair before the family Bible. Still, all had to wait, for the governess was tarrying in the school-room. Either Fräulein Schmidt was seeking her knitting, to turn a stocking-heel industriously during the morning-chapter's reading, to Rebecca's horror; or else the simple, learned lady was entranced 'in a mind pursuit as to the origin, by the ablest professors not yet discovered, of some small as an atom, but equally indestructible grammatical particle.' At last would come a thundering sound overhead—a heavy flopping.

'I never knew a Madame Moselle with a light foot on the stairs yet,' muttered the old man-servant to the old women-servants, 'and we wore out seven of them in three years, before Master Hector's father went to school. Yon was a lad; but the old man broke his spirit, too, at the end.'

This said, just as the good instructress shambled in sight; her worn carpet-slipper, feeling itself ill-used at heel, escaped thraldom, and leaping lightly before its owner downstairs, skimmed right into the middle of the polished hall, just under the children's noses. At that, Robert the Ancient, whose manners were stiff-starched though his visage unwashed (and who had been only stable-helper in Black Abbey's grand days, but was now coachman by courtesy and also butler of necessity), came to the front. Seizing the offended object, he placed it upon the large (always empty) card-tray, and solemnly awaited therewith the poor, shamefaced female pedagogue's descent. And though his mouth was close as an oyster-shell when presenting it, the leer in that humourous old eye provoked the little girls all through prayer-time to eruptive bursts of sacrilegious giggling, solemnly checked by Rebecca; but only heard as from far away, and not heeded, by the Fräulein.

The chaplain, however, was too oppressed with the long names that were coming in his chapter of Genesis, and the importance of his present position, to do more than splutter and lose himself in the geography of Judea. While he spelt on his laborious way, the good governess would be again lost in a reverie about what she considered 'these wonder-beautiful allegories, that human fancy had woven through long ages around a nucleus of infinitely ancient truth.' But she conscientiously never thus spoke to the little ones, Rebecca having implored her anxiously to refer all biblical questions to the latter's authority, who regarded all foreign glosses with suspicion. The Fräulein had generally to be informed when Hector's painful task was over; but then would heartily attempt to read the morning prayers in a correct English accent, ably aided herein by each of the old servants, whose voices, all in different inflections of correction, chimed in one after another, much after the manner of singing a catch.

Breakfast afterwards was of a pattern with the other household arrangements, being a slender meal on a small table set in the middle of a fine long dining-room. Here, full-length portraits of bygone magnificently dressed De Burgos gazed down on their shabby, merry little descendants supping porridge and milk, and slyly fighting with their spoons; whilst old Rebecca hovered behind them like a hen round her chickens, exhorting them alternately to 'be good, now!' and 'eat plenty!' The Fräulein was meanwhile dreaming as ever, for the care of the children's bodies she left to the nurse. She herself only sighed that they might grow quickly older, that she could feed their minds full of strong and beautiful wisdom, O, most soul-comforting food! as she had found it. Hector would go to Harrow, and his education be lost to her; but happily she could still inform the little girls' intellects after the pattern of her own. 'It was a most beautiful situation for a true-born teacher,' she would rapturously exclaim. These two should grow up typical women under her fostering hand, nourished on learning, sound to the core; deep and thorough in their knowledge; and ignorant only of the foolish prejudices (so far as in her lay!) which hinder women from becoming as perfect philosophers and ardent scholars as men, by shackling them with foolish duties only fit for uneducated slaves.

'Ach! Hypatia, Hypatia!' she would utter in ecstasy; the figure of that fair, white-robed teacher gleaming to her imagination like a ray of far-off light through the mists of ages. The young Alexandrian's supposed scorn of earthly love as degrading, moving more than even her profound learning the admiration of this her latter-day worshipper.

So, for a good deal longer time, and with a far more earnest oversight than is generally given to such young children—now that the days of Lady Jane Grey's education are in the far, severe past—these little ones of Black Abbey were kept studying by their enthusiast of an instructress. Nevertheless, she was of so patient a nature with their rebellious fidgeting, and so kindly-hearted, that they really disliked their lessons less than might be believed; although always wild as their hours of freedom drew near.

During these hours, they were indeed free as the swallows. 'Liberty was the life of them,' declared Rebecca, who secretly pitied the little ones for being forced to know so much more than herself. And though Rebecca found it her duty to scold them soundly for such rare misdeeds as came under her eye, the children understood remarkably well how to spare her fond feelings, and their own, when any particular mischief was on hand. As for the Fräulein, she was easily avoided; her leisure hours being spent in playing on the grand piano in the deserted drawing-room, or making an undeviating track up and down one particular shrubbery walk; which indeed for years she never deserted, since there 'her thoughts were shut in with her.' The day of the sugar robbery may, then, be taken as a fair sample of how these freed school-captives—at once outlaws—spent their sweet liberty till evening, when the village schoolmaster came to give them lessons in English. All the wide demesne, woods, mere, and meadows—ay! even all the surrounding farms far and near—were harried by them. In the latter, indeed, their raids were held as honouring visits.

Old Mr. De Burgo's visits, also, to his home were as few and brief as angels' ones (but there such resemblance ends). In his far-away youth, as it was still whispered by the tenants around Black Abbey, he had been 'a wild yun! a bad boy, who got the beautiful estate free when he come of age, but made the money fly; till his sins brought his widow mother's hairs in sorrow till the grave.' The county neighbours, yet, were charitably willing even then to forgive the young man's faults, if he had but taken to wife one of their daughters and reformed. Such charity is still so often observable, that the world is not perhaps as harsh as folks say. When Mr. De Burgo, however, married in another county, the neighbours took (as was natural!) less interest in him.

The country around Black Abbey was quiet, and the gentry homely. Mr. De Burgo found existence there dull and always duller, so grew to stay more and more away during his married life. His wife, indeed, had often come home to spend periods of retirement, as was supposed, from choice and haughtiness; but when, before her death, it became known that she had long been an injured and broken-hearted woman, the domestically inclined neighbours around ceased to consider Mr. De Burgo as an eligible guest of their hearths and hearts. In some ways, the world was severer at that particular time than now; and morality, too, seems to have its cycling seasons.

After that, young De Burgo, an only son, had run away with a girl of old family but slender fortune; a marriage to which his father had tyrannically refused consent; and by-and-by the young man died.

It might *not* be true, the neighbours repeated to each other, that old Mr. De Burgo's resentment had made him withhold from his son even the means of going to a warmer climate, when the young man was threatened with that consumption of which he died. Still, there was a vague rumour that the father being in debt then, had vainly tried to persuade the son into joining in the sale of some property, and thereby prejudicing the interests of the latter's children. And it might *not* be true, that when the young widow, between grief at her loss and previous trouble, fell into the brain fever from which her reason never perfectly recovered, that the stern old father-in-law had shown her little pity. And yet it was not altogether unlikely; for he was known to be as hard as a nether millstone* to those who offended him. Certainly, he gave her an asylum at Black Abbey, where she, however, soon languished and died.

The neighbours, after that, spoke very pitifully of the children, whom they yet hardly ever saw, since the society of Black Abbey's master was now a good deal shunned. The good people

* nether millstone = the lower, fixed and hardest millstone of a working mill. Greyabbey had a water-mill and a windmill in the 19th century.

acknowledged that Mr. De Burgo was still 'in society' in England and abroad, they believed; where certain small home-scandals concerning him were not much known, it was quietly added. Of course, a man like him, of old family and good estate, who had highly stately and agreeable manners and kept a fine yacht, could always be pretty sure of a certain amount of acquaintances. But the neighbourhood thought his closest intimates were somewhat—well, peculiar! Persons with stories; or doubtful foreign titles; society's damaged goods, though of superior quality. Some few friendships in a more outside circle, of undoubted worth and lustre, Mr. De Burgo had, however, kept or made by that charm of old-world breeding; notably, Nannie's father, who had been a poor but petted favourite in the great world. He, dying in a sad and sudden way, left his little one with grateful security to the charge of the fine old gentleman, who spoke with such good feeling of the young grandchildren left also, alas! under his care.

Thenceforth, little Nan was quite a trump card in her guardian's conversation, among his best set of acquaintances. Thenceforth Nan and Rebecca, her good nurse, lived at Black Abbey; and a blessing that was to the two little orphans there, who had just become motherless, and were lonely, untended, and untaught.

Mr. De Burgo was, undoubtedly, still a handsome, well-preserved old beau. A face of dark bronze complexion, with a short aquiline nose; gleaming hawk eyes; and snow-white hair, thick, closely waved, and so daintily arranged that his head always seemed to his grandchildren's awed but fascinated gaze freshly frosted by the pastrycook's art. He kept his figure still wonderfully active and spare by careful exercise; while his eye and hand in cover-shooting, once excellent, were still so steady that he spent most of his autumns and winters in a round of country-house visits during the pheasant season. His old-world courtesy still pleased women, and the strongly-spiced stories for which he had gained a reputation languidly amused the younger generation of men, to whom he laughed loudly against old fogies, cheerily declaring he only liked the society of 'young fellows.' Besides, people had acquired a habit of inviting him; and it seemed unkind to cease doing so.

Thus Mr. De Burgo spent his passing years gaily; what also with seasons in London, summers at Cowes, trips to Homburg and Baden-Baden.

'An ould sinner!' was Rebecca's blunt verdict, firmly believing that her master's diversions were all—whatever his foreign courier might assert of their fine acquaintances—of the unholiest description. Good Rebecca! She was not of Black Abbey, but yet was a northern Irishwoman, born and bred several counties' distance away, like her poor mistress—Nan's mother—to whose fortune, as to whose child, she had faithfully clung. And it was precisely this community of northern birth that had been the long, almost-forgotten cause of the first intimacy between little Nannie's parents and her present guardian.

'Wheels within wheels! Och! the worse for my lamb!' groaned the good nurse.

For, though Mr. De Burgo interested many a distant lady friend by feeling, if brief, allusions to his grandchildren—the subject of their orphanage being supposed too painful for him to dwell upon—whilst he made it understood that he had only thus partially shut up Black Abbey ('a fine place!') because its loneliness and memories were inexpressibly sad; yet, when the grandfather and master did go to his home, his grandchildren and dependents had cause to hold very different impressions.

Tenacious and hardened, old De Burgo always took grim pleasure in making a practice of reappearing like a comet among the fixed stars of magnitude, his county equals, at grand-jury times, or any such public meetings, by way of proving that he still held his rightful position amongst them. The neighbours were then mostly very quietly civil; but did not ask him to their homes, amongst their wives and families. And Mr. De Burgo was grandly polite in return, with secret bitterness; but whenever, as sometimes happened, some of his few fine and flawless English acquaintances paid Black Abbey a flying visit, he in return did not invite the tender-conscienced neighbours—'respecting too much,' as he said to himself with a chuckle, 'their domestic feelings.'

CHAPTER 4

A HIGHWAY ROBBERY; LEADING TO FAR-OFF CONSEQUENCES

'I HAVE a grand plan,' said Hector, who was lying on the grass of the outlaws' den, one summer day. 'Let us have black mail from any strangers that dare to come up to our house. We'll hide every day near the lodges in the woods, then jump out and demand their money.'

This idea was received with a squeal of delight from Aileen, the lesser brigand; but Nannie, the least one, was a weaker spirit, and demurred somewhat.

'Not from poor people,' said the little maid, shrinking delicately from that idea. 'It wouldn't be nice to ask them for money.'

'Of course not; we'll *give* them some,' cheerfully returned Hector, with the air of a generous benefactor. 'We'll take it from the rich ones, and give it to them; and if there's any over, I'll buy a black horse and be Dick Turpin.'

'But we should have some, too—ah! now, Hector ... That's not fair,' excitedly expostulated the inferior outlaws, feeling it their right to share the plunder.

'Well, but I thought of Dick Turpin *first* — so none of you can take him,' replied Hector doggedly. And as original ideas were sacredly held private property in this small community, and that the captain furthermore condescendingly promised them rides upon his future steed whenever he had 'tamed its spirit' (with a wave of his chubby arm), they grew pacified.

'Old Mr. Cosby is coming up this afternoon to see about

buying the moily* cow,' burst out Aileen, then; 'dare we stop him? Would grandpapa be raging?'

The bright little gipsy hesitated and looked awed at that thought, almost to pallor.

'No; for Mr. Cosby is only the Presbyterian minister. And besides, HE won't be back for weeks,' cried Hector, with a joyous air.

'If we robbed *our* clergyman there might be rows. Gracious! he might talk about it in his sermon. But they'll never know who we are, when we're disguised.'

So they laid their wicked plans.

A cartroad to the Black Abbey farm passed, at one spot, through a young plantation of larches that thickly covered with their feathery branches the steep banks on either side.

These banks were edged by a low wall; and the road was narrow. Could there be a better place for the perpetration of a highway robbery? And up there, hidden in the green, pleasant shade, lay the highwaymen that sunny afternoon, grasping long saplings, and wearing masks of black stuff (rags they had begged from Rebecca) tied over each face, with slits through which their eyes goggled fearfully. They had grown very tired of waiting, when, at last, came the sound of wheels, and the robbers' hearts thumped, as they afterwards expressed it, 'like clock-ticks.'

'Here's his gig,' whispered little Nan, peering through the cover and turning inwardly cowardly.

'His *shandrydan*† you mean,' burst out Aileen contemptuously.

'Men!' ordered the captain with flurried authority. 'Look out—I mean—lie still.'

An awful silence followed. Now they could hear their unsuspecting victim talking gaily to some one. (He had a companion,

* moily = hornless

† shandrydan = rickety conveyance

then, in his fate; but they dared not even peep!) Half with fiendish glee, half in terrible suspense, they listened to the slow wheel-creaks, till—

'*Now!!*' roared the captain, and with a diabolical yell all sprang from ambush; jumped into the road below, nearly lighting on their noses, and barred the way.

'Your money or your life!' growled Hector, so deeply that it gave him a fit of coughing.

'Money or life!' ferociously murmured the Tomboy and Moonyface in the background.

Agitating their terrible weapons, that indeed were very heavy to wield and cumbersome, they expected to hear an agonised appeal to spare the existence of a poor old man (which they mercifully intended to grant). But what odious words, instead, came back from the gig?

'Ho, ho, ho! … Highwaymen, no less! … Oh, he, he, he! but this is fun. Isn't it, my wee Bella? Wait now, my little dears, till I look for coppers.'

And the good minister stretched himself sideways, to grope in one pocket with all the difficulty of the corpulent. It was almost humiliating. Out rolled one penny in the cart ruts.

'Wait a bit. Mister Hector. We must get one apiece,' cried the kind old man, who still went on fumbling slowly.

This was too much; the waiting robbers felt, meanwhile, turned to little beggars.

'Tell him to take back his nasty pence,' murmured the little girls in distress; while Hector pulling his mask down about his neck, disclosed a fair, open face, all flushed, exclaiming:

'Oh! please, no! Mr. Cosby. We—we only did it for fun. … We were only *pretending*, you know.'

'Oh! but please go on,' entreated a childish voice, in such really imploring accents that the Black Abbey children gazed up surprised at the gig.

There, the minister's little grand-daughter, of whose existence they had only lately vaguely heard, was clasping her hands, her feet dancing with eagerness.

'Oh! *do go on pretending*, and let me be a robber, too. Grandpapa, you always say they wouldn't let me play with them; but I'm sure they would, they look so nice;' then, with beseeching humility to the little De Burgos, 'Please, let me; I've nobody to play with.'

She was the prettiest little pleader imaginable, with her speaking brown eyes and rose-tinted face; and she wore a good black frock and new straw hat; whilst the outlaws rather resembled aristocratic tatter-demalions.

'A woman! a very wee woman—determined, since! a month, to have her own way in this,' laughed the old minister, yet his spirit grieved that he must, as usual, deny this one wish to his treasure. But the Black Abbey children looked at each other, flattered, captivated, and caring not a fig for social station. The glory of their enterprise had suddenly turned to shame: then, with an impetuous wish to make all reparation to those whom they had so lately considered their lawful prey, they so eagerly begged the minister to let Bella join them, that the good man's secret fears of unsettling his little one's content with home were soon overborne.

So, the Black Abbey children promptly bore off their young visitor to the wood's recesses in triumph; Nannie and Aileen feeling, at first—so unused were they to a single strange face—like shy, if gentle, little savages; but Hector pompously trying to mimic his grandfather's grand air when receiving rare visitors at home. But Bella's artless prattle and utter delight soon put them all at their ease. She already knew their names, and soon told them how every night from her crib she looked out at the park-wall just opposite the manse, and felt 'dreadful' longings to see the demesne inside, and the children of whom she had heard.

Her young hosts were at once generously touched with extreme pity for this lonely dweller outside the walls of their enchanting and beloved Black Abbey. Her fate must be alleviated as far as possible, by granting her initiation into the lesser mysteries of their games. They brought her to certain secret 'houses' they had in the woods: and played at visiting each other.

'I'm a prince, and Nan is always my princess,' exclaimed Hector, suppressing, by the latter clause, an evident inclination on the part of their humbler guest to offer herself for that post of honour, which the heir of Black Abbey, with all his kindly condescension, felt was too exalted for her.

'And Aileen is a duchess; because we can't all be the same.'

'Then, I'll be a duchess, too,' declared Bella, but stopped, seeing embarrassed disapproval on all faces.

'I don't think you ought to be the same as me, because you're only a Presbyterian minister's daughter, you know,' blurted out Aileen after a serious silence, feeling conscientiously obliged to utter this disagreeable truth.

'You can be a countess, dear.'

'No, I won't—I'll be a queen from America,' returned the offended guest (What! greater than a prince and princess. There was severe silence.)

Then Nan murmured aside, 'Poor thing, she's a visitor. … Let's *pretend* she's a duchess too; just to please her.'

This being agreed on in whispers, the mock and real duchesses took up their abode in a wigwam of dead bushes. The princess, however, had a palace hard by, built of two layers of bricks carried laboriously to those forest depths. It was three feet square and floored with slates, and an approach between two elegant rows of smashed glass and crockery led thereunto.

'Please come in,' said royalty, squeezing herself up, as the duchess came to court. 'It's a wee bit small, but it's very comfy.'

Then the conversation became exceedingly polite. And how

were the duchesses' papas and mammas?

'My mamma is dead,' said Bella, with a sudden look of grief that produced consternation among the distinguished company. 'My papa is alive, though; but he's gone away to California, and sent me home to my old grandpapa.'

'We're so sorry; but we were only pretending, you know,' explained the other little ones in eager consolation, having since some years outgrown much memory of their own afflictions. Poor children! whom a sad likeness in sorrow had drifted together to grow up among the pleasant Black Abbey woods.

The prince now came in, with a heavy game-bag of matter in the wrong place (to adopt the celebrated definition of dirt), and, fatigued by hunting, joined in the agreeably melancholy talk.

'Nannie's papa was an officer in the Blues; and our papa was a gentleman and did nothing at all,' observed the little De Burgos, proudly puffing themselves with vanity like innocent pigeons, feeling the double fascination of talking fine, and trying to be gloomy.

'Well, my papa is a big storekeeper,' promptly quoth Bella, not to be outdone.

This was received with a puzzled silence, till Aileen adroitly covered the De Burgo ignorance by inquiring, 'What do you have for breakfast? We have porridge and milk every morning, but on Sundays we get tea, and eggs apiece. I do like Sunday for that.'

'I think of it all the week, till it comes,' gently observed greedy little Nan.

The humbler guest looked bewildered that these children, whose higher station and stately home she had envied from a distance, should he reared on food she despised; and said, staring, 'Why, I get tea and bacon every morning, just like grandpapa and Luke. And treacle if I'm good—sometimes honey, if I'm very good.'

'Well,' returned Hector severely, with a great effort, for envy and mortification made the poor outlaws feel somehow 'bad inside.' 'Our grandpapa rears *us* like the young Spartans, you know. He'd turn Rebecca off if she dared give us anything but porridge' (which was strictly true), 'but she lets us eat plenty, anyway; and he says we ought to feel always, when we've finished, as if we'd like more … I say!' (suddenly) 'do you like brown sugar?'

'Not much, but old Mary, our servant, gives me some,' carelessly replied Bella, wrinkling her pretty nose. 'Do you?'

'No,' replied Hector, with a gloomy, disappointed air. 'We're—we're sick of it!'

On this the other outlaws, feeling their chief required support, hastened gravely to turn the talk to a less secretly disagreeable topic. A long, long, happy June day those children played, while 'from bush to bush the cuckoo flew,' and the song-birds warbled about them. When the sun-beams slipped more slantwise between the great tree-boles, and the cows were being driven back from the big meadows for milking, they parted; having built, on the foundations of that highway attack, a friendship destined to have lasting consequences.

CHAPTER 5

'GOLDEN LADS AND GIRLS'

On many occasions, after this first meeting, the children from the great house played with the little one from the manse. They would have gladly done so constantly, but for old Mr. Cosby, who timidly dreaded that the terrible old master of Black Abbey might, on his return, disapprove of any such close intimacy.

Little Bella had, however, by her winning blandishments, won the open hearts of the children; and even the dreamy, approving gaze of the governess. For she was not only the grandchild of the only person of cultivated intellect whom the lonely lady met there, utterly isolated as she was, but had, on once being honoured by an invitation to school-room tea, behaved on a trying occasion with engaging tact. Fräulein Schmidt, who sat beside her, began meditatively drinking Bella's tea, and, besides that, devouring the little girl's bread and butter, till roused by shrieks of childish laughter from the rest. Then, how caressingly, even with actually an embrace, the little stranger had ended the matter; the others gazing wonderingly at the supple gracefulness which they could no more have affected, when not natural, than could wild birds in the thickets the manners of a trained canary.

Little Nannie White was a painfully sensitive child; delicate and quiet, unlike the De Burgos. Being of a dreamy, almost melancholy temperament, her brain and fancy worked more than was good for the body. But, at rare moments, animal spirits and imagination combining, caused a ferment within her already deep child's soul. Aileen resembled her only so far as the same mould of circumstances impressed a light nature and a gay heart. But both little girls led such secluded lives in the old house among the woods—allowed to run wild by good Rebecca's indulgence, being taught learning alone by the governess, and cowed to terror whenever Mr. De Burgo came home—that, so far from understanding how to show the prettiest wares of their behaviour for strangers' admiration, they closed up all the sweetness of their souls in a foreign presence, and seemed dull or rude. Hector alone was civilized, being at times taken visiting, by his grandfather. The old man, indeed, treated the child with capricious indulgence, as 'the heir of Black Abbey,' although not showing him love, sated desire had long since deadened that time-worn disposition to any such freshness of feeling. But all pride of family he centred in the noble boy. The early lessons in the De Burgo catechism of: What is your name or future inheritance? What duty, therefore, do your neighbours owe you?—might have dizzied young Hector's brain, with the British divine right of primogeniture. Only the loving, big child's heart balanced the wrong, and, as the upshot, the little lad believed that generosity in giving and promising, as well as spending, and childish good fellowship—a futile mimicry of his grandfather's fine manners that delighted all by its natural failure—were expected of an only son and a De Burgo.

Quite different was the small lass from the manse, whose head was troubled by no pride of birth. No shyness nor fear did she know, whom grandfather and Luke treasured with most loving reverence of the young woman-soul confided to what they termed their 'rude care.' She ruled over the learned, simple old man and fiery boy-student, with the calm assurance of an only child that her claim to all good things was indisputable; since to pleasure the world, like the French seigneur in the *Mariage de Figaro* she 'took the trouble of being born.' With strangers, her pliant nature and ambition to be loved taught her a thousand wiles.

With all three Black Abbey children this captivating

newcomer was the rage; even although Hector tried the young female minds by teasing admiration of Bella's superior prettiness. Then little Nan would cry, hotly jealous for her adopted sister, though resigned to the fact of her own pale moon-face—

'Aileen is just as nice-looking—and nicer.'

'Aileen—pooh! She's scraggy, with her legs and arms like broom sticks, and her hair cut short,' scoffed Hector; like any truthful brother. The accusation being such as a mastiff pup might bring against an Italian greyhound.

On this, Rebecca—being rushed to as umpire—would briefly express, in stern dudgeon, her vast surprise at Mr. Hector speaking so of his sister, 'who was a De Burgo born, and had the look of it.'

Poor Rebecca! The foster-mother could not bring herself to put away a jealousy of this plump and rosy manse child, since all her own loving tending could not bring similar colour to little Nan's cheek, or cover Aileen's sharp bones. Still, Rebecca's remark went to the core of the matter. Gawky and wild-spirited as she was, the Tomboy had still an air of refinement that would have singled her out among a crowd of other children. On her slender sunburnt neck, that had already the true 'antelope curve,' was poised a sweet little head, covered with dark lovelocks; and lit by a pair of wondering eyes so deeply blue they glorified the other, as yet, insignificant features. Nannie, on the other hand, was still merely a soft dumpling, with a shy, small voice, and tow-coloured hair; whilst Hector, big and chubby, with his fair hair and light blue eyes, had only the attractions of the splendid health of a schoolboy or a savage to boast of, as yet.

Again, little Bella had beautiful hair that matched her brilliant brown eyes, and waved over her shoulders holding pent warm lights. It was Hector's pure admiration, and that of the little Black Abbey girls mingled with innocent envy. For, by old Mr. De Burgo's orders, both wore their own hair cropped to the ears. 'It would grow all the better,' he said, taking a curious delight even in such petty tyrannies, and loving to exercise his crotchets unchecked upon these infants.

Thus, the higher-born children took to Bella with admiration and delightful sense of patronage, which their inbred feeling of courtesy led them to conceal. The little stranger responded even more delighted—with a flattering sense of being flattered; while her love was quite effusive.

Only in one matter, however, did the others find Bella sadly wanting; and they felt regretfully obliged to tell her so. Her name was vulgar. Why, they had one Bella, the kitchen-drudge, and another the old hen-wife. The Bella from the manse was so deeply chagrined at this discovery that Hector, in pity, searched out a big dictionary in the great deserted library, to find some other B-beginning name which might replace the baptismal affiction.

'I'll be called Beauty!' then announced the victim, glancing up from the pages with a sudden air of determination and bright deliverance.

The Black Abbey little maids, in the slightly severe manner of future leaders of society, suggested Bee as *more* fitting.

'Hullo!—I have it,' shouted Hector, breaking in; '"*Bonnibel—a handsome lass*," That's it! It doesn't sound so vain to other people, you see, Bella; and you'll know, any way, what it means.'

So this was satisfactorily settled.

Although Rebecca never 'took quite kindly' to the little stranger, yet, for the old minister's sake, she acted kindly enough. Even one day, she felt moved to do more, and asked gently, with an inward craving for any sympathy, even a child's—

'I wonder, did ye ever meet my husband out in America, down at a place they call Ohio?'

'No, Mrs. Steenson, I never did. Ohio was far away from us;' and Bella stretched out her little arms widely in illustration.

'Ach! weel! I just thought. His name was John Stevenson, though the people here give me Steenson, for short. Ye knew none of that name?' went on poor Rebecca; trying to speak unconcernedly as she moved away, but with a lingering gaze even after the soft childish lips uttered that cruel word—'No.'

The old coachman put his tongue derisively in his cheek, and scoured a bit with sand to the tune of, 'Whistle, and I'll come to you, my lad.' For that same question was put by Rebecca to every one who had been north, south, east, or west, across the green Atlantic water. But the children gazed after their nurse, awed-eyed; whispering to their new friend with shocked breath, how that Rebecca had once had a husband who had run away from her; and how that she was sometimes heard to bewail him to the other servants, to the children's infinite pity. Indeed, in extreme youth, Hector was so moved that he freely offered to marry her and not run away—if Rebecca would wait for him. Later, he was doubtless glad that she had declined; increased age teaching him how untenable was the latter clause of the promise, whenever Rebecca seemed likely to find it her duty to scold.

After that day, Rebecca's inner heart was again closed to the manse-child; who, however, beloved, well-fed, and well-dressed, gaily satisfied herself with its outer common court. Well-dressed! Yes, that went to Rebecca's heart!—to see this meaner child always in good, if stout, attire; in which she took, indeed, what old Mr. De Burgo once called, a vulgar pride. Her stuff frocks, however homely, were no homelier than those of which the little Black Abbey girls left tatters on a thousand brambles. Her boots were not patched, like theirs, till the village shoemaker declared he could mend them no more; when Rebecca would sorrowfully bid her charges 'take a few more turns out of them, and never mind the holes.' Often, the poor children were glad to get Hector's old boots, and hoped if these were too large, that they would 'grow into them.' Often they wished to each other, in sorrow, that they might run barefoot; and were ashamed that Mr. Cosby's grandchild should see their wants.

But Hector, the heir, might claim imperiously so many new suits a year, and show such lordly carelessness about climbing up trees in his best jacket, that the little girls, shocked at his extravagance, yet wished themselves most fervently to have been also born boys—nay! eldest sons. As long ago as they could remember, they had understood, only too well, that Mr. De Burgo regarded Hector as being in the world with good reason; as having a real necessity, a preordained place, for him to plead as to the cause of his existence. But Aileen knew she was a superfluity; poor Nannie worse—an encumbrance! For—so held Mr. De Burgo, towards his little grandson—country gentlemen of large estate cannot, unfortunately, live for ever. Therefore, they can alone console themselves, by perpetuating their privileged positions in their eldest-born; and these, by a lesser sort of sacred prescription, should be reared up in notions befitting their future semi-divine right over their brethren; as young queen-bees are pampered into difference from their kind.

'My dear madam, it would be absurd—in fact *wrong*—to be stingy with Hector now, when he must have Black Abbey some day,' Mr. De Burgo would majestically reply, if the governess ever ventured to entreat warm, winter frocks for her shivering charges; hinting that, to her mind, Hector was allowed to be too careless of his clothes. 'No,' continued the grandfather, with an air of thoughtful justice, tapping his brilliant-set gold snuff-box—visible proof to the world that he was a fine old gentleman of the past school; 'stint the boy now, and he will go to the dogs when he gets his fling! My good lady, I shall teach him the value of money; do not trouble yourself on that point But the little girls *must* learn economy; for, as they need never expect to be well-off, the sooner they become used to poverty the better.' Then the terrible hawk-eyes would carelessly glance at the pair of frightened children in the background, who had outgrown their thin, worn frocks in every way, and whose chilly blue arms were half-bared. They crept away with hanging heads, bitterly grieved in their small feminine hearts. And the Fräulein, good but simple person, who did not understand the excellencies (in such workings as these) of the system of primogeniture, thought that the teaching as to money's value which Hector was to receive would be, to extract therefrom the greatest possible amount of pleasure—for himself!

Was it any wonder that Rebecca's motherly heart, feeling bitter for her foster-children's wants, thought jealously of comfortably-reared little bourgeoise Bella?

Once—having given half-audible utterance with a perturbed face to some lamentations on this subject, she rose heavily, and, walking across the room still called the nursery, then used as a work-room by herself, and as a City of refuge from the Avengers by her charges, she took down her Bible from amongst the tea-cups.

'Are you going to read?' inquired little Nan with awed surprise. For it seemed so unusual to open one's Bible at midday that she feared Rebecca must be feeling ill.

'I'm going to find your proverb for life, child dear,' answered Rebecca with most mysterious affection. 'On what day were ye born, now—the 30th of September?' Then, turning the pages to the last chapter of Proverbs, she looked round the expectant children with uplifted finger, explaining impressively, that, as there were thirty-one days in the longest months, so there were just as many verses in this chapter. Whichever of these one's birthday corresponded with, was meant to guide us in life. 'And here is Miss Nannie's—deary me, yes: "Favour is deceitful, and beauty is vain; but a woman that feareth the Lord, she shall be praised."

… 'Och! my wee white lamb;' and the old woman stooped

to kiss her especial charge, with a mingling of regret at this prophecy of Nannie's indubitably plain features, yet a sense that her future evident goodness ought to be an all-sufficient consolation.

'Mine!' yelled the Tomboy, flinging her arms round Rebecca's neck.

'Gracious goodness, child!—be at peace for any sake. What's yours—the first? "The words of King Lemuel, the prophesy that his mother taught him."'

'That's horrid!—that isn't nothing at all!' cried the bitterly disappointed one.

'Hush! Would ye take on yourself to say that of a Bible-verse, Miss Aileen? Lay it to heart now. As ye grow up, the meaning of it will come plain; *for it's your proverb,*' sternly answered Rebecca, with a reverent faith that communicated itself to all the children, though poor Aileen still dreaded being called Mrs. Lemuel. 'Now, Master Hector,' soberly continued the augur—'"Let him drink, and forget his poverty, and remember his misery no more." '

Hector was dismayed. Then an animated discussion ensued—was he to be poor and miserable? that *couldn't* be!

'And to get tipsy!' added the Tomboy.

This last suggestion naturally roused Rebecca's wrath, though made in perfect good faith. So, like a Presbyterian divine, gifted in exegesis, she expounded all possible meanings of the verse. It might mean 'the cup of cold water' Hector would give to poor Christian brethren; it might be this charity, or that, towards those in misery.

'But, whatever it is, the truth of it will come to ye.'

'And now, Bonnibel's,' shrieked Aileen.

'Is it wee Bella, Mr. Cosby's grandchild?'

'Yes; but she likes to be called Bonnibel, because Bella sounds so common.'

'Cock her up, indeed!' exclaimed the scornful nurse; but a small voice broke in:

'It was me put it into her head; for we didn't think her own one nice at all. Tell us her verse, Rebecca.'

'Well!—well, dear child.' And Rebecca reluctantly read, that the Presbyterian minister's grandchild should make herself coverings of tapestry, and have clothing of silk and purple! But, instead of expounding this, the fortune-teller hastily rose, pleading employment, and bustled away.

'So she'll be rich—I wish *I* was,' sighed Aileen.

'And I'm to be ugly,' chimed in Nannie, still more dismally.

'Handsome is that handsome does! Cheer up, old girl! I'll give *you* a fortune. And, Moonie, I'll have you for my wife, some day!' shouted Hector, triumphant, as ever for his good fortune, anyhow, was well assured. How could he feel very sorry for the others, when his lines would be in pleasant places? and then, of course, he would have the pleasure of succouring them.

After the outlaws' crowning exploit of stealing the sugar, their sweet booty soon began to grow very nauseous.

For days and days they would say to each other with a sigh, or a sickly smile, 'we must go and eat some more.' Then, when, in the recesses of their hay-nest, each had received their daily portion, they would silently pocket what their palates refused, and separate, each hoping that the others believed they meant to eat it.

But Nannie used to repair to a sand-heap in a back-yard, where, with an air of studying the charms of the locality, she would meditatively allow her sugar to sift through her fingers and be thus disposed of. She suffered agonies of apprehension when Aileen discovered her secret, and insisted with glee on doing likewise, for the traces of two sugar-wasters ran a double risk of discovery.

'Come along,' said Captain H., one day, with a forced air of cheerfulness, 'we MUST finish that old sugar, for grand-papa is coming to-morrow.'

There was a suppressed groan at this, as the robbers reluctantly rose and followed him. Alas! there was still far more sugar left than all three could have now crammed down their throats in several days; yet the horses had eaten so much hay, that soon the nest and its hidden plunder would be ruthlessly bared. In this terrible dilemma, it was resolved to carry off and bury the sugar in the woods, as robbers were supposed to do with their superfluous gold.

That late afternoon beheld Nannie labouring toil fully with the candle-box along a secluded wood-path. Hector and Aileen had already carried it in turns whilst danger lasted, but now it was considered safe to leave it with their youngest comrade; and, running ahead with their spades, these two were presumably already digging in some gloomy thicket. So Nannie panted along, wary still, but with a feeling of comparative safety and inexpressible thankfulness that, at last, she dared to leave without constant dread that her sin would be brought to daylight and blared abroad in all ears. The sun was shining as if it delighted in its office; the little birds singing in the green boughs; the grass soft under her feet. Suddenly, a voice behind her said, 'Ye are my darlin', dearie! … ye are so! … ye are so!'

With difficulty, the child suppressed a scream, as she saw a barefoot, half-idiotic man following her, smiling. He was a mixture of ragman and pedlar, and well known thereabouts. But the little Black Abbey girls had been made to believe that his trade consisted in kidnapping children, carrying them off in his huge wallet. From morning till night, on sight of women or children (the latter of whom he especially loved), the poor daft body would chant his harmless rhyme of, 'Ye are my darlin', dearie! ye are so!'—Now, its sing-song began again, and the fearful child, glancing over her shoulder, saw him holding out some sticky sweeties towards her with an inviting air. That was the lure for his victims, so she had been told by Hector. Something living seemed, to her fancy, kicking in the sack. Setting down her boxful of sugar in his path, the child shrieked, 'Take it! take it! it's for you!—and escaped into the brushwood in such fear that her knees almost failed under her.

A faint, jubilant cry of gratitude reached her ears as she fled, filling her infant soul with fresh alarms. But Darlin' dearie was only gloating over the gift in ecstasy, and never again saw Nan without peculiar affection. Long afterwards, indeed, that devotion, springing from the trivial act, brought about the climax—the day of days, to be remembered, whether as blessing or curse—of Nannie White's life.

To the other children, their playfellow's adventure more than balanced the loss of the sugar. With ever-growing delight they listened to the ever-growing tale; while the little lass, proud of being a heroine, recounted it with such vividness of colouring, that she herself grew awestruck at having come out unharmed from such a terrible adventure.

CHAPTER 6

'COMPANY TIME' AT BLACK ABBEY

WHENEVER the master of Black Abbey was expected home, one knew as much by the air of suppressed disquietude on the faces of all the household, and a general alacrity in what was termed, without distinction, 'cleaning-up.' Indoors and outdoors, man and beast, had a share in it. The sturdy steward, who ruled his men with a rod of iron, might now be seen surveying the big meadows with a gloomy, wrinkled brow, as if he could make two blades of grass grow for every one, or put more flesh on his young bullocks' bones by eyeing them. Then he would turn away, muttering to himself, 'Och, well! no matter! Sure he's *always* raging; so it may as well be about the one thing as another;' and console himself with the reflection that his old master, who could skin a flint as well as most men in the matter of farm expenses, knew too well that his steward's wages were not great, and the latter's labour worth that of two men, to part with him.

Indeed, the old man was well served, though neither for love nor pay. The steward had been born and bred on the place, and had a foolish idea that he loved the very brown earth of its fields, and every tree, hedgerow, and gatepost on it. Rebecca had come to Black Abbey with her little charge Nannie, to whom she clung with almost maternal yearnings. Seeing this with keen eyes, Mr. De Burgo had offered to take her as nurse to all three children, and Rebecca had accepted with such alacrity as might Jochebed when offered the charge of the Princess of Egypt's newly-adopted babe. Faithfully, meekly, she bore up under her new master's stintings and terrible temper. She was with her nursling.

But she grew to love the other two children dearly also. The good soul used to pray aloud for them every night on her knees, quite unaware that the little girls, while pretending to be asleep in their cribs, had their ears pricked in ecstatic interest; while roguish Hector's ear was certain to be at the key-hole. They knew it was naughty; but the delight of hearing Rebecca supplicate that '*Grandpapa's crossness might be cured*,' was too unspeakably, entrancingly solemn; while it was still more ravishing to hear her always end in earnest entreaty, and pious conviction that her prayer would be granted, '*that Master Hector might marry Miss Nannie—and that Miss Aileen might get the next best match in the county! Amen.*'

Again, as to the German governess—although she was a considerable item in the old man's calculations of how little he could decently spend on the children and how much on his own pleasures, he yet knew what he was about, when he engaged such a learned, philosophic-minded woman to teach little children.

In youth, Fräulein Schmidt had known what she termed 'heart misfortunes.' Later, the solid pleasures of knowledge, the excitements, though rare, of scientific discoveries, the calm of philosophy, solaced her deeply wounded spirit. Then, although possessing some small means, having an enthusiastic desire to teach, considering the right training of young minds the highest and holiest of professions, as the greatest service she could render to the human race, she went to England as a governess. In England, with her mind severely trained and full of learning, her brain teeming with beautiful visionary schemes for imparting the latter, she was required to 'finish the education' of some giggling middle-class misses, whose wealthy parents had caused them to be taught a little of everything; to her worse than nothing of anything—a universal smatter! Her soul was soon vexed within her. How could she build on bad foundations? she asked; or conscientiously send forth from the schoolroom, as perfected, minds that were in some parts blank with ignorance, in others choked with masses of raw, undigested facts. She must begin over again from the beginning with them, she cried! Dismayed mothers looked on her as a fanatic; smug British respectability was shocked at her sublime indifference to dress, at her strange morality, which was truly of the spirit, but too scornful of the use of the letter. Then she met Mr. De Burgo, and—mistaking his old-world, universal courtesy in society to all women for true sympathy—told him part of her troubles.

Old De Burgo snatched at the golden chance. He offered her unlimited freedom in teaching the little Black Abbey recluses from their earliest years; in the disposal of her spare hours. He gained, thus, for an insignificant salary, a teacher who worked from devotion, not for pay. And she found a home; the work she most desired; and liberty, leisure, seclusion—rest!

The rabbits in the woods did not heed, if in her rambles she was dressed not unlike Robinson Crusoe; no mistress of the house grumbled that she burned too late the midnight oil, or woke the echoes of the still house with some great master's music in the small hours.

And thus she lived many years, happy; 'the world forgetting,' by the world unknown; lonely sometimes, till her pupils grew older, but holding all the closer communion with those silent companions, the great minds whose thoughts made noble, lining to the walls of the Black Abbey library.

Certainly, when Mr. De Burgo did come home, his refined taste was offended at the good governess's slatternliness. But he considered careful Rebecca as a counterbalance; a corrective to the children. Indeed, though none of Mr. De Burgo's lady-friends had ever seen his grandchildren, he could talk fluently to any with motherly hearts upon the excellent nurse, the unrivalled, devoted governess, he had for his little ones. And, when so speaking warming to the subject, as he charmed his hearers, he, it may be—it is even most likely—convinced himself he was doing his best. But on some occasions of Mr. De Burgo's home-coming, now notably on one, he brought some gentlemen back with him, for a day or two, at most. Then how the children watched, with mixed awe and glee, the unlocking of the best silver, linen, and china, beforehand; the good things prepared with difficulty and anxiety by the aged cook, who dreaded dismissal, since at her years no one else would employ her. How Robert, the aged sinner, groaned, washed, and shaved, and aroused from his normal state of laziness, that was varied by giving a hand's-turn at any job *not* his own work. This last quality precisely gave him what small value he possessed in his master's eyes; since he was never 'above' whitewashing, ivy-cutting, or vermin-trapping in the Black Abbey woods; or even light farm work, done with an easy air of condescension, whilst whistling Tate and Brady's psalm tunes*. His old horse, kept for going errands to the market-town and harrowing, was, meanwhile, seldom enough cleaned down; laziest of old hypocrites was this truly Irish 'decent creature!'

The children, at such times, would steal off on little expeditions round the house; wander into the bedrooms prepared for the 'comp'ny'—as they called the coming guests—much as they might follow fairies' footsteps, who had furnished and garnished the usually bare and closed rooms, and wondered if the strangers would not think the house as 'beautiful as did themselves. It was a pleasant stir in their lives. Already they felt, without understanding, that change is the soul of life. But it must be an easy, natural transition; not those sudden convulsions that

* Tate and Brady Psalms. Nahum Tate and Nicholas Brady produced a metrical version of the Psalms in 1696, later sometimes used in Episcopalian worship, in contrast to the tunes of the Scottish Metrical Psalter used in Presbyterian churches.

are rather like removes towards death. Then, on the morning of the last day, Rebecca would begin to examine the little girls' black Sunday frocks, emitting sighs like wind blasts, poor old soul! would iron, turn a second time, rub them with hot beer, to freshen them, muttering, 'Such *duds* for my wee lambs to be dressed in! Och! och!—I could just sit down and cry.'

Later in the day, Nannie and Aileen were solemnly dressed in these same garments; they heard carriage-wheels grinding the gravel, announcing their grandfather's arrival, and peeped past the blinds, feeling that their sacred home was invaded, that a master had come to sway in its very secretest precinct, and their innocent little vanities of governing in his absence had utterly vanished. By-and-by the children would be sent for, and creep downstairs rigid with shyness, whispering to Hector to 'go in first' Affecting an air of bravery which the poor little man was far from feeling, and repeating to his smaller companions, 'You OUGHT NOT to be afraid of grandpapa!' Hector would turn the drawing-room door-handle.

Then, it was considered quite a charming sight, to see fine old Bob De Burgo, with his snowy hair and handsome figure, advancing cheerily from amidst a group of gentlemen, and exclaiming, in a voice full of dignity yet affection, 'Hector, my boy! my dear boy! God bless you!' laying his hand on his grandson's head; then to the girls, who clung together as shyly as if he and his friends were so many ogres:

'Ah! little mice, you are not afraid of grandpapa, are you, my sweet Aileen—my white Nannie?' and this courteous old gentleman stooped to kiss their foreheads with a polished gallantry, mingled with paternal affection, that was itself a lesson in fine manners to be remembered.

'Little pale one! where are the roses fled?' he went on, pinching Nannie's cheek gently; then, turning himself about, observed, with a sorrowful shake of the head, to his friends, 'Poor

Jack White's child, you know.'

'No?—indeed!' said several; and one, raising his eyebrows by way of expressing caution, asked in a loud whisper, as if he thought because Nannie was small she was also wanting in hearing and comprehension:

'Didn't leave her much money, did he?'

'Not a rap,' said Mr. De Burgo, raising his eyebrows also airily, and doing even that with peculiar old-fashioned grace; whilst Nannie listened with both her ears to the talk above her downbent little head. 'But,' went on her guardian, tapping his gold snuff-box with most stately gravity, in a changed tone of deep feeling, 'Jack White's child shall always be like my own, whilst I am above-ground.'

An approving murmur passed round.

Then Nannie felt herself patted, caressed, 'for her father's sake,' they said; lifted kindly on one ogre's knee, who told her what a good, gallant gentleman, how loved and lamented her father had been, till her heart ceased fluttering, and swelled with pride.

Alas! a terribly big darn in Aileen's frock, meanwhile, caught her grandfather's keen eye.

'So, my little harum-scarum has torn her dress,' he said, with his sweetest smile (though the child shivered); then, with a shrug to an old friend beside him: 'Ah, well! I like them to appear in just whatever old clothes they have romped about in all day, rather than dress up finely for strangers.'

The little girls looked up amazed. Was it possible grandpapa did not know these were their best frocks? Just as Aileen's lips were unclosing (for the first time) in necessary correction, her grandfather added with bland, gliding promptness, 'And now, dear little ones, I shall see you soon again, and you would like to run away' (this last was, perhaps, the truest word he had spoken since they came in). 'Let me open the door for them.

Hector, my boy. … You can have that pleasure another time.'

And so, with an air of as courtly homage towards these small women-children as he would have used to very great ladies, Mr. De Burgo smiled them out.

As the door closed behind all three, the children sped away like arrows from a bow, still going noiselessly. In a few breathless seconds they were at the top of the house, raced down a long passage, and were safe in Rebecca's room. Only then they laughed aloud, so delighted at having done with the horrible ordeal of meeting grandpapa. Their joy could hardly get enough vent. They jumped, they flung themselves panting on chairs.

'What were they like, Nannie?' cried Aileen, 'I didn't dare see much higher than their feet.'

'Oh, I saw as high as their watch-chains, and I looked in the face of the one who took me on his knee,' answered Nannie, proud of her past courage.

'Let's mimic them! I can do the old fat lord,' cried Aileen wildly, in her glee trying to force a gruff bass from her slender throat.

'No, don't! he's a lord! You never hear grandpapa making fun of lords,' suddenly interposed Hector, with momentary pompous gravity; for he was not well satisfied with his own share in the interview below-stairs, especially as he loved to shine before the little girls; and, at this juncture, it struck him that further participation in their mirth was undignified, not to say unseemly.

'It doesn't seem right to go mimicking grandpapa's friends and mine, when they come to see us.'

'Oh yes, *your* friends,' jeered Aileen.

'So they are. Didn't you hear Lord William call me his old friend; and haven't I met him on board the yacht several times?' retorted her brother, with angry superiority.

'Oh, of course they're all friends with the heir,' struck in a foolish housemaid, overhearing the colloquy.

There was a steady succession of housemaids at Black Abbey, of whom Rebecca averred, 'each was younger and foolisher nor the last;' and their departures might be invariably prophesied by their master's flying visit to his home. Hector, not knowing whether to feel flattered or the reverse, walked off with his head high.

'He thinks himself a big man, I can tell ye,' said the housemaid, with vulgar sarcasm, looking after him, yet as if she thought his claims to importance well founded, too.

Feeling hurt and insignificant, the little girls crept away to a great empty attic, used by both as a sort of hermitage when sick of the vile world. There, crouched side by side, they called the housemaid a nasty thing; bewailed Hector's displeasure, though too proud to solicit its remission; and sated themselves with a luxury of imaginary woe.

Guests, indeed, were seldom pressed to stay longer than two days at Black Abbey. Their host always regretted their departure much, whilst yet declaring that with his mere bachelor establishment, and such a dull neighbourhood, where the natives were barbarians, he could not wish his dear friends for their own sakes to remain longer. In this manner were the prodigious efforts of the poor old servants, who had toiled indefatigably with wonderful results, disposed of.

'We made a big show, anyhow,' said the cook to Rebecca, when the above remark was reported to her.

'Ay—if they could only see how much barer things generally is,' replied the latter grimly.

'"You've just had pot-luck—taken things rough and ready with me," says he, when Lord William was bidding good-bye.'

'Rough and ready indeed! and me slaving at the rooms for days.'

'Pot-luck indeed!' quoth the wearied-out aged cook.

CHAPTER 7

THE OTHER SIDE OF THE PICTURE

At the breakfast-table, on the morning after the strangers had all left, the children reappeared downstairs, and supped their porridge and milk cautiously, lest a lapping sound should offend the fastidious ear of the old house-tyrant, whose close presence awed them terribly.

Their grandfather was bilious this morning after a course of late hours, and much eating and drinking with his friends; but he had a wonderful knack of keeping back his indigestions till suitable days. He toyed delicately with some dry toast, then pushed away his plate disgusted, and silently eyed the children, who felt 'creeps up their backs' as they expressed it, but dared not raise their glances, and supped on.

'Egad! I wish I had as fine an appetite as you. It takes plenty to keep you!' he said at last, with a still sneer, and a semi-amusement that did not sound at all cheerful in the little girls' ears; to whom, especially Nannie, he addressed himself.

'Go on' (as the latter's spoon wavered and turned back unemptied to her plate); 'you had better make the most of it, while you can eat at my expense. I can tell you, when you grow up, you will find it hard enough to feed yourself, if you go on at that rate—Miss Glutton.'

Nannie's porridge tasted now like ashes in her mouth; the milk sickened her, yet she dared not desist from swallowing it. Certainly, she was not suffering, like Mr. De Burgo, from a surfeit of the best wines in his costly cellar. Yet poor Nan's present disturbance of mind, caused by those cutting words, made her feel quite as bodily indisposed at that moment.

'As to Aileen, she may be a little better off than you, but not much,' continued the venerable head of the family with a displeasing smile, impartially bent on troubling them all, though his little granddaughter's sweet face made her his favourite, in some degree. 'If your mother *had* had any fortune that could have gone to you; but just like her! she had the impudence to entrap your father when she hadn't a penny. As it is, Hector and I will have to give you something, I suppose—not much.'

Aileen melted into tears.

'Stop—stop! I'll box your ears if I see any of that,' said the old man warningly, with a look of latent savagery in his blue eye.

Aileen did her best to obey, and gulped down sobs instead of breakfast.

The Fräulein, who had sat hitherto silent, huddled together as if trying to draw into herself from uncongenial surroundings, now attempted a remark that it was a fine day, with suddenness; and swallowing some tea, choked herself and coughed violently.

'My dear madam,' said Mr. De Burgo, with extremest politeness, 'you are nervous this morning, I fear.'

The poor lady did not utter another syllable.

'Total silence!' observed the grandfather grimly after a few minutes. 'I regret that you children do not try to be more agreeable in your conversation, when with me. You could all laugh enough yesterday, by yourselves.'

A tremor ran through all; where? how? had he over-heard them?

'My puppies is* growing big,' uttered poor Hector, trying to be brave; but, in his flutter of mind, using the bad grammar he heard among the labourers.

'Is they?' mimicked his grandfather, with a withering expression. 'Those are no doubt the expressions you pick up from the

---

* grammar rule (see glossary)

low company you are so fond of; from that old brute Robert and the rest. I am thinking of giving those puppies a present to Lord William, and if you use such language again I shall.'

'But they were given to *me*,' the little lad dared to object with quivering lips, after a moment's pause of horror. For he loved the dogs passionately; and their private possessions were so sacredly respected amongst each other by the children, that he felt no less than that his grandfather meant to rob him by superior force. Yet he forced back rising tears doggedly and bravely, believing that to make him cry like a baby was the old man's unkind wish.

'Let me tell you, sir, that if you think you have a right to call even *your soul* your own, while you are under my care, you are uncommonly mistaken,' replied Mr. De Burgo in a voice certainly calm, but as keen as knives, bending forward to transfix the chubby boy with eyes that seemed to hold his, a moment, in a glance like a vice.

A perfect stillness now prevailed.

The charming old gentleman smiled; took snuff; and rose, expressing an agreeable hope to meet the Fräulein at luncheon again. Then he descended the hall-door steps, leaning on his heavy gold-topped cane, looking in his spick and span attire a Dresden-china aged beau; a fine specimen of the good old school, going round his farm and his gardens in the early morning.

Hector rushed from the governess's presence, in which he especially hated betraying weakness, as he always tried to impress her with respect for his manliness; but ready to burst into a relieving howl, if he met an old friend. He met Robert the lounger, luckily.

'Don't ye believe a ha'porth he says, Master Hector,' quoth that Unclean but now sympathizing One reassuringly. 'Sure! didn't I hear Lord William offering to *buy* them the other day;

and the master saying he meant to shoot over them himself in Scotland, next year. *Give* them!—Bless your heart, no!' Hector came upstairs again with his broad fair face quite cheered; and naturally could see no great cause, now, for Aileen's excessive grief, whom he found hotly bathed in tears, with Nannie standing over her, outwardly quiet, inwardly brimful with suppressed emotion, calm with desperate resolve.

'I—I wish I never had been born,' cried Aileen. In the excitement of the moment, she felt herself an intruder in the world, a pariah to her family. Her childish mind was outraged at the insult to her mother, whom, not remembering, she invested with the tenderest thoughts her little brain could conceive.

'Oh!—shut up! Girls cry about a word. I didn't cry when he said he'd take my puppies; and that would be something to cry about,' preached Hector, trying to puff his virtues into an example for Aileen's imitation. But, seeing his consolation was indignantly rejected—there being no analogy in the cases to his sister's mind—he put his arm affectionately round her neck, and with a thump on her shoulder, meant to destroy any imagined sentimentality in the action, cried out lustily, 'Never mind about your fortune, old girl. I'll make it all right! I wouldn't mind how many more of you there were; no! not though it would be ever so much more out of my pocket!'

Aileen's eyes brightened like bits of blue sky through rain-clouds at this magnanimity. Nannie looked up, her gloom of soul somewhat dispersed by such generosity. Hector felt quite pleased and proud of himself. Off went brother and sister to the school-room, and then sounded a little laugh from Aileen, like a bird's twitter. Nannie heard it, and was glad in her solemn, small soul that her friend was light-minded enough to be so soon comforted. With her it should be otherwise.

CHAPTER 8

'UNDER A HAYCOCK, FAST ASLEEP'

THAT afternoon was sacrificed, unwillingly, by Mr. De Burgo to the yearly ceremony of visiting a few of his richest tenants' farms; the poorer ones were never thus shone upon by the light of their landlord's face. He ordered the children to accompany him. 'It is proper to look as if one took an interest in these sort of people,' said he, waving his gold-headed cane with didactic majesty; 'I make it a point, always, to do what is correct. You must all learn to do the same.'

The little ones felt quite surprised at receiving injunctions to continue as a solemn duty what, without their grandfather's knowledge, was already their greatest delight. For weekly they harried the farms around, of all which they were made free, being everywhere welcomed with hearty greetings, and oatmeal or griddle-cakes baked expressly in their honour. But, either from instinct or awe, they were now mute.

Curiously, too, at the first farm, when the landlord, calling but its mistress to the threshold (which was his manner of visiting), informed her, for lack of other conversation, of the children's respective names and ages, the farmer's wife, who knew infinitely more about them than himself, only answered with canny reserve, 'Dear, yes! yer honour. … Sure, we know the young ladies and Master Hector, when we see them.'

Aileen immediately giggled. Hector was obliged to frown, and little Nan to pinch her into terrified silence; timid little plotters, fearful of losing their liberties.

At the second farm, Mr. De Burgo deigned, magnificently, to compliment the farmer on his young calves. The latter grinned:

'O, ay, yer honour—but troth I'm thinking *your rearings*' (pointing to the children, with a great haw-haw) 'does you more credit, *considering how much less ye see after them!*'

The old gentleman smiled, took snuff, and answered with Grandisonian jocularity, but—remembered that tenant's familiarity next quarter-day.

On they went, at once, to other farms; Mr. De Burgo, like a fine old patriarch, heading the troop of children and dogs, for he walked fast and far for a man of his age, loving to astonish by his feats younger men of what he considered a weak generation. He himself seemed made of iron; and the little girls now trotted hand in hand after him, with weary legs.

Hector, as the eldest and the boy, mindful of the morning's warning, racked his young brain, continually asking himself, 'Oh, *bother!* what shall I say next?' and as often blighted with a sarcasm, beyond his understanding. If silenced, he was presently asked, 'Well—speak, sir! where's your tongue? Are you sulking?' The little inferior beings behind were not expected to talk much, but a keener fear of consequences had endued them with far greater tact than their brave champion, and they exchanged agonized glances at his many blunders.

They were hurried, averting their noses, past the stench-pools of neglected, outlying hamlets, rotten and squalid. One or two mothers ran after the lord of the soil, seizing the yearly chance of imploring a blessing, as that a roof should be mended, or some grace for the wretched rent. Their harsh angel of Bethesda waved all back. 'I never interfere in these matters—go to my man of business.' Then, laughing under his breath, muttered, 'Good gad! what swarms of children do they raise all the same! Those smells ought to have weeded out some of the surplus, one would think.' On they went past poorer farms where, if a labouring tenant raised his hat, the landlord cheerily cried, 'Glad to see you're so well! —sorry I can't stay today. Hope to come round soon, again,' and walked rapidly on. The children wondered why he chuckled so, after such meetings.

At last, they came again in sight of the woods of home, were out of sight of all signs that a hard landlord, vampire-like, was pitilessly draining the life-blood of the estate.

The pleasantly shaded high road here ran beneath the demesne wall, overtopped by the Black Abbey trees. A lad of about seventeen, with a gun on his shoulder, now passed them, wearing a shabby shooting-coat and a straw hat, which last he raised in frank, though awkward recognition to the little girls, answering a broad grin from Hector with a friendly glance. But the grandfather took the civility as meant for himself, and with infinite condescension, touched his own hat, affably inquiring, 'who is that fine young fellow?'

Instantly a glad chorus arose. 'Oh, that is Luke Cosby. He is so kind to us. He made me a kite.—He mended my doll—'

'Mend!—did he? … He'd better *mend his ways*, the poaching young blackguard, or I'll teach him a lesson he'll remember all his life. I've heard of him,' responded the benignant old gentleman of a few moments before, in a sudden rage, his eyes and nose assuming the hawk-like, hard expression most feared by his dependents. The children cowered, and his gaze hovered over them, as it were gloatingly.

By and by, they came in sight of the manse, which, lying between the two Black Abbey gates, snugly nested amidst its orchard and shadowing trees that hot day, blinked with small, sunshiny windows quite contentedly across its garden-strip and the dusty strip and the dusty road at the high wall and haughty wood just opposite.

'Hush!' suddenly commanded Mr. De Burgo, peering through the orchard hedge; and the children, mute as mice, at once looked too.

In the dappling light and shadow of that pleasant place were some low haycocks, and against one reclined the Reverend Joseph Cosby, with his toes pointed to the sun. The good man's eyes were closed, his mouth open to the perdition of small flies, and a sermon escaped from his relaxed grasp; while his rusty black waistcoat heaved blissfully to a more timeful than tuneful breathing.

Suddenly, just overhead, appeared a charming little girl peeping over the haycock. Utterly unconscious of being watched, she peered down in apparent ecstasy on the sleeper, clasped her hands, tossed back her hair as if such joy unshared was too great, then—oversetting the whole summit of the cock, which was loosely piled, with one shriek of triumph, she sprang down herself with the ruin, burying the poor minister in an indiscriminate mass of hay, legs and arms.

Mr. De Burgo burst into a laugh of such loud, unartificial pleasure at his old neighbour's ill plight that the children, taking permission, ventured to scream with delight, too. This speedily brought Mr. Cosby trotting to the gate to greet his landlord; leading his naughty grandchild, with a proud air and fond, pretended chiding, by the hand.

'Rosy-cheeks: you are the most charming and the prettiest child I have seen for many a day,' said Mr. De Burgo, who did not deign to go further than just to the garden wicket. 'Will you give me a kiss?'

Bella at once hid her face in grandfather's coat—but the moment after peeped out with such a coy glance of rustic coquetry, that the old gentleman caught her and kissed her several times with all the gusto of a decaying beau.

'Would you like *me* for your grandpapa, pretty one?' he asked, chucking her under the chin; then took his snuff with the air of a latter-day Chesterfield.

'Oh, you are far prettier than my grandpapa!' answered Bella, staring at him wide-eyed; then, cunning little minx, immediately fondled Mr. Cosby's hand, adding, 'But I like my own old one, to play with.'

'My wee pussy! Oh, she sees at once the difference. She guesses you would not care to be buried alive in the hay, Mr. De Burgo—ha, ha!' chuckled old Cosby, with sincere pride in that infant wisdom.

'On the contrary, nothing gives me more pleasure than to see my own grandchildren playing round me. But it should be a warning to you not to leave your hay out so long. Why, in England it would have been saved long ago! but in Ireland everything is so mismanaged.'

'Dear, dear, I am sorry—yet, Mr. De Burgo, the weather was very backward. And last year, too, was more severe; as no doubt, sir, the poor among your tenants——'

'Ah! indeed, yes. By the way, we passed a nephew of yours, just now, Mr. Cosby,' blandly interposed the old landlord, who evaded carefully all observations to poverty on his estate. 'He seems a fine young fellow.'

'Well, indeed, he is so, thank you, Mr. De Burgo,' said the innocent old pastor, quite touched. 'A little thin and rawboned, yet; but a good lad—the best!'

'Ah! I am delighted to hear it; delighted. Still, you must forgive me, Mr. Cosby, if, with all good-will and respect to you, I am sorry to feel obliged to say, that, from inquiries I have made, information has been given me that your grand-nephew is always roaming over the country—and never without a gun on his shoulder.' Mr De Burgo's tone, from being terribly courteous, was rapidly becoming as terribly biting, finer manners being superfluous 'Of course, were he any one else, I should have stopped this, as poaching, before now; but liking for *you*——'

'Indeed, indeed, Mr. De Burgo, he always has his license,' the old uncle attempted to put in, much pained.

'Granted—' his landlord caught him up with still more

severity, the hawk likeness showing strongly as he bent his brows. 'Still, as I rear some pheasants behind that wall with expense and trouble' (little enough of any of the three!) 'for my friends' sport next winter, Mr. Cosby, I should resent their being knocked over, if they come to feed in your stubble—you understand.'

'Oh, now Mr. De Burgo!—do you think my boy would do that?' cried the poor minister, so hurt that his eyes (he being a simple soul) absolutely filled with tears. 'He has never so much as shot a blackbird, hereabouts, for fear you should hear of it, and think it was more, sir. But Colonel Alexander, at Ballyboly*, gave him free leave to shoot over every foot of his land, being more kind than I can say to my boy; and the Demerics†, too, for they have all such a wonderful liking for him—'

'Say no more! That will do my good friend. It is all right, no doubt; as I was sure it would be, with you,' interrupted Mr. De Burgo soothingly, laying his hand on the minister's shoulder with almost affectionate condescension, so soon as he heard of his neighbour's different behaviour. Although these last had almost cut his acquiantance, and that he affected to despise them as 'natives' to his occasional guests, it was curious that he yet did not care to oppose them, in such matters, with the fine tyrannical spirit he displayed in his own family.

His manner now imposed on the innocent little ones, whose hearts had been swelling with grief because grandpapa was so cross to kind Mr. Cosby; and on the latter, too, who was, indeed,

---

* In *Orange Lily*, May Crommelin calls Carrowdore where the novel is set, 'Ballyboly', and the occupants of Carrowdore Castle (where she herself lived) the 'Alexanders.'

† In *Queenie: A Novel*, May Crommelin calls Ballywalter where the novel is set, 'Ballymore', and the occupants of Ballwalter House the 'Demerics.'

only a grown-up child. Mr. De Burgo went on, 'I should have thought, however, that—ahem—literary pursuits would be more suitable for this young man, since I understand he is to follow your profession; and I believe … ah! … I told you so before.'

'Very true—yes, indeed—so you did, sir,' replied the minister in confusion, yet smiling, fears being banished. 'And what do you think he said? "Uncle Joe," said he, "please tell Mr. de Burgo, if ever he speaks of this again, that *Shakespaere was a poacher!"* Indeed, he did; and yet, really now, he never meant it for conceit. But it's a notion he has, that every true man has the love of sport in him—somewhere. "And the Persians," says he, "were brought up to ride and to hunt, and speak the truth. You would like me, surely, to be a many-sided man, Uncle Joe," he said; "and not a lopsided creature."'

Many! … ah! … very good,' murmured his patron, raising his frosted eyebrows airily as he took snuff; and thinking in his heart that the young rascal in question, must be a 'very queer customer!' 'Talking of teaching, Mr. Cosby, could you … ah! … undertake to put some Latin into the head of this grandson of mine, before he goes to Harrow? Could you … ahem, ah! … come up to Black Abbey every day?'

'Surely, surely, Mr. de Burgo, did I not teach his dear young father, and never loved a pupil better' (and was still unpaid). 'Dear me! … I *beg* pardon; I should not have reminded you … why teaching Master Hector will be quite a pleasure.'

'Are you going up to Black Abbey? O, let me go too!' besought a small voice.

'No, no, Bella. Be good, now, dearie; and I'll ask some nice little children to play with you.'

'I don't want nice little children; they're always nasty farmer's children. I want to play with little ladies like Miss Aileen and Miss Nannie, and learn to talk French, too,' retorted Bella, in a temper; then stamping passionately on the ground, 'If I mayn't go to Black Abbey, I wish you would dig a big hole here and bury me.'

Old de Burgo was vastly tickled. 'Why do you want to go to my house, my beauty?—tell *me*.'

'Because it is so *beau-oo-tiful!* not like this ugly house,' replied Bella, won by his apparent sympathy; then, stretching out her chubby arms to him with all the fearlessness of a petted child and the grace of a cherub, 'O let me go there, sometimes—very often. You are such a nice, pretty grand-papa; not cross, like my bad one to-day. You *will* let me go.'

Had she been an ugly, even a common-place child, who so clasped Mr. de Burgo's very coat-hem, farewell favour! she would have been shaken off like a muddy puppy; but, 'Egad! the impertinence of the pretty little wretch,' almost made Mr. de Burgo laugh. Next moment, he had lifted her on the gate, to the mingled momentary horror, then utter amazement of his own grandchildren, who had expected their humbler friend's utter annihilation. 'Yes, she must come up to Black Abbey, Mr. Cosby,' he loftily decided; 'I insist upon it she shall come up and play with my little girls, sometimes.'

'Thank you, sir, thank you,' replied the worthy pastor, quite flustered and flattered. 'Indeed, she has been once or twice; but Mrs. Rebecca and I agreed' (here he lowered his voice) 'that as, hereafter, they will be in somewhat different positions in society, it might be only future disappointment to my wee girl to encourage a close friendship, now.'

'Bah! Humbug! Nonsense. Mine may learn, now, at all events, not to be upsetting; a very good lesson. Do you hear, children, you are to let this little Rosy-cheeks play with you sometimes—and be civil to her.'

Whereupon Mr. de Burgo crumpled up the little manse-maid's bright face with his old hand, kissed her red rosebud mouth with the more satisfaction that he saw his own little ones staring wide-eyed, rather jealously, and turning away, cut short the pastor's half-gratified remonstrances and the child's jubilee of delight.

'Isn't she very pretty, grandpapa?' Hector ventured to observe, by way of safe remark; after some silence, as they were being herded at a very rapid pace homeward.

'Humph!—An animal beauty,' was the sneering, musing remark that only followed; one which puzzled the little lad.

Thenceforth Bella Cosby went often up to Black Abbey, a welcome playmate to the little girls there, who also in their generosity, not liking to feel superior to their friend, eagerly tried to impart to her as much as they could teach of French and German—more, indeed, than their pupil, though docile and flexible, often cared to learn.

'She just wriggles out of her lessons,' quoth Aileen, with righteous indignation, in her absence.

'Ah! well,' peaceably replied the other little task-mistress, 'she's rather stupid, poor thing! though she is pretty.'

CHAPTER 9

'A WOMAN, A DOG, AND A WALNUT-TREE'

THERE was an immense neglected garden at Black Abbey, but it lay in such a sunny hollow, sheltered by high walls and environing trees, that the flowering bushes, and even many an old-fashioned more fragile blossom planted by dead and gone De Burgo dames, still flourished luxuriantly, almost uncared-for. Copses of lilacs and laburnums grew here and there. The grass-plots were rough round the fish-ponds, and the sun-dial slanted awry. The fuchsias, rejoicing in the mild sea-breezes, grew into very thickets. And though the fruit-trees were as old 'as the hills,' said the gardener the children thought Eve's apples could not have been more delicious'

Going there one blazing noon to play, when the air was heavy with scents and the hot hum of bees, little Aileen and Nan hailed young Hector, whom they met armed with a sling, his pocket bulging with pebbles.

'Come with us,' they cried, springing on him like kittens. 'We've dug up Nannie's doll' (Hector had buried it the week before.) 'So, as it's born again, we're going to christen it.'

'That's a stupid girls' game,' said the youthful Trojan loftily. 'I'm going to kill magpies. I heard grandpapa tell Lord William that they sucked all our pheasants' eggs, and that our old fool of a keeper never destroyed them.' (The poor man's duties were more numerous than the eggs.)

'Well, you needn't fire stones in the garden then; for Robert said you would break the glass-houses,' gibingly retorted Aileen, to take down his conceit.

Hector's pleasant face flushed.

'I've just been there; and Robert has no right to order me,' he rejoined, trying to look big, adding with a somewhat suspicious suavity. 'But, anyway, I'm off to the loneliest parts of the woods all by myself. You two would be frightened! but with my knife in my pocket, and a big stick, I'm ready for any robber.'

The feebler sex quickly consoled themselves for his absence by the solemn ceremony they engaged in at the garden pump. Having dowered the doll nobly with polysyllabic names (being most careful to say nothing irreverent in their invented service), and uttering wishes for her future goodness, with their eyes devoutly tight-shut, Nannie deputed herself, on the vinery steps, to deliver a sermon—to the special delight of her grave small soul. She made her nursery text, 'Little chillens should be good!' the ingenious means of bringing many of the sins of her congregation into painful evidence; first solemnly adjuring 'my dear brezrens,' (Aileen and the doll) to think a great deal about her preaching, and beginning, 'It's very nasty of little chillens to slap each other.'

'Well! you scratched me afterwards!' fired up poor Aileen, recognising an allusion to late events.

'Now, Aileen! it isn't right to stop a clergyman in his sermon—*and you know it isn't!*' wailed the preacher, with righteous indignation.

Whereupon, the congregation, having a deep reverence for the rules of the game, tried to calm itself.

'And when little chillens takes' (*i.e.* steal) 'cakes or jam, I don't think it's nice to eat it all up; and not give some to other little chillens.'

'That was Hector; and you know there wasn't enough for you,' wrathfully shrieked the poor congregation, conscious of generous impulses, and springing from its pew in a wheelbarrow.

'Oh—my! stop!' ejaculated the preacher in a natural tone

with alarm, and with her everyday lisp. 'What *is* dis?'

There was a small pane broken in the vinery door close by, and the fragments lay around.

'We couldn't have done it!' uttered Aileen, after a pause of round-eyed dismay. 'But if grandpapa sees it—!'

'It must have been poor Hector—Oh poor Hector!' softly murmured Nan, with extremest pity for the possible punishment of her worshipped hero.

Feeling convinced that this was the case, both loving little hearts agreed, they 'must mend the pane immejently; and never, *never* tell!'

So, eagerly manufacturing some mud putty at the pump, Aileen, as the adventurous spirit, tried to plaster in the biggest bits of glass, whilst the more timid Nannie acted hodman; and soon both became quite hotly happy over their labour of love, their sweet baby-faces flushed with excitement, and themselves no more heedful than the bees or butterflies of the broad noon-blaze the sun was pouring down on that delightful, world-forgotten garden.

'It *only* looks as if somebody had putted some mud there; but the glass is really in, at least two bits is,' observed Nan, trying to excuse some inward qualms as to the dirty appearance of the work, which both poor little things had now stepped back to examine.

'And grandpapa is going away to-morrow, and won't never see it,' cried Aileen, excuting a dance of delight.

'*Won't he?*' said a dreaded voice behind them.

Years afterwards, when both little girls had become grown women, they distinctly recalled how their knees had knocked together, how their hearts wildly beat like startled birds against the bars of a cage on hearing the sardonically cruel ring of their grandfather's voice that day, which made them know at once that severe vengeance was coming. He had stolen upon them with as light a step as an old panther, perceiving that they were intent upon some mischief, and wishing to amuse himself by first watching his unconscious victims at play. He was angered now, doubly, at overhearing those who should have been the tender objects of his care expressing their natural joy at his speedy departure; and that still more by their gestures than their words. Tyrant-like, he almost hated them for it. Perhaps, in his heart, he yet would have liked the children to love him; though why they should do so, beyond the bare fact that they called him grandfather and guardian, heaven knows! for, certainly, he gave them no other cause.

Seizing them in turn, then, 'by the scruff of the neck' as he termed it, the old man shook both the little girls as he might a couple of terriers. Then he reproached them bitterly for their deceit in attempting to hide their breakage of the pane. What had most angered him, he never mentioned. Gasping, almost breathless, yet strong still in their sense of innocence, both anxiously cried out that they were blameless; appealing to each other, poor infants, for confirmation.

Ha! So they were liars, besides; Mr. de Burgo asked no better than the chance of beating *that* out of them.

So, under a storm of abuse which seemed to lash their ears like hail, both were driven before him to the house. Naturally the poor baby-hearts quailed, knowing of old that a whipping was in store; naturally the little feet lagged as they went to punishment, sobbing so painfully that the gardener, generally considered a gruesome specimen of crossness, felt his human feelings give a sudden heave within his body, and, 'thinking it a peety of the wee yuns,' uttered a curse.

'So you can't walk faster, eh, Miss Aileen? *I'll* teach you! Got the sulks, Miss Nannie, I see. *I'll* take them out of you,' were the jesting remarks, backed by a running accompaniment of kicks delivered daintily, with which this fascinating old gentleman made the culprits hasten their pace. While hurrying on himself, with grim satisfaction, he observed occasionally gaily—

> 'A woman, a dog, and a walnut-tree,
> The more you beat them, the better they be.'

He quite rejoiced, indeed, in the disobedience of a dog, giving him a plea for seizing the poor brute by one hind-leg, and thrashing it almost to death, reiterating between his teeth, 'I'll break your spirit,—if I have to kill you!'

With just the same feeling, he now began a painfully similar scene, which need not be described. But both little victims, though so young, had high tempers, being as the old man swore 'unbroken;' and being bred to a strict sense of truth by their governess and Rebecca, or rather never cowed into being untruthful, both felt themselves martyrs in a sacred cause. First, Mr. de Burgo observed that, not for the worth of the pane, but for their continued lying, he meant to chastise them. This, though uttered with an air of severely scrupulous justice, seemed utter mockery to the quaking infants, who believed he was *glad of the chance*. Then the wails, shrieks, and sobbing heard from the study made poor Rebecca's blood curdle, as she hastened to the spot; believing some one of her children must be killed by mischance—till stopped outside by all the eaves-dropping servants, who knew what was going on, and were boiling with indignation—even fish-hearted Robert.

'Och, och! my poor babes! Oanee! my wee lambs! … he's murdering them,' wailed the old woman; not venturing to go in, lest she herself might be dismissed and worse happen to her darlings. Then, with bitter hatred, clenching her fist at the door, 'Ah! ye bad ould Turk! blathering to Lord William about the "*dear*" childer, as if butter wouldn't melt in your mouth.

It's blarney for strangers with you; but bloody wars at home!'

'Listen,' growled sullen Robert. 'Ay! he's carrying on in there finely; as he did with his own ones, till he broke their hearts—clean and clever!'

'A curse'll surely come upon him for it, sooner *or* later,' solemnly prophesied the cook, wagging her head.

The good governess rushed out of doors in a state of mental agitation defying philosophy; her plans for training these tender souls by the sole force of moral persuasion ruthlessly shattered; the womanhood in her, which she termed a profound abstract reverence for youth, so pained, that to her own infinite surprise she found herself weeping.

Meanwhile, inside the study, Aileen's hysterical nature, like that of many a poor would-be martyr, had so nearly betrayed her, that she screamed out her readiness to say anything she was bid. At that, little Nannie, who would have died rather than let a false confession be wrung from her, and whose rather dull bodily appearance concealed a large heroic soul—such as is seen, indeed, in some few children destined to answer for more talents to the King than their fellows, but oftenest in those strangely precocious young spirits that early die—stopped her own wailing to cry, in a tone that pierced deeper into her little comrade's heart than pain into her body, 'No, no, Ailie! you must not be a coward—look at me!' And poor Aileen, shame-stricken and agonized, recanted again; becoming so choked with convulsive emotion that, despite her grandfather's rage, he saw nothing more could be extracted from her. Turning his wrath on the weak little mortal who had so robbed him of victory, old De Burgo beat Nan till his arm was tired, but could not now elicit a scream from her. Fearful that her companion might again give way, the child took her awful punishment in almost utter silence; and with a passive endurance marvellous in such an infant. Then the study-door was flung open; and while the servants scattered like small birds before a hawk, their old master, passing through them, dragged his two limp victims upstairs, and thrust each into one of the big empty bed-rooms; locking the doors, that solitary confinement might prevent their encouraging each other in the dashed resistance which, as he told both—'Egad! he would lash out of them if he kept them there on bread and water for a twelve month!' He had had some thought of tying each to the leg of a bed, remembering old episodes when Hector's father had defied him; but as both seemed half dead, and certainly incapable of much motion, he left them.

CHAPTER 10

THE TAIL OF THE STORM

LEFT each alone, in pain and terror, the poor little girls although of different tempers, were yet in two respects suffering alike. Both maid-babes felt a sense of horrible degradation at having suffered such bodily chastisement at the hands of one of the other sex; and this they could afterwards remember to their dying day. Both white souls knew for the first time what was hate; and for many and many a month afterwards could not think of Mr. de Burgo without it.

He had beaten them before; and each time their shame and horror of it was a mystery to Hector, who took his (far lighter) canings with sturdy light-heartedness; but those hitherto had never been so cruel, and had been caused by faults, although so diminutive that the punishment was utterly disproportionate, yet that had given an air of justice to the matter in the children's simple minds. They looked upon old Mr. de Burgo as a sort of awful male Nemesis who exacted perfection in them, and they even supposed they *ought* therefore, to be immaculate.

Unhappy Aileen, whose too excitable mind was almost overset by the brutal treatment she had received, writhed and rolled on the floor in her loneliness, wishing her grand-father dead!—wishing that she could see him beaten and tortured, as he had tortured her.

Nan, in fellow-solitude, lay still and white as a small corpse, feeling too sick and weak in body to stir the hundredth part of an inch, but her mind only too active. The sweet baby face was all smeared with tears, as she infinitely pitied herself and her dear fellow-sufferer; but no revenge was there. That was an impossible sin to her mind; unlike Aileen, she only wished herself dead and safe from harm. Then came the thought … *why not?* Not thinking now of her dear nurse's sorrow at losing her, of Hector and Aileen—the timid child only had one idea in her small soul, what an escape it would be from Mr. de Burgo's barbarity to go to God. Her ideas of death were extremely vague, but the Fräulein's great effort was to teach the little ones not to fear it ('true philosophy,' she quoted, 'is to know how to die'); and then Rebecca always talked of Heaven as a most 'lovely, nice place' where Nan's papa and mamma lived. Yes! once free, Nannie would slip to that one deep place she knew of in the great rushy mere, where the wild ducks paddled unharmed, and the teal flew in winter. There, laying down her hat on the brink, she would sit on the edge and slip softly in; then all woes would be over with poor little Nan.

The imaginative child felt a deliciously mysterious shudder at so tragic yet happy an escape for herself as this seemed. Next she seemed to see searchers finding her body, all bewailing her, and saying what a bad man Mr. de Burgo had been. 'And he'd be so 'shamed; and maybe zat would teach big men not to whip little chil'ren,' reflected his infant victim, with a thrill of satisfaction at that requital *that* quite did her good. After death, existence seemed to be a placid contemplation of her tormentor's vain remorse, and everybody's sorrow for a child of so many virtues. Before now, she had several times thought of starving herself, and so making her old guardian 'sorry' for his taunts on her appetite; but, alas for heroines! her six-year old strength of will could never resist the temptations of smoking hot tea and bread and butter. The mere was best.

During this time, Mr. de Burgo had gone out for a long walk over his estate, not meaning to come back till late afternoon, since he never lunched. The day was fine; he annihilated the hopes of some tenants; he felt a grim enjoyment, on the whole.

The children had had a sound 'leathering,' and though they still showed extraordinary obstinacy, good! it would give him all the greater satisfaction to break them in. All women and inferiors needed breaking in. And, to prove it, he idly struck the setter that followed him. It cringed. Then he caressed it; and the poor creature fawned and licked his hand, looking up at him with gentle brown eyes.

The old man was alone in the fields, and he laughed out aloud. That was how he would have liked women to be; soulless, submissive, caressed whilst young and pretty, discarded when old. Some he had loved (or thought he loved) in hot youth, he still knew, and privately called 'ugly old devils!' Still, he valued a veneer of courtesy so highly, since to seem what he was not and say oftenest other than he thought, were 'in his mind society's tactics,' that most women only thought him a fine specimen of the old school—who cared little for their society after dinner.

Coming home, he cut himself a supple young ash-stick, and tried it with satisfaction. Two of the workmen met him, and each said, 'Master Hector is looking everywhere for you, sir.' What a bore these brats were!

Going upstairs, with a heavy determined tread, he first unlocked Aileen's door, who had sprung up in fear and uttered a wild shriek. 'Stop that, and come here,' said the grand-father, inviting her to approach with a threatening wave of the stick. Aileen, almost beside herself with terror, only shrieked again at this grand-paternal gesture, and rushed behind the bed. Ha! so she required disobedience to be whipped out of her. A short chase ensued; a scuffle; two switching lashes—then, the agonized child, not knowing what she did, caught Mr. de Burgo's arm with her teeth. He tore her off, when she fell on the floor in convulsions. Rebecca now rushing in, though unbidden, was just in time to catch up and carry her off; being bidden by her master, white with rage, to take the horrid little wretch out of his sight!

Now it was Nannie's turn. The child lay still even when the old man stood close over her. Solitary, bruised, feeling pain and hunger, the young creature's wonderful endurance had not lessened but increased and soured into utter obstinacy, so that she would have been torn in pieces, now, rather than give way. 'Will you say, now, that you told a lie, miss?' said the voice that made her timorous flesh creep. 'No—no—no! I didn't tell no lie,' the little one murmured. Then the cruel blow-shower seemed to rain upon her again. But despite each stroke of pain seeming worse than the last. Nan hardly cried aloud only moaned. Her infant mind suddenly conceived the thought that soon she would be certainly killed, and then her guardian would indeed be sorry!—and this strangely enabled her to bear up for a few more seconds, but might hardly have helped fortitude longer—when suddenly it all ceased.

The old man stood looking down on the small figure that was almost like a corpse, so motionless, and the pallid little face that had assumed a startling resemblance. 'Egad!' he muttered, drawing unconsciously back; then slowly, as if becoming unwillingly possessed by some overmastering thought—'Egad! … she does look half dead … and so like her father!' Then again, after a pause, still looking how still she lay, only her eyes under their half-closed lids seeming conscious of his presence, he muttered, in strange self-justification of his weakness, 'You maybe thankful you are no child of mine; or I would see you in your grave before you got the better of me! … but it wouldn't do!'

He went slowly, and called down agitated, hysterical Rebecca; who, poor soul, had been mistakenly supposing that because her dearest nursling was silent, she was not suffering.

Then, with his mouth like a thin line of living wrath, the old master almost shrivelled the nurse with the reproachful abuse poured on her for the disgraceful up-bringing of the children, which had resulted in such glaring disobedience that he had been forced to punish them heavily. Threatening her, next, with instant dismissal, if her charges ever again showed such symptoms of temper, Mr. de Burgo left the poor scape-goat utterly crushed by that last menace, and descended somewhat relieved by this outpouring of black choler.

About an hour afterwards—when cold disgust had taken the place of anger's boiling heat, and when Mr. de Burgo felt that he would be best pleased never to be tormented more with hearing or sight of those girl-brats, whose weakness of body prevented him from punishing their tenacity of spirit—young Hector burst into the study like a red-hot grape-shot, 'Beat me, grandpapa! Beat me!—it was me that broke the pane! The boy's face was flushed; tears had been streaming down his face most of the afternoon, which last he had been spending in hunting for his grandfather to set matters right. He now fairly howled, at thoughts of his little girl companions, like a mastiff-pup. 'Stop blubbering' ordered old De Burgo, who felt that this whole business was really becoming quite offensive. But Hector was a boy—was his heir—was a male De Burgo. Treatment for girls was not fit for him, whom his grand-father certainly chastised, but still would have suffered no meaner mortal to do so. Hector's punishments too were rare, and from caprice, not part of a system of oppression; he was to the old man as a little prince brought up with two small beggar-maids. So, laying his hand on the boy's head, the grandfather blandly remarked—to stop the noise without more disagreeability—'This is … ah! … an unfortunate misunderstanding, but we will say no more about it; you have been punishing yourself enough, I see.' Hector, however, refused to be so easily comforted. Therefore old De Burgo was obliged to lecture him for doubting the right of anything done by his grandfather; adding, with magnificent but extreme vagueness, that it was for faults inherent in the female race he had been forced to punish the little girls. 'You will be a man, my dear boy,' he ended, 'and if ever you misbehave, I shall appeal to your good sense and honesty; but girls—like all women—are very different: and I shall expect you, Hector, to help me in teaching them that they must obey without a word—without a murmur—in anything! everything!' His little grandson—and no wonder!—soon looked big with his own importance as a future man, yet still showed such signs of absurd distress at each mention of Nan and Ailie's beating, that Mr. de Burgo suddenly promised to buy him Farmer Muckle's white pony, and to forgive the little girls for his sake, since he had behaved so finely in confessing his fault.

Out shot Hector, delighted, to tell dirty Robert, the steward, and all the men-world, his news—a happy little sky-rocket, this time; was it any wonder? Such a white pony of ponies as he had often sighed for!

Old De Burgo yawned mightily with relief, thinking he had just behaved like an angel of patience. Thank heaven! to-morrow he would be off for another half-year's freedom; had cleverly tided over much disagreeable business owing to late bad harvests, and dashed poor tenants who would get poorer and poorer, and confounded richer ones that were unsqueezable. He would have a big gamble at Homburg to console himself.

Big he called it, beforehand; but it might not be ruinous; for he was cold-blooded in this as in his other vices. Nevertheless, it was now his favourite one; all other passions had palled. Play he had taken to, somewhat late in life; had often had runs of luck; and now it seemed likely that his devotion to it would last as long as he lived, or that the Black Abbey woods were standing.

And the Black Abbey estate was not entailed.

CHAPTER 11

'A WEE WOMAN!'

Mr. de Burgo had taken himself (and, it seemed, a big shadow also) away from Black Abbey; every one breathed freely again, rejoicing like small birds when the hawk is gone. Hector daily rode his white pony; and till he should come home again in the evening, and give them a turn upon this wonder of an animal, Nan and Aileen played much with the little lassie from the manse. The latter was invited up by old Rebecca, to give spirits to her poor little charges, who moped for many a day after their beating, even when bodily recovered. Their minds were indeed so impressed, that neither ever forgot that scene; and, till her life's end, the more imaginative Nannie could never see her guardian look at her full in the face, without the feeling that he would be glad to strike her.

It was no wonder that little Bella, therefore, with her great gift of sympathy with all those in her sight, and pretty if vulgar curiosity, soon wheedled both her loftier friends out of the secret they had meant to keep hidden as a disgrace. Of course, also, her own too open little mind, could no more keep the tale than a passage-way can passers by—according unto her nature.

The minister, his little grandchild, and young Luke, were all at tea one night in the manse-parlour, which, though too odorous of bygone bacon, was still homely and snug to its bachelor masters; and little Bella was as usual on her gran'dad's knee. The spoiled child, at this evening meal, was a small but constant temptation to sin through selfishness, to the good old pastor; for most even holy-minded men having a besetting sin, that of the reverend Joseph Cosby was—self-indulgence in buttered toast. He loved smacking his lips over the most buttery, hot bits; and when one specially so was uncovered midmost in the pile, seldom could resist bolting his own share and snatching hastily at it. But next instant, with what a conscience-stricken air he would withhold himself and offer the dainty to the rest. Luke, suppressing a smile, always refused; but Bonnibel's plump small fists never failed unhesitatingly to grasp it; when the good man would try to take patiently both his disappointment and the next piece.

Assuredly, when nightly praying to be cleansed from the sins, however small, that, as says an old divine, our souls gather in the daily walk of life as our feet do dust—explaining thus the sacred saying, 'He that is washed, needeth not save to wash his feet, but is clean every whit'—this, of such petty greediness, was not unlamented by the good and childlike man. Excess in the matter of cream and buttered toast may seem ridiculous to some—no matter! it was a sign to him of worse he might come to; and he conquered it—most nobly! It had to be watched sternly, however, since sometimes it did get the better of him.

This night it was evident that Miss Bonnibel, from her important air, was almost bursting with some huge secret.

'Oh, gran'da!' she whispered by-and-by with round eyes, 'isn't it awful how that bad old Mr. de Burgo beated his poor little girls?'

Thereupon, the lucky cherished little grand-daughter told the whole story, to the great indignation of her two listeners—who, however, only looked silently at each other—adding strict injunctions to secrecy because, as she ingenuously confessed to her grandfather, she had herself taken similar pledges. And when the old man mildly reproached her for such a breach of confidence, the little one hugged him tight, explaining, with kisses, 'Oh, well I did promise not—but I've only told *you*!'

'A wee woman! a wee woman! Isn't that, for all the world, the way her sex keep secrets?' ejaculated old Mr. Cosby as Bonnibel smiled herself off to bed, softening even the grim face of old Mary the maid-of-all-work, as, clasping the latter's horny hand, she danced upstairs to her crib in the best bed-room overhead (for that she should have the best of all they had, was a matter of course in that little household); and with the absence of her ringing laugh and bounding, often bouncing tread, the pleasant home-noises and human sunshine of the manse seemed to those in the parlour below vanished with her under the bed-clothes.

But then young Luke exclaimed, while tying flies, 'I wouldn't give a farthing for a woman who couldn't keep a secret—and that wasn't *true*. I'd whistle her to the winds.'

Whereupon he laid down his work and threw his lanky arms above his head energetically,—then, with a softer manner—for indeed, as old Mary affirmed, young Luke's anger was 'just a puff and a blaze—and over!'—he continued gravely, 'And we must really be more strict with our child, Uncle Joe, or she will begin to prevaricate. Did you notice how she tried to evade acknowledging her promise?' (For Miss Bonnibel had tried laughably to shuffle round the pitfall she had dug for herself, although she would by no means have jumped over it—that would have been a lie!)

The doting grandfather rather helplessly rubbed his bald pate with his red cotton handkerchief, quite disturbed that Luke should really find fault with their joint treasure. It might have been two parents consulting together, from their earnest air, and the younger the sterner one.

'Ah! well, well! my boy,' apologized the old man, 'she'll grow out of it. Take my word for it, there's nothing drives little children, ay! and even women, so much to untruth as just fear, being timid creatures.'

'That's God's truth, I do believe,' cried young Luke, who in those days was given to using strong expressions, according to his nature; and who, though righteously severe like all youth, yet spoiled Bonnibel to the full as much as, if differently from, his uncle. Then he relieved his mind of pent wrath by such denunciations of old Mr. de Burgo as would have considerably astonished that fine old beau, coming from a raw and uncouth Presbyterian student of divinity, who had absolutely his own ideas of chivalry.

The minister's face grew redder as, with his plump hands planted on his stout knees, he gave big sighs over the poor little Black Abbey orphans, at the end of Luke's every fresh sentence—although himself would not speak of the matter, fearing, good soul! he might judge too harshly. It lay heavy on the benevolent old man's mind, that since he taught Hector Latin, he had thereby had a daily opportunity of inculcating better lessons into the little lad than were set by Mr. de Burgo's example; whereas, hitherto, the tutor's eagerness to fill the pupil's brain with verbs had alone occupied him. 'And, as Mrs. Rebecca says, the boy is like a half-baked cake, more than any of the others; just dough-marked by the last one that fingered him. So, if he grows up and takes after the old man, when I might have taught him to do better, I should never forgive myself,' he said sadly.

'He'll never do that. Cheer up, Uncle Joe; and you'll see he'll turn out a fine country gentleman, though he is slow enough at his lessons,' cried Luke. 'You should have seen how keen he was, when I took him out fishing one day.'

The minister smiled broadly: then apologetically rubbed the shapeless old nose in his round face—a nose to which ill-treatment made no difference whatsoever—and observed with gentle insinuation:

"Deed now, Mrs. Rebecca and I were curiously speaking of that very thing; for, as she says, the little fellow wearies of girls' play, and the garden-boys and such-like are no fit companions for him. Ye couldn't, now, Luke ... indeed, I suppose, my dear boy, you'd hardly care to do it ... but still, if you could take him at times with yourself, when you go shooting, or for a long walk, Luke, it would be a good deed—it would, indeed.'

'Humph! Turn bear-leader,' growled Luke, yet good humouredly, though the prospect of curtailing his free, lengthy rambles to suit a child's capacity—of giving up the long afternoons spent lying silently behind a cover, to get a shot at some rare bird, to listen to a small boy's prattle, was a sudden trial to his temper. So it was slowly that he added:

'Well, Uncle Joe, I'll always do my best to please you.'

'You always do please me, my boy.' And Mr. Cosby gazed at the tall youth with a look of touched affection that ill-natured folk might have thought ridiculously incompatible with his comic figure.

'And it will just delight Mrs. Rebecca's heart A good Christian that is; no eye-service about her,' soliloquised the pastor. 'Strange! that she should be always fretting after that husband of hers, that so ill-used her ... if it wasn't for wee Miss Nannie, I verily believe she'd be off to America to search for him, but her heart-strings have grown round that child; and 'deed, no wonder, when she told me the story of how it came to be left with Mr. de Burgo—the more shame to him for abusing the fatherless little one!'

'How was it, Uncle Joe?'

'Well, it seems Mr, de Burgo fell ill of a terrible fever, in some small Italian town, where her father and mother were. The young couple might have left the inn, but thought shame to desert a countryman; so her father nursed him well. But then both sickened of that very fever, and died within a few hours of each other, and had only time, with their last breath, to ask him to take charge of their babe; for they had not a near relation in the world.'

'The old scoundrel; and this is how he repays them,' gnashed Luke, spoiling two flies. 'After that, Uncle Joe, I promise you I'll do my best to make a different man of young Hector.'

By-and-by, rising and striding up and down the little parlour like a young caged warrior, Luke, changing the subject, began suddenly talking of himself, as excitement, at times, made him do; a rambling discourse, but such as the elder's soul loved, to be thus openly told of the youth's secret ambitions, young hopes—yet fears. Then, just as on hearing the last, the elder's sundial face would be immediately overcast, while he would murmur distressfully—'My boy—my dear boy!' (for Luke to him was *his* boy)—the gawky, wild-spirited young student, would pull his hands out of the depths of the pockets they had despairingly sought, and with an ever-recurring determination to make his way in life nevertheless—give a great, deep laugh at himself, and his Uncle Joe, that did one's heart good to hear.

Much as the simple old man loved to have the thoughts of his honest lad's soul thus poured out to him, it made him often tremble. For Luke was young, clever, and rash, and though orthodox—yes, surely orthodox enough! yet given to gaze fearlessly about him, and seeing other truth-seekers besides himself striving to go heavenwards also by many different paths, question whether his were in reality the straightest one. The poor minister had himself nourished Luke on sound Presbyterian doctrine; fitted him out, before entering the big world, with his own stoutest arguments; and were the lad to change their creed ever for one seemingly more suited to his large nature and hot emotions, the excellent old uncle would have bitterly reproached himself as an unworthy teacher.

However, his fears were groundless now; although in after-years, Luke was destined to meet, and gallantly be victorious over, the mind-attack that so many fearless thinkers, like himself, must be tried with.

CHAPTER 12

THE KING OF THE COMPANY

YOUNG Luke kept his promise.

The next day saw him start, with delighted Bonnibel, for Black Abbey, first vaulting over the low garden-wall into the road, in wild school-boy spirits. His chubby small cousin, meanwhile, trotted soberly through the wicket-gate; calling back with a benign wave of her hand, 'Isn't he a naughty boy, grandpapa? but I'll not let him get into mis-chuff.' For, this miniature woman considered that all the common-sense in the manse was contained in her own complacent self; and, although she was certainly taught, by what she heard people say, to revere her grandfather's goodness and solemn profession, and her student-cousin's already brilliant attainments in learning, yet she knew they were but ordinary mortals, manageable by plaguing and kissing.

While the old minister went off through the parish (thinking that he ought to deliver a scolding to certain ill-behaved persons, yet feeling, beforehand, a longing to turn his exhortations into mere love and pity), the other two entered the Black Abbey demesne by the quiet farm-gate, just hidden from the manse by a curve in the park-wall. Then they struck through the woods, to reach the house straighter, Luke said; as if he did not go twice as much out of his way through the great white-boled beeches, and down the pleasant sward of the rides, cut through bracken coverts and resin-scented spruce copses, to enjoy all this—and more, to see the old chapel ruins*. These last were, in truth, very

* The ruins of the Cistercian Abbey of Grey abbey, within the

small, and almost hidden in ivy; but lay most picturesquely in a small hollow, wooded all around, and amid which slid quietly the brook that laughed through the meadows near the house, having its source in the great rushy mere. Some higher portions of wall still remained, however: one pierced with a fine chapel window; another, in which a low arched doorway, with zigzag carved edging*, faintly bore witness to the chapel's hey-day of fresh-built fairness seven hundred long years ago†, when, in the now still hollow, proudly uprose—

'Three gables great and fair,
That slender rows of columns do upbear
Over the minster doors, and imagery
Of kings and flowers no summer field doth see.'

And the glad, listening Black Abbey monks, just installed—

'Heard withal
In the fresh morning air, the trowels fall
Upon the stone, a thin noise far away,
For high up wrought the masons on that day.'‡

But now, through the wood, children's voices sounded in wrangling.

'Girls, you know it is your duty to do what *I* tell you; so give me up the king's seat, or—or else I'll have to push you out.'

---

grounds of Greyabbey House (Rosemount), had been the site of the Parish Church (in the re-roofed Nave of the Abbey) until a new Parish church was built on its present site in 1770.

* The Romanesque west door of Grey Abbey has a zig-zag carved edging.

† The Cisterician Abbey of Grey Abbey was founded in 1197, seven hundred years before May Crommelin's day.

‡ Lines from a William Morris poem, *The Proud King* (1868), describing the building of Peterborough Cathedral.

A shrill shriek of defiance, another plaintive, but resolute wail of—

'No, no—we will *not!*' told that two of the weaker sex, of different natures but of the same mind, were at bay. As Luke, a righteous young judge, appeared through the bushes, he was sprung upon with glad acclaim by the little pack.

'Whoever sits on that seat is king of the company; so, of course, as I'm a boy, and the eldest, it ought always to be mine,' explained Hector, showing a stone seat in the arched doorway, on which how many a dark prior or lay brother, successive inmates of those walls, how many a yellow-shirted kerne begging at the gate, must have sat on just such a warm, still afternoon centuries ago, when the round earth, the sun and moon, looked even as now they do. 'But to-day Aileen wants it, and Nan backs her up, though she never disobeyed me in her life before. But Aileen's such a spitfire. You are! Grandpapa said so, and that Nan was as obstinate as our donkey—and that they had better learn now to do as I choose, always, for they'd only have to do so later' (prophetic words!—to one, at least).

'He must have meant that Miss Nannie was very patient, and that Miss Aileen had spirit, I think; and that they were to look to you, as a gentleman, to protect, and give up to them,' replied Luke, under whose gaze little Hector's honest face flushed red with ready shame, feeling that he was considered a bully, when trying to practise, really for almost the first time, old Mr. de Burgo's lessons. All three children idolised Luke, since to the little maids he was the model of manly courtesy, to Hector the hero of the most daring exploits in birds' nesting and shooting that could be imagined. But whilst the boy looked down, utterly abashed, up spoke little Nan.

'Hector is very good to us generally, Mr. Luke. Yesterday, he purtected me from the gander that bited at my legs, and had an awful fight wis him. Only to-day, Hector, you know you were *too* bad!'

Luke laughed in his heart at the woman-child, who, according to nature, after long patience, indeed reproached her tyrant, but if others dared to likewise condemn, flew to protect him against the world. Then he unfolded his plans for the afternoon's amusement. With the governess's leave, the little girls might repair to the manse, there to have tea; first baking indigestible cakes to their hearts' delight. Meanwhile, he would take Hector on his pony to the shore, teach him to sit Snowball over a jump like a man, and to shoot curlew (and much more, lecture the little lad into behaving chivalrously in future). Outcries of delight at once testified to the Black Abbey children's previous experience of such pleasures. And, so with general satisfaction, the plan was carried out that day; and somewhat similarly on many a succeeding one.

The poor Fräulein, indeed, gladly took her pupils to the manse, thinking it well they should see for themselves, in that humble, happy household, that 'Better is a dinner of herbs where love is, than a stalled ox and hatred therewith.' To the philosophic, learned recluse herself, a gentle discourse with the mild pastor, or, better still, a grim argument with young Luke on some weighty topic of the day, was her only real intercourse and exercise with other living minds—while as yet, her pupils were so young.

Still, for a summer or two, the college stripling returned, and used his influence for good on these young souls who one day, later, would have such power for joy or woe on the souls surrounding them; still, for many a summer, the children lived happily in the old hall and at the manse. Hector, indeed, soon became a schoolboy; but his presence was only all the more longed for and delighted in by the two little lonely maidens left at home in the shelter of the woods. There they grew up, changing from childhood into girlhood without perceiving it:

and long the poor Tomboy in especial struggled, failingly, to join in Hector's ever-manlier pursuits when the holidays came round. Without perceiving it, their minds widened more and more under the Fräulein's steady teaching; she laid ever heavier tasks upon their mental powers, secretly delighting in the fulfilment of her dream, in her soul-pupils; whilst they, secluded as any woodland-reared maidens in a fairy tale, did not guess that others such as they were differently reared in the unknown world beyond their still home woods and park wall.

And meanwhile, just outside that wall little Bella Hawthorn, too, grew up comfortably—well satisfied to be less highly learned than the companions of her childhood, since she led so much more easy and snug, if humbler, a life.

PART II

'I was glad, that day
The June was in me, with its multitudes
Of nightingales all singing in the dark.
And rosebuds reddening where the calyx split—
I felt so young, so strong, so sure of God!'

E. B. Browning.

CHAPTER 13

THE SLEEPING PRINCESS

The world has grown fourteen years older!

Once more the Black Abbey woods have felt spring's secret power stirring the sap in their rough trunks, till now over-head the leafy covert spreads fresh and green.

The old house among them still wears bravely. Its many gables and steep-slanting roofs are a little more lichened; if possible, more heavily hung with ivy; but these only disguise the want of paint on its woodwork, and give a still quainter charm to the walls that seem imbued with some sense of dull, dumb life—so lovingly they seem to hold their inmates—so perfectly Black Abbey fulfils to the latter the idea of a true home.

Thus Nannie White was thinking, as she came to the front door, and stood outside on the curved horse-shoe steps, whose stones so many generations of De Burgos had hollowed with their feet. Behind her, indoors, the old saloon looked almost gay, since her own hands had helped to dust and polish, to pull up the blinds, and uncover the dimmed splendour of the ancient embroidered satin furniture, and especially to adorn the whole apartment with flowers, glowing like an indoor garden with such subtle surprises of disposal as showed rare taste, and the love of one to whom flowers were real joys in a grey dull life. It was not for the expected guest that she had so lavished them there. No! selfish or not, it was assuredly only for her own pleasure; though small pleasure, otherwise, she expected this night. Indeed, now, the cracked voice of motherly old Rebecca was heard, uttering from within the dark oak hall in dubious accents:

'Well, the house all looks as nice as a nosegay, and as neat as—as—ninepence!'

The old woman, it must be explained, was much given to adorning her language by alliteration's artful aid, but frequently, as in her last sentence, was a little puzzled to gratify that taste. She was now, in a manner, housekeeper, since her charges had outgrown the nursery; but pleased herself by imagining that she was still, likewise, maid to her foster-child, and as useful as if younger; and new-fangled.

The latter now answered, with a wicked small smile curving her gentle mouth, '*You* think everything is nice, Rebecca dear; but wait till *he* comes!' (This meant that the old master of Black Abbey was expected back on one of his short annual visits—and that with small joy.)

'Och! good gracious deliver us, my lamb! And d'ye think, he'll give us many *parables?** sighed the old soul, her broad face, that had befitted the summer evening, suddenly troubled as she came out and anxiously regarded her young mistress.

Nannie hastily repented, understanding Rebecca's euphemism to signify one of those home discourses used by old Mr. de Burgo as a safety-valve, apparently, to rid himself of all his accumulated bile, ill-humour, and evil thinking of the past year, till—no wonder, since he never spoke otherwise—he seemed possessed by a devilish spirit to these quiet, peace-loving women—storms that each seemed to shear away weeks from aged Rebecca's life.

So the young girl answered, 'Cheer up! you silly dear old woman. Don't you know that Mr. de Burgo tells us he always likes to do what's "correct"?' (a large note of interrogation was here instantly inserted by both the women-minds). 'And so, I am sure, he ought to tell you this time that you are a very pattern and treasure of housekeepers; and he will roar like a sucking-dove, if he does find any fault at all.' The speaker's

* parable = a long winded account of misdeeds or short-comings

lips curved slightly as she spoke, in a manner showing she was humorous—a somewhat rare gift in a woman.

'Och! come now, child dear!' smiled the old dame, 'don't I know rightly you're laughing at me with your blarneying! *If* he finds fault, do ye say? As if he didn't find as many, every day in the week, as a sieve is full of holes. But it'll keep him busy to find much fault with you this night,' she continued, in admiring affection. 'Who could ever think I'd washed and ironed that blessed old muslin dud so often with my own hands?'

Her young mistress, indeed, was a comely sight, in a white gown, with loose, flowing skirts, after the fashion of those days (*crinoline?—well, perhaps*) and just one crimson rose fastened at her breast.

'But 'deed, instead of himself, I wish it was Miss Aileen he was bringing; for it's terribly lonely here for a young creature like you,' went on the old woman.

'Ah!' said Nannie sadly, but quite under her breath, 'I wish so, too.' Rebecca, not hearing her, turned back indoors; but she, coming forward, leant her elbows on the stone baluster-coping, and let thoughts come that Rebecca's wish had roused. For, three years ago, Aileen had un-happily shown such symptoms of delicacy that a maiden aunt, eccentric and poor, had come forward to save the girl's life, taking her off from Mr. de Burgo's rule to warmer climates abroad—and so Nannie White, like the poor stone, was 'left all alone.' Lonely and long indeed the months had seemed, without her heart's sister—not seeing Hector ever, either, who was now in a cavalry regiment, and had been for four years in India; and yet she was young, and life was new and fair, and full of consolation. Nannie had grown into a tall, slim maiden, with a sweetly reserved air at most times—at moments dignified and gently sarcastic; yet again whose wide-curved tender mouth would almost immediately relax into still laughter, or restful good-humour. For, in those days, the girl thought she must laugh silently (with a sweet laughter akin to tears) till she gave up her last breath—laugh at her neighbours' little sins, shams, shabbinesses, their virtues that became weaknesses, their wrong deeds that seemed virtues; but far, far more at her own! Well for her, if she could keep that gay humour, to brighten her earnest thought, as now, till life's end!

As to her features, but yesterday there had been a warm discussion on that point between her nurse and old Mary, at the manse.

'She won't wear. It's just pig's beauty, as they say in the west,' quoth the latter sour soul, in her vinegar voice.

'Pig's beauty, indeed!' shrieked Rebecca, wrathful that the homely term, meaning mere tender fairness of extreme youth, dared be applied to her darling. Then, with severe significance, 'Well! *I say nothing*—but handsome is that handsome does; and I wouldn't change my young lady's looks for Miss Bella Hawthorn's, no day.'

Old Mary's judgment might be so far true, as that Nannie shared with hundreds of fair, fresh island-daughters her gifts of sun-tipped light-brown hair, soft hue of complexion, and the figure's pliant grace. But her eyes!—They were her chief beauty now, and would never, till they closed at last, suffer the face they lit to fade into the great crowd of commonplace human physiognomy; great grey eyes, so tender, they seemed to love all things, not utterly vile, they looked on. They were looking, now, beyond the gravel court, and shrubbery thickets from which came the glad evening twittering of birds, whose mates covered their eggs warm in many a snug nest—looking over the rich green meadows, from which the milch-kine were slowly coming homewards, to where beyond the western woods the sky was wealthy with the gold and Tyrian-purple of the departing day-king. She was drinking in gladly all the evening's beauty—the scent of the white-flowered rowan-tree, down the grass slope, that perfumed all the air—setting wide, as it were, all the windows of her soul, with intensest enjoyment of this nature outside her; for in a few more minutes the tyrant of the house would be here, and her liberty, and this exquisite pleasure, vanish into the past.

What a pity this, their only visitor at Black Abbey, ever *did* come home! Nannie lived so peacefully and happily here all the rest of the year; without keen joys, but without keen pain; having the green world and her books, the great thoughts of her dead, and the kindly presence of her few living friends, to rejoice in. Her living companions were the good German governess, who still remained here, Rebecca, and the inmates of the manse; the dead—all the poets of the past, and many a master-mind. Still, she was no chill recluse, but a girl with red blood in her young veins, and a heart capable of passionate loving. She surely should have known some younger, more kindred spirits, young men and maidens. At that, she would have smiled, as at an impossible wish. She did see indeed daily as many such, in 'the mirror clear' of her imagination, as ever the Lady of Shalott:

'Sometimes a troop of damsels glad,
An abbot on an ambling pad,
. . . . .
Or long-hair'd page in crimson clad.'

All these, and many more, visited this girl, who could see her youthful kind in no other way; and who had, whether for her own happiness or pain, received as mental dowry a full-pressed measure of the 'terrible gift, imagination;' so, though she loved dearly the stillness of the woods, the tranquil life far from the world's roar and hurrying crowd, yet hers was a large and many-sided capacity of enjoyment. Was it foolish thus to ramble under the greenwood for idle hours, and dream of untasted bliss?

Of 'damsels glad' she knew, indeed, few in real life; one down here at the manse; and Aileen, dearest of all, with whom she always daily held sweet intercourse in fancy. The 'abbots' might be philosophers, or great scholars and thinkers of the day, whom she, longing to know, thus met and discoursed with. Of shepherd-lads and pages she took small account; but she, too, saw an unknown Lancelot come riding through the barley-sheaves, whilst the sky was blue, and the sun blazed high, and all the world with her was young. This was her nineteenth-century knight, the ideal of her girl's poet mind; one day she should see him, and recognize him, in however common daily life. And so Nannie White lived and dreamed, like the Sleeping Princess, among the old woods; through which, as yet, came no adventurous fair prince to claim a bride.

Pity! that all this gentle life should be so rudely interrupted; for now—! yes, … the wheels that brought home her old, disliked guardian could be heard clearly up the drive.

Sighing, Nannie slipped back into the hall's recesses. Groaning in heart, old Rebecca and Robert (who had now grown wall-eyed, and, as an allowable consequence, was always covered with snuff) hurried to the steps; for Mr. de Burgo, curiously enough they thought, used to remark that he liked his old retainers 'to *look* as if they were glad to see him home again.'

Up drove the carriage, and, O wonder! out lightly sprang—not tottered—its sole occupant. This was a tall young man, with a fashionable dust-coat, and a man-of-the-world air, such as Nannie in her seclusion had never seen the like of before. He clapped Robert on the back; hugged Rebecca, who made outcries between laughing and crying; and next moment, bounding up the steps, dashed into the hall like a joyous young Boreas; then, exclaiming 'Dear old Nan!' flung his arms about the girl, and would have kissed her, but that she sprang back, startled, so that his lips barely touched her cheek.

'Is it—Hector?' she doubtingly ejaculated, quite breathless.

'Of course it is. Who else should it be?' he heartily answered, yet a little taken aback himself at his lost embrace, as he surveyed her. Overcoming shyness, out Nannie stretched both hands in warmest cordiality—though inexplicably making him aware no second kiss was therein included.

'It is such a surprise! … such a pleasure! … Come into the saloon now, and tell me how you came, instead of—*him*.'

'*He* took gout badly,' explained Hector, laughing, as he also fell into their former significant childhood's habit of designating their home tyrant. 'So, since there was business here to be seen to, and he can't move for some days yet, why, I came! I was only too glad of the chance of seeing you and the dear old home again; for, I do assure you, this is the first leave I have had since we came back from India (except for running up to town, sometimes), or, of course, I would have been over long ago.' His regiment had only returned two or three months before.

'I am *so* glad you have been able to come now, anyway,' softly replied the young girl.

Then, as they still surveyed each other, he burst out quite naturally, like the old Hector of their schoolroom, with—

'Bless me, Moony-face, how you have altered! I should hardly have known you, if I had had time to look.'

'I hardly did know you—and yet I did,' shyly laughed Nannie. 'But I had not the faintest idea you were coming; and you know it is five years since we met.'

'Nonsense! can it be so much? But, of course, you must be right. I remember quite well you were just recovering from scarlet fever, and your hair was cropped short, and your frocks were not very long.'

'A gawky, sick school-girl! I remember,' she gently answered, recalling the childish mortification of having had thus to meet her hero, with her wrists red and bared and her frocks shrunk to her knees, owing to her guardian's stinginess.

'Well, no matter, you could not look nicer than you do now; and evidently your hair has grown again, as much as you could wish.'

'Are you not hungry? Dinner will be ready in a few minutes,' said Nannie, answering this utterance of affectionate admiration by a shrewd smile up at the yellow-haired young giant above her, with his blue eyes and blonde moustache—implying that his creature comforts were, just at present, much more important matters than her own looks.

Off went Hector at that, cheerfully willing. Nannie quite laughed low to herself this time; his gait, that had been formerly like that of a mastiff puppy, having, though steadied, lost none of its old honesty and carelessness. Yes, he was '*just the same!*'—their very same warm-hearted Hector of old.

Now, he had run full tilt against the Fräulein on the old wide stairs, and shaking both her hands ever so long, dallied, inquiring tenderly after her last pet cat, and complimenting her on looking younger than ever, till quite a tinge of pleasure came in those sallow cheeks. Of course, therefore, he was late for dinner, and kept everyone waiting; while everyone was delighted that Mr. Hector should do as he pleased. Instead of their finical, wrinkled, crisply-hoary despot, here was come a fair young prince, to gladden their hearts.

What a merry little dinner followed, then! while the last red rays of the sleepy sun blinked through the fresh green layers of beech branches westward, just outside the windows; and the cuckoo's evening cry came from the snowy big hawthorn on the slope; and there seemed a down-weighing roof of heavy care lifted off the very old house, and all felt an upspring of lightheartedness, and rejoiced.

'Do you remember, how we all used to eat our porridge breakfasts here, whenever grandfather came home, and that we were half-starved little wretches, longing for more?' laughed Hector.

'And how Rebecca used to put sugar on our bread on the sly, and smear it all over with butter lest he should catch her?' chimed in Nannie.

'And the lunch for Lord William, that day when the boy was brought in from the cart, and rough-trained beforehand to act footman! And Fräulein, you thanked him so politely for every dish, that at last he said confidentially, "*Don't mention it, ma'am,*" and electrified grandfather with anger.'

How they all three laughed now at the remembrance! They were so cheerful, they would have laughed at the most feebly amusing trifle this night.

And then the sallow, solemn Fräulein, with her earnest eyes glaring from behind her spectacles, giving her a resemblance to Athene's owl, began putting Hector 'through his facings,' as he expressed it, as to what he had learnt of the Indian languages during all the while he had been in the land of the sun. Did he know what Professors Schultz and Weiss, the great philologists, had discovered concerning the dialect spoken in that very district in which his regiment had been quartered?—but of course he did!—What, *not!* Ach! was it possible?—How was it possible? The shy and now ageing learned lady straightened the bent bow of her back, and, forgetting dinner, burst out with such a flood of vehement information concerning the sacred Vedas, the Sanskrit language—elder brother of its European relations—and the Aryan speech—mysterious ancestor of them all—that the young man at last cried for mercy; especially as the roast meat just then came in.

'But Mr. Luke—the Minister Luke Cosby—he knows all that; and we often have long discourses together upon such subjects,' mildly expostulated the poor Fräulein; subsiding, nevertheless, as she saw that Hector's appetite, always fine, was after his journey simply voracious.

'Oh, Luke! he was always clever at thinking. But my thinking is a mere *façon de parler*. I can only *do* things, Fräulein—*if that, even*,' laughed honest Hector, like a young Viking, whose knowledge was of man and the wide world, his sword, and what old sages he had learned at Harrow. Little for new-fangled learning cared he! 'Dear old Luke!' he added, 'what a good fellow he used to be! What a pity he is only a Presbyterian minister!'

'But, ach! you had such OPPORTUNITIES!—how is it *poss*ible? Though, truly, when one remembers what a—an *uninstructible* boy you were in the schoolroom, everything is possible,' plaintively observed the old Fräulein, yet with a laughing, weakly-affectionate look at her handsome former pupil's face, like any woman. It was the longest speech Nannie had heard her make on an unphilosophic subject for some time. Hector broke in with a gay smile: 'I had my opportunities! Yes; and I used them too—in shooting big game. I killed more tigers last year than anybody for five years before in that part of the country. You force me to say so in self-defence, Fräulein. Only I am afraid you don't care to hear about my opportunities, now—ha! ha!'

'But *I* should,' hastily put in Nannie; and Hector's eyes, mirthfully quitting the grievedly-scientific visage of the preceptress, saw the soft face to which almost all their allegiance had been paid during dinner looking at him with great, though subdued, eagerness. Had not she and Aileen been his constant comrades when little, and when they two had so heartily wished themselves boys that they might always so go with him: while they were as proud as himself when he shot his first woodcock? Had they not gloated, later, over even the faint reports through others of the doings of their Nimrod—their mighty hunter—in India? since Hector hated letter-writing, even to those he loved best, being quite an ordinary young man; and when he did scrawl one, wrote plenty about the climate, and next to nothing about himself.

He smiled at Nan now, secretly flattered by her genuine interest; for, though still estranged by shyness, they nevertheless felt like brother and sister to each other. Encouraged, she added:

'And you will tell us too, *won't* you, about that time when you volunteered—'

Hector raised his hand in laughing warning.

'No, no—at least not now, Nan' (in a lower tone). For, in a disturbance with some hill-tribes a year ago, Hector, in the same spirit that sent him killing tigers, must needs volunteer; and had his name honourably mentioned in some of the papers, as the young sister hearts at home had exulted to read. But his own doing in this matter, Hector, writing at the time, had barely mentioned, being apparently more eager to know how his pet retriever's puppies had turned out, and whether the colt at home had been broken in yet.

But now did he tell of scenes in his hunting expeditions that delighted both the elderly woman and the young girl; for, in a rough-and-ready way, Hector had the gift of description; fire body in his talk, not words of smoke—real sense in his fun. Though not mentioning himself more than would any young Briton hating bragging, he amused them with such divertings, little camp episodes, and comic reminiscences of 'roughing it,' till the good Fräulein actually so laughed that she felt obliged to hide the contortions of her face in her handkerchief, her risible muscles working so stiffly, after long disuse, that her features seemed galvanised; and even nannie, whose laughter was mostly silent, joined in with as clear a sound as that of a happy child.

They lingered long at dinner, that pleasant spring evening.

CHAPTER 14

THE YOUNG PRINCE

THE sun had long set, the shadows deepened, the dew dropped, the sweet tender night had come, and one star, out yonder over the sea, quivered in the sky.

Together, outside on the top-most garden terrace, Hector and Nannie were seated, side by side, enjoying the faint half moonlight, half twilight, that made the old-fashioned garden, with its terraced flower-pots and flights of steps, its glittering fish-pond and massive yews, seem mysteriously beautiful under the spell that enchants us, spring after spring; while, —

> 'Here and there
> The cloud-like laurel clumps sleep, soft and fast,
> Pillow'd by their own shadows.'

From the open glass door of the saloon, meanwhile, streamed out lamplight, and the grandly harmonious sounds of Beethoven's thoughts, which the Fräulein was reciting in there on the piano, with all her soul.

How had it come about, that she had thus left the young man and maiden alone together for the whole evening; since, after dinner, armed with her knitting needles, and a coarse white stocking, she had sat down with an evident intention of making Hector's evening pass in pleasant instruction, although the good soul had seemed, as she did so, somewhat wistful? By-and-by, the instruction in her conversation had predominated, to Hector's mind, over the amusement; and bending down to Nannie, as she poured out his tea, he murmured, 'I thought Fräulein played to herself every evening; she used always to do so.'

'Yes, except when your grandfather is here; but to-night, of course, she is sacrificing her music to your amusement, on your coming home,' answered Nannie, in all good faith; crediting the elder woman, perhaps, with her own warmth of feeling too unhesitatingly.

Had Hector been a ploughman, he would have scratched his head at this juncture; his grandfather would have taken snuff; being young De Burgo of this generation, he thoughtfully pulled his blonde moustache. Then he rose, and with an insinuating smile approached his withered preceptress. 'This is, somehow, not like the dear old evenings at home I remember, when I used to come back for the holidays, before going to India … How is it we have no music, Fräulein? I think that is what I miss. You used to play so delightfully, till midnight.'

'Ach, ja!' the Fräulein bounded from her seat, as if she had been till then on thorns, and her kindly grey face quite glowed upon Hector. 'Yes, those indeed were heavenly nights! Yes, yes; you always liked music (not like your grandfather), although, I imagine still, it is to you only beautiful noise. Nevertheless—as you wish it—oh yes, you shall have it!'

She seated herself at the instrument, for which she had been secretly yearning, like a poor smoker for his forbidden weed; and, her desire fulfilled, began to play as if possessed by a full band.

'And now you and I will go and chat together outside,' said Hector, at once, to Nannie, with the smile of a young Hercules who has for once played Ulysses successfully. She looked up at him, quite surprised at his triumphant undertone; for she had been in a sort of blissful dream, and hardly knew what he had been doing—as was indeed often the case, without such delightful cause as to-night. But, once roused, Nannie could notice so-called trifles even as keenly as any poet's vision, who in common things proverbially see more than do common men. And so now, raising her grey gaze that was oftenest downcast, in still happy musing, to Hector, two little mocking sprites laughed in his eyes, hidden in another swift moment by her dropped lids. 'You are not one bit changed, Nan!' he cried out joyously. 'I remember you used to have that very look when you were a mere baby.'

'And you are not changed either,' echoed the girl, at the masterful ring of affectionate praise in his voice she remembered so well; and both young souls were unfeignedly glad to have found each other again in the world, as it were.

Hector insisted on wrapping his fair companion carefully in a warm shawl, for a sort of caressing kindness and fond condescension was his natural manner towards women; it might be, with some, a dangerous one. The night-air was soft and lulling, as they two wandered together among the roses, or sat on the terrace, while the brown earth slept beneath them; but overhead, little by little, life seemed to begin to pulse above in the grey heavens, and the constellations shone afar off, and the stats sang in their courses. 'And so you have seen Aileen, lately. Do tell me what she has been doing in London, since she came back from Cannes,' Nannie was saying with a little loving envy in her voice; for Aileen was the core of her heart, and alas! was never now suffered to come home for more than two or three summer months, by the aunt who had apparently appropriated her.

'Doing, Nan? She and Aunt Prue never are doing anything, it strikes me, but scampering about, from artists' studios to concerts given by the newest and biggest foreign musical stars. I declare, I got quite vexed with them. My Aunt Prue is not at all a good guide for a girl like Aileen.'

'Oh, Hector! *is* she not? Aileen thinks her so clever and excellent; I thought she was like a cheese made from the milk of human kindness.'

'Ha! ha! Nannie. No; she is rather too dried-up and peppery for that. A little old maid, dowdily dressed, who, nevertheless, is hand-in-glove with goodness knows how many very great people! But then she *is* clever, certainly, and a recognized oddity. She is a perfect Bohemian in heart, too; so can coax a sulky genius to come to a duchess's gathering, when few other powers on earth (or out of it) could make him put on a dress-coat; and she takes good care that he gets the best of the bargain.'

'I see; though poor, she is a power, in a small way. But, Hector, what is there to object to, in all that, for Aileen?'

'Because'—and this young man of the world took a confidential tone, as appealing to his hearer's common-sense—'Aileen, between ourselves. Nan, is rather a beauty; but there is Aunt Prue, teaching her to laugh at every poor fellow that may have birth and fortune, but not brains enough to satisfy their High Mightinesses. Why, everybody can't be a genius! … And then abroad, instead of keeping to English society, there they are, chattering French, and German, and Italian, exactly like foreigners.'

'Oh, you thorough-born Briton!' cried Nannie, laughing outright. 'No wonder Aileen rebels! I am sure I should do the same in her case.'

'No, no; I could not allow that,' laughed Hector, in turn. 'How Aileen has become such a little democrat, after being brought up at home here, I do not know; but I must keep one of you two of my way of thinking. Do you hear, Miss White?'

'I hear,' murmured Nannie, with smiling, sedate face, but a mocking sound in her voice. It was pleasant to be spoken to by Hector in such a tone of authority; for this young woman's opinion carried so much weight in their small household, that she was secretly weary of being always thought the wisest.

Hector, looking at her, felt tempted to draw his chair closer; so of course did so. Her face, if not striking, was wonderfully sympathetic; what a pliant grace there was about her figure! He was glad that his dear little former companion had grown up so—well, just thus. 'And now, 1 want to hear about yourself. Tell me all you do,' he said caressingly. 'But I suppose you visit a good deal among our neighbours, the Veres, and the Hares, and the Desboroughs?'

'I have never met any one of them; and I do not suppose they know there is such a being in existence.'

'Nonsense! Is it possible?' exclaimed Hector, astonished.

'Of course, I know my grandfather never cared for them much—I can't tell why. But since I came home, I have met several of them in London, and found them extremely kind.'

(Nannie was not likely to remind him that he was a marriageable young bachelor, though she slightly smiled.) Hector pursued, 'But it must be terribly lonely for you, then; now that Aileen is away.'

'Well, rather,' said the girl softly. 'She sent home a box of books, and things she did not want, the other day; and when I unpacked it, I looked at each as if it was a friend.'

She did not add, that she had cried over them with heartache and loneliness: still, her voice shook a little.

Hector impulsively put out his hand and stroked hers, saying, 'Poor little Nan.' He felt just like a brother, as he did it; though, a moment before, he had remembered how long it was since they two had been as brother and sister to each other.

At that moment, the Fräulein, most unsympathizing surely of women, burst—bang! clang! thump! into quite a lively, rattling air; which, perhaps, helped to rouse Nannie out of any chance momentary sentimentality. Forcing a light laugh, she soon regained her entire self-possession, and therewith her hand, saying, 'Oh, you need not pity me. After all, I may have been lonely here, sometimes; but I have never been *dull* … And then I went on a visit, for two months each year, to my old, and indeed only cousin (twice removed), Miss White. Dear me I what funny visits they were, without being amusing.'

'Tell me about it all,' demanded Hector, who liked sitting out here in the evening's cool, after his journey, beside this soft, fair girl, with the loving eyes and mocking voice; and who was lazy, and wanted to be entertained.

'She was very stout,' said Nannie, 'and she lived in a little house, in a little street, in the most gossiping little Irish town imaginable; and little linen paths were laid over the carpets, from chair to chair, in her drawing room; woe to any persons who diverged from them in a giddy fit! They had to spring to the oasis on the hearth-rug—and be thankful if they escaped Cousin White's tongue, telling them roundly and loudly how stupid and awkward they were.'

'It must have been rather like practising for the tight-rope.'

'Yes, indeed; but luckily, in her hours of private life the old lady enjoyed life in a more comfortable, though very untidy, little den. She was not refined; she said that was not the fashion when she was young: but she was all kindness to me, and believed I was buried alive here, and came to her to be "brisked up, and meet some nice young beaux."'

'Capital! And did you meet any nice young beaux, Nan? And did not they think you a very nice young woman?'

'Fie, Hector! They never called girls in our position anything but "young ladies." There were several of them; they came to my old cousin's little friendly evenings, and had "sherry white wine, and seed cake." Some tried to be high-souled, and some tried to be funny; but all only ended in being underbred. 'Bah!'—with a little disgusted expression, that made Hector break into a great laugh, conscious of being a well-born and well-bred young Antinous.

'Still, it would be a shame not to be grateful to her. Poor Cousin White! she meant to do her best for me; and now she is dead, and I have not another relation left in the world—'

'But you have friends that are surely more. Stay, Nannie; you are not going? It is too early. Oh, don't! The Fräulein has not finished yet'

'The Fräulein may play till long after midnight, Hector; and you will go and smoke; and I must go now, indeed.'

Then the girl offered him her hand, with a sweet little air of decision, and as if she were really in a hurry, seeing it was truly rather late; but then felt that either she was a bad actress, or that Hector, knowing her so long, had divined her mind, for, though he shook hands with her warmly, it was with an indefinable sudden deference she felt, but could not have described; and a curious, lingering smile followed her, as he said, 'You have certainly grown out of my last recollection of you in short frocks—eh, Nan? And yet it was not so very long ago, either.'

Going upstairs alone, and through the still, old house, a rosy flush mounted to the delicate face of its girlish inmate, for she feared—and she tormented herself—that young De Burgo had guessed her agony of difficulty. Always hitherto she had, of course, kissed Hector on saying good-night, just like Aileen, being his adopted sister; and school-boy like, he always grumbled, or only passively endured the affectionate hugs he received from both madcaps. But now! what ought she to have done? Which action would have been most truly modest? She had puzzled over that with a maidenly timidity, growing to perfect agony, while they had sat out there, apparently so void of inner trouble, in the gathering dusk, and the sweet later moonlight of the garden. She had resolved first, that to offer her former boy-brother her cheek, as to a present brother, would at once restore their old simple relations; but when it came to the point she suddenly could not! And now it was bitter to feel that she was really less to Hector than was Aileen. *And no coquette could have done worse!* she lamented low to herself. The

Sleeping Princess was awaking from her long dream, with a dim trouble; but after some moments she saw her own face reflected in the mirror, and it looked so fair and sweetly serious that she involuntarily smiled back, and, without asking herself why, felt somewhat comforted. "Nannie! Nan!" Hector had called her by her name so often, as if he liked it. Surely he did like herself as much as ever. Somehow—somehow—they would be to each other again just what they had been of old.

Again, fickle-minded, she looked at her glass and sighed. 'Only good-looking!—What a neutral face to have! better almost to be plain.'

On which the awakened Princess burst out laughing at her own foolishness, and letting down her soft, shining hair, knew it was pretty. What a Launcelot he might be, this handsome hussar—this former boy-brother of hers—for any dreaming Lady of Shalott, such as herself had been! Ay! far handsomer, and with a higher head, than even the visions of her fancy … and she had thought of him these four years only as the honest, noisy schoolboy last seen.

She opened her window, and in came the spring night, full of blessing; and there was as restful a spring-time in her heart. 'It is worth being born, *whatever comes*, to have known what living is,' she softly murmured to herself, after she had gazed out long in a reverie at the dim, dewy earth below, and the sky brooding tenderly over it above; then turned away to sleep.

CHAPTER 15

THE 'SOUL OF THE HOUSE'

How the next fortnight passed Nannie did not know; the light-winged hours had flown so jocundly one after another since the first moment when Hector's voice and step had roused the echoes of the old house, and brought with the spring, as it were, a new life thrilling through it and all its inmates. For the first time since many a still, monotonous month, Nannie knew again what it was to be merry.

It was like her glad childhood come back again. How gay old Black Abbey seemed!

The poor young girl had been enduring her loneliness too long, without knowing *how lonely she was*; while now—

'It cannot last long,' she said to herself with sorrowful warning, while the other half of her heart was yet palpitating with the gladness of being glad on one of those blissful June mornings. 'It cannot last long!' For this girl's nature was serious already, and could not lightly enjoy the summer sun without taking forethought of future winter. Some natures need to be hollowed by adversity, but hers was deeper than most others by far, to hold and know what like is the water of affliction, or life's wine—joy; so, even whilst the latter was throbbing in her pulses and brimming in her heart, unused to such a delicious draught, the orphan reminded herself, with shy, sweet wonderment at the miraculous change, how she had long only looked forward to a lonely life whilst here in the dear woods, and afterwards to a hard life of greater loneliness—of work, and pain, and uncomplaining self-command: and so her present joy might only make coming forlornness the harder to bear. Ah!—

'Pleasure has cramped dwelling in our souls,
And when full Being comes, must call on Pain
To lend it liberal space.'

No matter!—she would say to herself bravely; when the time came, she would know how to brace herself to the old life again. Nevertheless, she knew in her heart it could never be borne so easily as before.

It was as if the happy Golden Age had come back for this young couple; even in Arcadia they could not have been more free from the world's petty laws, than in the grand old Black Abbey greenwood. Together they two rambled, not long after the sun had begun to kiss away with warmth the dew that glistened down the grassy rides and on the flowers that seemed thick-showered over the whole earth; while, above the grass-meadows, the larks' song seemed music suspended a moment in the blue blinding sky above their heads; and in the woods and every thicket twittered a continual, if less tuneful, full-throated chorus. Together they two rode in the late afternoons, when the sunbeams slanted low over the white loneliness of the wide sea-strand; or they galloped along the close-turfed, bordering down. Together, under the sickle-moon, a strong, broad-shouldered figure, and a white more shadowy form wandered side by side through the sleeping gardens and down shadowy wood-paths; where, if Robert the ancient, prowling through the shrubberies because he had no business there, as he smoked his short pipe by stealth, espied them from afar, he told Rebecca with a saturnine chuckle, and she laughed in her heart.

'It does me good to be happy; it makes one feel better, body and soul,' mused Nannie White one early morning, standing barefoot, just as she had risen, at her open, high window, and seeing far off, beyond terrace and gardens, the mere flash in the sunlight as the wild fowl fluttered over it, dipping here and there into the reed-beds. 'If it is good for women to bear the yoke in youth, as says the son of Sirach, surely I *have* borne it long enough: and now it is good to be happy again—at last'

Remembering how hardly her guardian's yoke had pressed her, the young girl's face darkened; for she had been meagrely kept, and long insulted with taunts upon that keep, until lately she had come of age, and found, to her surprise, that if she owned little it was yet enough to live on; and that her father had by no means left her as the charge upon Mr. de Burgo which the latter had been pleased to represent; who, quite on the contrary, had always received a sufficient and suitable allowance for his pains. Her temper might have been soured, and her hope turned to morbidness, in those early years, when her painfully sensitive nature was most impressionable, had it not been for the Fräulein's high-toned if too transcendental companionship, and for Aileen's enthusiastic affection and sunny gaiety; and not least from knowing now intimately a humble, Christ-like old man, the reverend Joseph Cosby—and through him the far deeper distresses of the poor, those living examples to patience whom we have 'with us always.'

The Black Abbey poorer tenants were still a scandal, and the mismanaged estate a disgrace, in the otherwise prosperous country around.

Now, at one-and-twenty, Nannie White was still an untried girl, a beginner in life; but one who in the last four years had been led, in loneliness, through close, loving communion with nature up to perceive and give ever more glory to nature's God. Her young mind had not been giddied in the world's whirl, nor her heart too early troubled, before she rightly understood herself. Grown to womanhood in this green solitude, high ideals, only, had impassioned her thoughts when her mind roved from the frequent study of those great intellects and holy hearts who being dead yet speak to us, whose good works live after them.

She heard them with ears not dull; she, too, declared to herself she would taste the true toilful happiness of ever striving to lead the highest life of which she was capable.

Alas! how difficult it is to keep up that striving, and not to stand still at times, or descend to others' level!

So Nannie mused, but then quickly roused up and hastened her dressing; for she had promised to be out early with Hector to see the haymaking begun this morning. Later, both had so much work to do till afternoon that they were saved from wearying of the honeyed hours. Young De Burgo was busy, between agent, bailiff, and steward; more busy and bewildered, indeed, than he had bargained for. As to Nannie—the old servants called her 'the soul of the house,' not thinking how pretty was the name.

The fact was, that Rebecca, to save herself from dismissal when her services to her loved children were no longer needed, had become housekeeper by courtesy, and in reality a sort of upper cook and head housemaid; feebly trying to rule two cheap-waged, red-handed wenches, who, as she averred, were always breaking her heart and the china. But she was growing old; and to help to conceal this fact, her young mistress, as she always styled Nannie, had to be not only eyes and memory to her, but constantly hands.

So, on this especial morning, Hector, standing on the door-steps in the scented morning breeze, was urging in vain—

'Come, Nannie; you are going for a ride with me now. You cut short our walk this morning to hurry back about some absurd preparations for dinner, when I have told you every day that what would do for the Fräulein and you, would certainly do for me.' (Would it indeed, dear Hector? the womankind knew better.) 'So now,' the young man gaily added, 'if I let my work slide, you surely can yours.'

'I don't know what your work is,' said the maiden demurely; 'but if you had twenty-six cows under your management, and meant to make the dairy pay, and knew this was churning-day, that would be important'

'But, surely you don't see it done *yourself?*'

'But surely I do. I have two men and a maid waiting now for me—Nethinims* all three, hewers of wood and drawers of water, whose brains seem utterly fallow.'

'What a poor man's wife you would make!' enthusiastically exclaimed Hector.

A slow flush, whether of pleasure or displeasure it would have been hard to say, faintly tinged Nannie's softly outlined cheeks; but she answered with a light sarcastic tone: 'Exactly; nothing more. So don't keep me, my dear Hector, from training myself for my future lot.' And catching up a pail that stood beside her, she would have flitted down the steps, but that Hector, also grasping it, detained her.

'You are not vexed, Nan? You surely can't imagine that I don't think you fit to be a duchess—to be fitted to grace any position you choose? Say you are not vexed. Say you believe me.'

'I will say anything you like,' hastily answered Nannie, whom the young man's low hurried tone and eager beseeching eyes suddenly disconcerted. 'Anything—if only you will let me get to my temple before the week's churning is sacrificed to you, instead of being offered to the divinities of the market.' She hurried on through the fresh, green shrubberies to the farmyard, but as Hector would not relinquish his hold on the pail any more than herself, it was carried between them.

'And so this is food for the chickens. Are they to *pay* too?'

'Of course; you have hens by the hundreds in that rambling old farmyard of yours. That ought to pay—though it is not always an easy matter,' replied the girl, with a very natural

* 'Nethinims' were Old Testament hereditary temple assistants in Jerusalem.

housekeeper's sigh.

'Well, Nan! my grandfather certainly ought to be obliged to you. I can't think why you should trouble yourself about these matters,' exclaimed young De Burgo, looking at her admiringly; though, indeed he had hardly taken his eyes off her since they had set out.

Shifting his hold on the pail, as he spoke, he placed his other hand fondly over her shapely fingers. Nannie's was neither a tiny hand, nor yet one of the plump and snowy order. Still it was a pleasant one to look at, and seemingly typical of the rest of her—with a liberal breadth of palm, good for work and endurance, yet with a sensitive touch and a timid clasp. At Hector's caress now, it quivered and shrank away; but she only said with quiet dignity, rather as if she felt his sign of brotherly praise undeserved than that she rebuked a freedom—

'Now, Hector, that is nonsense; you are flattering me too much. Who else ought to look after these things, now Aileen is away?'

'But why does my grandfather not get proper servants to do all this work, instead of allowing you to slave in this way, to save his pocket?' persevered the young man, with an annoyed air. 'This sort of scratch establishment did well enough while we were children: but now it is too bad not to have a proper one for you. I shall certainly speak to him about it'

'Pray don't,' said Nannie, with a sudden earnestness that impressed him. 'You see, I understand your grandfather's ways,' with a little laugh, 'and—and I like doing all this work here … for a little time longer, at least.'

They had passed under the old archway into the courtyard, before Hector, recalling his somewhat vague remembrances of old Mr. de Burgo's miserliness at home, had time to do more than wonder in his lordly way; for spending money, and having life made easy, came naturally to the young heir of Black

Abbey. Then he watched the poultry flock to the call of their breadgiver, and the rough faces of the Nethinims (as she called them) brighten as their young self-made mistress approached; and he himself followed her round the shady dairy, whilst she inspected crockfuls of bubbling buttermilk, and the piles of golden butter on the cool slabs.

'Will you soon have finished here? he murmured, loth to go, yet conscious that his presence there was a cause of wonder.

'I am afraid not, indeed. Hector. Martha, please put up those twenty pounds *very* carefully; or stay, perhaps you had better, please, let me show you what I mean.'

'After lunch, then?' put in the young man, with suppressed impatience. Nannie's eyes met his with grave earnestness that this time had not a shade of her occasional demure coquetry.

'There are some poor sick creatures in the village I have promised to visit this afternoon, so of course I *could not* disappoint them,' she said in low apology.

'Ah, well!' and the tall young squire turned on his heel, nodding to the Nethinims, as if he had come there merely to overlook their labours as an act of extreme condescension; then, biting at the tip of his fair moustache a second, muttered carelessly, 'Coming back by the farm-gate, I suppose, Nan?'

'No; well, ah!—yes,' was the hesitating answer; for it was weak-minded, indeed; to come back by the nearer farm-gate to please Hector, Nannie knew, when she had meant to go down the road, and see her lately much-neglected friend, Bonnibel Hawthorn, at the manse. Still, Bonnibel was here always; and Hector—ah! how little!

CHAPTER 16

'UNDER THE GREENWOOD TREE'

THAT was one of those sunny June afternoons, when from a laughing sky dropped tiny, dazzling showers, blinding one a second with what seemed only warm drops of light.

Down one of the most secluded woodpaths, the heir of Black Abbey and his grandfather's ward were strolling side by side.

'I thought you were never coming. I must have waited a good two hours for you' (barely half a one). 'Those people cannot have wanted you half as much as I did,' said the young man with a playful tone of reproach, as he looked down at his companion.

'They wanted me dreadfully,' said Nannie, with a little heart-tired sigh, feeling her vitality as if drawn away by the late great drains upon her sympathy. Then her grey eyes turned large and wistfully upon him:—

'Oh, Hector! that village seems plague-stricken with sickness and poverty, and no better for all the food and medicine one pours into it.' 'It does seem very bad, certainly,' acknowledged its future owner, with regret; but not an idea that to be a young nineteenth century knight meant fighting such dragons as disease and want; next moment, his thoughts (who can blame him?) took a pleasanter turn.

'But how they must bless you, Nan! Widow Murphy confided to me the other day that you had just given her daughter something to start housekeeping on, for her marriage—she spoke of you as an angel of light—'

'Yes! and they spent it all on whisky and a fiddler for a dance, that night; though they are utter paupers,' drily returned Nannie, as who should say she was thoroughly disillusioned now as to human nature—not that *that* made her dislike it any the more.

'What a shame!' exclaimed young De Burgo, astonished. 'After all that advice I heard you giving them so kindly, too. They are a dirty set, certainly, at Ballymore*, where she lives; and drunken also, from what I hear. I don't know how you have such patience with them.'

'How can they wash without water? And when there is only one mud-hole as a well for a half-mile around, what can they drink but whisky? Even buttermilk is too dear,' murmured the girl bitterly. 'Oh, Hector, I beg your pardon for saying so, as it belongs to your grandfather; but that is the truth. And it will be your property—would you not try to do something for them?' And Nannie, who had almost an undue horror of seeming to lecture, gave a beseeching glance up at the debonair, manly young face, that seemed always to have seen only the sunny side of all things: 'You are not angry with me?'

'Angry with *you!* ... Well, yes. Nan, I am a bit. For, after all, Ballymore is no business of mine; and there is no use asking my grandfather, now—he don't mind it. ... No; don't look so sorry, dear,' and Hector caught the girl's hand. 'The truth is—I did not like to tell you before—but Ballymore is to be sold.'

'Sold! Oh, Hector, why?'

Ballymore was a large outlying townland.

'Sit down here, and I will tell you all about it,' said the young man, flinging away his cigar end, and speaking consolingly, as if Nannie was the person whom the loss concerned—not himself.

He drew her, silent and sorry, to a fallen tree-trunk, and threw himself down at her feet. Beside them, pine-trees sent up a grateful resinous incense to the summer sky; behind, young bracken

---

* 'Ballymore' is the name given by May Crommelin to Ballywalter in *Queenie: A Novel.*

uncurled their tender green fronds in the sandy bank beloved by the rabbits. Violets gushed out along the edges of the wood-path, like a purple libation poured by the hand of some lavish goddess. Everywhere were fresh-dropped bud husks, whiffs of gorse, the tender bronze of oak leaflets contrasting with the dotted young greenery of the beech, while the rosy flush of sycamore buds had changed into tassel flowers. It was a pleasant place.

'And so much of the estate was sold, too, when you came of age,' Nannie murmured, with very real sadness in her voice, since she was as proud of Black Abbey's wide domain as the De Burgos themselves—proud *for* them.

'The poor old man was so hard up, then,' apologetically explained Hector, with a soothing air. 'Besides, dear, to tell you the whole truth, I had got tremendously into debt. However, as he had brought me up in his own sublime indifference to money, neither of us can much reproach the other.'

'Yes, so sublime on his part that he does not mind ruining your prospects for life so long as he enjoys himself and that you make him no present reproaches. Oh! Aileen and I know him better than you do, Hector. Why did he never look after you? He has always even encouraged you to go headlong into debt,' uttered Nannie with a flush of passion.

'Hush, my dear girl!' and young De Burgo momentarily roused himself from his lazy posture, and looked more earnestly at her. 'Remember, he is my grandfather; and though I grant it is his nature to be hard on womankind, still to me he has always been indulgence itself. While as to my morals,' continued this easy-going grandson, with a quiet laugh as he resumed his recumbent attitude, worshipping at his divinity's feet very much at his ease—'as to my morals, I suspect it must take him all his time *to look after his own!*'

'Hector, you are incorrigible. But why must poor Ballymore go now?'

'Because its owner was at Homburg last year,' explained the young man, with a laughing but wry face. 'Then there was my step in the regiment—though that is not lost money; but I have been rather extravagant in hunters since the regiment came home from India this winter. Certainly his expenses dwarf mine into nothing, but that is all fair enough. Black Abbey is not entailed, and he could make ducks and drakes of it if he pleased, but for my sake. Not that all he loses is likely to do more than reduce this rambling old property of his to more then nicely compact proportions. … How you would have laughed the other day, when he explained it all to me before sending me here. It was quite refreshing to understand that these far townlands were only a trouble, and that it was a real gain to get rid of them. … I said yes to everything. And now I am here, I say yes to everything the agent and steward think, in their turn, they are explaining to me; whilst I am thinking—well, of something very different.'

'But, Hector, surely you ought to take more interest in the estate that must be yours—that was in the possession of your ancestors for generations, when all the other gentry around were mushrooms,' ejaculated Nannie, almost horror-stricken at his want of the deep reverence for the De Burgo family, in which she and Aileen had grown up undisturbed by other influences from the great world outside.

'*Cui bono?* All these things, my dear, will come right of themselves; and if not—I can't alter them. Besides, remember my grandfather is alive yet; and it would not, therefore, be very polite to poke my nose into what are really only his concerns.'

'But it will be your work on earth to live here amongst your tenantry—to know, to understand them; and if you know nothing of it beforehand—'

'Work! work! What are you always wanting me to work for? Who would work if they could help it?' murmured the lazy young giant, turning on his other side; as if to lie in the sun were to him, just now, the sum of bliss in life. Nannie, who was excitable and in earnest, and who had seen so little of young men she did not understand he was laughing at her, almost sprang up—flashed a look at his big idle body, as who should say she would give anything to strike out a spark of the divine fire that *did* exist in him, if she but knew how to awaken it.

'Why do I want you to work?—why? Because work is the salt of life; because it only keeps- your pleasures from corrupting; because without it, as Carlyle says, we have no right to exist in God's fair task-garden! Hector, Black Abbey will be yours; you would not neglect it, and live upon earth a human drone!'

That was enough. The sting of her voice pierced through the padding of good-humoured inertness which young De Burgo had assumed only to tease her; and, raising himself upright, he replied, only allowing his hurt feeling to show itself in a sudden sobered earnestness of voice:

'Come, Nannie! you are a little hard upon me. I was talking humbug a moment, not thinking you would take it seriously. We none of us made ourselves; and if I was born without much gifts for head work, *is that my fault?* I hope, nevertheless, to go through life as a gentleman and a good soldier; which last is the one thing on earth I care to be—therefore, I suppose, my appointed task, as you call it … And if I succeed, will not that be doing my duty to God and my neighbour, although this lawyer's work as to selling Ballymore is rather beyond me at times?'

'I beg your pardon. Hector,' said the girl, almost with tears in her eyes. 'It was very wrong of me; most presumptuous—and—conceited; as if no one but myself thought here of their duties to those around them. But, indeed, your grandfather never has thought; and so I did not reflect that all other men were not made selfish; and I do feel so bitterly for these poor people. … But please forgive me;—you do forgive me, do you not?'

'Who could help it, when you look so pretty?' responded De Burgo with returning warmth, becoming suddenly his usual self again, with all the caressing fondness, the gently masterful protection in his voice, that he had shown less or more to Nan all his life—less in childhood, more of late; always much. But this shy, wayward maiden shrank back, saying reproachfully—

'Now, Hector, that is too bad. You want to punish me, for preaching to you, by quizzing me. Did I not tell you twice the other day how much I dislike your saying such nonsense, when I know—'

'Don't you know how good-looking you are?—for if not—'

'Stop, Hector! You may say nice-looking, if you like. That is a good neutral expression' ('Which I hate,' *sotto voce*), interrupted the gentle cynic, with a secret bitter feeling that for herself she would rather be wise than pretty; but as regarded other persons—ah! well, that was different.

'Nice-looking! good-looking! Yes, you do look good and nice; and—well, I may think what I please, if I am not to speak, my white queen,' laughed the young man at her feet, gazing up with furtively admiring eyes; for to him that constantly changing expression, betraying ever transitory shade of thought, gave an unwearying charm of face that was more—far more!—than crude beauty.

'But come, tell me now about your projects for Black Abbey, and our poor people. I almost think, though I am not clever like you, that I could be of practical use. Even when we were little, do you remember, Nan, it was your brain used to hatch our schemes, but you had to come for my arm to carry them out?'

'Indeed, Hector, it was not so. Our ideas were different, that was all—as those of man and woman might be; but that never made mine better,' contradicted Nannie in a quick distressed voice, surely beyond the occasion; but it vexed her always more than she could explain when Hector, even in jest, asserted her superiority over himself.

'No matter; I am not despising myself. Hercules was not as wise as Ulysses, if I remember right, but he could clean the Augean stables when he was put to it. So be my goddess of wisdom, and tell me what is wanted here.'

So Nannie began. It was a cause that, for the last several years, since she had begun to look round her and understand, had made her heart burn. She had thought over it in loneliness, and long; and now, at last, she could tell it all to sympathetic ears—to one who in the good time coming *could* help. Till the sun sank lower, tipping the fir-tops with fire, they two sat there side by side; and while a passer-by would have surely thought they were talking of love, the maiden was all the time eagerly, pitifully, and only speaking of her secret schemes for bettering the earthly lives of the Black Abbey poor; while young De Burgo, listening to her as to a sweet divinity, said 'yes' to everything suggested to him, as was his amiable weakness—but not now from carelessness; as usual, but with his whole heart.

It was Utopia they had planned together, when they rose. The blessed isles of which sweet-tongued old Horace sang, were hardly more favoured than should be the land their imaginations foresaw smiling around them; where now were, in too many hamlets, as Nannie described it, mud-wells, whisky-shops, and underlet dirt-hovels—all curses old De Burgo had brought upon his fair inheritance.

Going home, they had to cross the little trout stream, bridged by two rough logs, slippery after the rain, under the trees' thick shade here. Nannie paused half-way, a mere second—not from timidity; but next instant Hector, who was beside her, passed his arm closely round her waist, and so drew her to the other side. Then she disengaged herself at once, saying haughtily, though her heart was beating:

'Your help was not necessary. Hector.'

Hector looked at her a moment, taken aback in his tide of different feeling, and then said, exasperated:

'You need not be so offended, Nannie. That, between us, surely is not necessary either.'

Both went on silent and hurt. It was their first quarrel, and they apparently meant to make the worst of it. He was angered, thinking he had discovered her to be cold and proud. She was angered at secretly discovering, that instant, that she was neither.

CHAPTER 17

A LAST DAY'S RIDE

Two young people gazing at each other with disconsolate faces; a letter open in the hand of one.

'Yes, my grandfather is coming to-morrow, he says,' Hector repeated, '"and looking forward to the pleasure of a little feminine society." A compliment to you, Nannie.'

'The ould Turk!' murmured Rebecca inaudibly, from the side-table where she had been proudly placing her breakfast dishes. In her heart, she believed her master was just made for the midst of a harem, where he might have petted in turn its unworthiest pretty members, delighted in exciting jealousies, and bowstringing the recalcitrant.

Under this common calamity. Hector and Nannie seemed suddenly tacitly agreed to bury their quarrel of the preceding day, although they had not yet made it up.

'Only this one more day for you and me to spend alone together; so let us make the most of it,' Hector said in an affectionate undertone, pleading for reconciliation with his handsome, honest eyes, and ungallantly ignoring the Fräulein's existence.

'I will do whatever you like, to-day,' sweetly murmured Nannie in reply.

So, though both faces a few minutes ago had been so blankly joyless, what now could be more amiable and mutually pleasing than the behaviour of these two beings?

Still, strangely enough, as this last happy day wore on, Nannie, whose spirits sank ever more and more with the approach of her tyrant's home-coming, could not but perceive that Hector's had correspondingly risen. It vexed her in her innermost heart. How could she know that her present sorrowful mood—her dread, by experience, of coming daily petty insults and annoyances, seemed to bring her down from the position of a shy, wise divinity to that of a human orphan girl, needing her companion's protection, he thought; and, therefore, he was glad. Besides, another idea gave him an additional secret elation.

They rode out together that afternoon that was what it always pleased both best to do, without asking themselves why. But there was less opportunity, in truth, for conversation, and more for action; and during those long hours, when both talked together, it had often been a fine secret pain to the girl that so many of the topics that had naturally suggested themselves to her thoughts were beyond the young man's ken; she not at all understanding that the common food of other minds was meaner fare. Love-guided, she now by habit always avoided those subjects on which her knowledge shone above his, seeking those wherein the man's different experience made him the wiser. But, at times, she dimly felt a want—naturally; and had no other friendly intellects near to supply the lack. When head and heart go together, that is perfect love; complete and all-sufficient. But how seldom can that be the case, O poor human nature!

On the other hand—from the first moment he swung her into the saddle, Hector, too, felt happier, hardly understanding why. He was a very son of Mars in heart; and the god when in energetic action could not have felt oppressed by the superior, sweet wisdom of grey-eyed Pallas Athené. Well-known as a good rider himself, De Burgo delighted in instructing Nannie when on horseback; and she was as proud of his superiority as in the days long ago, when he had first taught her to ride fat Snowball—and loved his teaching. Besides, she had not had the great pleasure, to her, of riding, for years; since her old guardian would not, of course, indulge a poor orphan in such a luxury; and these now were Hector's horses, that he had lately sent home after the hunting season.

As they turned out of the park gates, a distant view of the manse chimneys, snugly nestling in greenery, along yonder, under the wall, made Nannie exclaim in sudden recollection, 'Do you know, Hector, that I heard Mr. Luke Cosby came yesterday, on a visit to the dear old man; and he brought Bonnibel home, too (she went away for a week, just after you came). Would you not like to go and see them, for the sake of auld lang syne?'*

'Bonnibel? ...' repeated the young man inquiringly. 'O, I remember now; the little girl who used to play with us, long ago. I had almost forgotten her. She was at school the last few times I came home, before going out to India; but Luke happened to be here, and went out fishing with me, as eagerly as any apostle. Yet, I should like to see him again. A Scotch friend of mine told me he was quite a fashionable preacher in Edinburgh' (condescendingly). 'Fancy old Luke be-slippered by the foolish virgins!'

'I can fancy nothing more unlikely; and though *he* is a great preacher, he would hate to be called a fashionable one,' answered Nannie, somewhat indignantly. 'Why, Hector, have you never read, in even the great English newspapers, how that he is considered one of the most scholarly divines his Church has? besides being so fiery a preacher that they say he will revive the pulpit fame of Chalmers, and equal Guthrie? I have, often. Besides, old Mr. Cosby always brings all the references to "his boy" to show me, with such pride!'

'Dear, the world is big and crowded; and I am afraid, among my circle of acquaintance, no Presbyterian minister little short of the fame of Moses would be likely to be known,' replied

* 'for the sake of auld lang syne' = for old time's sake (as in the Burns' song).

Hector, in candid self-excuse. 'But come; tell me all about him. One ought to know of one's old neighbour's success in life, if we are to call at the manse on our way back ... though I think I should rather not do it, this—last day.

'But we *ought* to do it,' hastily replied Nan, avoiding the honeyed, laughing beseeching in Hector's eyes; for with her, duty always mastered liking. 'As to his fame, it has been steadily rising all these years. But I am afraid that in Scotland he is beginning to be called new-fangled, and dangerous in doctrine—unorthodox, in fact; while he is in reality only liberal, like most great minds. His last book "Light beyond the Grave," made a sensation*; it was like a breeze of fresh air in a close

* A late 18th century controversy in Irish Presbyterianism between 'New Light' and 'Old Light' factions that reflected the emergence of (and reaction against) the 'Scottish Enlightenment', eventually resulted in the formation of a relatively small breakaway 'Remonstrant' or Non-Subscribing Presbyterian denomination in the 1820s. In Greyabbey, however, the New-Light Remonstrants with their minister Rev. John Watson, were in the congregational majority, while the Orthodox Presbyterian Assembly attempted to instal their own 'othodox' minister and assert legal ownership of the Meeting House. Disturbances at the Meeting House between the two factions in 1830 prompted the arrest of the 'New Light' minister by the local JP (William Montgomery of Greyabbey House), and the minister was marched off under armed guard to Carrowdore Castle (then the home of May Crommelin's grandfather, D. Crommelin, J.P.). Eventually, however the Greyabbey minister was confirmed as the legitimate incumbent by William Montgomery, who also provided a lough-shore site for the orthodox minority of the congregation to build their own 'Old Light Meeting House' (later Trinity Presbyterian Church) and their old building is now the 'Orange Tree' Wedding venue. The original Presbyterian Meeting House in Greyabbey has, since 1830, been known as 'First Greyabbey' Non-Subscribing Presbyterian Church.

death-chamber, one of the reviews said, but it brought him almost into persecution. Of course the old minister is very sad about this—and he himself feels it greatly, but he is too brave to complain. … He is thinking of leaving Edinburgh; going over to America, where he has been invited to lecture; and afterwards he thinks he would be happier in London—if even he has to begin afresh. Thought is freer where there are many minds.'

Just then, they rode by the manse garden-plot, and saw a gaunt, big man, in waistcoat and shirt-sleeves, mowing the grass with a will. It was long-backed Luke himself.

'Why, there he is! A muscular Christian, by all the powers. I like the fellow for it!' exclaimed young De Burgo, and gave Luke a shout of cheery greeting; on which the latter, looking up, burst into one of the great, unrestrained laughs they remembered so well, and waved his straw hat.

'And, look quick—Bonnibel!' whispered Nannie, as tall, and apparently sturdy young woman, wheeling a large barrow laden with fresh-cut grass, hastily escaped round the house-corner.

'What a strong-armed country-lassie!' cried Hector, vastly entertained. 'Why, last time I remember her, you and Aileen used to be giving her secret lessons in French and German in the woods …; because you pitied her devouring anxiety to be as accomplished as the young ladies of Black Abbey.'

'Yes, and what righteously severe little teachers we were; and how indignant when we discovered that her real wish was to be thought like us, without the strictness of our education. Still, after having only been to a second-class school, it is wonderful how much she makes of even her little—acquirements' ('smattering' had been the word on Nannie's lips, restrained by friendship). 'She is not clever, but so wonderfully sympathetic, that every one thinks her so. She can be all things to all men.'

'Except a companion to her poor old grandfather apparently.'

'Why, Hector! who told you that?'

'Yourself, my white queen. Was she not away last week, and only came home with Luke? And when I asked, had she not been at least another human being for you to speak to, during the last year or two, it appeared that she was always having second-rate school-friends to visit her, whom you did not care to meet, or else she was gadding off to them for weeks, while *you* took charge of the good old minister in his "walks abroad." It was very good of you. Nan—'

'Och! she is my darlin' deary. She is so; she is so!' came in a tremulous pipe from under the hedge.

Hector burst into a startled laugh; and then, as he saw the poor 'daft body' of the countryside resting there with his rag-bag, cried cheerily, 'Right you are, darlin' deary; she is so,' and flung him half-a-crown.

'He has never forgotten the time when I gave him our sugar in the wood; do you remember?' hastily exclaimed Nannie, trying not to blush, as she could just catch the sound of some very confusing blessings which the beggar-man, with cunning in his madness, was calling out after the young heir to Black Abbey and the slim maiden riding at his side. For the next half-mile, while Hector smilingly half-listened, she nervously talked continually of the accused Bonnibel Hawthorn, excusing the latter's frequent absences; explaining that the loneliness of living under the shadow of the Black Abbey woods (which to herself had a wonderful charm, if at moments oppressive), might be—nay! did seem, unspeakably dull to the gay-hearted manse lassie; of whom Nannie spoke with even more of the tender lovingness than she mostly extended to all her friends, humble or high, and less of the gentle satire she playfully exercised on all but the two or three who had gained the innermost sanctuary of her heart.

'But how is it she has become such a friend of yours?' asked Hector, suddenly waking up, as it seemed, from a happy reverie to the knowledge of what the dear lips he was listening to were really saying.

'I do not really know that she is a friend, if that means one whom one chooses to be a soul's companion; but Providence placed her there', and me at Black Abbey, both lonely—and, you know, something man must love.'

'Ah, yes: and you must have been lonely, poor Nannie. You had not—I mean, you do not know the Veres, or the Hares, or the Desboroughs.'

It was such a warm sleepy afternoon: by mute consent they let their horses idle when they rode down on the warm white tide-strand, where nothing living seemed to be but the pert, pattering sandlarks, and the gulls sleeping on the blue swell of the great, ever-living heart of the sea itself. Softly they paced just where the ripples, with accustomed lazy lips, kissed the sand. The June land behind them seemed melted into the quivering warm haze that hung over it; away at the great broken ring of the horizon, the summer sea was merged in the illimitable blue that softly veiled in grey their meeting; while these two human souls moved as if lost likewise in a day-dream.

Nannie's heart was sad, with the low fear of coming change. And yet!—she felt, at other moments, a passionate delight in her gladness, that had not yet quite vanished—that filled her with some of the spirit of divine madness. At such moments she would have sung aloud, if she had but had singing voice, of that which so possessed her. But this night, when in solitude, it must find expression from the overfull heart and bursting brain; that had felt and thought, before, far more than most of her kind, but never so much as now.

And Hector? With more earthly human, if in his own degree as warm feelings, he rode by her side—handsome, honest, and, if not clever of brain, strong now in his simple resolve to be led by her beside him, who had the more heaven-sent wisdom, to do the right with all his sturdy might. But what his ideas were in the delicious dream that now possessed him, he could not have told; he only knew he *felt*. He was no poet, to sing in a thrill of passionate emotion to the fair face beside him—

> 'The sunlight clasps the earth,
> And the moonbeams kiss the sea—
> What are all these kissings worth,
> If thou kiss not me?'

Turning her head by chance, Nannie saw her companion smiling to himself; and felt on a sudden a little bitter that he should be so complacent, and she full of hidden trouble like man, like woman, so often in the world!

So, forcing herself to seem as if she shared his gaiety, she remarked, to try him, 'You will have no more of our dull companionship soon. Hector. This will be the last day of it now; and that, for good and all.'

'The last! why so? My grandfather is coming to-morrow, and of course the worse luck for us! But—after that … we may have many another such day yet, Nan, you and I.'

'And the Fräulein,' added his fair companion, in all good faith supplying what he had not thought at all a necessity.

'Ah! no Hector—

> "Life is never the same again,"

you know; and the poor old Fräulein will soon have to go away from Black Abbey.'

'To go away! Why, I thought she would live and die with us—that she was a sort of heirloom that would come to pieces if removed. Impossible! But, without nonsense, Nannie, does she really mean it? My grandfather told me, after Aileen left, that she herself wished to stay on as a companion to you; and because the rest and quiet of Black Abbey were a help to her in writing some great book that was to be the work of a lifetime.'

'It is finished; and has failed,' said Nannie sadly. 'Failed, at least, in so far that the publishers are afraid of venturing on such a ponderous work on metaphysics by a woman. Perhaps they were right. It was to have come out both in English and in German (I helped her by translating all the first); but now it will in neither; and her labour of years for human good, as she meant it to be, seems useless, and her life wasted. I am very sorry for her.'

'And so am I, most truly. Poor old Fräulein! What an unfeeling brute she must have thought I was, not to have asked! Why—she never said a word about it to me.'

'It is good not to "let our griefs spread far." But it may still be published in the time to come, at her own expense. That is why she is thinking of going to London, to give lessons, and live with her brother, a professor of Sanskrit, who is coming there soon. She will not earn much, I fear, but it will help to boil the pot. And then even here she wrote for some scientific German papers: she can still do that, too.'

'But why not stay on here, and only do that—here, where she has her lodging for nothing …? Why, what is it? You looked as if something was wrong that I said: *does she not?*

For Nannie's speaking eyes and delicately-hued, changeable face reflected too faithfully, to her own regret, every rise and fall, each quick emotion though but of the slightest, in her changeful heart.

So, now she had to answer—reluctantly—yet thinking the truth perhaps best, 'It is generous, but Quixotic of you, dear Hector, to think that she could stay on here without being of use, and as a charge on Mr. de Burgo. She could not have done that.'

'Then how—why *has* she stayed?' asked Hector, getting rather red.

'When your aunt took Aileen abroad, Mr. de Burgo considered my education already sufficient, and naturally objected to keeping the Fräulein only for my advantage. But she—she was fond of the place, you know—'

'The place! … Not of you, whom she calls her own child so often! I beg your pardon; go on, Nannie.'

'And so she came to an agreement, also naturally, with your grandfather, by which she could still enjoy such a quiet, pleasant time for her studies, and yet not feel chargeable to him. You know she has a little annuity.'

'A paltry pittance! What is it? … Thirty or forty pounds a year. Nannie, how can you back her up in such ridiculous pride? She must have forced my grandfather to it. Why do you not tell her, she ought not to think of such a thing, after all the years she has spent with us?'

'How can I?' said Nannie, very low, but smiling firmly. 'She feels as I do, since I have been one-and-twenty. We have neither of us any more right here.'

Hector, interrupting her, caught her bridle, and stopped both horses suddenly. He was red now to the roots of his hair.

'You don't mean that you—you also—actually pay my grandfather for keeping you here; and keeping you in such a way?' demanded the young man with hoarse exasperation, while yet he foresaw the answer in her face.

'Only since I have come of age. Hector,' soothingly answered the girl, with a tone soft as healing to a wound.

'And before that he paid himself,' uttered Hector, with a passionate though subdued oath. He remembered how well how the orphan had been ill-treated, like his own little sister—taunted even more bitterly; and, leniently though he generally felt bound to think of the old man who was lavish to himself, his blood boiled.

Just then his young horse turned restive at the sharp halt

Hector's good-humoured soul seldom knew anger; but when it did come, as now, it was with a great sullen wave that overwhelmed all reason. And so now, being wrathful, he sharply chid the poor animal, that, catching his own spirit more and more, after a few moments of mutual irritation, angrily reared. There might have been a scene; since Hector, in his present mood, would have punished whatever dared to oppose him, but that a little terrified ejaculation Nannie could not restrain (it was of fear for him) pierced through his thick passion—although just then he would have turned a deaf ear to outcries of others.

With one hasty glance at her frightened face and parted lips, Hector mastered himself, and then subdued his hot young thorough-bred, whose distended nostrils and fretting heart were soon quieted, when its master's hand resumed its accustomed gentle firmness.

Still not a word was spoken. Nannie knew of old this was best when Hector was in such a black mood. He worked it off sooner in silence, when not goaded from outside also with words. Then, reaching the end of the sandy bay, they turned on to the grassy down, and cantered homewards. As was their wont, they rode through the fields; Nannie, careless of the intervening grass banks, that she now took in Hector's wake with unhesitation, as she would have taken the most yawning of ditches had he bidden her.

And thus, in silence still, but a softer tenderer silence again, as both felt—since they knew each other too well to need much speech—they reached the manse by the wayside.

CHAPTER 18

MIDSUMMER EVE

THEY had hardly ridden up to the side-door, when out ran the little minister himself, beaming with greeting: 'Ah, Mr. Hector, this is indeed a pleasure—this is indeed!' cried the good man. 'And Miss Nannie, too—though that is a more accustomed one; but none the less a happiness for that, my dear young lady, as our daily blessings are the greatest.'

The old pastor had just been making a sermon after the ordinary receipt: take a little text, cover it almost out of sight with your own moralizing, as much as you can get; bake it, or not, in your own brain to pleasure; and finally serve it up cold.

He was not good at sermons, this good old man, who had to make so many long ones; his daily deeds were his true and grand preaching.

'It is very kind of you, Mr. Hector, to come in this friendly way to see your old tutor, who first taught you your Latin.' Then the minister's voice changed, and with a sudden impulse of emotion, laying his hand on the arm of the handsome stalwart figure that had so outstripped him in height, since those days long ago, he uttered simply, 'Dear, dear! Forgive me, my dear lad, but what a fine man you have grown!'

His eyes absolutely watered; and Hector seeing that, laid his own herculean young hand kindly on his old teacher's shoulder, reproaching himself for not having paid an earlier visit to the manse.

'And now, if you will not mind going round by the back of the house here—ah! *you* know the way of old—we will come on the young folk, Luke and my Bonnibel; as, indeed, you first called her, Mr. Hector,' rambled on the old man, trotting away by yard and back kitchen, and past the hedge on which the family washing was having a thorny time of it, in happy oblivion of the scolding Bonnibel would surely give him, for bringing such a visitor by such a way.

There was a little grassy close, framed in privet, just under the parlour-window, at this gable-end; and before entering it by a wicket Mr. Cosby stopped, with a sign of caution, and screwed up his rubicund old physiognomy into a most comical facial moon. 'My boy, Luke, is asked to give a lecture in aid of the blind, in Belfast, next week—invited in the most flattering way,' he whispered. 'And I believe he is reading part of it aloud, at this very minute, for Bonnibel to criticise; as indeed I begged them; for I can assure you both, I think more of that girl's opinion than I would of that of many other people. Ah! you don't know, Mr. Hector, how clever my granddaughter is. Miss Nannie does know; but, bless her! she knows everything.'

Softly entering the close, they all approached and heard, indeed, the grand, thrilling tones of a true orator—a very Boanerges—one born to move men's minds, as if he played on the key-board of a mighty, manifold instrument; being answerable for his gift, as he makes the responsive chords sound to heaven for good, or to hell for evil. It was difficult to catch the whole, though they all stood silenced: yet words reached their ears of passionate appeal on behalf of our brothers and sisters, by whom the blood-red glories of sunset cannot be more imagined than as the sound of a trumpet—to whom the great, green outer world is not, and they are thrown inward upon that of the mind; and who, whilst even embraced by those they love, may not yet behold that light which 'never shone on sea or shore.'

> 'O dark, dark, dark, amid the blaze of noon!
> Irrecoverably dark! total eclipse,
> Without all hope of day!'

The speaker's voice at the last words had passed away from its intense impassioned vibration, into a low, deep tenderness that hushed the listeners' hearts, as with the calm of a hallowed place. There was silence within the parlour, where the preacher was; there was silence outside in the summer close, for some few respectful moments.

Then Luke Cosby called out cheerfully, in his hearty voice, but still with a ring of deep feeling in it, 'Well, Bonnibel, what do you think of it? Shall I end there, or add an anti-climax?' (No answer.) 'Why won't you speak, my dear? Come, criticise it; don't spare me. That's why I read it to you. There! you ought to be flattered.' (Still, no answer.) 'Why, Bonnibel, Uncle Joe said you were an excellent critic; but you are the severest, certainly, I ever knew.' With which, and a quiet laugh, Luke stepped to the window. A little on one side of it, perhaps so placed for the shade, perhaps to be out of his sight, was a low chair; a woman's workbox and its contents lay scattered heedlessly on the grass. But Bonnibel, the excellent critic, where was she? The other lookers-on already knew, with half-indignant amusement.

Several yards away, she knelt under the hedge, tempting out with a ball of worsted a coy kitten that evaded her reach; and smothering little bursts of merriment over their silent game. Suddenly becoming aware of the silence, she looked round, and perceiving how she was detected, seemed transfixed; assuming such a guiltily-innocent expression that neither grandfather nor cousin could withstand it, and both burst out into indulgent mirth.

Then she came slowly forward—a tall, voluptuously formed girl, with just now a shame-stricken expression; such a woman, of fair, red and white, tender flesh, and lustrous brown eyes and hair, as Rubens would have loved to paint, not perhaps for his own more austere countrymen, but for the French court.

Young De Burgo stepped forward to shake hands, with a friendly readiness that, however, to Nannie's keenly fastidious mind, was only saved from being admiring condescension by his charm of good address. Hector was too proud, she thought.

'Ha! Miss Hawthorn,' said the young man, 'I am delighted to renew my acquaintance. We were just seeing what an admirable critic you make to my old friend, Luke Cosby, here.'

'Oh, Mr. Hector! how do you do?' was all the girl softly murmured; and lifted up her full brown orbs just as mildly to meet his gaze. Then she looked at Luke without one word, but an expression of unutterable penitence, like a grown-up naughty child.

For a moment or two gaunt Luke shook his head; then, overcome by a comical twinkle that crept into the corner of the fair culprit's eye, his rugged features relaxed, and with one of his great laughs, that startled people, nowadays, as if bursting loose from his usually strong gravity, and restoring the uncontrolled, wild joyousness of youth, he exclaimed, 'Well, well, Bonnibel! after all, you are a genuine critic, and took the gentlest way you could of showing me I was long-winded. But I must be even with you, some day.'

Shriven! and feeling now free to sin again soon, Bonnibel turned gaily to the rest; and as the conversation became general, she several times ventured to address 'Mr. Hector'—as she from the first called their future landlord—with a shy humility, yet gladness on seeing him again, that was very pretty. But the guest seemed preoccupied; and charming though the manse-mistress no doubt was, he soon moved away with the two men, showing more real interest, to inspect a litter of black pigs, of which the old minister was extremely proud.

Bonnibel wrinkled her pretty nose in disgust. Faugh! Fancy looking at a pig, when she was by!

Left alone together, Nannie, unheeding her companion's bewitching graces, forthwith reproached her. 'Oh, Bonnibel,—how could you?'

Miss Hawthorn seized her hands deferentially, yet eagerly, and drew her to the garden-chair. 'Now *don't*, please, look at me so severely,' she cried, half-laughing. 'You know that I dread your little frown far worse than other persons' worst scoldings.'

'Luke is too good for you. You don't appreciate how great a man he really is, or will be.'

'Nobody was ever great to—well, in this case, to the little cousin who sews on his shirt-buttons. There! I will be really sensible now.'

'I am glad to hear it, and that you are more useful than I could have believed,' said the Black Abbey lady, with a sly, doubting smile; as Bonnibel sank comfortably on the grass at her feet, with an easy grace, despite largeness of mould, which the other eyes, that ever noticed all things beautiful, admired.

They did talk now 'sensibly:' Bonnibel addressing her visitor as a beloved patroness, however, rather than as an intimate friend, long as she had known her; yet with a tact that avoided all appearance of fawning.

Suddenly, after an indifferent pause, she said, with a dawning smile, 'How handsome Mr. Hector is!'

Nannie, although she tried hard not to seem so, felt taken aback, and foolishly troubled; all the more that Bonnibel's eyes were steadily turned upon her face, in a calm, brown stare.

'Is he?—I hardly know. … Do you think so?'

'Who could think anything else?'

And then, Bonnibel, removing her gaze, spoke in enthusiastic praise of young De Burgo; but, as it were, only taking interest in their future lord of the manor, and from her humbler, and indeed, she owned, momentary view-point. Also, she did not look again at Nannie, who soon no longer felt embarrassed—whose heart quite warmed. No one, neither Rebecca nor the Fräulein, had thought of so freely speaking as did this other girl of her own age, with divining sympathy. Nannie's reserve kept herself back from speech; but she wanted indeed to hear Hector spoken of—much spoken of—and the soft curves of her mouth grew glad. She felt, as says the great master of novelists, that she had never been so disposed to think highly of her friend (Hector) as when she found him standing higher than she expected in the esteem of others.

'But, what I like him best for,' said Bonnibel softly, but suddenly again, 'is, that one can see he thinks so much of you.'

Poor Nannie started again, and tried to draw herself up; but felt most unusually weak against this friendly attack.

'What do you mean? … But of course, if—if he does, it would be natural. We have always been like brother and sister together.'

'Brother and sister—yes; but would he follow Miss Aileen so continually with his eyes,' murmured Bonnibel inquiringly. 'I *beg* your pardon, if it is forward in me; but, indeed, it is because I do care so much for you myself, that I can quite understand a man loving the dust under your feet.' Plucking a daisy, she began pulling off its petals, not carefully one by one, but several at a time in haste, 'This year … next year … *nev—!* Ah! you naughty broken one left, you don't count. It is *next year!*'

'What do you mean, Bonnibel? … What are you doing?' Nannie found, tremulously, voice to ask. She could not have spoken before; all she had been able to do, was to preserve herself from betrayal by silence. She felt strangely moved—glad, angry; ashamed to ask, yet longing to be certain.

'Ah! Here they are, coming back,' only answered Bonnibel, rising with lazy alacrity—if the expression may be used.

It was time to go now, the riders thought; and the others went to see them get on their horses.

'Did you know that this is John the Baptist's eve, Miss Nannie?' called out Luke. 'This ought, by all legends, to be a night of vigil and rejoicing.'

'St John's eve, Luke,' his cousin interposed, correcting his Presbyterianism. (She herself secretly thought her sect unfortunately wanting in *haut ton.**)

Luke smiled, and went on, 'Think of the midnight fires, round which the young people danced†; the towns lit up and garlanded; the burning wheels rolled down all the hills around, to typify the sun's decline. It might be well described, if any poet felt inspired on such a night.'

A quick understanding smile passed between him and their gentle guest, unseen by the others.

'And one should gather fern-seed with ceremonies—dear, dear, not that I know them—to make ye invisible,' cried old Joseph Cosby, chuckling at his own feat of memory.

'And each girl ought to gather a red rose, and keep it till new year, for some reason or other,' innocently added Bonnibel, gazing up at the riders, now mounted. Hector laughed; Nannie, half-blushing, frowned as they rode off; for both knew what it meant, if the withered rose kept its colour.

'What do you think of her—of Bonnibel?' asked Nannie, when they two were out of earshot, in a tone expecting admiration as a matter of course.

Hector, who seemed happy again, answered to tease her, 'I think she might have preferred poor Luke's lecture to the kitten.'

'Well, she might; but indeed she is wonderfully simple in some of her ways. I believe she could amuse herself playing with that kitten all day long.'

'I think she could flirt not a little, too. Don't look so shocked, Nan—where is the harm? Or rather, dear, remember other women are not all such sweet saintlike recluses as yourself.'

---

* high fashion.

† St. John's Eve, or midsummers eve (23 June) was a traditional time for bonfire celebrations.

'Did the ladies you met out in India flirt?' asked Nan, with the first pang of jealousy she had ever yet felt traversing her breast.

'I told you that there were hardly any at the last station we were at—for two years. Tiger-hunting consoled me,' replied young Hercules, to whom the open field had been dearer than Omphale's chamber.

'But you think Bonnibel Hawthorn handsome?' said Nannie hastily, recurring to an indifferent subject.

'O yes, beautiful!' answered Hector, but as if not caring a halfpenny for such beauty; the refined charm of his dear companion's face, that was soul's beauty permeating and making lovely the body, not the body's beauty embarrassing a small soul, being then more, far more, to him.

But Nannie wondered why he could think thus of the girl who had always seemed so quiet in manner, soft as her own pet kitten. She knew nothing, in real life, of flirting.

And then, once more, they two rode happily homeward through the June bean-fields, and under the opulent glory of the evening sky.

CHAPTER 19

'IT WAS A LOVER AND HIS LASS'

NIGHT had come. A young moon, passion-pale, rose imperceptibly through the tender gloom of the summer sky; looking from far away down on the sleeping earth and wooing ocean, and two young figures wandering, side by side, in Black Abbey's old demesne.

'And this is our last evening ramble together—for a while,' Hector was saying low, as they went along a shrubbery path, long deserted, and interlaced thickly with wild roses and hazel branches.

'Our last—for years,' faltered the girl.

'What do you mean?' asked the young man with a start, bending to look anxiously in her face. 'It shall not be our last; no, not even for a while. I take back my words. Why should it be? Have we not both power over our own actions?'

'Dear Hector, I must leave Black Abbey soon,' murmured Nannie. Then, while he made a startled exclamation, she went on hurriedly in an explanation which some feeling, she hardly knew what, had hitherto restrained—emboldened to speak, now, her secret thoughts by the mysterious dusk that transformed their work-a-day world into a shadowy silvery land, where all was refined, though real; fit time and place for soul-secrets to be uttered—'I must go. ... I have felt so long what my work was to be in the world; and now that the Fräulein is leaving here I cannot stay either, but will go to London with her, and earn my own bread.'

'Nannie! ... Child, you don't know what life you are proposing to yourself!' exclaimed young De Burgo, in a tone of pitying protection towards a weakling. Then he could only trust himself to add, 'What could you do? Would you go out as a governess too?'

'No,' answered the girl, in a low small voice, yet one so clear as showed her certainty of mind; 'but I will be a poet … however small a one.'

'*No—!!*' uttered Hector in turn; but this time it was an outburst of simple admiring astonishment, that sent a warm rush of pleasure through his companion's heart. 'Well! you are clever enough for that—or anything else; that much is a certainty to me.'

Poor Nannie, who had been quivering with excitement, laughed a little, but then begged, 'Ah! please don't call me clever, Hector. It reminds me too much that one may have all the necessary qualities to be great, except the one small divine spark to fire the mass.'

'What, not clever! nor talented—you dislike the word, nor a genius! Then I can only call you—my poet! my "moon of poets,"' jested the young man daringly, with gaiety roused by and surpassing hers. And, though she shrank from him with half-displeased pleasure, he bent his handsome fair head down towards her browner hair in merry confidence, as they went side by side along the narrow leafy path: 'But come back now! I will tell you a bit of a secret; *last night I tried to write poetry too!*' Then, in answer to her incredulous outcry of curiosity, 'It was your eyes and nothing else, that made me do it. They kept haunting me, and so did a line that rhymed on and on in my memory, most inexplicably:—

> 'Sweetest eyes were ever seen.'

I thought it would inspire me, but somehow there was no getting beyond it, though I tried hard … I stuck fast, and that was the end of it!'

'Oh Hector! Hector! Because that is what Camoens wrote to his wife, and if I *had* been a second Caterina, you might have written more,' expostulated Nannie, as if against such admiration of herself, feeling inclined both to laugh and yet cry—touched, entertained, yet angry with herself for a darting wish that this honest, soft soul of Hector's had been wedded to keener intellectual fibre, and the man made more for thought as well as action.

Meanwhile, Hector went on with common sense enough, but some dulness, 'Plenty of fellows at school and even later, whom I have known, used to think they could write poetry too; but it never lasted. It was only while they were in love,'

> '"Young men, aye, and maids,
> Too often sow their wild oats in tame verse,
> Before they sit down under their own vine,
> And live for use,"'

quoted Nannie, to free herself from some embarrassment.

'Just so,' quoth Hector, approvingly. 'Just like my friends, as I said. Now don't be vexed, dear; only, don't you think the liking for it may pass with you too.'

'But I am not—in love!' retorted poor Nannie, with quick fiery answer, though breathed in bitterly chill tones, like fire burning under snow.

What had she said?

A sudden shock of feeling, like a hidden revelation, sent a thrill through here from head to feet; even outwardly she was trembling.

But it was dark; Hector could not see that. And her freezing words—the wounded haughtiness with which she had drawn back, made him pause too with a sensation of recoil, as if an icy touch had been laid on his hot heart.

'I only said that a time *might* come—no matter when—when you will rather, too, sit down under your vine and live for use,' he said in an estranged voice.

'For use!' repeated Nannie, with a poet's overmastering emotion. She felt, indeed, hoist with her own petard. The consciousness of her one gift, her treasure, burned in her breast; however small her one confided talent, to her it was a sacred charge.

'Oh, who dare say what is not of use, that we feel bidden to do by the Power on high that directs even the butterflies to flutter, and the birds to sing? A little brown wren's note may not seem of use when there are so many nightingales, but "it sings because it must" That is what I feel—because I must! although I do not know what good it can do.'

'I did not know that people had such revelations—that one was to stitch, and another to make sonnets,' replied Hector, almost brutally, yet feeling as if she were a being of a different order from himself, bent on ascending to heights beyond the straining hold of his earthly arms. 'And yours is puzzling, I confess, since you can look after the house here well enough; and you say, you don't write poetry very well.'

'No; but even that very inability to be like those great minds one longs to resemble, may be a probation here below. Need our gifts perish after we have used them on earth?' she answered low, and in pain of mind. 'After all, the impulse to do the best we can in all circumstances is a revelation of will. I did the housework here, as you say; but now I am going away, and what other work can I do then but write?'

'Do? You can do something better than go and starve in a garret, as you most likely will,' with caustic emphasis.

Nannie, midway in the shadowy path, stood transfixed for a few full moments. Covering her face with her hands, she sobbed low, 'Oh, Hector. You! of all others. How can you speak so cruelly?'

Then she darted past him. The trees there, neglected for years, had so overgrown the path, it had seemed as if it ended. She, however, pushing her way between the cool green branches that closed protectingly upon her track, passed out of sight by a way she knew. But in one second Hector sprang after; in a few more had caught her to his breast, under the dark boscage. 'Why did I speak so? Why? Because, Nan, I want you myself—to be my guide, my star in life. My love, I cannot do without you. I will not let you go out into the world alone. Ever since we were little, have we not felt made for each other? And now it is the same. I can do nothing good in life without you. *Oh, Nannie, I know it! Speak.*'

But she could not speak to him. Only, as she gave up her lips to meet Hector's rapturous kisses, he knew she loved him; and so, at that same instant, she gave up her soul, to be knit with his indeed, as he asked, in jointly earnest life-long striving to do the right, and strain towards the highest aims possible in their lives, helping each other therein. To her, the fulness of her whole life's bliss had come in that one unutterably exquisite, highest-attuned moment.

As to Hector, he knew he had gained his dear divinity—his sweet-counselling Egeria. Nay! but he had all along known he would! So he thought, strong in his sense of love, and youth, and power; not thinking much, rather feeling that—

> 'The sunshine kisses mount and vale,
> The stars they kiss the sea,
> The west-winds kiss the clover blooms,
> But I kiss—thee!'

It was all as it should be. Had this not been agreed upon by them twain in sunny childhood, and that with the true wisdom of babes—foretold of them by others? It all seemed natural, however new.

'The oriole weds his mottled mate,
The lily's bride o' the bee;
Heaven's marriage-ring is round the earth;
Shall I wed—thee?'*

The path just beyond the thicket ended in an open space, where four greensward rides met; while all around lay the dark, slumbering woods. Midmost in this space was a small and very ancient ruin, the base of one of those round towers erected by a bygone race; to what purpose none now rightly know.

Loving, yet misunderstanding, this human pair had passed under those dark boughs;—when they passed out they were most solemnly engaged to each other to be man and wife.

The clear pale moon overhead witnessed it; the faint summer stars and deep-hearted woods, and that ancient, mysterious tower, which must have seen many another solemn rite.

Side by side—close—just beyond the edge of the wood, just on the verge of the moonlight—thus a moment Hector and Nannie, newly-affianced, stood!

* Lines from a poem by Bayard Taylor, 'Proposal' (1865)

CHAPTER 20

MIDSUMMER DAY

MIDSUMMER Day! When Nannie rose next morning it was indeed after a night of happy vigil—of wakeful rejoicing; for all that night long, till the grey dawn upspread, and the birds twittered, and another loud, sunny, glad day began again, happiness had kept her wide-eyed.

She was so unused to it, it almost frightened her. And into her memory came, and stayed, and often repeated itself, a German poet's exquisite warning once heard from the Fräulein:—

'Zwei Kammem hat das Herz;
  Drin wohnen
Die Freude und der Schmerz.
Wacht die Freude in der Einen,
  So achlummert
Der Schmerz still in der Seinen.
O Freude, habe Acht;
  Sprich leise,
Dass nicht der Schmerz erwacht.'

She was in this mood as she waited with Hector upon the grey stone terrace before the door for old Mr. de Burgo's arrival. Her lover rallied her upon her fears of his grandfather's anger.

'You have me to fight your battles now,' he said, while her hand was clasped in his. 'And my shoulders are broad enough to bear any reproaches, if he could be displeased at the only wise action I ever did in all my life.'

And indeed, to Nannie's loving eyes, they were broad enough for all her and his joint burdens to come. But she knew the old man would be angry. Nothing less than a fine match would have pleased his vanity for Hector. She felt in a painful and false position.

The railway station* was a good many miles from Black Abbey; therefore old Robert had been grumblingly obliged to start very early, as Mr. de Burgo was coming in time for a late breakfast. He was secretly consoled, however, by the fact that, as the ancient phaeton was the only vehicle (except the great, yellow chariot) which had survived from the past glories of the coach-houses, his master would be obliged to sit beside himself for an hour and a half, during which time—Hereupon, the wrinkled sinner put his tongue in his cheek, and began crooning a psalm tune to himself, as he harnessed the horse. It happened to be that one beginning, according to Robert, 'O, all ye p*a*ple, clap yer hauns—'†

The steward, passing through the stable-yard, heard him with a gloomy brow, and said an hour later to Rebecca, 'I'll warrant ye, thon ould Judas is just thinking he'll have *the first of it* now with the master, about those oats I accused him of wasting—if he was not making clean away with them. … Not one of us but he'll have his hint against, and shake his head over.'

'Not one!' echoed Rebecca, sighing as housekeeper; and as being well aware that, though very reticent in words, the enemy's winks and mutterings seemed to insinuate such dark suspicions, that everyone would have preferred being accused of far worse crimes than their real, or supposed, slight offences against old

---

* Newtownards railway station (7 miles from Greyabbey) was opened by the Belfast and County Down Railway Co. in 1858.

† Psalm 47: 'O all ye people clap your hands … (Episcopalian Hymnary - as sung in Church of Ireland churches); 'All people, clap your hands; to God … (Scottish Metrical Psalms - as sung in Presbyterian churches).

Robert himself, in plain language.

As the carriage drove up, and Mr. de Burgo was carefully helped out, the change in his appearance struck Nannie very much, since she had not met him, now, for a year. He was no longer the well-preserved, crisply snowy-haired old beau she had last seen. Now the hair was thinning; his face grown grey and pinched; while his figure, never tall, had become shrunken, so that his clothes no longer sat upon him with the neat jauntiness of yore.

Even while cursing his Italian valet, who supported him upon one side, while Hector gave him his arm upon the other, Nannie fancied—or was it fancy?—that his eyes ranged piercingly from the young man to herself. They, at least, had lost none of their keenness, whilst the aquiline nose was more sharp-pointed than ever.

'Where is Fräulein Schmidt?' were his first words to his late ward, as she received him on the steps; and he looked round with that raising of the eyebrows showing that one of the household, already, had failed in the deep deference that he called due respect, and with which he liked to be met.

Nannie hastened to find the Fräulein, who was reluctantly persuaded to make her instant appearance in the Saloon, where she was received indeed with a lowering brow and very scanty courtesy by the master of the house; and whence, to Nannie's secretly extreme vexation, she took the first opportunity of shambling away, after sitting in silence, with a look as if on Mr. de Burgo's arrival her spirit had slunk to the innermost recesses of its clay house, while her features had little more expression than the lid of a mummy-case.

Meanwhile, the two young people remained in dutiful attendance upon the autocrat of the house, who leisurely began his breakfast, and proceeded to put searching questions to Nannie as to the state of household affairs during his absence—evidently implying that, as a matter of course, they had all gone wrong. The girl grew inwardly more and more convinced that all this time she herself and Hector were the objects of a furtive but more than usually keen scrutiny. Honest Hector, on the other hand, becoming much more at ease as some small jokes of his were graciously received, soon forgot discretion, and *would* fix his eyes occasionally in fatuous admiration upon the face of his lady love, who grew paler and paler, full of inward tremors.

'Old Robert tells me the dairy woman left six months ago, and that he did not know that any one was got to replace her. What is the meaning of that?' demanded the old man, with an air of searching investigation.

'She went away only because she was ill, Mr. de Burgo; and as the poor woman was very anxious to come back, I have been superintending the dairy for her. You need not be afraid that it has suffered' (with a faint smile, as that suspicion became evident on the sharp face opposite her); 'the profits are larger, indeed.'

'Humph! Very likely. No doubt she robbed right and left. The whole of them do. But I hope she has got no wages, since she chose to go?'

'No,' duly replied Nannie, who had helped the poor soul, an old servant about the place, out of her private purse.

'Well; at least that will repay some of her pickings. But why was no gardener got, as I wrote desiring should be done, after that old fool's death?'

'Brown, the steward, could get none to come for the wages, Mr. de Burgo, as yet. I have been trying to give the garden-boy all the necessary directions, during the last month or two, myself. You may not find things in as good order, of course; but I did my best.'

'Brown is a fool.' And Mr. de Burgo indeed inserted a very violent expletive or two, with which, in the old-fashioned style, he garnished his speech on all occasions; though, had he been one of this latter-day generation, he would more probably have reserved them for effective use in the bosom of his family. Nannie's replies had secretly pleased him, in so far as his determined selfishness on being miserly to the last pinch at home, so as to be more extravagant upon himself abroad, was gratified. They had also set him thinking in another direction than before; two opposing interests were balancing each other in his mind. 'Brown is a fool! and from what I could gather from Robert this morning, has had a quarrel with my new bailiff, and one or other mean to leave. A pretty piece of trouble that will give me.'

'Robert makes too much of things, Mr. de Burgo. They are quite reconciled now. I was able to smooth over the misunderstanding.'

As the examination was now ended—with a sound from Mr. de Burgo that might have been a suppressed snarl, although meant as an acknowledgment of indebtedness—Hector, who had been listening with amazement and some indignation to these revelations of his grandfather's household economy, which absence in India and good-humoured inertness had prevented him from rightly understanding hitherto, now tried to assist Nannie in some teapot duties that plainly required little help; and that with so undisguised an affection, by way of reparation for his grandfather's ingratitude, that the latter looked up and rather pointedly asked, 'Well, my boy, and have you been over often to see your friends, the Veres, or the Hares, or the Desboroughs; since I believe they are at home?'

'No, sir, not yet.'

'And yet I thought you liked them in London; not that I ever affected their society much,' observed the old gentleman with a sugared sarcasm, who hated his neighbours, but, unless it were necessary, had no wish to offend his handsome grandson, his heir—the one being for whom he now perhaps entertained some warmer sentiments in his frozen heart, and his last link with that set of young fellows to whom he still struggled, with difficulty, to attach himself, declaring he had not lost his appetite for their pleasures, and was no old fogey, yet. 'Well, Miss Nannie,' he now went on, turning to favour her, 'and so, no doubt, you have been trying to make this young gentleman's country banishment pass as pleasantly as possible. No need to ask, ha, ha! Young men's comforts are always more attended to by womankind than those of old ones.'

'I think, sir, she tries her best to please both, and be all goodness and kindness to everybody. If she does not succeed in making everyone happy, that is not her fault. She certainly has done so with me,' warmly responded Hector.

'Hum! Well, I hope the Fräulein, however, has honoured you both with more of her company than she has me; otherwise I should certainly not have considered it proper to have allowed a young hussar to come over here and be always in the company of a young lady under my charge,' went on the old gentleman, assuming an air of intensely dignified gallantry as he made a little bow to Nan that made her shrink; remembering what the children had called his "scoldings before company," and their general sequel, long ago. Then, as both young people felt intensely uncomfortable, he added, with a smile, that was to poor Nannie no more hilarious than a partial display of his false teeth, 'Young ladies that lead a retired life in the country do not always rightly understand the little attentions that a man of the world would pay, only as a matter of course, to any young person of the other sex in whose society he was thrown.'

There was no mistaking her guardian's kind intention of making her know her own position at once on his arrival, and nipping in the bud any wild hopes that his grandson's behaviour might have raised. The slender girl's figure his gaze transfixed seemed to bend like a reed before the bitter breath of an east wind; the sensitive poet's-face mutely looked towards Hector, with pained, timid pleading. The latter had flushed dark-red while his grandfather was speaking. His honest young face looked as if the anger, that was always slow to come but long to go with him, had begun to rise. He now said, with prompt bluntness, 'Miss White, sir, can make no mistake in thinking that my attentions to herself mean entire devotion on my part, for they do. And I am ready to explain them to you, whenever you will listen to me.'

Nannie, keenly noticing, saw that the old man started a little; but, controlling himself, he answered with unnatural blandness, lightly tapping his snuff box, and then very deliberately relishing his pinch with a *grand seigneur* air, 'My dear fellow, you forget that I was not addressing you all along. I have no doubt that your behaviour has been, as you say—ahem—perfectly explicable. But why insist upon answering always for this young lady, who no doubt could speak much better for herself? Never knew a woman that couldn't!'

'Because,' said Hector, with deep feeling—and, turning, he put his arm protectingly round Nannie's waist—'she has given me the right to speak for her. She has, God bless her! promised to become my wife. Grandfather, ever since we were little children we have always cared for each other, more than for anyone else. I tried to wait until she was under your charge again, to tell her how much I loved her; but last night it was too much for me.'

As he paused in true emotion, Nannie gave one quick, proud glance up at him. Whatever came now, she need not care; her knight had spoken, and she felt that she could trust him to defend her. To the utter astonishment of both young people came a low laugh of quite peculiar zest from Mr. de Burgo, as he raised his eyebrows very much: 'He, he, he! , . he, he! Fell in love like the birds in spring-time, eh, just because you were together? Well, it is a very pretty amusement, and not at all uncommon.'

'Have you nothing more to say, sir? Am I to understand that you give your consent?' asked—after a few moments' bewildered pause, while trying to repress the excitement of his feelings—the heretofore indulged heir to Black Abbey. The venerable head of his family had always treated him, hitherto, with sublime graciousness. It was the proper thing to have an heir to Black Abbey; and Hector had given promise of being a fine young prince, worthy of that still finer ancestor who had petted the handsome boy, been proud of his prowess as a soldier and sportsman, and shown him an example of extravagance with the complacent feeling that the property would see himself through life luxuriously anyhow. *Après lui le déluge!* But now the latter only took more snuff, though his hand trembled very much.

'My good sir, since it appears you have both already settled the matter to your mutual satisfaction, I really fail to see what my opinion can signify to you.'

'Then it is a matter of utter indifference to you. I am free to do as I please,' burst out poor Hector, with heaven knows what quick visions, and determinations of marrying upon the little private income that had accrued to him on his coming of age—the legacy of an aunt, ill-treated by her father, like all the latter female De Burgos.

'Oh, Hector, hush! Have patience, for my sake!' murmured Nannie, laying a light hand on his arm. Then turning, with tears running down her face—tears of over-excited feeling and womanly deep emotion—she said, 'Ah, Mr. de Burgo, I know—I feel—that you do not think me good enough for Hector. But, remember, I was brought up with your grandchildren—as one of them; and I do not think anyone else could ever care so much for them, or for dear old Black Abbey.'

She ceased, alarmed; for her old guardian turned livid as

he looked at her, and leaning back in his chair, feebly tried to loosen his neckcloth. Hector, also perturbed at this, tried to help him, but was waved back. 'Leave me, sir. I desire, I command, that you leave me to die! … Don't pretend to help me. Do you think I don't see what you are both aiming at—that the old man may die, and you two step into his shoes? … Oh, go and tell the sexton to dig a grave for me at once. Go—go! stammering and spluttering with rage and weakness. '*I beg, I desire* you to order me one at once.'

'There is no use in your staying, dear; better go. I have seen him like this once or twice before,' whispered Hector, with deep wrinkles on his broad brow; for to see his grandfather almost in a fit, and know that he had brought this on, and could not cure, but indeed very likely must aggravate matters by his future conduct, was a troubling thought to his kind big heart.

After half an hour he rejoined Nannie, who had remained waiting, trembling, in the saloon, which still retained its old name, being indeed too ancient and stiff in its furnishing for a modern morning-room.

'Well, dear, he is better now, and quiet, you will be glad to hear,' exclaimed the young man, his face free from almost all cloud now, like a lusty morning sun, rejoicing in the assurance that he has only to put forth his strength, and all obstacles must scatter before his victorious march. 'I soothed him; and he said of his own accord that we will talk all this over quietly, when he is stronger. But nothing will please him but that I should ride over to Redbay* and see the yacht this morning. It

* Redbay, near Cushendun on the Antrim Coast Road. In 1816 May Crommelin's grandfather (Nicholas De la Cherois-Crommelin) purchased land at Cushendun where he built a large house for summer residence called 'Cave House' entered through a red cave near the harbour. Behind this, across the Antrim Plateau, is Newton

must have come in, he says; and he wants to go off for a trip, as soon as he can move. … It will be a very dull day for you, my poor little Nan! But you see, poor old fellow, after all one must please him, as he is evidently rapidly coming round to our way of thinking,' ended Hector, caressing her joyously and fondly, with a certainty, born of his youth and strength, that all must go well with them.

Nannie would not damp his feelings; though the smile on her face was a pale one, and in her heart, womanlike, she doubted.

But she watched him from her window ride out under the high archway and down the shady elm-walk that led towards the sea, and waved her hand to him, as he looked up with a cheerful glance. Indoors was the dreaming, still-lived lady; below, in the sunshine, light-hearted Lancelot rode on, but without sin or care, in his life full of action. She thought of Shalott.

Crommelin, where a family mining enterprise was located. 'Redbay' was familiar to May Crommelin and here she set another 'Ulster' novel: *A Jewel of a Girl* (1879). However, in this novel, 'Redbay' town and harbour appears to be much closer to 'Black Abbey' than Cushendun.

CHAPTER 21

THE LESSON OF LIFE

A QUARTER of an hour had not passed before Paolo, the sleek-mannered Italian valet, came to find Nannie, who indeed still stood in a dream at the same high window, gazing down the shadowy road under the patriarchal elms, or away to the peep of rich land and deep-hued ocean she could just descry beyond the sea of greenery.

His master wished to see Miss White in his study, said the man.

See her; so soon! He was sufficiently recovered, then, to fight a defenceless woman; but poor Nannie, on the contrary, had none of her usual strength. Her emotional nature had been too highly strung yesterday, and after her wide-eyed night, and from excess of late happiness, she was weak. The morning's scene had painfully reminded her, too, of her false position under this roof; but friendless, homeless, where else could she go?

So she approached what was always considered the household torture-chamber with reluctant footsteps; wishing, as one so often in life vainly wishes, that this day she had not had to endure what must be coming, and she so ill- prepared to meet it!—that she might have had a lull to rest in.

Mr. de Burgo was seated at his ease, in a deep leathern chair, and seemed indeed wonderfully recovered. But there was no seat near for Nannie, nor did he offer her one. She was obliged to stand, like a menial awaiting orders, or a culprit receiving sentence, looking down, with an inward repulsion she vainly tried to overcome, at the wizened, wrinkled old man, who received her with quietness that was horrible to her, and a silence for a perceptible space—which she felt she could not be the first to break. Then he nodded at her, like a China mandarin figure, but with a much more satyr-like expression of countenance. After two or three moments of this, he sneered: 'Well, Miss White! … well, Miss White! I congratulate you; I do, 'pon my honour. Egad! a pretty mess this is you have got yourself into! As nice a little bit of scandal will soon be going through the country about you, young lady, as ever I have heard.' He helped himself to snuff as he spoke, and raised his eyebrows in a manner so insulting that the light leapt into Nannie's grey eyes, and her pale face grew warm with quick blood.

'What scandal could there be, Mr. de Burgo? No one dare say that I have acted wrongly—otherwise than any woman in my place might have done.'

'Hush, hush! Stop now! … Take care! Remember I stand no impertinence. No, none; by George!' hastily interrupted the old man in a still more suppressed, warning voice, with a look as of a devil in his eye at her opposition. Then he went on: '*I* tell you so. Why the very servants, madam, are laughing together over your love-making. Your conduct with Hector is common talk among them. Old Robert told me, this very morning, of having seen you together last night kissing—'

'Stop,' said poor Nannie with difficulty. 'This is too much. Hector told you that it was last night I promised to marry him.' She had herself, before she could sleep, hastened with the tale of her happiness to her old foster-mother, Rebecca, whose heart she knew would be overjoyed at such news from her nursling. The Fräulein had locked herself into her room to compose a sonata that, haunting her soul, had seemed in its dim first conception music worthy of the spheres; and Nan had not had the heart to disturb her with such human matters as a love-story. Old Robert was a traitor; and as to the few other servants, the mere Nethinims, they were devoted to Nannie, and feared and disliked Mr. de Burgo. Nevertheless, by the coarseness of his words, all the bloom seemed rubbed from her romance, and her fastidious, almost self-fearful mind, began even to query whether she had not indeed done something unseemly—something, in her ignorance, that the world would cavil at. She could not speak, but she could have cried.

The old man saw the effect he had produced, and went on more gently; 'For your sake I … hum … said nothing of this before Hector this morning. You have, on the whole—on the whole—always seemed to me modestly behaved, hitherto. It would have been a greater disgrace than I cared to inflict on any young lady—*dash it!*—to say in plain terms before a young man like him, what every one would think of your having allowed him to make love to you during my absence—playing, what's their names?—Paul and Virginia here—without a proper chaperon. For, begad! that Fräulein is the most utter old fool as to any notions of propriety I ever saw.'

Nannie White had grown pale again, and her lips were set. After a long pause, during which Mr de Burgo (secretly vastly pleased with himself) had time to alter slightly his mental attitude, and Nannie to strengthen her's, she succeeded in asking, with a face the muscles of which were rigidly set:

'And what do you now propose, since I have made myself a subject of scandal to all persons of propriety?'

'Well, well … not exactly that yet,' hummed and hawed the old gentleman, taking snuff again, and looking curiously at her. The mental pain Nannie plainly suffered after merely hearing a few strong words, was so much greater than he, even with his experience of womanish hysteria, could have supposed possible, that Mr. de Burgo put her down mentally as a weak fool. She had, however, luckily for himself, ridiculously old-fashioned ideas as to womanly pride and duty, which would make her plastic as dough in his hands.

'It need not be so bad as all that yet,' he went on. 'Matters like this are hushed up every day. … It would be most painful to me to hear the daughter of my old friend spoken of as having tried to catch my grandson: and that, by George! without having a single recommendation of either birth, or beauty, or fortune; and after having sheltered and brought you up under this roof! Of course Hector means all he says for the moment; but the fellow has been in and out of love a dozen times before, bless you! and meant it just as much.' (Whether this had been so or no Mr. de Burgo neither knew nor cared; but experience in human affairs, perhaps, warranted the assertion.)

'However, as of course I could not hear of such a thing, the moment he found he would have to live on his own wretched pittance, poor devil, he would let you drop quietly, as soon as he conveniently could; and then, Miss Nannie, you would look blue. No, no! Egad, with poor Jack White's daughter I can't stand seeing her prospects ruined like that; for a jilted girl is always more or less pointed at.

'We will hush it up,' went on old Mr. Worldly-Wisdom, in a consoling tone. 'Hector can come off in the yacht at once with me till his leave is spent; and you had better stay on here, for then no one can suppose I have any grounds for complaint against your conduct. And indeed, on the whole, I must say I am satisfied—fairly satisfied with the way in which you manage my household affairs.'

A look as of a revelation her opponent had unwittingly made came into Nannie's eyes: she was too good a house-keeper to be lightly parted with. Then, as she still seemed unable to speak, this experienced old beau, who knew, as he used to aver, a 'doosid deal about *affaires de cœur,*' went on with an air of gallantry:

'Come, come, my dear; after all, everybody—yes, begad, nearly everybody—has had similar little stories told of them, and it.does no one any harm. But nothing cures a first attachment like a second, ha, ha! I declare, I will promise to look out for a husband for you. Come now! there is Smithson, the lawyer, who ought to be married; and the Veres' agent, and—'

'Stop, Mr. de Burgo. Remember, if you please, that you are speaking to your grandson's promised wife,' cried Nannie, flaming out upon him, her soul afire now with indignation. 'How can you imagine that I would be weak enough to give him up because of any foolish or malicious gossip, when in my heart I know I acted rightly? No; not even for your anger, though I am truly grieved at it. I promised to marry Hector, because I believe in my very soul that it *will be* for his good! But, if ever he *wishes it*, I love him so much that I am equally ready to set him free.'

'Marry Hector! penniless pauper that you are, madam! Never!' almost screamed Mr. de Burgo at her, grinding his teeth in a frenzy of passion, while all the muscles of his pallid face seemed strained, and he breathed with difficulty. Then followed a string of epithets that need not be described, nor the scene that followed. Under the storm of insult—of evil imputation that tried to blacken her love for Hector into a vulgar sordid attempt to ensnare a rich man's heir—poor Nannie bore up, though she trembled greatly. Her face was tortured with a pain that, although she knew herself to be blameless, was to her sensitive nature bitter to bear.

For the first time in her life, the woman that was so proud of her white motives—who had without knowing it gone daintily, like a moral Pharisee, in her unsullied robes of a pure memory, a purposeful present, and high, lone life, found herself bespattered with mud, like the poor, lower-living sisters she had so often stooped to pity. In her bewilderment, it almost seemed to her as if she must have in a manner deserved some of it. Only once, when the old man threatened her with having the power of leaving Black Abbey to Aileen, she faintly smiled. They three—Hector, Aileen, and herself—had grown up too closely bound together in heart and soul for that menace to have much effect. It was only for Hector's sake she waited; hoping that when the whirlwind had passed over her head, she might venture to speak a small word of gentleness—peace—that might possibly be heard, and so take root to a better end than its evil predecessors—words being living things, sparks struck from the soul.

But, before the end, it was too much for her.

With a face like a ghost, and almost as noiseless a footfall, Nannie White entered her room again, and there found Rebecca. The old woman was sitting on a chair planted in the middle of the room, with her hands folded over each other on the lower part of her body, in an unconscious attitude of resignation, whilst she rocked to and fro. She was waiting to hear the result of the interview, which her motherly instinct made the poor old soul dread for her darling.

'Oh, Rebecca, Rebecca!' exclaimed poor Nan; and sinking on her knees, she buried her head in that dear lap to which, as a babe, she had so often toddled for consolation. Then she burst into a terrible flood of tears. 'We must go; we must go away! … I told him I would not stay another day under his roof.'

'Yes, yes, my lamb, we'll go; we'll go. But ochone! oh—where to?' sobbed the old nurse, obedient at once, without further questioning. Nannie raised her wet face, trying to think; arresting, by pure strength of will, the passionate grief that still shook her body—

'We can go to Redbay to-night; and then—then on to London, as the Fräulein and I meant to do; only we have so little money.'

'Hut, child! sure I've five pounds put past, in the first wee sock that ever went on your foot; blessings on it!' cried out Rebecca, recovering from her first almost speechless bewilderment. 'But we'll not can* walk the distance. And, Oh, gracious

* 'will not can' = will not be able to

deliver us! what'll become of your clothes?'

'Perhaps—perhaps good old Mr. Cosby would lend us his gig,' slowly suggested Nannie, holding her head, since her brain seemed reeling with all that had to be considered.

There was not a car to be had for love or money, near; at the worst, they might maybe borrow a cart.

'I'll be off and ask him!' ejaculated Rebecca, rising in a jiffy, and wiping the tears that were chasing each other rapidly down her cheeks, which were like withered winter apples. 'Oh, but it is sore to get *the turn-out* like this!—after all these years. My lamb, my lamb! what will Master Hector say?'

'He will say that I did right,' said Nannie quickly, with a proud glow of confidence. 'But hurry, dear Rebecca, for time is precious; and I must go and find the Fräulein.'

'Oh, ay! find her. She must come too; we'll all clear out together,' gabbled the old nurse, as, short of breath, she hastened away down through the park; making no more preparation than to throw a shawl over her head, as when she had been a barefoot country girl.

But this time both reckoned wrongly, although about one whom they had known during so much of their lives.

The governess was found, after some little difficulty by Nannie, in a strange retreat—a dismal walk at the rear of the stables, between two ugly beech hedges used unfastidiously for drying the household washing. But these exactly, she declared, helped to keep her thoughts in bounds, which otherwise, with a more open view, would stray wide as the horizon, instead of dwelling sufficiently long on, and exhausting, one subject. She was now pacing up and down with unequal strides, accordingly as she was excited or puzzled by whatever occupied her thoughts. It might have been Goethe's wonder-beautiful theory of the leaf-type—that not-yet-even-fully-appreciated, however admired, godlike philosopher no less than noble poet. Or, it might have been the great doctrine of Dr. Darwin as to the origin of species—about that time beginning to be first heard of—and of whom she was so ardent a disciple as to be heard exclaiming often to herself aloud over his book, with clasped worshipping hands, 'Ach!—*that* is a man! that *is* a man!'

Whatever it. was, although she saw her beloved pupil's grave face and pallor, it was with difficulty that she could withdraw her mind from its preoccupations with abstract philosophy, to interest itself in her companion's living love and pain. But when, at last, she was made to understand all that had passed, the sallow woman stood still and groaned aloud. 'Ach! mine unfortunate child! leaf of my heart!' she exclaimed, half in English, half in her native tongue.

'Has this most silly but dangerous thought-disease, this mind-fever of mere youth, seized upon you too? Ach, ach! how it attacks all; and how many it makes miserable! But you must resist it. You must strengthen yourself against it, as against any bodily epidemic, say the small-pox, that the foolish and vulgar believe is a necessity; but not you, who understand vaccination. Have I not always taught you that the only divine in us—thought—must evermore strive against the tyranny of nature, of this environing matter, through which with difficulty it has struggled upwards from its first faint beginnings until it conquers all? Have I not armed you; filled your memory; shown you how to use your mind; been so proud of you, as a woman who would be a model to the foolish of our sex, and a proof of what right education would do?'—the poor preceptress's voice broke down with emotion—'And now, if you give way … alas! what do I say, seeing you have already given way? Farewell mind-rest! Adieu to the tranquil enjoyment of science, till the crisis is past. … Nannie, my mind-child! be warned by me. I know—I have suffered.'

Silent, with a sort of sad amusement, Nannie White stood

beside her old friend; longing for the latter to take some present decision, yet hardly liking to urge her to leave in such haste the retreat which had grown so dear to her, although knowing that would be best.

'Do any of us ever really learn from the experience of others in such matters?' she gently asked. 'No: I think we must all learn the lessons of life for ourselves. But when the crisis of the fever is past, as you call it, why should I not turn to more intellectual pursuits again?'

'Because you will awake from a dream, and find yourself chained for life!' cried out the Fräulein, in such excitement that she tried to relieve her emotion by violently rubbing her outspread hand all over her face, and even began twitching out some of the hairs from her thick eyebrows, accompanying each uprootal with an *ach!*

There stood poor Nannie, tremulous, oppressed, turned out of her beloved childhood's home, and longing for if it were only one word of friendly encouragement from one of her so few friends; but she was only to hear urgent remonstrances, affectionate imploring entreaties to vow herself to her art alone—to science and spinsterhood.

'Oh,' uttered the Fräulein finally, in desperation, 'I am fond myself of Hector—I admit it. He is a most excellent young man. He has all the everyday virtues. But you—you are his superior in mind; you have a poet's soul; and how could you accept him as your *master?* for that is what marriage too often, alas! means in our still benighted age. If, indeed, you could meet with a master-mind, who would treat you as a friend and comrade, and encourage you to work—not for his mere selfish comfort, but, with a truer larger love, for the good of the whole human race—some great soul, with great heart and great intellect—*then* you might be happy.'

'And where on earth is she to find this man-miracle? Not

in Black Abbey, anyway, ha, ha!' cried out a cheerful laughing voice behind them.

Both the others started, and looking round saw Bonnibel Hawthorn, with dancing brown eyes, and rosy cheeks, whose heaving breast showed that she had been running up most of the way from the manse through the woods.

'My poor—poor dear! Rebecca has told us all about it,' she now added, stretching out her arms and warmly embracing Nannie, yet with deference. 'Don't be offended with me, for I can't help it. I am so sorry for you. But don't mind them, dear; don't mind any of them, excepting Mr. Hector. (*Shouldn't* I just like to see his face, when he hears how this old wretch has treated you!) And grand-papa begs and prays you to come down now, and stay with us. Oh, do; there is a room for you, and Rebecca too, as long as ever you like. Say you will, dear! … You could not break our hearts by going away to London as if you had not a friend in the world.'

'Bonnibel, Bonnibel, you are far too good to me—I am quite bewildered. May I think for a moment or two?' uttered poor Nannie, so touched by this unexpected kindness that she could hardly speak from fresh emotion. But her friend in need drew her down on a bench, and softly caressed and cheered her till she was soothed; whilst the poor Fräulein stood by with a disconcerted expression, again severely rubbing her unoffending face.

Bonnibel was enraptured at the fulfilment of an attachment which she now repeatedly declared she had foreseen 'from the very first;' and she also hastened to explain, with pride, that hers had been the first eager proposal to offer at once shelter and welcome to the friend who was expelled from so much more lordly a home. 'But, never mind; you will come back and be mistress here, yet,' she added. 'And poor old grandpapa, the moment I said it, was so eager for me to run up. Only, at first, he was utterly bewildered between sorrow for you, and joy at the good news about you and Mr. Hector; and indignation with your grandfather; and regret that he owes it to his conscience to offend this fellow-Christian by taking you in, so that he nearly cried. Isn't he a silly old dear?'

'But your cousin, Mr. Luke; what did he think I should do?' asked Nannie, still hesitating, who set great store by the opinion of Luke Cosby in all matters involving a question of right or wrong; aye! and even many (more than one might think) concerning good taste and feeling too, from the rhyme of a verse to the fashionable follies of that bygone day; although one would not, certainly, consult the gaunt eager Presbyterian minister as to a puzzle in etiquette or the hue of a ribbon.

'Oh, Luke is out fishing, as usual; but no matter what you decide, it is sure to be right in his eyes. He thinks you—oh, well, I can hardly describe what, but something between Sappho and a saint!'

'Go, go, my child,' now broke in the deep voice of the Fräulein, as Nannie, with a half-smile on her trembling lips, which was indeed but another phase of the emotion that trembled also in a tear or two on her eyelashes, still faltered.

'Go to your good friends, and do not keep looking at me—for you are troubling your heart about what I shall do. Ach! child of my soul, I go to London to-morrow or the next day; and when my brother the professor comes over, there will be another home for you, if you like to follow. … And as to what I said of marriage to you, see! I have been thinking again—perhaps you are right, that in this you must learn your experience for yourself. After all, what we each seek is only happiness; and "a man's desire is his paradise." So you would never be truly satisfied with the love of science like me, unless you had found mere human passion insufficient. Ah! if you would but believe that an artist, a poet, a philosopher, ought to live only for the good of all mankind, and so be far happier in truth—although they may think themselves miserable—than if they gave themselves up to mere family life, poor private duties, the good of only the few. So marry: and may you never repent it. But if you do, be more courageous than other women.'

A strange blessing.

Nannie, however, calmly smiled, with a bright look of trust as to her future. Not that she was foolishly confident as to married above single bliss, or indeed any earthly bliss; but that she held the old-fashioned belief that we are all sent down to the earth as a probation-place, wherein the happiness or misery, which we call fate, that befalls us, is not chance-work at all, but our preordained trials according to our different characters. So, only anxious to do the fight, she could be brave. But the Fräulein! whatever she held, it was no such simple explanation of life. Vague and misty, perhaps, were her ideas in comparison—like those of many people; unlike those of most in that this was caused by too much and too subtle thought, not by too little.

And now as Nannie, with thanks from her heart, at last said she accepted Bonnibel's offer, there was no time to be lost; and all began bestirring themselves in helping her; hers was the head, theirs the hands, in the rapid plans that followed. Before they had ended, up came old Rebecca, sadly blown after her hurried expedition. She began at once stripping their clothes from the hedge in hot haste.

'Let me help you,' cried Bonnibel, who seemed to consider the excitement of the whole matter a capital joke.

'Ay, do,' said the old woman, 'for listen to Miss Nannie now. It's only how to leave the house and everything about it in order, she minds. Not a thought to herself, or her bits of clothes. But I'll not leave a rag nor a *stitch* behind for yon old *rough-yun* to lay his hands on' (Rebecca believed that the word 'ruffian' was a mere corruption of rough-one, it must be explained).

'If it was me,' cordially uttered Bonnibel, regardless of

grammar, 'I'd turn the house topsy-turvy; and then dance down the steps.'

Nannie had gone indoors to more important work before this time; her gentle presence somehow inspired these two with a certain sense of reverence, so that they tried to show the best of their minds as to a mind superior. Alone together, however, both these sinners, it is to be feared, almost joyfully relapsed at times; glad to feel they were, if meaner souls, yet such in common.

After a while, nevertheless, Rebecca's brave resolutions grew weak, on a message being conveyed to her that Mr. de Burgo wished to see her.

'I'll give him a piece of my mind that will warm his heart for him,' she at first valiantly declared; yet went very much like the famous progress of the snail up the wall to that study door.

'I am told that *you* are packing up your things as well as Miss White. Is that true? What is the meaning of it? How dare you do so without my consent?' demanded the terrible voice, which Rebecca declared always 'gave her a turn.'

The still more terrible eyes were upon her, for in a lesser degree like Domitian, the worst punishment Mr. de Burgo could inflict, in Rebecca's opinion, was his indignant look. But, being a wise woman, she kept her own gaze steadily glued to the floor.

('I was up to his tricks,' she said afterwards, recounting the tale with a glee she had by no means felt at the time.)

'Please, sir, I came with Miss Nannie, and I wish to go with her.'

'You may go,' vociferated her master, in a tone, she thought, as if he were going to grip her by the back of the neck. 'You may go to—!' (a certain place, of which, scholars tell us the name is derived from the valley of Hinnom, otherwise Gehenna).

'Thank ye, sir; *I will*,' murmured poor Rebecca, so flustered she did not know how she was expressing her thankfulness at getting leave to quit the premises. Only this part of the interview she always subsequently forgot to narrate; and then, after meekly enduring being mulcted of as much of her wages as could be, consequent upon her audacity in leaving without a month's due warning, she crept away quaking like any criminal just let off with a fine.

And so, before the summer afternoon had much lengthened, Nannie White and the old nurse went out of the fine old house that had sheltered them both so many years, and down to the humbler manse, outside the wall. Their light boxes were being easily trundled down the road on a wheelbarrow, by the minister's red-haired boy-of-all-work. Down the quaint horseshoe steps they two went; crossed the smooth lawns and the low meadows where knee-deep in golden buttercups the sweet-breathed milch kine fed; and on through the deep green-hearted woods, and by the chapel ruins in their shade. At the quiet little gate near the manse, Bonnibel and her old grandfather could be seen waiting for them; the minister's face beaming from afar with a blaze of kindness, hot pity, and eagerness to console.

But before reaching these kind friends, Nannie stopped. Looking back, she could see the roof-tree she had left, its quaint old chimneys cutting with sharp straight outlines the rolling curves of woodland that stretched on either side; she could just still descry the white pigeons, like specks sunning themselves on the grey steep-sloping slates. And she said with a choking voice, 'Good-bye, dear Black Abbey! Dear old home, good-bye!'

CHAPTER 22

PRAISE A FAIR DAY AT EVE

THE world's great timekeeper was drawing to the western verge of its vast half-dial overhead, but still illumining with its red refulgence the two manse meadows, waving high with their summer's pride, the flower o' the grass—and beyond them, a corner of dusty road below the Black Abbey park wall—was gleaming like fire through the branches of the last trees there, the outstanding sentinels of the great dark masses behind.

And now Miss Hawthorn, who had been lying asleep under the garden hedge for the last two hours, woke up; and guessing how late it was, yawned like a Penelope by day. After the exciting events of the morning, she had been obliged to leave Nannie White alone in her little bedroom, there just under the manse slates, suffering from a violent headache, and evidently, above all other cures, longing for perfect stillness; although her poor troubled face tried to hide all weary feelings, and to smile at Bonnibel's chatter. It was provoking. Bonnibel was so longing for a *good* gossip over the past, present, and, above all, the future of this most interesting love-affair; the first she had ever seen with her own eyes, in which *he*, as she termed young de Burgo, with emphatic simplicity, was of higher rank than an attorney's clerk, or a young man in a grain-merchant's business—the recognised beaux of her two dearest school-friends.

Rebecca had betaken herself to the double consolations of crying and a three-o'clock cup of tea; no amusement to be had, there.

So, after looking into the manse-parlour, with a shrug at the effect its old horsehair-covered furniture would have daily on their guest from the great house; then stuffing half-a-heap of the minister's socks that lay waiting being darned behind a shutter, and the rest under a sofa-cushion, Bonnibel salved her conscience by begging old Mary to 'give the place a wipe up,' and danced out with a light heart. Like a modern nymph, she comfortably lay down in a nook much frequented by her lazy self, where the grass was soft, and the hedge hid out the road close by; and here, with her arms under her head, gave herself up to dreams of bliss—of a good time coming! What luck that their highborn but poor Black Abbey saint (in this light she regarded Nannie, with whom she was never quite at ease), should be engaged to Mr. Hector and then turned out of doors. What wisdom in Bonnibel herself, although she really loved Nannie White, to have received her with such outspread arms! For now, in future, the young mistress, who would of course revive the glories of Black Abbey, would never forget the lowlier friends who had sheltered her outside its wall. '*Catch her!*'—complacently smiled Miss Bonnibel, with perfect assurance, meaning thereby that she knew Nannie too well.

Indeed, she herself often silently marvelled at the lofty ideas as to right and wrong, and the fastidiously delicate nature, of the outcast princess they had just sheltered. Pride, as well as real friendship, would keep Nannie White from resting till she had repaid all the kindness ever shown her, to the uttermost farthing. Bonnibel herself would doubtless be continually up at the great house; and—O thought of bliss!—would also get introduced to the county families. These must, she decided, as a matter of course call on the young de Burgos, who had done nothing amiss. It was sad that she herself was only a Presbyterian minister's granddaughter; but still, gentlemen would not mind that. She was determined to make a perfect sensation, when only once seen in the county. They would speak of her as the beautiful Miss Hawthorn—Mrs. Hector de Burgo's inseparable companion and friend ... and—and then the pretty day-dreamer fell by degrees asleep; and so dreamt on, sleeping, of similar delights—only momentarily marred by vague, tiny troubles, doubtless suggested by the brush of a bee's wing, or the tickling of the grass-crests against her rosy healthy cheek.

At last she was roused by her pet kitten that was purring away like a simmering kettle beside her ear: and so rose up, yawned, as we saw—and betook herself indoors.

A hasty brush to her brown hair, a wonderfully rapid washing of her hands, a blue bow pinned to her collar, a good shake to her other garments, and Bonnibel's toilette for tea was finished! With refreshed sympathy she eagerly knocked at the door of Nannie's room, requesting to be allowed to carry her up a tray. Nannie, however, opening the door, met her on the threshold, already neatly dressed to go downstairs, and with a calm though sad face. Her buxom young hostess broke out into expostulations, then wonder, then congratulation.

'You must have slept well, you poor dear; and I have been thinking of you all the time, and so afraid you would not be able to rest, and would find the room uncomfortable—there is a feather bed, though!' she exclaimed, with effusive warmth and clinging caresses.

'Indeed, I really wish you had not given me up your room,' replied Nannie, who had been truly concerned at this; Bonnibel having already shown her with pride how she had pulled half her own possessions helter-skelter into an attic close by.

'Not at all; we know how to honour such a guest, when we get one, you see. And besides, dear, you don't mind me running in here whenever I want the glass here, which is bigger than mine, or any of my clothes? And so you do like it? looking round with a sort of dubious pride. The room was sunny and large enough, but there had not been time, in old Mary's opinion, to give it the 'wipe up' it sadly needed. It was rather dusty, decidedly dirty in sequestered nooks, and generally untidy. Still, had not Bonnibel chuckling stolen Mary's best Sunday muslin apron, and therewith draped the back of the glass, tucking the strings away from the old woman's purblind but suspicious eyes? Had she not piled the table and mantel-piece with all the cheap keep-sakes, and photographs—such as we at first remember—of young persons with blurred features, wide sleeves, and hair puffed over their ears (photography was then a new art), given her by loving school-friends?

'That is a really beautiful print,' said Nannie, hesitating, seeing she must say something, and looking in sincere admiration at one above the chimney-piece. It was a proof before the letter—and exquisite copy of one of the most beautiful of the many representations of one lowly Galilean mother and her babe—

> 'A child with eyes divine, a little child,
> A little child—no more.'

Tired as she was, poor Nannie looked at it now with a soothing sense of being calmed and comforted.

'That is Luke's. He bought it as something out of the common, at a great sale; so I just stole it out of his room, to cover a hole in the wall-paper,' explained cheerful Bonnibel. (It was fastened up by a corking-pin at each corner. Poor Luke!)

'O, never mind! I'll pull it down again for him,' unheeding her guest's remonstrances. 'Don't keep looking at it any more, dear; look at this, instead.' And with unabashed glee Miss Hawthorn displayed a hammer that adorned the mantel-piece, amongst the shell pincushions and other objects of taste.

'That! What is that for?'

'To kill the cockroaches with! They come crawling out at night. It is great fun,' Bonnibel explained, her mirth fairly overflowing. But, nevertheless, her high spirits were so natural to her that one could seldom feel jarred by them. And even at the same time as the girl wound her arm round her guest's waist to lead her downstairs, there seemed to be such a world of loving sympathy in that clinging soft clasp and coaxingly cheerful face, that another person, who believed he or she *felt* really more, might have bitterly envied her—for Bonnibel expressed so easily what she *did* feel. It was not hypocrisy, but she could call up her emotions and dismiss them almost at will, whilst others struggled in vain for such power of expression or self-possession. Such people said at times that she had not their own depth of feeling; but that may have been from jealousy—perhaps.

As Nannie White entered the little parlour, it was with a shrinking feeling that she did not wish her trouble and presence to embarrass these kind friends who had received her—to damp Bonnibel's gaiety, and the good minister's homely accustomed mirth. And yet she could not seem gay: and hardly knew how to look.

A tall, raw-boned figure, however, met her at once, and with Luke's hearty hand-grasp, and a few rapid but cordial low words, wishing her the best of blessings and future happiness, all awkwardness vanished from her thoughts, although shyness nevertheless remained. She did not like to say very much, nor did either of the two ministers, the good elder one or his nephew. And indeed old Mary was bustling in and out of the parlour with the black kettle for 'Miss Bella to wet the tay'* and then the buttered toast and one thing or another, with her ears pricked sharp as needles all the time. Neither could any of them remain silent when Nannie for the first time met the two men, since on entering the house she had been too overcome with emotion to speak. Now she could thank them with most earnest, though

* 'wet the tay' = leave the tea to 'draw'.

somewhat trembling accents, for both the good wishes of the one and kindly deeds of the other, hoping—and here her voice faltered more—that all might yet turn out well. She had tried to do what seemed right—she was not sure, however … above all things she wished to do her duty.

'Why should it not be right? said Luke, in his deep indignant voice. 'Mr. de Burgo is a very rich man; does he want his grandson to marry an heiress that they may join "house to house" and "lay field to field that they may be placed alone in the midst of the earth?' And as to what you say of his wishing Mr. Hector to marry some one of greater rank, you are a lady of good family and breeding, and one, though I say so to your face, who will prove a blessing, I hope and believe, to those on the Black Abbey estate as well as to their young master, and Mr. de Burgo has no right to ask more. Still, you will both bear with him, and have patience—of that we may feel sure—and so do right, whatever he may do.'

Nannie White only gave a little mute assent, but there was a decision in her slight nod and pale smile that said as much as volumes of words to those who understood her.

Old Mr. Cosby, who was all mildness and humility, looked somewhat aghast at his nephew's out-spokenness, but must needs do his best, too, in consolation.

'Ah! there's a silver lining to every cloud; and, my dear Miss Nannie, remember it's a long lane that has no turning,' said he. 'And in fact there is a world of proverbs to remind us that we are never tried above that we are able, although we may be refined like silver seven times in the fire … Ah, yes! look at myself now—contented and most thankful for my blessings, and yet many a day in my life, deary me, I have been, *that* sad, *that* melancholy, ye would hardly believe—'

'No indeed, grandad! No one does believe that melancholy ever cast its gloom over your dear, old, rubicund face. So don't be making Miss Nannie unhappy, and come to tea—come to tea!' interrupted his grand-daughter, swooping down upon him. The old man looked quite taken aback and reproachful, for indeed he had been thinking of the girl's own dear dead mother, and troops of his brothers and sisters and friends, whose dust lay under many a green mound, while their spirits had gone before him over the great river, as sweet-tongued Horace sings:

> 'In the dark passage-boat which comes back
> To the sweet native land never more.'

And yet his grand-daughter never could, apparently, be brought to believe he had ever shed tears, or felt life a burden that seemed too heavy to be borne. But he only shook his gentle head, and murmured with injured affection, 'Ah! well now, my Bonnibel—well now; you don't know!'

'Well now, I do know, grandpapa,' exclaimed Bonnibel; 'but haven't you *got me?* Whereupon she gave him a hug, as if that thought should be an effectual consolation for all woes; then sat down behind her teapot straightway with a beaming air. And, indeed, as the rest obeyed her summons, and took their seats at the table too, she looked such a smiling queen of rustic beauty, of ruddiest red and milkiest white, with such boldly brilliant brown eyes and softly coaxing voice—(a combination that often caused an inward puzzle to some, as of an incongruity which was not immediately discoverable)—that unconsciously the eyes of the other three kept turned to her, as to a pleasant magnet. Youth, good looks, good spirits were her attraction; and pleasant indeed while they last.

During the meal, old Mr. Cosby, with tender solicitude, was continually seeking out the most buttery bits of hot toast he could find, and piling them on Nannie's plate. 'Ah! this one more little bit, my dear young lady—ah, do now!'

Luke and Bonnibel smiled furtively at each other meanwhile, knowing the good minister's hospitality could no further go.

The small square table in the small square parlour was piled high with hot potato-cake and cold meat, for both the ministers had healthy appetites; the tea was good, the eggs and bacon cooked excellently well, and yet all could see with sorrow that their guest was unable to eat. The distressed host could only try to think, in his regret, of what else he could offer to tempt her with, but his granddaughter promptly stopped him.

'Now, you must not worry Miss Nannie any more, grand-papa dear. She is not like you; she can't keep her appetite, no matter what trouble she is in—and a very good thing that is for you.'

The poor old minister looked quite aghast for almost ten seconds, at the idea of his having been worrying Nannie, and at such an accusation of materialism; seeing which, Bonnibel patted his shoulder, and pulled his neckcloth straight, to make him smile again.

The manse maiden was adroit in avoiding the mention of their guest's name, and called her Miss Nannie in a playfully affectionate tone when obliged to speak to her; the fact being, that although Nannie had led such a companionless, secluded life up at the great house, she had, nevertheless, always kept unconsciously a little aloof, seeming to Bonnibel one of a higher sphere in thought and ways than herself, as she was by birth; and that proud, delicate nature encouraged no familiarity. So the latter did not want to call her Miss White, yet hardly dared call her by her Christian name—loved and looked up to her as to a sweet patron saint, yet was aware she did not quite understand, and a little feared her.

She felt the same, oddly enough, with even Luke, although her cousin.

And now Luke, seeing Nannie grow more and more faint

and silent, did the best of all for her; and, without any ado, opened wide the window, letting in me sweet evening air and chirping of birds from the garden hedges.

'You would be better outside,' he kindly said. 'I almost think this room is close.'

Almost! it was redolent of many meals. Bonnibel, however, always out of doors, healthy and heedless, never minded that; her good old grandfather, utterly contented of disposition, accepted everything around him in life so placidly that Luke used to declare, laughing, he would never have made a martyr, so unconscious was he of ever being ill-treated. Luke himself used to create a thorough untidying draught in the little manse whenever he came in; and would then look round with a comic air of discomfort he tried to combat, feeling that things were somehow wrong, but not knowing how to right them. Now he himself took Nannie out of doors, who went with him, relieved and thankful.

The old minister, however, tucked the milk-jug under his arm unobserved, and trotted down the lane with it, in mortal terror lest old Mary should espy and upbraid him. He always stole what he could of his own property to supply the needs of a poor begging wretch down the lane, who, Mary declared, imposed upon him; and indeed the good man was often tempted to believe Mary was right; yet still he went.

Bonnibel also, as soon as her cousin had taken their guest out, softly slipped away.

'Those two are too clever for me. Luke doesn't care for what he called my "shallow sparkle" the other day, if he has got Miss Nannie to talk deep to him,' thought this young woman, with a perfectly bright, satisfied smile. So she went and calmly purloined poor Mary's big work-scissors, with which she began in the flower-plot pruning away dead twigs and snipping off faded roses, whilst that distraught crone was vainly hunting through the house for her lost property. The young manse-mistress, indeed, made such a picture of smiling industry that Luke stopped involuntarily with Nannie White, as they paced to and fro, to admire her.

'Lazybones! lazybones! you are wonderfully busy tonight,' said the big man, with a surprised laugh, in the fond tone that he and his old uncle always adopted towards their house-treasure. She had her faults, this bright, careless girl, and they perhaps knew them; but they loved her dearly all the same, and there they were right. If we did not love imperfect human nature, it would be a cold world.

'Will you let me help you?' offered Nan, to whom—though her thoughts were far away—helping everyone came naturally. But Bonnibel shook her scissors at them both laughing, and declared there was hardly enough work for herself. No doubt they were both talking, as usual, of old Greeks and new poets whose names she could not remember. No; none of either? Well, of odes and epodes or some such nonsense, with which they had once puzzled her.

But if they went into the orchard, they might find a little listener trotting after them very soon. Nevertheless, the little listener, as the finely-built big lassie called herself, had small intention of doing so. They looked too anxious and grave, and then the garden was such a splendid post of observation! —

Nannie, as she moved away had no heart for talking of even the sweetest of odes, mellifluous as honey of Hybla; she was listening with intenseness to catch a sound from a distance. Luke, too—good, awkward Luke—hardly knew what to say, or whether to say anything; for thundering from the pulpit against special sins, large-hearted tolerance towards all sinners, or lectures on science and theology, were all more familiar to him than the delicate mysteries of a lady's love. So he strode up and down silently by Nannie's side; or now and then, in his earnest, kindly, deep voice, would say something advocating patience; and still patience, and more patience. 'Ah!' murmured poor Nannie, now growing almost heartsick with listening and waiting. '"*Tout vient Ã ceux qui savent attendre*," they say. I wonder—shall I find it so in my life?'

She stopped, and the crimson came to her cheek; for down the road they could hear the gallop of a horse.

'It is Mr. Hector; he is coming this way,' exclaimed Luke, in joyful haste. 'Will you go to the arbour, Miss Nannie? You can talk to him more undisturbed, there; and I will go and take his horse, and tell him where to find you.'

The arbour was at the end of the orchard in which they were, and was almost the only spot in the little manse domain not more or less open to public gaze. It faced the manse meadow looking seaward, and was a mere rustic seat between two ashes, embowered in a little thicket screening it from the high road; but 'at least it was secluded,' as Bonnibel declared, who liked it for lazy reasons of her own. As Nannie waited, she could almost hear the beating of her own heart; the only sound in that still, late eve, save a call perhaps from the village across the fields, or the rustle of a belated bird in the bushes close by. She stood self-possessed, but lily white—waiting. Then Hector's tall figure came striding through the orchard, between the gnarled low apple-trees that age had downbent like patriarchs. How handsome he looked! how manly! The powerful influence of her lover's physical attractions which Nannie's reason declared formed no essential part of her love, yet gladdened her heart, as if in despite of that reason. He looked to her, as he came, a king among men—amongst such men as she had seen in her simple round of life. The next minute the colour rushed back to her face, however, as Hector came up—for, with a movement of eager fondness, he caught her to him, exclaiming, 'Poor little Nan! it is very evident you want me to protect you. What a trouble you have got into, the instant my back is turned! But you must never run away again from me, like this.'

Nannie was fairly astonished. She had prepared herself for stormy passion; for possibly despairing impotence on Hector's part, like a young giant meshed in a wizard's toils. But this tone of defiant, almost loud-mirthful raillery, was unexpected. Looking closer, however, she could guess he had been angry; his face was still flushed, his breast heaved, and he had plainly ridden long and fast, and had dismounted at Black Abbey only to throw himself on his wearied horse again. Gently half-disengaging herself from his hold, she looked at him with surprised, large eyes. 'Do you quite understand what has happened? Hector, do you know that I was obliged to leave your grandfather's house, owing to what he said to me about our engagement?'

'Well, and so have I left it, because you left it; and here we are together. I could not show our identity of feeling better, could I, dear? although, by his account, you were such a proud, sensitive, little mortal you took umbrage at a mere nothing and blazed up.'

'A mere nothing! Hector, he so insulted me that I cannot—I could not ever—tell you all that passed,' cried poor Nannie, almost breaking down, her voice failing her with the shame and horror of the recollection. Hector's face grew black at that. He consoled, yet urged her to speak and tell him all; and soon—although she could not and would not have repeated to him, by near, the whole of what had passed—the young man knew and guessed enough to make him passionately angry. Then, in her turn, Nannie soothed—implored him not to mind what had been done to her. A curiously similar scene it was, only of deeper meaning, to a hundred such that had taken place between these two in their dawn of childhood, when, how often! Hector had thus consoled his little playfellow for some harsh treatment by the grandfather, who had been carelessly indulgent enough to himself.

'But this is too much! To have treated you so! I *cannot* forgive him now. He might have said what he liked to myself,' burst out the young man.

'Do not say that, dear Hector; none of us dare say that. I forgive him; and so must you, far more. For see how evident it is that he did not wish to bring on a quarrel with you, when he tried to explain away what had happened between him and myself,' uttered poor Nannie; thinking it was her duty to say so, although perhaps against her own interest.

'Because he likes having an heir; and he has no second one,' said Hector, with a bitter laugh. 'He does *not* want to quarrel with me, because I am like the second appetite to him that the old gourmand bought, or the *débutante* that an old chaperon takes out into society to keep her afloat still. Yes, he tried to gloze it over. But now I shall certainly not go back to his house till he has apologized sufficiently to my wife. For I am not going to leave you at his mercy, or that of strangers any longer, Nannie. You have had too lonely a life, as it is.'

But Nannie shrank back a little, and forced herself to utter firmly, though there was a piteous look in her eyes, 'Ah! Hector, how can you marry without your grandfather's consent, when you are almost entirely dependent on him. I—I made up my mind this afternoon, that for this reason I ought to set you free from your engagement.' (The last words were uttered very low.)

Hector started, unable to believe his ears.

'What! Nannie? You would throw me over because my grandfather won't give me an allowance—may disinherit me, even? And yet I am ready to risk it all for you. And you, who seemed to me so far above other women, so little mercenary, not to care for society: I could never have believed it possible.'

He was almost blinded with rage and sorrow, or he would have seen his words contradicted in her changing face, even before she softly answered, pained—

'Do you not understand me better, after our being together so many years Hector? It was on your account I spoke. For what would being poor with you signify to me, who have been accustomed to being so much poorer all my life? But you have been used to being extravagant, dear Hector; and it might seem, after a while, hard to you to live differently from all the ways you were accustomed to. And—and—it is just because I do care so much for you, that I cannot bear to think you should make such a terrible sacrifice for me.'

'Is that all?' cried the young man, joyously. Certainly, big-hearted, soft-souled Hector cared little for money;—spent it because he had it, but thought he could shoulder his way through the world very fairly without it.

'O, if that is all, Nannie, we will be married to-morrow—next week' (and he laughed outright in his relief). 'You poor little thing! Fancy your wanting to give me up for my own interests! You are so good, that is why I did not understand you.'

'But indeed it is not all, Hector, It would surely not be right for us to marry at once, without your grandfather's consent—without giving him time to change his mind. We ought to be patient. You ought to have time too, to make sure that you may not repent; for you may meet with so many handsomer and richer women, better fitted to be your wife, in the fashionable world—'

But Hector was so excited at that, he would not let her finish. He stormed—pleaded—urged their long attachment to each other since childhood—his grandfather's no less invariable selfishness.

It was all to no purpose. Nannie's resolution was immovable; and little by little the influence her high, sensitive, but wonderfully self controlled mind, had always had upon his honest plastic nature, quieted and persuaded him. They had been attached to each other as brother and sister so long, that it seemed to her not at all difficult thus to continue for a while longer. Life moved so slowly at Black Abbey that it begot great patience, as in the days of our ancestors; and to her, living on uneventfully and calmly among these woods since childhood, Hector had always seemed present in memory and thought, and their present love only the fulfilment of their life-long attachment. But he felt differently; his life had been varied; he had almost forgotten his little playfellow when in India; and now he felt all the impatience for a closer union of a first love. He even believed his love greater by far than hers, because the more ardent and unreasonable.

'You are so cold, Nannie—so cold!' he exclaimed, his own heart hot and selfish in his passion. 'You do care a little for me, I believe; but still you can talk calmly of giving me up, and are as cold as ice.'

This was too much: Nannie burst into tears. She had kept up for his sake; had tried, out of her great, true love, to make her lover see his real position, and to hide the agony at thought of losing him that made life seem a dreariness she could never live through. Her grief was so poignant, her breaking down was such an unusual event—since, gentle and meek though she was, her fine fibre of nature had a marvellous power of endurance—that Hector was at once regretful, and soon overpowered with remorse and dismay, as he saw how terribly she had lost her usually high self-control. He threw himself on his knees beside her; caressed her; implored forgiveness, and vowed utter conformity with everything she desired in their engagement.

'Only promise me one thing, Nannie. Promise never to give me up for my own good, as you call it,' exclaimed the young man, in an outburst of most genuine and impetuous feeling; and then he earnestly repeated all he had said on the evening before. She had been his good angel even in childhood, and if she were not his high guiding star in future life he knew it would be the ruin of all his better aspirations—of all the good resolves she had revived in him to be no longer a selfish drone on earth, but to lead a useful life in 'God's fair task-garden.' He was violently in love; honest in self-abasement. No one else could ever have such a peculiar influence over him for good as this pale, grey-eyed girl—making him feel a man with a soul, of which the life extended far beyond the little limit of existence on earth.—He won his suit!

'I promise then. Hector,' said Nannie, gently, 'never to give you up because it may seem to me best for you, *unless you wish it yourself*; and then, remember, you are free. I shall never reproach you.'

Longer they sat on, now understanding, and quieted in spirit again, till the stealing moonlight imperceptibly began to brighten all the grassy meadows before them, down to the glimmering sea. Their crazy, wooden seat was a bower of bliss; the prospect towards the far horizon, in which some of heaven's lights faintly began to burn, an outlook into a world of mysterious beauty and peace.

'And where will you go to-night?' pitifully asked the sheltered though wandering princess of the outcast, home-less prince.

He laughed cheerily. 'I shall ride over to Redbay, and put up for a week at the hotel. I met, to-day, several men I know, staying there for the salmon-fishing in the river; and they say they are having a very jolly time of it. Then I shall ride over and see you, to-morrow and the day after, and every day this week, till my leave expires—worse luck!—at the end of it.'

So he rode away down the road, Luke Cosby walking a considerable way by his side; the earnest divine and his former pupil in field-sports renewing their old confidence And Luke seemed so impressed when he came back by the warm-heartedness and honesty of the young heir of Black Abbey, that he could not help saying, as he gave Nannie's hand an earnest shake that night, 'I believe in my heart, Miss Nannie, you have made a good choice, if you will not be offended at my saying so; and that Mr. Hector, as I always thought, has it in him to make a fine landlord—a blessing to all around. And I congratulate you both, most truly, on having resolved to be patient.'

'Amen,' said the devout old minister. 'But let patience have her perfect work—' We all know the rest of those grand words, the even awful height of that standard to which we are bidden attain; and Nannie bowed her head to them in silence.

As to Bonnibel! Her fervent sympathy, warmth of friendship, yet humility as a hostess that night, after Hector left, made Nannie, in surprised gratitude, feel scarcely sorry she had been forced to leave her old home—to have learnt the unfeigned kindness of these friends and especially of this impulsive girl.

So ended a day in which Nannie White had lived through more, by having felt more, than in many previous months. So fair a dawn! so stormy a noon! Praise a fair day at eve.

CHAPTER 23

ALL IS FAIR IN LOVE OR WAR

During the next few days the little household of the manse took such a lively interest in the love-drama which was being enacted in their midst, that, as Bonnibel declared, it was to them all 'as good as a play.' The two persons most concerned were, however, too much absorbed in each other's society to see the comical element that mingles so often—and sometimes grimly enough—in our human affairs.

Hector rode over as he had said each day, impatient, and anxious to make the most of the short time now left them to be together; while Nannie, now more at peace, seemed in a happy, fevered dream, as one conscious of inward excitement, yet whom a sweet spell enthralled in stillness. On the other hand, Rebecca, as the out-thrust housekeeper, was burning with curiosity to know how matters went on inside 'our house,' as she called the now lonely grey home in yonder woods; and on the very first evening managed to wipe her weeping eyes, and indulge in fat giggles of glee, when thinking how her Blouzelinda, the red-fisted scullery-wench, would have to cook Mr. de Burgo's dinner her blessed self; and be free to accomplish her fell, apparently daily desires of burning one half of the food, while flavouring the rest with smoke. Each serving-maid and man up at Black Abbey was also a staunch secret adherent to the cause of the much-pitied young lovers; excepting, of course, that time-server, old Robert, who was in high favour at present with his master. So most noons, and every evening in the dusk, some of the Nethinims would come down to hold whispered conferences with Rebecca in the lane; whilst Miss Hawthorn's bonny face might have been espied peeping through some bush, awaiting their departure, to hear from the garrulous old nurse all about the 'last tricks of the ould tyrant' up at Black Abbey. On this matter these two had become close gossips and cronies, and would chuckle together over some piece of ill-gotten eaves-dropped intelligence which both fellow-sinners judged it wiser not to impart to Nannie, who was over dainty as to the means used in obtaining their interesting information.

'But you see, poor dear, as her head is in the clouds, it is quite necessary for you and me to look after her interests, Mrs. Rebecca; a poet's friend always must,' said Bonnibel, self-excusingly.

Rebecca quite laid aside her old distrust of the young manse-mistress on this topic, although in other ways she never could quite forget or forgive how 'the minister's Bella' had surpassed her own bairn in childhood in rosy cheeks and vigorous growth.

It seemed, from the spies' accounts, that Hector's departure had sent his old grandfather into paroxysms of rage, during which, observed Rebecca, he must have felt 'clean lost for want of herself and Miss Nannie to worry.' Blouzelinda's cooking, too, next put him into what was reported as 'the biggest tantrums had *ever* been seen!' He declared himself poisoned between two dishes, that had seemed a bran-mash and a mustard-poultice—mildly supposed by the dispassionate judges at the manse to have been meant for mutton-broth and perhaps curry. Next day a first-rate cook, and no expense spared, was sent for post-haste from the nearest town; the Black Abbey cellars were ransacked for what good wine still remained in them; and the apothecary, the attorney, two squireens, and a well-to-do hunting farmer were invited to dinner by Mr. de Burgo, who was determined to show that he could dispense with the society of both his family and his county compeers. The dinner was jovial enough, by all accounts from outsiders. The guests' own memories of the latter part of the feast were, however, hazy; possibly obscured by sleep, as they only clattered homewards past the quiet manse in broad morning light. Unfortunately, the new cook was found to have partaken so much of the general festivity at Black Abbey as to be hopelessly intoxicated next day. With wrath and anathemas, the old gentleman sent for another one immediately, a reign of terror meanwhile prevailing, that made the underlings declare him as not fit to be gone near with safety.

'I hear tell he has sent for a religious cook this time,' repeated Rebecca. Then piously,—

'Dear knows, poor soul, her religion will be wanted!'

When the desired substitute, however, was provided, good character was found to have been more regarded in the matter than good cookery. One day passed, on the master's part, in subdued growlings and unfavourable comparisons of the righteous manna with the flesh-pots of wicked Egypt; then the eruption of anger burst forth again—such, seemingly, as necessary occasionally to Mr. de Burgo's bodily well-being, as those of Vesuvius are to its existence as a living volcano. The fish-sauce was declared to be infamous, and the cook called up to the dining-room to hear, without any possible softening by message, Mr. de Burgo's true opinion of her conduct. She was desired to say how, as a professing Christian woman, she could answer it to her conscience thus to poison her fellow-beings. She ought to be made to swallow it herself. By heavens! she seemed hardened (the poor woman was quite dumb with confusion, and had a nervous grin on her face that was far from being caused by amusement)—she seemed hardened, and *should* swallow it!

This the cook, though a meek person, flatly refused with spirit. Enraged by opposition, Mr. de Burgo snatched at the sauce-boat, and getting up, despite difficulty, with wonderful alacrity, screamed in a senile rage that he would put it down her throat. Round to the other side of the table nimbly scuttled the cook. After her hobbled excitedly the infuriated old man—dignity, age, gout, all forgotten in the enraged desire to have his will. Then followed dodges to either side—half rushes, and stops—while the opponents' eyes glowered upon each other, till Mr. de Burgo unfairly called his Italian valet to his aid to 'stop her!' On this the cook fairly took her courage in her two hands, and therewith boxing Paolo's ears—urged thereto by Blouzelinda's sympathetic outcries, whom the noise of the affray had brought up hot-foot and heavy-booted from the scullery—all three servants disappeared together in a noisy group, by apparently understood consent; having indeed no common quarrel, but a common cause among them.

Of course, the insulted good woman at once packed her box, and betook herself back to the town, where she spread such stories of Mr. de Burgo's behaviour, that these, added, to his previous reputation, made him seem absolutely Satanic; so no one could be found courageous enough to replace her. Hereupon, the obsequious Italian valet was reported to have placed himself in the breach, and to be daily concocting omelets and salads to the best of his abilities. Nay, worse! the nasty foreign thief, as Rebecca brought word, quivering with anger, had wrung the necks of Miss Nannie's pair of young prize fowls in his sinful ignorance, because they happened to be the plumpest. The yacht still lay at Redbay, but there seemed little chance of its owner being able as yet to leave Black Abbey; for what between all the anger and excitement he had gone through, and the effects of his dinner-party, a fresh attack of gout made it necessary for him to see his friend the apothecary daily.

It must not be supposed, however, that he was not almost as well informed of what took place in the little manse outside his park wall, as Rebecca was herself of his doings. Her trusty allies certainly did not mean to play false; but in stable-talks or kitchen gossip before Robert, that temporising adherent of the evil powers that be, it was natural to brag of the coming rising sun, and warn old Judas of how things were going on at the manse between the lovers, and that he had cut away the ground from under his own feet; and Robert, in self-interest, warned his master. The latter made a fresh move in the game by despatching a letter, marked private and confidential, to the Reverend Joseph Cosby. In this, while he desired the minister not to widen the breach between himself and his grandson further by mentioning this correspondence, he bitterly reproached Mr. Cosby with looking to his own future supposed advantage, by harbouring a young person who had repaid the de Burgo parental care with ingratitude and deceit. Worse! he charged him with conduct so unseemly and scandalous in a minister of the gospel, in encouraging interviews between the lovers in defiance of his grand-paternal wishes, that the meek old man who received it positively wept softly over the distasteful missive, wondering what indeed was his duty now.

Luckily for his peace of mind, Luke entered just then, and insisted on knowing something of the matter. On hearing—he gave such an outburst of righteous wrath against the past and present conduct of the ancient hypocrite up yonder that Mr. de Burgo's ears should have been on fire in his dismal study in the lonely house, where only memories—mind-ghosts—trod the silent floors; and neither the summer sun nor sweet outside air could bring much pleasure to that sick head and frozen heart.

During the first day or two. Hector's sunny temper had made him easily believe that all would come right in his love affairs. He was one of those royally-reared children of good fortune to whom it seems so natural that they should be blest, that perhaps from that very audacity of trust in fortune, perhaps from their glad natures, unsoured in youth, it actually does often happen that luck or the world befriends them to a surprising extent.

Luck this time failing. Hector grew troubled and moody by-and-by, for want of a settled purpose to hold to. If, as Nannie thought (his own ideas he knew being vague on the subject), his small private patrimony was not sufficient for both to live upon as he lived now, in case his grandfather remained obdurate, why should he not try to make his fortune like others—leave the army, emigrate, go with his friend young Desborough to the gold diggings for a year—heaven knows what? He was hardly serious; but still enough so to make Nannie uneasy. For, like a true woman, being ready to think her own geese swans, she rated Hector's capabilities very highly, perhaps a good deal more than need be; yet did not believe he was a man able to turn his hand to anything, or fit easily into any other grooves than those he had been prepared for by youthful anticipation and education; namely, first the life of a rather luxurious cavalry officer, and afterwards that of a thorough country gentleman. She timidly ventured to suggest that perhaps Mr. Luke Cosby could give him particulars as to emigration; hoping, the little deceiver, that Luke would help to dissuade Black Abbey's headstrong, handsome heir from any such wild project. She was only a country mouse—a rural poetess; and her acquaintance with living men being almost bounded by the parish limits, Luke Cosby was the wisest man and best friend she knew.

But Hector laughed outright at her. He was very fond of old Luke, really, who was a capital sportsman, and no doubt a fine muscular Christian; but the idea of consulting a Presbyterian minister as to the difficulties of a man of the world, of a young man of fashion, seemed absurd!

Nannie agreed with him that this was true of old Mr. Cosby, but, gently, still held there was a difference between an obscure old minister living in this sheltered nook in the black north, and a rising town preacher, who could attract his thousands for the other's tens; a scholarly divine, an already well-known writer.

'Still, every man to his trade,' put in Hector lightly. 'If I want to know more of theology, I promise you I'll go to him, though perhaps I ought to consult our own wheezy, forty-minute preacher at Redbay.' (The nearest church to the De Burgos was some miles away, which accounted for Mr. Cosby's almost sole influence in the Black Abbey neighbourhood.) 'But, otherwise, I hardly think the day will ever come when he could have anything to say in the affairs of the De Burgo family.'

Would it not. Hector? We cannot see far ahead in our lives, truly.

So Nannie meekly said no more, dutifully supposing Hector knew best on such matters, and understanding that the easy frankness with which he spoke to Luke and the old minister, and even Bonnibel, about his affairs, arose from the same honest warmth of heart which made him likewise so speak to even Rebecca; while yet in his good-humoured pride he never thought, apparently, that they could have any opinion on the subject but such as overflowed from his own eager lips—seeing this matter was so far out of their sphere.

CHAPTER 24

MAKE HAY WHILE THE SUN SHINES

NANNIE and young De Burgo were standing side by side in the breeze and sunshine, on the last morning but one of the latter's possible stay. Over some tree-tops before them was the glint of the bright, tossing sea, joyous to look at this morning; but nearer in front was the minister's meadow, in which since cock-crow had been heard the steady swish of Luke's cheerful scythe, while behind him went the red-haired boy-of-all-work, and Bonnibel in a large sun-bonnet, tossing the hay with all their might

'How that girl can work, when she pleases!' remarked Hector, from where they watched her unobserved at the fence. 'Why, I thought she was as idle as could be.'

'Not when her cousin asks her to help him,' smiled Nannie, significantly glancing towards Luke. 'I suppose they two will come together some day or other.'

'Whew! Is that it? Well, I never remarked much tenderness between them,' uttered Hector with surprise. 'Poor Luke! What a handful he will have to manage, as Rebecca used to say long ago of me; ha, ha, ha!'

'Now, Hector, you must not turn my good friends here into ridicule. I am fond—yes, really fond of them all, as I told you the other day,' returned Nannie, not without deeper meaning. For Hector had chafed a little at his future wife having to take refuge in the manse, as if she had no other friends; and would have had her go to London, to live with his maiden aunt and Aileen. And Nannie had softly chidden him as too proud; being too proud herself to go to a stranger, although his relative.

Bonnibel had heard the laugh, and looking up saw that Hector had arrived—he having just ridden over. She sauntered over the field to wish their future lord of the manor a good morning; and, being hot and tired, to rest her arms a few moments on the fence. She was not going to be a *fâcheuse troisième* to the lovers; oh, no! she knew better than that But it was only civil to greet such a guest; and she vastly enjoyed the playful teasing she generally received from him, and the more familiar footing it seemed to place them on.

'That sun-bonnet is certainly a capital shade—a perfect extinguisher, so far as your face is concerned, Miss Hawthorn,' said Hector, who, although hardly in a humour for joking this morning, knew his fair rustic hostess expected some such feeble attempt from him. Then he added, 'But I wonder you are not equally careful of your hands; they are getting all sunburnt.'

'Ah, indeed, yes—and my wrists. It is too stupid of me, especially when my arms are really the one good point about me,' self-pityingly assented Bonnibel, with a most naive expression.

Hector was much tickled by her simple air, although hardly believing in it. 'Let us see them,' he gaily exclaimed. 'How are we to take only your word for it? We must be judges.'

Forthwith Bonnibel, as innocently as could be, pulled up her sleeves and exposed two milk-white arms. They were very pretty, it was true; large, but well-moulded; soft as an infant's, and with dimples at the elbow that little loves might have played hide and seek in.

Even whilst quizzing Bonnibel on her own appreciation of her charms, and pretending to grant very deliberately that she was right, the young man, in truth, admired them so much that involuntarily he glanced at Nannie. But she, dear soul, was too proud to be jealous. One instant a fine satirical glance, questioning their hostess's good taste, crossed her expressive features; the next, it vanished, and only calm acknowledgment of what was in reality fair to see, remained. Was she a female Pharisee? was ever in her mind, that she should say of others' behaviour, I am better than thou! She had read, she even in her small experience knew, that other girls often stooped to petty warfare amongst each other, pretty deceits to please men; making the weakness of their sex their self-excuse. But she was too high-minded; and felt she could never respect herself were she to do likewise. Nature also had given her a keen sense of the ludicrous—tipped her tongue with satire. Still she strove not to judge, and though she must laugh at human follies, tried to do so softly in her heart, with all sympathy even for the snobbish as well as the merely foolish; and humour in her was never far apart from the pathetic.

What a contrast! thought Hector. On one side of the fence red-and-white rusticity, with fairest buxom charms. Beside him—could he rightly describe his gentle guiding-star, the woman he loved, and who influenced him beyond all others? Except this, that her every look bore out the elder poet's description of a perfect mistress, being:

> 'A little proud, but full of pity.'

While he hardly knew whether her features might be called fair by others, only that they were most fair to him, while those grey poet-eyes lit them with that upward large gaze and tenderly exquisite charm.

As he thus thought, Bonnibel was likewise busy drawing comparisons betwixt Luke, who was still toiling as if for dear livelihood in the melting sun, with his grave browned face, and long body so roughly jointed together—toiling in his shirt-sleeves; bent double, with a red handkerchief tied round his waist—and Hector de Burgo there, on the far side of the fence, the very pattern of a fresh and fine young British gentleman, as he smoked his cigar in idleness.

At that moment, a lad came up, panting, with a note for young De Burgo.

It was from his grandfather's Italian valet, saying that the old man was dangerously ill; and that having sent for the doctor and a clergyman, he wished to see his grandson also for the last time.

'Dying!—I believe it is all a hoax,' muttered Bonnibel; but no one heard or heeded her.

Away strode Hector, across the field homewards, in anxious haste, with a sudden utter change of feelings—with horror and pity in his open, impressionable heart.

And Nannie White too was under the sway of that awe and great sympathy which seizes most of us, when anyone of those we know has been called to come away from among the children of men, leave the green smiling earth, and go—in such a case as this, we dare not truly guess whither.

'She is so high-strung, or high-flown—which is the word?' thought Bonnibel in her heart.

All that summer's day, the inmates of the manse waited in vain for news from the great house up in the woods. Evening came; and still they knew nothing for certain. Night fell; and then, at last, Hector's slow step brushed the dew from the grass in the dim orchard, where Nannie rose up, almost ghostlike in the twilight, to meet him.

'He is better … he will live, they say,' said the young man in a suffocated voice; 'but—O Nan, I hardly know how to tell you all … and to look at you.'

'Does he want to part us? and you have consented?' she asked in an almost soundless voice.

'No—never! How could you think such a thing possible?' cried out the young man vehemently. 'But he … he wished us to know our own minds for certain, he said. … He made it a death-bed request, Nan, that we should not see each other, nor write, for—two years!'

'*Is that all?*' she answered, and a tone of even great joy, of intense relief, thrilled through her words.

'All! Ah, Nannie,' uttered Hector de Burgo, almost reproachfully, though lovingly, 'it seems nothing to you, because you are so good and patient, and like a saint—but so cold.'

CHAPTER 25

BY THE SUMMER SEA

The two girls from the manse were sitting among the rocks of the Black Abbey shore, by the summer sea.

It was late August; and to one of them, to Nannie White, the summer seemed dusty, sterile, and slow of dying. Every year before, she had loved each warm long-drawn day, spent up at her old home yonder—grieved that each was past at eve. But now, she wanted freshening autumn to come quickly and pass into cold winter; and then for the new year to begin, that it too might be sooner lived through.

The shore was utterly lonely; tempted by which consideration, both girls had taken off their shoes and stockings idly. Bonnibel was wading like a big child, perfectly amused with gathering shells, weeds, and suchlike glistening sea-stuff, which, when dry, would presently be flung away as ugly. There was no fear of the tide playing tricks, since there the beach sloped so gently—

> 'To the sea;
> The nymphs are hidden only to the knee,
> Where half a mile of rippling water is
> Between the waves that their white limbs do kiss
> And the last wave that washes shells ashore.'

Nannie preferred sitting on a rock overhanging the water, like a modern silver-footed Thetis, who had not altogether left her native element whilst sunning herself. She had slipped away, to be in comparative solitude a few moments, apart from Bonnibel's gay but ceaseless chatter—to look in silence at the illimitable blue of the sky mingling with the darker heaving blue of the sea, and listening hear:

> 'The first wave of the rising tide
> Rush onward with uninterrupted sweep;
> A voice out of the silence of the deep —'

It was cool and refreshing here. Accustomed to much silence, Nan now at times fairly longed for it, when yet feeling herself obliged by gratitude to answer the lightsome babbling of her friend.

Back waded Bonnibel, and began for the twentieth time to wonder what could have brought old Mr. de Burgo again to Black Abbey. He had arrived suddenly home the evening before, after a two months' absence in his yacht, which now lay in Redbay awaiting him.

'He has come back, as I told you, about the sale of a good deal of timber,' answered Nannie, rousing up not altogether gladly from her thoughts. 'Is not that reason enough?'

'You foolish dear! it must be more than that. He is after no good—*that* we may be sure of. Still I almost wish we could meet him, for one feels just buried in dulness, and a battle would be enlivening.'

'To tell the truth, I prefer keeping out of his path. The rapid way in which he recovered from his supposed death-sickness last June, and hobbled back to the cheerful haunts of men, was too instructive; although I hardly thought I needed any more such lessons. He is too clever for us, Bonnibel.'

'It was a shameful cheat; so why do you keep to that ridiculous bargain? Why don't you write a few little lines to poor Mr. Hector? *I* should, I know.' The pretty temptress gave a side-long roguish glance, trying her companion's firmness just for the fun of the thing.

'You would not, I am sure, Bonnibel. Why will you always make out the worst of yourself? Hector believes thoroughly in his grandfather's illness, and I respect the feeling in him. But even if he did not, we gave our word!'

'And so the wicked is to get all the good of his deceit, and virtue is *your* only reward,' uttered Miss Hawthorn, tragi-comically. 'You won't be able to keep to it'

But though disliking the discussion, Nannie quietly answered—though with the momentary look on her changeable, sensitively expressive face that sometimes made her gentlest words seem an irrevocable dictum to the other of lighter mind:

"'And because right is right, to do the right
Were wisdom, in the scorn of consequence.'"

Bonnibel was silent one moment, then, always ductile, warmly answered with quick conviction, 'Of course, dear, that is the right way of looking at it, isn't it? You are right; quite right. Honesty is the best policy.'

Nannie hid a smile at this supposed echo of her own thoughts.

Silence for a little while; then a change of ideas. Said the neater nymph, although the one of wandering fancies, to the prettier one, whose 'sweet neglect' of dress was often more than even would have pleased Ben Jonson, 'Your hair has all fallen down under your sun-bonnet Shall I twist it up for you?'

'Oh no, dear; don't take the trouble, dear. There's nobody here to see me, that's a blessing!'

'You only keep it tidy for your cousin Luke,' Nannie a little wickedly remarked.

Bonnibel laughed, but with a great, healthy blush; seeing which, the other good-naturedly went on:

'It is very becoming, certainly. You might sit for the picture of fair Chloë or Delia, only the shepherd swain is wanting—Listen!

What is that?'

For her delicate ear seemed to catch an approaching sound on the sands behind.

'Oh—nothing,' said her lazy fellow, yawning.

But Nannie, not convinced, slipped over the rocks to peer. Then she hastily uttered a warning whisper, 'Quick! quick! Fly! It is old Mr. de Burgo!' and herself vanished into a friendly cleft.

'Where? … which way?' uttered Bonnibel; and, apparently quite stupidly for her, made an attempt to rush one way, then turned back undecided. Next instant, Nannie peering back, caught a glimpse of the old man, riding slowly round the corner on ancient Snowball, that was now quiet as a doting snail, but still sure-footed enough to carry him. She saw Bonnibel stand—a blushing image of charming confusion—caught with her brown hair just falling on her shoulders, some wavy locks seeming gilded by the sun, and her pretty feet half peeping out from her down-dropped gown. Slowly raising her eyes the maiden softly murmured, 'Oh, Mr. de Burgo. I am just *buried in shame!*'

Then came a chuckle of vast enjoyment from the grey-beard; compliments suitable to his old-fashioned gallantry, and the occasion, no doubt; but Nannie, retiring into deeper shelter, heard no more.

A quarter of an hour afterwards, Nannie White, dressed and somewhat disgusted, sat alone by the sea—gravely gazing over the wide-curved sandy bay to where she could just see moving specks on its white-ribbed surface. These were old Mr. de Burgo on his pony, and Bonnibel herself going, with a step as free as Diana's, by his side. They passed out of sight.

Half an hour went by, during which Nan might have enjoyed her utter loneliness certainly, and the sea-view; but no longer did so, being puzzled and even perturbed. Then came a joyous cry from overhead; and down the rocks scrambled the strayed nymph, panting, and plumped down at her friend's side on the sand.

'Oh, dear! I'm quite exhausted!' she exclaimed, beginning to laugh violently. 'What an old wretch that is for paying compliments; but I could just turn him round my little finger.'

'Is that what induced you to take such a long walk with him?' asked Nannie, rather drily. 'I see you managed to get shod again, however.'

'Yes, I told him to go out of the way till I put on my shoes and stockings again,' answered Bonnibel, in unabashed good-humour with herself. 'He asked me particularly to come and show him the only place in the sandy bank along there, where he and his old pony could scramble up from the shore. He didn't know it, so I couldn't refuse; could I?'

'He knew it before you were born.'

'Well, then he must have forgotten it … It's very likely, as he's so old. I didn't think he was so very dangerous at all, dear; except the danger that he would topple off and break his neck when the pony climbed up with him. He was so shaky that I had to give him my arm to hold by, too; ha, ha!'

'And then you walked back with him along the high-road this far? … Did he never speak of me?' asked Nannie with a good deal of constraint; being far from humanly perfect, quick to feel hurt, and her friend's adventure almost seeming to her like a sudden desertion to the enemy; slightly disloyal in its ending, anyway.

'Oh, yes, dear, he did ask after you. I told him you were somewhere among the rocks; and he said he would not disturb you for worlds—that was all.'

Nannie's fine upper lip curled; she could imagine the ironical emphasis.

'And then,' eagerly recited the girl, so utterly taken up with what had happened to herself, she did not well perceive the change in her companion, 'he was so kind. He asked me why I never went to walk in his demesne, and begged me to go—'

'When?' with an alarmed air.

'Whenever I like,' with a triumphant nod.

'Bonnibel!—I advise you not to go till he has left'

'Oh, no, dear … er … of course not,' was the slower, indeed evasive, answer; the young manse mistress being, secretly, rather taken aback. What a blessing it was! she thought to herself (after a few moments of inward pause and reflection) that in her outburst of eager confidence she had just stopped short from telling what had passed at parting. For the old beau had looked down quite ridiculously into her bright eyes, suggesting in an insinuating tone, 'Then you might perhaps, sometimes, take a walk through the Chapel Wood.' And when she, laughing, rather vaguely assented, he had held her hand tenderly in his shaking grasp, murmuring, 'Then to-morrow—*at three!*'

Well! and where was the harm of going to the wood? Bonnibel asked of herself, with injured righteousness. Was it not just sacrificing an hour to that silly old squire, all for the sake of prudish Nan here, who did not know her own interests? For when old De Burgo had asked his pretty guide, with a searching look, what she thought of his grandson, had not Bonnibel, scenting war, at once unfurled her colours, and with amused relish for the fray, expressed herself in enthusiastic praise of Hector? Whereupon her hoary catechist, chuckling to himself, had patted her shoulder; observing flatteringly, that if his boy had any eyes in his head, he no doubt returned her admiration. Adding, 'You and I ought to talk over this business of his together quietly, Miss Cosby—Hawthorn, I beg pardon. By Jove, such a pretty name suits its owner.'

There! see what good she might do. Nevertheless, when Bella skilfully sought again to make her friend see that adventure with Mr. de Burgo in a better light, pluming herself on the wise strategy of opening peaceful negotiations with the foe, had not Nannie quite damped her enthusiasm by seeming to doubt her discretion although not her affection. Any momentary questioning of the latter had been easily caressed away from her guest's mind by Bonnibel, so soon as perceived. Her hurt warmth of feeling was shown in weeping kisses; her sympathy, was like the deep sea. And Nannie, if she had been easily ruffled on the surface, was in the depths below full of goodness, forgiveness, and especially justice; besides feeling true and warm gratitude towards her friends in the manse.

But still that night Bonnibel, when alone, gave way to some indignation against her friend; disliking, she declared to herself, what some people thought high-breeding, but which was to her mind stiffness. Was it to be thus kept in order, as it were, that she had given up to her guest, as the future Mrs. Hector de Burgo, her own larger room, with its feather-bed, and best glass, and hanging wardrobe? (though, truly, she still altogether monopolized these two latter luxuries, to the continual invasion of Nannie's privacy).

CHAPTER 26

'OH MISTRESS MINE, WHERE ARE YOU ROAMING?'

BUT next morning Miss Hawthorn arose, beaming upon everyone like a noonday sun. By-and-by, Nannie heard her carrying on a lively discussion, through two open doors, with old Mary. It was impossible to avoid overhearing most of Bonnibel's household secrets, since they were generally cheerfully shouted from a distance in her fresh young voice.

'Mary, have you any time to-day?'

'*Time!* I've har'ly time in *this* house even to say my prayers,' came in sourly-aggrieved answer. (Mary had never been in another situation.)

'Because,' in seductive tones, 'the little muslin curtains in Miss White's room want washing badly …' (very badly! movement of much joy on Nannie's part, who saw delightful visions of her chamber getting its much needed 'wipe-up') … 'and I've taken them off.'

'Is it *stripped* them off?' ejaculated the old woman in a towering rage. 'Then ye may just land them back again. Isn't it enough for a Christian woman to have to put clean clothes on all of your backs every week, without washing for dumb furniture. Not a hand's turn will I put to them.'

'But, what have you got to do?' demanded her young mistress, quitting the tones of blandishment, and preparing for a trial of her authority.

'I've got to baste the roast mate, and put buttons till the minister's shirt for Sabbath … and darn your stockings, which ye might very well do yourself,' etc, etc., came back in shrill, unshrinking truthfulness.

'Well, Mary, never mind those things; but you must wash the curtains.'

'I will *nawt!*'

Nannie fled, to avoid playing eavesdropping to an indignantly usual altercation between the young mistress accusing the old maid of insubordination, whilst the latter was defiantly secure in the knowledge that she was as indispensable to the minister and the manse as the meeting-house itself.

On this, Bonnibel disappeared; but, before the mid-day dinner, emerged triumphant from her room, which, the door being left open, seemed filled with an atmosphere of soap-suds.

'I've done them! I've beaten Mary. I washed the curtains in my bath!' she exclaimed triumphantly.

'No!' exclaimed the minister and Nannie, in an admiring chorus.

'Yes!' replied Bonnibel, sinking exhausted into her seat; 'but now I have such a headache! Poor grandpapa! I did want to walk with you this afternoon too; it is so lonely for you always going about visiting alone.'

'Don't mind me—don't mind me, my dear child,' said the good old man, much flattered by this rather unusual interest in his lonely parish work.

What could Nannie do, in gratitude, but offer herself as a substitute; although she happened that very day to have a more real headache than her friend? At other times she often gladly accompanied the simple, Christlike old man, who was blessed as he passed every threshold, and whose talk refreshed her by its genuine worth, although his accent was by no means irreproachable, and his black velvet waist-coat might bear the marks of yesterday's dinner-gravy. She herself knew, and few better, the wants of all the people round Black Abbey, far and wide. These, in their unenthusiastic way, had always shown they "liked well" Miss Nannie from the big house; but now grateful gladness at the prospect of having her always among them broke through even their self-restraint, and found hearty expression from these dour-seeming, decided natures—for the good news of her engagement to Hector had spread like wildfire. Bonnibel hardly ever went on parish walks, generally alleging her household duties, with a lazy laugh, in excuse. If Nannie did not thus go with him, she seldom saw the minister again till evening, when, overcome with fatigue, he generally snored in his arm-chair; and so, more was the pity! she had no other conversation the livelong day, but that of his grand-daughter, although that indeed was gaily incessant. Luke Cosby had been obliged to end his holiday at the manse, a few days after Nannie came there.

When they returned homeward that evening, Bonnibel met them at tea, brimming with smiles.

'What *do* you think has happened to me?' she cried. 'You must guess—guess both of you. No, I can't keep it in! Well, I met Mr. de Burgo by chance, and he was *ever* so kind! and has invited me to go with a party next week, for a trip in his yacht.'

Mr. Cosby stopped blowing his tea, and expended the remainder of his breath, dear old man! in a long-drawn sound, vaguely resembling the noise of an astonished porpoise. Nannie was simply thunderstruck; so wisely remained dumb. As soon as the old minister had partly recovered himself, he uttered a series of interrogatory ejaculations, such as '*The which?* … When? … What for, now?' while his grandchild, laughing with a disenburthened air, gave voluble but not very clear replies. She had happened to go out for a few minutes, wanting fresh air for her head; and so she had happened to meet Mr. de Burgo; and he had happened to talk of yachting, which, she had observed, must be delightful … and so he had kindly invited her … and so forth … and so forth. There was really nothing in it at all; now, was there? but it was so kind and delightful of him.

'But it was so strange you met him, since he almost never comes this way. Where was it you did meet him?' asked Nannie, breaking silence at last, and asking in good faith; but Bonnibel felt indignant, suspecting she was suspected.

'Where? Oh, just outside there,' she lightly answered, as if so eager about the gist of the matter that it was annoying to be questioned upon details. 'It is to be a trip to the south coast of England. He has asked Mrs. Heavyside to go with him; but of course she would like another lady to be on board. So, you see, it will be quite a kindness my going with them, and by *miles* too delightful for me!' ended Bonnibel, smiling triumphantly at the masterly stroke she had made in requesting her friends to take this last view of the subject.

'Mrs. Heavyside! But you surely are not going?' asked Nannie gravely, in a tone meant to convey (as it did) more to Bonnibel than to the minister. She could hardly believe, at first, that the girl seriously meant to go in any case; had quickly seen it was indeed so; and had just presence of mind enough to suppress any expression of opinion. But with such a companion it was truly worse and worse!

'But I surely am going—why not?' cried her young hostess loudly, like a vexed child; in one second all the sunshine being blotted out of her pretty face, that began to pout and redden. 'Oh, gran'pa, *say* I may—say I may. I told Mr. de Burgo that of course you would let me go.

You never would think of stopping me unless some one put you against it. … And of course you can't go, Miss Nannie; so why should you grudge it to poor me? And he said that unfortunately Miss Aileen couldn't go with him either just now.'

'Aileen! No, I should think she would not care to go now, if even she ever did go with him,' answered Nannie, with a slight quiver of her lip, and faint inflection of scorn in her tone, that told the other girl why—though the good minister heard the words said in blissful simplicity. Nannie was bitterly disappointed in her friend.

It must be explained that although Mrs. Heavyside's home was in a distant county, she was known to Black Abbey doubtfully, as one of old Mr. de Burgo's favourite lady-friends, who often made one of his party on short cruises, and had landed once or twice at Redbay and driven to see his home. To be intimate with him would have made an angel seem a questionable person in Black Abbey. Besides, she was fast, it was said; looked on coldly in society; was too wandering a star. And Bonnibel herself knew, or thought she knew, far more about her than Nannie; having, to the latter's astonishment, repeated but lately some rather scandalous gossip about this lady, whom she had never seen, which how she had picked up was a wonder. She, laughing very much, refused to explain, however—and Nannie had thought it best perhaps not to ask further.

Apparently Bonnibel quite understood, but would not take the hint; for she bitterly kept repeating, '*Why shouldn't I go?* … I don't suppose Mrs. Heavyside will poison me! … and when Mr. de Burgo did mean to be so kind, at last—like—like repenting and holding out the olive-leaf, it seems quite wicked, so it does, to go on suspecting him and holding back. It's not much amusement, either, going with one married lady and an old, old man; but it's very likely the only chance of any *I'll* ever get in my whole life. It's very different for you, who will be rich, and able to go about anywhere; but—but! Oh dear! I was just up to my eyes in happiness a minute ago, and now you've gone and spoilt it all.' And here Bonnibel burst out crying violently, without in the least trying to stop her grief. Nannie, against whom the last reproach had been bitterly hurled, was deeply annoyed; but strove to keep her own self-possession, and explain with reasonableness that she had not wished by any means to dictate.

'There now, Bonnibel; there now, my dearie! you hear what Miss Nannie says; you took her up quite wrong. … Drink some tea. Hush, now! hush! Well talk it all over quietly by-and-by,' interposed the poor minister, terribly distressed; and striving to console his spoilt grandchild by making soothing noises such as nurses use to babies, whilst he pulled out his own red cotton handkerchief to wipe her tears, and his round face looked as troubled as a moon's reflection in broken water. His peacemaking so far consoled the weeping mourner, that she consented by-and-by to swallow both her tears and her tea together, and deigned to accept Nannie's assurances of kindly feeling; but still the meal ended in constraint.

As soon as she could, Nannie slipped upstairs, to let her host and his granddaughter discuss the matter, freed from her presence; feeling sure that the instant she was gone Bonnibel would spring to her grandfather's side, and, lacing her arms round his neck, shower kisses on his bald crown, until she had coaxed him into perfect acquiescence to her wishes.

Once by herself, Nannie sat down at her open little casement in the darkening evening to think the matter out. After trying to look at it every way, she came to the conclusion that old Mr. de Burgo's strange invitation could have nothing to do with herself; it must have been given purely on account of Bonnibel's pretty face, and because no one else could easily be found to go so lightly with Mrs. Heavyside. The whole thing, therefore, now concerned Bonnibel alone; and Nannie, having an almost too great hatred of meddling, arising from, in this case, mistaken delicacy, said to herself sorrowfully that if the girl would go—why she would! She always was given, or managed to get, her own way, and could not bear being thwarted. The finer-minded woman was very greatly disappointed in her friend—but still was fond of her. Experience must teach Bonnibel, for all advice seemed to glance off the girl's gay mind. Indeed, what could Nannie herself allege against Mrs. Heavyside? Nothing but some stories which might be calumnies; and a vague doubt on the part of the world, it was said—and the world was often unkind. And lastly, with a rare sense of justice that made her always try to look at both sides of the question, and often made her seem lukewarm, Nannie told herself that the manse-life was indeed dull for a girl whose pleasures came almost altogether through her senses, and not from her intellect—a nature made to love society, idleness, colour, warmth, luxury, yet so greatly debarred from all such in her past and future life.

'Where—are—you?' was now mildly shouted through the dusk house; and after a few seconds Bonnibel's large, softly-rounded figure appeared in Nannie's doorway. 'What! all in the dark—all alone?' she uttered in so gentle a voice that it was plain her rage had quickly spent itself, 'Are you angry with me? Oh, I do hope you are not—I am so ashamed of myself.'

Who could indeed seem angry with such a big, bonny, soft-spoken maiden, whose look of repentance was accompanied with a deferential but warm caress; and whose one plain fault was only too great a love of pleasure?

'Angry! No,' said Nannie, cheerfully. 'Well, have you made up your mind that you really like going to see only miles of salt water for several days, and then the edges of the land?'

'You dear, funny creature! what a way to put it! Why yes … we, that is grandpapa thinks so, and —' answered Bonnibel, hesitating, her brown eyes beginning to shine again, however, and the fog to disperse from her face.

'Well, and what are you going to wear?'

'Oh, you darling! Yes, isn't that always the first question?' cried Bonnibel, now fairly delighted, and venturing to give Nan a hug. 'You are an angeL Yes, do let us talk about that.'

And thereupon, with one bound, she sprang into the middle of Nannie's bed, to the utter destruction of its subsequent smoothness, for Bonnibel was no light weight. Then she began reviewing in mind all her dresses, which were rather many and gaudy for a Presbyterian minister's daughter. 'What do you think I shall require most?' she asked, with an anxious air.

'Boots and gloves!' replied Nannie, with secretly severe truthfulness.

After a careful discussion of yachting apparel, Nannie quite regained her young hostess's warm goodwill; and the latter began to bethink herself, in turn, of pleasing the other. 'By the way, dear, there was something else I had to say—that you might not have liked me to say before grandpapa; it is that perhaps—mind it is not certain—but *perhaps* Mr. Hector might come on board for a day or so, as his regiment is at Brighton; and if so I will tell you everything, every single little thing I can about him. And he will be so glad to hear of you, won't he, if he does come?' In uttering this soft, flattering tale of hope, Bonnibel had to suppress some twinges of conscience, truly, since when she had asked that terrible old man whether his grandson was likely to come on board or no, he had pitilessly quizzed her, asking if his own company was not a sufficient attraction, and left her in doubt, not saying more than that his grandson might come or might not. Well, the chances were he might; so why should not Bonnibel give that innocent pleasure of anticipation to her poor friend? she asked herself Nannie felt only too well the subtle charm of this suggestion, and succumbed inwardly before it, her secret objections to Bonnibel's trip rapidly melting. She was indeed already craving for some news of Hector de Burgo; if only one word. It seemed so long since June, though it was not yet September. If two months seemed long, how dreary, how terrible, how unending would not two years be?

'And you can send him heaps of love-messages by me, you

know,' went on Bonnibel, coaxingly. 'Fancy me flying to meet him like one of those little Cupids on the valentines, with "Forget-me-not," or "Still fondly thine own," printed on a blue scarf! Ha! ha! ha!'

'Oh, thank you,' said poor Nannie, drawing back. 'But I think he would rather imagine my messages. *I* should in his place, I know.'

The very idea of sending her inmost, her sacred thoughts to Hector, by even the most intimate third person, would have made her shrink; but by such an outspoken, heedlessly merry messenger, however warm-hearted, it seemed verily desecration. And yet—if it could have been!

Well, it could not; so, with a silent sigh, Nannie turned the conversation to Mrs. Heavyside, trying to warn Bonnibel delicately of the carefulness she might have need of to avoid being lured into sharing her companion's possible follies; as some birds, once caught, will act as decoys to others, liking 'companions in their woe.'

But Nannie was so gently mild in trying to avoid lecturing, and so inexperienced herself, Bonnibel so engrossed with thinking of a new dress, that the advice (like most) might almost as well have been spoken up the chimney.

'Oh yes, dear—certainly, dear—I quite agree,' Bonnibel uttered warmly at due intervals, till suddenly remembering it was time to answer something more, she apologetically murmured, with soft pleading in her brown eyes, 'Of course, you are too particular to go with her; but remember how different your position will be, while I am only an insignificant little nobody, that nobody minds. Bless me, beggars can't be choosers! ... And for all the amusement I get in this little manse with grandpapa, one might as well be a frog built up in a wall I've heard of them living for years so. And afterwards it will only be another manse, with—with Luke, I suppose. But he is so headstrong and foolish with these new views of his, that he may never get "called" again! and then he'll be very poor, for writers never get much, do they? And it was *such* a large parish that he said his conscience made him resign in Edinburgh. … Bother his conscience!' (vehemently.)

'With Mr. Luke? Then I congratulate you with all my heart, no matter whether he has a ministry or not,' said Nannie, gravely.

Bonnibel had the grace to flush like a poppy, and plucking tufts off the Marseilles quilt, spread rumpled ruin around her. Then she laughed, recovered from her embarrassment, and, with the air of one who has an amusing confidence to make, volubly went on, 'Shall I tell you a secret? One evening I overheard grandpapa talking to Luke in the arbour, and he said how anxious he was to see us two married; and Luke said he had always looked forward to it, but didn't like to hurry me. And there was I behind the bushes, on my knees, giggling so much at their solemnity I nearly choked. Oh, often I have heard them talking there. … *Don't* look so shocked! It was only once or twice, really, and quite by accident' And she bounced up gaily, pretending she must hurry away; in reality afraid lest Nannie, whose gentlest judgment she stood in awe of, should reproach her for eavesdropping.

'Oh, Bonnibel!' the latter called after her, laughing reproachfully, knowing perfectly what she was about; adding, as a parting shot, 'And so you did not go to the woods today, as my future grandpapa asked you?'

'No—'

That little, horrible, slippery word, somehow, got out of Bonnibel's lips before she knew (so she declared to herself) what it was about. In mute anger she left the room, and going alone into her dim attic, softly stamped with rage. The good old minister had striven to rear her with a horror of telling lies, and she disliked doing so. Fibs she had often found excusable, but this was such a big one! So she went to bed rather miserable, after all, that night, bitterly blaming her guest in heart, who had given her no breathing-time to make an evasive reply—had positively forced her into false-hood. And then, worse and worse!—What if that silly old de Burgo should come to-morrow, to call on his 'Bright-eyes'—as he had gaily threatened to do—and let out anything about having 'happened' to meet her in the Chapel Wood. Bonnibel's head whirled round and round; she tossed sleeplessly, thinking how she could stop—how warn him; she was, you see, quite a foolish novice in intrigues, and inclined even to utter sorrowfully, in her repentance, during the small hours—

> 'Oh, what a tangled web we weave,
> When first we practise to deceive!'

But falling asleep towards morning, the pretty deceptress woke refreshed, and 'stronger-minded,' as she told herself. Mr. de Burgo was seen by her, and cleverly stopped, when driving out of his lodge towards Redbay. The old man laughed heartily at her warning—uttered in boarding-school French—and, playfully tapping her cheek, asked. Did she take him for a stupid school-boy?—bidding her make haste, and be ready to start in two days. Old Robert, who drove him, looked meanwhile piously in the other direction, with his mouth closed as tight as an oyster-shell. All was well: and Bonnibel hastened home, finding Nannie busy working for her with flying shining needle. Her guest sat up late to sew for her indeed, and rose at cockcrow those two days; and yet many a little detail Nannie supplied herself that was lacking in her friend's wardrobe, wishing to shield the heedless girl from Mrs. Heavyside's dainty ridicule. Bonnibel was in highest spirits.

'Blithe, blithe and merry was she;
Blithe was she but and ben.'

Mr. Cosby, too, poor old soul, had been sorely troubled in mind, even after he had granted his darling's wish; and several times, with an air of deepest humility, he anxiously said to Nannie, 'It seems a very strange thing—doesn't it, now?—that my little girl should be invited on such a trip, and by Mr. de Burgo, of all people. 'Deed, I would have hung back. Miss Nannie—I would so, I own—but Bonnibel had so many things to say in favour of it, that maybe she knows best—for the wisdom of that girl passes belief. And it might do her own health good, for she has had so many headaches lately, that I've been secretly uneasy. Hasn't she, now?'

As Bonnibel always adorned her little fits of ill-temper with the title of headache, this was the case; and Nannie sweetly seeming to agree with him on the beneficial effects of sea-air, the old man became gradually happy again.

And so, two days later, out of the troubled sea she had made their late life, rose Bonnibel, like a fresh, rustic Venus, smiling to the last, and mounted into the old, old gig, driven by the red-haired boy-of-all-work.

Nannie and old Mr. Cosby were left alone.

CHAPTER 27

PEGASUS IN HARNESS

Left alone with the old minister in the manse, it cannot be said that Nannie was lonely. On the contrary, in the change of feeling—the sudden calm and idleness after the busy toil she had had in preparing for Bonnibel's departure—she, leaning over the garden-gate watching the gig recede from sight, felt almost inclined to sing softly in her heart.

It may seem ungrateful of her—unkind. But, in truth, she was just the reverse of either; only she was a poet, and she felt free. She looked across at the Black Abbey high wall opposite, overhung with the trees that each seemed to her a friend; and then round at the pleasant, square manse, backed by its little outhouses; its whitewashed walls staring at the sunshine, and at its feet the little garden-plot, and by its side the orchard; and still rejoicing in all these common sights, she looked further to the sea, across the whitening harvest fields, and said aloud, 'Delightful stillness!' … She was used from childhood to being alone—alone for hours, either with nature in the woods or open country, or else communing with the minds of the great dead, in the dim, well-furnished library of Black Abbey. Here she had neither silent companionship; but instead, for the past many weeks and all day long, Bonnibel was always with her—always prattling, as merrily truly, but as ceaselessly and often as noisily, as a canary sings; till her more thinking companion grew unutterably wearied of companionship. Nevertheless, though the minister's granddaughter was not as refined as Nannie might have wished in a friend—not very intellectual—still the latter had had small choice of friends in her life, and believed it her actual duty to love those who were given her as neighbours in life So she loved the much lovable in this girl, overlooking her human imperfections; but would have liked a change. Once or twice the guest had tried to absent herself by a country walk, but saw that, not understanding the longing that was almost a necessity, her young hostess was secretly hurt; at other times, when the poet pleaded the wish to be alone to write Bonnibel had certainly withdrawn from the room on tiptoe, with too ostentatious yet real good wishes. But half an hour could never pass before—forgetting all but the wish to impart some amusing trait in old Mary's or the kitten's behaviour, or simply (most maddeningly interrupting of all!) to ask how her friend 'was getting on'—her bright face would be seen peeping round the comer of the door. So, writing occasional verses, but with difficulty and badly, her heart being often troubled and unhappy, her mind unused to working under such different circumstances, Nannie had resigned herself to weeding the garden and sewing on the minister's shirt buttons, both duties much neglected by Bonnibel.

But now, delightful stillness—freedom! And yet—foolish poet-heart, always oscillating between love of solitude and the human craving for the rest of the humanity—had she not, in the close-hedged calm of her former passionless life at Black Abbey, longed at times for world-noises, for voices to break the hush? What words can so well describe her feelings as Matthew Arnold's? finding an echo surely in many a sensitive high-strung mind, as well as in the poet-brain itself, which driven forth, as it were, into the desert by genius, that possessing spirit, at last cries out:

'I have been enough alone!'

But then must, half despairingly, add:

'Where shall thy votary fly, then? Back to men?
But they will gladly welcome him once more,
And help him to unbend his too tense thought,
And rid him of the presence of himself,
And keep their friendly chatter at his ear.
And haunt him, till the absence from himself,
That other torment, grow unbearable;
And he will fly to solitude again.'

Nannie had hoped by now to have been working hard, if living also more hardly, in London, with her mind-mother, worthy Fräulein Schmidt, who, however sapless as to human feelings, had most understanding sympathy for the needs of the intellect But the old governess's brother, the Sanskrit professor, had been delayed in coming to London; she herself had taken a compatriot's work in a school meanwhile for three months. Nannie could only try to bide patiently in the little haven that had received her, having succeeded in quieting the scruples her delicate mind would otherwise have had, by making such an agreement with the old minister as the grasping owner of beautiful Black Abbey had not scorned to accept. Only now, what was simply offered was gratefully received, as between two early Christians to whom community of goods made giving and taking easy. The reverend old Joseph Cosby did grieve, indeed, a little at first, that his poverty made this arrangement, if not a necessity, yet an undeniable assistance; but consoled himself with the thought that his dear young guest, who was a household saint to him, would in two years, with the blessing of Providence, be secure from all fear of want. He would have shared his last crust, or only cup of water, with the poor around him; the only luxuries he had, the only temptation he ever felt towards such, were for Bonnibel.

Rebecca, too, was no more a possible burden in the frugal household. She had been but ten days or so in the manse when she came to her former nursling, her brow weighty with resolve, and discreetly closing the door with especial care, announced that, having heard that the doctor's wife in Redbay wanted a nurse, she had applied for the situation. For a moment Nannie was too startled to speak. How could Rebecca have guessed that her young mistress had wept silently in the previous night; being full of trouble as to how, out of a very slender purse, it would be possible to extract enough means to requite the good minister at all adequately for the charge of them both.

'Oh, Rebecca, you must not!' she cried out. 'You are too old to go out into strange service. I have money enough—quite enough—to pay for us both; and what should I do without you?'

'Hush, darling; d'ye think I don't know as well as yourself how much your little bit of money is?' said the old woman with dignity. 'And so long as I have breath in my body, I'll try to work for my keep. You'll do without me well enough—no fears.'

In vain Nannie begged and expostulated; Rebecca was inflexible, knowing, poor old soul, she was right. She even kept up her proud air when old Mary tried to humiliate her former superior by telling her that, in the opinion of all the village, 'such service with a dispensary doctor's wife was a sore comedown for her that had been nurse with de Burgo's children, and housekeeper of Black Abbey.'

Rebecca swallowed big and bitter tears in silence, but only relieved herself by observing to her former nursling with self-restraint, 'That old Mary is a bitter pill; I wouldn't like to have to swallow her every day. Maybe, it's as well I'm going.'

And so go she did, one wet July morning, in the minister's gig, as a token of his esteem, her withered face smiling back on her foster-child till the crazy vehicle was far down the road; while she still kept waving her hand cheerfully, though her heart felt just bursting with the feeling of degradation and the breaking up of old habits; and to herself she was inwardly wailing,

'It will be the death of me! … Oh, my lamb, you don't know how hard it is! You will have your good times yet, thank God, but I'll hardly live through to see them.' Poor old woman! she was terribly near the truth. She made the noblest struggle of her life that cold summer's morning, and no one knew it was a heroine that left them; even Nannie but dimly guessed the effort and pain: so unseen are our souls by even our dearest.

And now, Bonnibel gone and herself left alone in the little manse all day, Nannie White set to work with cheerful yet almost feverish earnestness to put Pegasus in harness. She had never written any but short poems before—little bursts of song that had been awakened by some simple happiness in her former lonely life among the Black Abbey trees; maybe to have heard the cuckoo's cry in blooming June; or maybe, since she was young and strong, to have rejoiced in winter-time to see the whole land white with snow, while the frost-birds flew in great flocks overhead. These she had sent diffidently to magazines, at good Luke Cosby's suggestion and with his help, telling herself humbly that she expected them to be refused; and lo! they had been accepted, even praised. But now she was sitting down to her first real work—with what care! with what pains! with what anxiety, yet fond pride! This was the book that should win her a name and place among poets, the young girl-poet secretly hoped. Why not? Her maiden effort, yet it might be her best; and like most maiden efforts, it was ambitious and somewhat long. How she saw it bud and grow to full being, in anticipation! The chosen kernel of it was a classic myth that had fascinated her mind long ago, being a grand, eternal truth hidden in Greek allegory. It should be sung by her now in modern, melodious verse, clothed with many thoughts that had lain long silent in her hot heart, and which, heedless of after-poems, she only thought of lavishing like a spendthrift, outpouring her all. How eagerly she dashed off the first lines—how she sat and worked at it, long and late, those first days, till by-and-by her tired brain refused to give shape to the misty images that over-crowded it, and writing began to mean only disgusted blotting out—a Penelope's brain-web, woven and unwoven! Then after a week, she re-read it all. It was when tired, at the end of a day's toil; and laying down her head, she could have cried; nay, did so a few moments, with that 'noble discontent,' as Charles Kingsley calls it, which those with high aims, and ever higher-raised standard, must feel to their lives' end. Alas! she felt it was not given to her to feel filled with that divine inspiration which glorifies even feebler human vessels than herself. She knew what poetry should be: what was this poor stuff? But she!—she could not write better. Hers was only one poor little talent, and she longed for five!

Next morning, refreshed, she skimmed again over the pages as with new eyes; they seemed, to her surprise, well written, deep-flowing in thought yet with surface sparkle; and a thrill of warm pleasure passed through her, at the thought that one day Hector de Burgo need not be ashamed that men spoke of his poet-wife. And more—she felt with humility and with thankfulness that—as sings a living poet truly and tunefully—

> 'Not only those
> Who hold clear echoes of the voice divine
> Are honourable— …
> … but those who hear
> Some fair faint echoes, though the crowd be deaf,
> And see the white god's garments on the hills,
> Which the crowd sees not; …
> … they are blest,
> Not pitiable.'

And so gladdened in mind, she set to her work again; weighing each line slowly, and ever more carefully polishing all to the minutest word, that, if severe, her poem might be faultless. It was for Hector's sake that, half unconsciously, she thus wrote and re-wrote with over-anxiety of refinement; since the thought worked ever also in her brain that, if her poem were criticized severely and cavilled at, she was lowly-minded enough to take it meekly, but how vexed Hector would be! For there was one small sore spot in her heart—human happiness being imperfect—that Hector's mind not having much liking for poetry, he would hardly under-stand hers, with the appreciation, that is, of kindred minds—would be inclined to judge it secretly by the popular verdict—be touchy, perhaps doubtful on the subject, in his jealous love.

So, her enthusiasm being thus schooled and hampered by anxiety and affection, while she strove not to make art thereby suffer, the work grew but slowly—in spite of that joyous beginning.

Meanwhile, Nannie did not neglect the good old minister. She gave him even more often her company in his walks, since his round face looked as depressed now as if his grand-daughter had been his constant companion. She attended to his comfort reverently and lovingly, in a hundred little ways, so that the manse parlour was soon a changed room in its sweetness and tidiness. She even—O, what Bonnibel never suffered—gave him a gracious permission, when he hesitatingly asked leave once, to cool his tea in his saucer. Every night, afterwards, this relapsed old offender against polite manners drank it thus, always with vast enjoyment; making a great noise, like the engulfing of a sea, and then biting broadly into his buttered toast, in a manner which ever since his granddaughter had returned from her boarding-school it had been her daily effort to correct. He should have been happier, indeed, being thus more cared for than under his grandchild's home-sway; but—unsatisfied human nature—he would confidentially observe to his guest that, like himself, she must be missing his dear girl continually; there was a something wanting in the house; and he trotted morning and evening to the village post-office himself, with an anxious, expectant air, and returned disappointed, long before it was possible to get a letter from Bonnibel. However, in due time a letter came, having been posted at the first English seaport they had touched at; and although it was but a mere scrap, ruefully telling she had been very seasick, but hoping, in a laughing tone, that the future would make amends, Mr. Cosby was perfectly satisfied. He strutted about as if no one else had ever got a letter before; and called on every one to admire the thoughtfulness of his child in not losing the first opportunity of writing home. The next letter, a few days later, was dated from Plymouth, and though hardly longer than the first, was in a scrawl so big and black with evident satisfaction, that the good old minister fairly feasted his eyes on it; and, chuckling, read it again; and, holding it further off, yet again. They had landed on the very first afternoon, and had listened to the band of the marines playing on the Hoe. Mrs Heavyside had met there several officers whom she knew—both naval and military—and had introduced them to Bonnibel. 'It was too heavenly!!' ended the letter, in a gush of delight that made one suspect she had quite given up her traditional belief in the whiteness of angels' attire, and would hardly consider them properly dressed unless they wore red coats or blue jackets. In a postscript was added: 'Old Mr. de Burgo rather bothered me, by keeping always glued at my side: one can't have perfect bliss!'

Nannie faintly bent her brows, as if the note, especially the addition, was not quite to her liking, but reminded herself soon that you must like your friends with their faults; ay, and perhaps ought to take them wherever you can find them. But old Mr. Cosby broadly wrinkled his, and with much sympathy for his spoiled darling, said, 'Tut! tut! Now that is very thoughtless of Mr. de Burgo. At his age he should remember that young people are young people, and like to talk together, naturally.

He is an older man than I am, and I'm sure *I* always try to put myself out of the way.'

It was most amusing to listen to simplicity thus taking ancient worldliness mentally to task; something like one of the Cheeryble brothers passing judgment on the Marquis of Steyne for a want of *savoir faire*. And then for a week—ten days—almost a fortnight, came no other letters from Bonnibel. Her grandfather began to hang his head, and was quite depressed in secret, as Nannie could see, although he bravely tried to hide the fact from his guest by hourly apologies for the delinquent. 'She began in too great eagerness at first, and wrote herself out. That's so like my deary!' And again, 'She is the life and soul of the party, no doubt, and they don't spare her a moment' How tenderly, how unutterably the old man loved his child! It made Nannie almost envious at moments, that she herself had never known similar affection. He was so fearful now that even she, although no stranger, should guess that he pined because his darling was happy away from him, that he affected a quite unusual gaiety at moments. At last his affection was rewarded There came another letter, addressed to 'The Rev. Joseph Cosby,'—so much fatter than its predecessors that its owner quite chuckled with glee, trying to prophecy its contents as he fingered it over and over, dallying with his enjoyment. Alas! there was but one poor morsel of paper for himself; the rest was marked 'Private,' and for Nannie. The minister's contained curt but loving excuses to Bonnibel's dearest old granddad. She had really been enjoying herself too much to write, so felt sure of his forgiveness. They had sailed from Plymouth, to her sorrow; but for consolation they were accompanied to Cowes by two other yachts, belonging to two 'very nice young men,' friends of Mr. de Burgo's—the latter seemed in favour again. Once at Cowes, they might go further; she did not know; was only sure those at home were not to expect her back to stupid old Black Abbey nearly as soon as had been thought when she went away. And so, with more loving assurances of writing volumes 'next time,' it ended.

In Nannie's letter—as to the contents of which the old man, out of delicacy, would not so much as even hint an inquiry—there was a fuller display of Bonnibel's real feelings, 'Oh, my *dear*—' it bluntly began, 'I do so want to be able to tell you everything, and to talk with you over all we have done since! You are always so good and sweet in listening, and advising me; it does seem such a shame to be staying away so long, for you must miss me terribly.' At both these latter remarks, written plainly out of the fulness of Bonnibel's heart, Nannie somewhat humourously smiled. 'Between ourselves, Mrs. Heavyside was not at all kind when I was sea-sick. She didn't want me to come on deck, I think; but when I did get well, as soon as she saw I had no wish to interfere between herself and old Mr. B— she was as sweet as sugar. Yesterday she gave me a new bonnet that she had only worn a few times, and that didn't become her. Poor thing! I am sure she has been very much maligned. Of course I have had cards to play, as the young men on these two yachts are quite DEVOTED to me, and the old gentleman doesn't always like that, or having so much of his dear Mrs. H—. I could die of laughing, sometimes.

'By the way, Mrs. Heavyside says the dress you made me is the only one that really fits, and that the others have all a market-town air. Only it is so plain, that I am not quite sure if one ought to believe her. Anyway, I have unpicked the tartan trimming off my green one.' And so forth, and so forth, upon her wardrobe to the end.

Two evenings later, as Nannie and the old minister sat at tea, and the parlour-window was open, a grimy hand appeared through the latter, holding another letter; while what the country-folk called a *drim-and-dru* voice* was heard to whine, 'Tay

* drim-and-dru = a droning, whinging lament

and shugger! Shugger and tay! Och, ye are my darlin'-dearies, both!'

'It's Darlin'-dearie himself,' said Mr. Cosby, rising with alacrity, knowing the beggarman was often trusted with any letter that the village postmistress, after spelling out the postmarks and asking the advice of a jury of gossips, believed would be welcomed at its destination if it arrived there without waiting 'to be called for;' whilst the carrier was generally rewarded with a sup of tea and a bite of oat-cake. But then the good minister's face slightly fell, whilst he murmured, 'It's only from Luke.' Only from Luke! Could devotion to his grandchild farther go? since only three weeks ago a letter from Luke, his 'boy,' would have been reckoned as the greatest of epistolary pleasures by old Joseph Cosby. Any way, two letters for himself in one week was quite an event, and heavy on the Black Abbey post-office. And now Nannie came forward with a large bowl full of tea, which she placed on the sill; while the minister, before he thought of touching his letter, began buttering hunches* of bread for the poor hungry creature at the window, whose eyes greedily followed him. But big and buttery though the slices were, the daft body pointed lovingly with one finger to Nannie, and between his bites frequently murmured, 'Ah! thon's the lassie for me. She's the lad to gimme shugger; aye, when she was a bit of a toddlin' wee thing. She *is* my darlin'-dearie!'

While Nannie smiled, wondering at the length of time that her childish adventure in the wood had remained in the grateful remembrance of this poor idiot, the gentle pastor beside her was trying, with as coaxing a tone as its nurse would use to a cosset-lamb, to entice this wandering sheep of his fold to meeting next Sabbath. No harsh shepherd was he. His rubicund face, at such moments actually glowed with intense care and

* hunch = a hunk or thick slice

fervent love for the souls given into his keeping; while to some reverent and imaginative eyes, like those of Nannie White, his bald head even seemed to shine as is prophesied shall those 'who turn many to righteousness, as the stars for ever and ever.'

As Darlin'-dearie, his mouth full, and considering the chances of being rewarded with a fresh 'whack'* of bread, was understood to murmur favouringly that 'he might maybe go *that* far,' the minister continued, 'And I was cut to the heart, Darlin'-dearie—now I really was! to hear that you gave some bad language to some men in the village here yesterday.'

The culprit shuffled, looked this way and that, and at last burst out half-crying, 'Then, why do they be always *gladiathering*† after me? (Where on earth had he picked up that word? wondered Nannie, quaint as were many of the local expressions.)

'Are you not afraid that God will punish you for cursing and swearing? went on Mr. Cosby impulsively, with grief, feeling it needful to appeal thus to the instinct of fear, since he had often before spoken of God's love, yet sometimes doubted whether he had ever pierced through the clouded wits that obscured this poor human soul.

'Na,' replied the beggarman, recovering a little, and putting his head consideringly on one side, 'Na. For I mean no harrm, *He* knows … so no harrm, I'm certain sure, will be put down to me.'

It suddenly struck both listeners that what some of the country people frequently averred was true, namely, that Darlin'-dearie, though half-witted certainly, yet simulated sometimes greater foolishness than was natural to him, with a dull, frightened idea that he would be 'let off more easy.'

---

* whack = large quantity

† gladiathering = attacking in unwarranted persecution (as a gladiator might a Christian)

The good minister eagerly bent forward to seize the first, maybe the last, such chance he might ever have, of making sure that the great truths of which he had often before spoken to this poor creature were understood. With one hand upraised, while Nannie listened with bated breath, and the half-idiot's wandering gaze even remained fixed, he spoke with hushed voice, like an old apostle, of eternity, of God's goodness; then tenderly reminded Darlin'-dearie of his sins (for the latter, though so gentle in deeds that he would not hurt a fly, was too often in a state of maudlin intoxication, and if unkindly tormented took revenge in very bad language while seeking flight). 'Are you not afraid of God, when you think of that?' went on Mr. Cosby, with a world of love in his face and voice, which he was now preparing the way to show. 'Do you feel ready to die—to stand up before *Him* and give an account of all you have done?'

The daft beggarman softly drew a long breath, raising his head. 'Aye,' said he, to their astonishment, '*like a lad!*'—Then he shambled hurriedly away, before the old minister, taken aback, had recovered; and they heard his plaintive sing-song borne on the evening breeze to them from far and farther down the road. 'A great faith—a great faith,' soliloquised the old preacher, gently shaking his head from side to side, and gazing in the direction he had taken.

Then after remaining a good while sunk in meditation, he roused himself, and said more briskly, 'Come now, Miss Nannie. Let us see what Luke says.'

But what Luke said, though it brightened the old man's face a moment, only brought, the next, a shadow of depression heavier than any Bonnibel's absence had yet caused. For Luke wrote he was going to America on his lecturing tour very soon, and was coming to pay them a farewell visit in a few days; adding emphatically the hope that Bonnibel would be back by then from her yachting trip, of which he had but just heard (and that, it seemed, with small pleasure).

CHAPTER 28

'WHY DID SHE LOVE HIM?'

In another few days it was autumn at the manse. Autumn could be seen outside, in the Black Abbey trees overhanging the roadside wall that were turning rust-red and yellow in patches, prophetic that all the leaves would soon alike pass away in sad dying glory; hollyhocks stood up stiff in the garden-plot, red-admiral butterflies hovered, blackberries ripened in hedgerows, dew and countless spiders' webs glistened thick in the grass in the cool mornings; thin grey mists rose up from the land in late evenings.

'Why, what good fairy has been at work here?' said Luke Cosby, with a delighted air, looking all round the old parlour. He had arrived on foot a few minutes ago, carrying a rather heavy black bag in his hand like a feather-weight; having in his liking for freedom in his actions, and with a touch of eccentricity, kept those at the manse unacquainted with the precise time of his arrival. After dashing off to cleanse himself from the dust of the journey, before tea, he had quickly returned, seeming to bring an atmosphere like an invigorating moorland breeze into the calm windless existence of the others. His face had plainly been well dipped in cold water as a refreshment, and his hair soundly brushed back, without any regard to the fact that his head already began to show bare through it at the top like a high mountain-peak. 'Ah! I see. It is the artist's touch that one perceives in the house,' Luke went on with a cheery laugh. 'Miss Nannie, I congratulate you. What the change is I cannot tell, but it makes itself felt. I love to see a room like this; but Bonnibel knows nothing of the art, and I can never explain to her what is wanting.'

'But then she is so busy—with other things,' quickly returned Nannie, seeing a hurt look come across the poor old grandfather's face.

Fond as he was of Nannie, he could never take it lightly that his darling should be thought surpassed; while Luke, like any brother, would criticise Bonnibel's shortcomings to all the world. There was no change after all in the brown-papered, low-ceilinged little parlour itself, with its dingy horsehair furniture and worn carpet. But there were flowers in it, now; a few sketches; a spirit of order and daintiness held sway; and the sweet evening air was invited to come in. Under Bonnibel's rule, her darning basket gaping wide, and muddy boots half-thrust under the sofa in merry haste were its most striking adornments; the steaming incense from each meal mingled with the lingering fragrance of its predecessors.

How eagerly Luke talked at tea. The home-loving nature of the man was shown in the keen interest he took in all the news of Black Abbey, where the happiest hours of his youth, he always said, had been spent; and in his hardly less ardour in describing all his own late life and plans for his long future tour in America, certain of sympathy in this one little spot of earth at least, were all the rest of mankind estranged from him. He seemed very cheerful in spite of Bonniber's absence; though the old minister confided to Nannie in the gloaming, when Luke had gone outside to smoke his favourite clay pipe, that 'his boy was terribly vexed that she had been allowed to go with Mr. de Burgo.' 'He told me so when we were alone a minute together,' said the old man. 'Dear, dear! it's hard to know sometimes what is best; and she was so set upon it.' And then, his heart being softened by Luke's coming, and the still hour, and the tea and buttered toast lately indulged in, Mr. Cosby let out all the thoughts and hopes of his innocent old heart, that the two he best loved should become man and wife—smiling all over and growing so rubicund with pleasure at Nannie's friendly sympathy, that his face loomed like a red moon through the dusk as he whispered, cautiously bending forward with a hand placed on each knee, 'He has always looked forward to it since a boy, when I told him, if I were called away from earth, I looked to him to take care of our little lass. It kept him from foolish will-o'-the-wisp attachments that hurt so many youths. Yes, my boy was blessed! He knew his treasure was safe here, and his mind has been free to work with all its might during all these best years of his first manhood, just when too many others are trammelled and heavy-laden with heart-troubles. Oh, I know well, to become at all nearly a perfect man he must have them yet, and work his best in spite of them; but he has had a good start in life, I am humbly thankful to say.'

Nannie, who knew how greatly Luke had taken to heart the troubles of his late ministry, wondered that the old grandfather should think that as nothing. Plainly, the blessedness of having Bonnibel for a wife outweighed with him all else. She could well believe that Luke, besides the great unworldly devotion of his life to his work, had, as yet, been troubled by no other passion that could interfere with his home affections, except the love of study—of classics, science, and literature—the different mistresses of his somewhat versatile mind.

'And Bonnibel herself … you are sure she will be perfectly happy and satisfied to marry him?' Nannie at last asked.

'She is—between ourselves, of course—even more devoted to Luke, I think, than he is to her—if that could be!' smiled the old man. Then, with his handkerchief over his face, he fell asleep by-and-by, as a gentle snoring announced.

When Luke soon afterwards came in, he found Nannie sitting quietly, thus companionless, in the dusk, waiting old Mary's pleasure to bring the lamp, that she might read or sew, not liking to slip out, being sure in the garden-plot to stumble on Luke, who might not wish for her company. She looked forlorn! But, sitting down, he began so earnestly, and with such cheerful understanding sympathy, to inquire about her new, her great work, that soon Nannie found herself not only shyly sketching its outlines, but, by-and-by, when the lamp was brought, giving the manuscripts into his hands, and submitting with gladness to that most trying ordeal, the examination of one's unfinished labour. To no other person she knew could she thus have borne to show it, except perhaps—even this being doubtful—to Aileen. It was her secret, her very own, as yet: what other brain could, like hers, see in vision the growth of this germ of thought into the perfect book? whose judgment else, among the few she knew, could she trust as better than her own? Not Hector's, alas! … and no, not Bonnibel's. But Luke *understood* the matter; he was besides that neutral being, a perfect friend. He was not disturbed, like Hector, by anxious jealousy or distrust of the poet's powers; nor by envy like possibly some others. He had read Nannie White's first poems, and, remembering them, sat down to scan these. Those had breathed a deep love of nature; of summer fields and summer skies, in which larks sang invisibly, each like a small living epitome of music gladdening the mid-air; of deep seas, sunset storms; of winter's restful sleep and sober hues again, little less than of nature's softer hours. But this was different.

He sat silent so long that Nannie, timidly hazarding a remark, said with discouragement, 'There is very little to judge by yet; I write so slowly.'

'I do not wonder at it,' said Luke, kindly, now at last raising his earnest gaze from the leaves he held. 'What does surprise me is the classic theme, the changed style—scholar-like, self-restrained. Before, you sang because you felt. Here the thoughts of most of your young life as yet the reading I might almost say of years—for this philosophy is drawn from many deep, pure wells, one can see—are distilled, and their essence given to the world in melodious, stately, but almost severe verse. … This might be a pure calm hymn to wisdom herself! … You have written it for the thinking few, but—' And here Luke, stopping short, abruptly began rubbing the thinning hair on his forehead with his old, troubled gesture, and a hesitating smile.

'But,' went on Nannie, 'you think it will not be rewarded by the coin of the million?'

'Perhaps, after all, that is not now a pressing consideration. And of one thing you may rest assured—Mr. Hector will not be annoyed by any cavilling of the critics at this,' answered Luke, implying assent to her question; adding the last with a little meaning smile that brought a faint red flush to Nannie's cheek, for he had gone to the core of the matter. 'I almost wish—as regards your present necessities for the next two years—that you could take to fiction or light magazine articles. Pegasus is a more amenable literary hack when in that harness.'

'Only I cannot. Great poets have been also great novelists; but I have only my one, poor little gift,' said Nannie sadly.

She would have been glad enough indeed if her work had lain in the fatter, easier, low plains of prose; but she felt instead the command was given her to climb, like others, in loneliness, the difficult heights of poetry. 'And now, tell me more of what you think, without hesitation. You know I am always glad to feel pruned.'

'One only prunes generous trees, that will strive to put forth all the more fruit for it,' smiled Luke.

And then he did indeed point out all the defects he could see, and bid her remember Milton's golden rule, that poetry should be 'simple, sensuous, passionate.' He hinted, too, so far as he dared, that while truly she had written well of the threefold love that burns in all heroic souls—the love of God, of country, of family—yet that the whole poem was, however correct, cold—'cold and chaste as Diana's kiss.'

That night, as Luke, when all the rest were gone to bed, smoked his last pipe in the kitchen that Mary always left swept up and bright for the 'young minister,' he thoughtfully shook his head: 'She is attempting what is beyond her strength. The lark wants to mount like the eagle, but it must drop tired into its grassy nest soon. One cannot interfere, however. Perhaps it is best to try to the utmost, however one may fall short.' For Luke was one of those who knew, although our living poet had not yet written these words—

> 'How far high failure overleaps the bound
> Of low successes.'

'And without knowing it, she is trammelling herself with love-fetters. Those little earlier poems had each a spark of the divine fire in them; but in this fuel and labour may smother the flame,' he went on, his thoughts turning upon Hector. He thought of the latter as he would be in future, an honest-hearted country gentleman , turning gladly to home life—most likely, according to his simple nature, disliking that his wife should be spoken of in public, though even in terms of highest praise; and she, a sensitive poet-soul, trying to please and obey the beloved idol made of coarser clay than her own porcelain material; blinding her eyes with love to his inferiority; her mind, conscious of its gift, struggling to obey the divine mandate to use its talent; two duties clashing—heart and brain tearing her asunder. It is easy enough perhaps to be a writer, thought the man who wrote himself; but it is difficult to be a poet.

'How will it end? and why did she love him?' Luke finally asked himself. Then, after a little musing, he smiled, knocked the ashes of his pipe into the red embers of the fire, and remembering he had used Byron's query, took his answer too—

'Curious fool! be still;
Is human love the growth of human will?'

'Maybe, there is some great law of compensation, still dim to us, that accounts for all such apparent mis-matches. Maybe, some such trial is necessary to perfect the noblest natures—maybe' ... the pipe having been soothing, and the warmth of the kitchen-fire pleasant, since it was late, a sleepy satisfaction began to steal all through Luke's gaunt, recumbent figure; and further distinct thought became difficult.

But upstairs, how differently Nannie was thinking of Hector de Burgo, as she sat by her bedside, with lightly clasped hands and down-cast eyes, lost in reverie. To herself she seemed but a poor, pale creature, with only one gift—one of the 'irritable race,' best fitted for study. And she blessed Hector, as ever, in her heart fervently, that he had cared to link his strong, easily-contented nature, made for stout action, with her troubled, ever-aspiring soul; that he had brought all the love, and light, and gladness that rejoiced her now into the previously grey, still utterly monotonous calm of her existence.

And then slipping downwards softly on her knees, she prayed for him as the August harvest moon rose slowly over the trees opposite her window, flooding them with silver light; as again she would pray for him when the red sun's rim should rise out of the sea next morning. It was all she could do, but the best she could do, to pray thus night and morning for the man she loved, till she saw his face again.

CHAPTER 29

THE ONLY VISITOR

'I PITY you, poor Miss Nannie, to -day,' said Luke Cosby, with a cheering laugh. It was ten days later, just before the afternoon dinner-hour. The parlour table was laid, and these two were waiting for Mr. Cosby to come home with a guest and neighbouring minister, Mr. McCoy; whom Nannie especially disliked. He was the only visitor that had come to the secluded little manse since Nannie had taken refuge there, three months ago. 'My cousin Bonnibel laughs at him under his very nose (it is really a shame of her!), but he never sees it, and laughs too, and praises her liveliness,' went on Luke. 'But you are so delicate-minded, you will be profoundly, miserably polite!'

'He is perhaps worthy, but certainly disagreeable,' said Nannie, always roused to a pleasant sense of fellow-feeling in Luke's friendly company. 'But I, at least, suffer in cool disgust, while you are inwardly a raging volcano.'

'Verily! he is my arch-enemy,' groaned poor Luke, looking round the parlour as if it would be his horsehair-and-mahogany furnished torture-chamber for the next two hours. 'He is always hoping to prove me unorthodox from some careless word I may let slip, and watches my lips like a terrier at a rat-hole. But I will disappoint him. … I will put a watch upon the door of my mouth to-day. It would grieve poor Uncle Joe too much to have some of my opinions declared sins to him; although he is placidly aware that they are different from his own in some matters not necessary to salvation.'

Their talk abruptly ended as the visitor, who was short and full-paunched, made his entrance with the sort of triumphal air often assumed by persons of his proportions. Soon the dinner began. Mr. McCoy, it is but truth to say, resembled a pig a good deal in his outline of head, expression of gaze, and manner of supping his mutton broth. His hands and nails, too, were dirty. What a contrast with Mr. Cosby, whose waistcoat might be stained indeed, like the pinafore of a careless child, but whose rosy, old, cherubic face beaming above it was a title-page of assurance that he might be untidy, but was never otherwise than clean. As to Luke, one almost liked to see the rather awkward way in which his clothes (scrupulously good, save when he went a-fishing) hung on his angular shoulders. He gave one the impression of having always just emerged from a bracing plunge in cold water, and then of having finished his dressing in a strong breeze. While losing whatever outward graces of youth he ever possessed, ugly Luke only showed the more a thorough gentleman to the heart and mind's core of him.

The meal had just begun when a surprised outcry was heard from the kitchen that was only divided from the parlour by a passage, and where old Mary generally reigned in severe solitude. Then followed confused laughter, hushed voices. When the old woman, carrying a dish, entered to the surprised company in the parlour, they saw besides that the big-frilled cap she wore tied under her chin was slightly awry, while her face wore a rare smile, like a touch of spring in a wintry landscape.

'What was that noise, Mary?' asked her old master. The old servant feigned not to hear. He repeated the question.

'It was—nawthing.' And therewith the speaker's smile vanished, and she apparently went after it, hastily quitting the room.

'If it were not outrageously impossible, I should believe Old Mary had got a follower,' laughed Luke aside to Nannie.

'May I give you a liver-wing?' asked Mr. Cosby now, generously, of his new guest, preparing to dissect the second chicken, and having already given the tit-bits of the first to Miss White. The guest seemed coy about answering; his eye twinkled, and an unsatisfied smile played over his thick lips. 'Where would you like it cut? What do you like best?' pressed his host, inviting him to point out his wishes. *'I'd like it cut here!'* and thrusting his own knife and fork into the fowl, Mr. McCoy conveyed it wholesale, its sauce dripping upon the table-cloth, to his own plate, with a loud roar of mirth at the exquisite humour of the joke. Then he added, leering round at the rest for applause, 'He asked me what I'd have; and I think—he! he! he!—that *all's best.*'

Poor Uncle Joe's discomfiture, as he gazed at the mutilated remains now alone left to appease his own appetite for roast chicken, touched the other two almost to tears. But, rallying from his disappointment like a good Christian, the old minister presently eked out his scanty share with some slices of cold boiled beef.

Next Old Mary's rice pudding was expected—the pudding, she boasted, that she had daily made for her master for forty years (never failing to please him). Everyone else owned indeed that no rice puddings were ever so deliciously burst and blended with milk; but these persons would sometimes have liked a change; even at the risk of future puddings being spoilt through want of daily practice. The pudding duly came, but, to the amazement of the manse inmates, it was accompanied by—an omelet! an excellent, savoury, smoking-hot omelet! such as had never been seen to come from Old Mary's kitchen before, during all her reign.

Mr. Cosby exclaimed in utter surprise, 'Why, Mary, did you make this?'

No answer except a reproving clearing of the throat.

Luke, urged by curiosity, broke in at that, 'Mary—who made this?'

There was no entire evasion possible of the young master's

question. Still, averting expressionless features, and with a vinegar voice, Old Mary only replied, 'It was—a young woman.'

Nannie fancied she heard a stifled, fine laugh in the passage, the door being half-open; but Mary's expression seemed that of one resolutely blind, dumb, and deaf to everything save her old routine of duties.

'She has a niece who sometimes visits her, whom I call Young Mary. She must have made the omelet,' confidentially exclaimed Old Mary's master when she had left, with much enjoyment of the dainty.

This was agreed upon, and universal praise given to the niece's accomplishments.

Mr. McCoy, smacking his lips, made what he was pleased to believe a joke about Old Mary and the old minister, and that Young Mary would suit the young minister.

Now Nannie had a sensitive abhorrance of vulgarity; but of all vulgar men, she thought a jocose one was worst. The humour of this joke was never perceptible to her; but it was so frequently repeated by Mr. McCoy during the following half-hour, that it soon became fairly nauseous.

When the hot water and tumblers for the after-dinner whisky punch were placed on the table, poor Nannie looked at the window dispairingly. It had been so sunny among the yellowing and reddening foliage, the heavy dahlias and hollyhocks out there; but now a sudden shower was falling betwixt her and the still green privet hedges. She was a captive plainly; for it seemed too rude to Mr. Cosby and Luke for her to seek refuge in her bedroom, the only with-drawing room left to her. A martyr to her manners, therefore, as Luke had prophesied, Nan sat on for another half-hour, till a second glass had been slowly sipped, made to perform a rinsing noise within the mouth, and then swallowed with maddeningly deliberate relish by Mr. McCoy. Luke did not join his elders in the punch; but thinking his own custom more wholesome, contented himself with a moderate allowance of cold whisky and water.

The unwelcome guest had a disagreeable manner of continually interrupting and trying to lead them all in conversation. This was, though they took it gently and were very civil, in reality a piece of offensive presumption; since his ways of thought were cabbage-garden paths compared with Luke's, that were as broad highways of science, the old minister's like hawthorn lanes, or the fair lone heights whereon Nannie's mind oftenest loved to stray. He was truly

'One
Who thinks the all-encircling sun
Rises and sets in his backyard.'

Luke had somehow got to speaking of the doctrine of evolution to Nannie, in the strong hearty voice that was to her an encouragement in the mind-battles, to the old man a comforting assurance of orthodoxy—and that, to both, by its sound. Should evolution come to be held scientifically true, Luke would not shrink, he said (and the theory was then new!) from holding it as therefore theologically so—not inconsistent with the original act of creation; the revelation of such aeons-long-enduring a plan and purpose in God's continuous action upon the universe as was to him a thought of immeasurable grandeur—

Mr. McCoy now broke in, with a humorous side-nod at Nannie, 'I haven't understood one word of all you've been favouring us with for the last half-hour, young man, he, he! nor, I'll venture to say, did others. 'Deed, I'm thinking ye've maybe blinded yourself with your own dust'

Luke looked up in amused surprise; Nannie's fair face flushed in gentle indignation; but both glances were alike lost on the speaker, who, with greedy relish, was plunging his doubtfully clean hand into a dish of nuts, and sorting out the finest.

'I'm thankful to say,' he went on with a pious air, 'that my heart is not haughty—"neither do I exercise myself in great matters, nor in things too high for me," as says good David.'

Luke, to Nannie's surprise, temperately refrained from useless answering.

'Have you lost your old love of discussion?' she murmured, aside.

'Not yet,' answered Luke in the same tone. 'But great questions won't go into little minds; and the minds did not make themselves. I am beginning to believe, though, what Newman has somewhere said: "When we have stated our terms and cleared our ground, all argument is generally either superfluous or fruitless."'

Next the good old minister tried to interfere to save Nannie from hearing all the unpleasant details as to the drunkards in Mr. McCoy's parish. The old man's talk was oftenest of bees and flowers, and he now grew quite animated in description, telling of a newly found plant that, according to botanists, was a fresh link between the animal and vegetable worlds.

Mr. McCoy constantly interposed a running fire of 'Well, buts'—which, in his ardour, Mr. Cosby only waved eagerly aside till, the nice explanation of how his plant devoured flies being finished, he turned with a hospitably penitent air, ' I beg your pardon, McCoy; you wanted to say that—?'

'I was going to say, that no matter what fine foreign shrubs ye may talk about, still the lily of the valley is a most be-u-tiful flower,' doggedly observed Mr. McCoy.

Nannie now tried, in her turn, to keep the guest from leading the conversation, and addressing Luke, innocently said, 'It is a pity there is no harmonium here, you are so fond of music; and the Fräulein has sent me some grand stirring German airs this morning, which Luther would certainly have set hymns to, and not, as he said, left to the devil'

She caught with surprise a look of sorrowful reproach from Mr. Cosby's mild face. But the stranger, patting his body, and then leaning back and stretching himself with a satisfied air as if assured he had laid in sufficient munition at dinner, said with a leer of aggressive insolence, as it seemed to Nannie's dainty discernment, 'It's to be hoped he'll keep his love of it to himself; and not be piping to his sheep in public worship, like too many false shepherds amongst us these days.'

'And why not in public worship?' cried Luke, who, like a war-horse scenting the fray, could no longer restrain himself, but rushed to battle.

The burning question, whether instrumental music was lawful or not in the Presbyterian form of worship, had begun between two opposing champions.

'He is too combative, that boy of mine; too combative!' murmured the poor old minister to Nannie in a mild agony, longing to pour oil on the troubled waters, but only it seemed, when he tried to intervene, pouring it on flames.

Mr. McCoy was rash enough at first to dare upon arguing out the matter, perhaps not rightly knowing how redoubtable was his opponent, nor that Luke was already considered one of the keenest in debate, as well as most eminent of scholars in his sect. His opponent was soon fairly overborne by the simoom-blast of that burning eloquence, which also silenced good Mr. Cosby into wondering admiration, and enchanted Nannie. But as soon as the storm was over, the asinine foe raised drooping ears and tried to show by a sarcastic bray that he was 'of the same opinion still.'

'Our young friend is apparently fond of musical boxes—he, he! He's of the rising generation you see, Miss White, and they like their play-toys.'

'Well,' said Nannie, whom he had addressed apparently as

one of those 'silly women' alluded to by St. Paul, and merely wishing to let him know she had a mind of her own, 'it has always seemed to me that as St. John saw harps in heaven, it cannot be wrong for us to have music in our houses of God on earth.'

'It's no business of ours what the angels choose to do,' stuttered Mr. McCoy, getting into a rage; 'what we want is scriptural precedent for all *we're* to do; ay, that's it—ay! that's it. Did Paul travel with a barrel-organ?' (fuming and snorting). 'And, pray, where is it mentioned that fine ladies screeched like opera-singers in the sanctuary, as—as they do I'm told in your church?'*

The eyes of both the other ministers were upon the fair and honoured guest; but she, though so wise and well-read in their eyes, made foolish answer with kindling grey eyes: 'When Miriam played and sang upon her timbrel before the Lord—'

'That will do. That will do. I thought you knew little about it,' interrupted Mr. McCoy, holding up an offensively obtrusive outspread palm in vast apparent pity of her ignorance. The two

* The debate between the 'liberal', urbane, intelligent and loveable New Light minister (Luke Cosby) and the neighbouring Old Light minister with all the opposite qualities (Rev. McCoy) here focusses on the late 19th century controversy of introducing instrumental music, hymns and choirs into Presbyterian 'Meeting Houses' – which in Scotland and Ulster had previously (since Calvin and Knox's day in the 16th century) exclusively practised unaccompanied 'psalmody' from the Scottish Psalter. In the mainstream Presbyterian churches this controversy didn't really manifest until after the 1880s. However in the Non-Subscribing Presbyterian church in Greyabbey, the minister (Rev. William Hall) was using a harmonium (played by his daughter), and hymns from a 'Unitarian' Hymn-book as early as the 1860s. Rev. William Hall indeed answers the description of Luke Crosby is many other ways, including undertaking a fund-raising lecture tour of America about 1864.

other ministers looked inclined to smile, though respectfully grieved for their discomfited spokeswoman.

'All that dancing and piping has no place nor divine sanction in the New Testament economy, young lady, having passed away with the beggarly elements of the ceremonial law.'

He drained his glass with loud suction, and looked round him victoriously. He might even have refilled the tumbler, but that Luke, as if such a thought never struck him, said rising, 'The shower is over, Miss White; here is the sun out again, and you would like to get some fresh air. May I open the window for you?'

Thanking him, Nannie stepped out daintily on the wet sparkling sward of the trim close. The afternoon sunlight fell pleasantly on her bared head, on the heavy-fruited orchard, the russet leaves, quivering overhead against the deep-blue sky, on the wet-laden roses against the wall. She drew a long breath of relief and looking round to Luke, who had silently followed her, just said, 'Nature is never vulgar.' He nodded, but being less fastidious then herself, or perhaps having learnt to open his heart in larger sympathy towards all of human race, gravely answered, 'Think what it will be, in the times you and I shall yet live through, when none of our fellows, in our love and better understanding of them, shall seem wearisome or disagreeable. ... Then, too, as poor Roscoe wrote, when poverty forced him to sell his treasured books, but he tried to console himself by reflecting that in the eternity coming he should meet with, and know their writers, which was better:

> '"Mind shall with mind direct communion hold,
> And kindred spirits meet to part no more."'

Mr. Cosby, who had stayed in the parlour to lock the whisky-caddy, now came out; but no one knew whither the neighbour preacher had vanished. By-and-by, however, he appeared waddling (no other word could express his walk) from the rear of the house, with a flushed face, grasping a swelling umbrella.

'Why, McCoy, where have you been, man?' cried the genial old minister, as his guest came up with a battle-light lingering in the corner of his little eye, and yet an elated smirk. Mr. McCoy, with emphatic side-nods, plunged breathlessly into the history of his short absence.

'I made my way,' said he, 'into your kitchen, Mr. Cosby. I wished to have the dust removed from my coat, sir; and there I saw a somewhat prepossessing female. Young Mary, thinks I, and had it in my mind to compliment her on her omelet; but first I bid her render me this service. Hoity-toity! miss drew back and says mincingly, "You've made a mistake—I'm not the servant." "The which—?" says I sternly, and transfixing her with my eye. "I never asked if you were the servant. *I asked you to brush my coat!"* (I had her there I can tell you.) "I'll give it to Old Mary, if you'll allow me," she says with a fine-lady, polite air. So with that I turned round upon her, "Young woman! young woman;" says I, "I'd have you to know, for all that you think such a mighty deal of yourself, that you ought to be proud to black the boots of a minister of the gospel, so you should—yes, ye should!—yes, ye should!" 'He paused, and looked over his shoulder, for past the beech hedge came a slight woman-figure, dressed in a plain but pretty stuff gown, and carrying the identical pastoral wrap-rascal.

Her face was almost concealed by one of the enormous, gipsy straw hats that most womankind wore in those days, and which was pulled down over her eyes.

'Ah! here comes the minx,' exclaimed Mr. McCoy, audibly, adding facetiously as he strutted to meet her, 'Let me tell you, if you hadn't such a pair of bright eyes in your head, miss, I'd have maybe given a worse account of you to Mr. Cosby, here, for an impudent little hussy.'

'Thank you, sir,' said a somehow familiar voice, checking a sound of faint mirth, as the girl dropped a curtsey.

An exclamation of 'Aileen!' burst from Nannie in a transport of delight; then, as two gloriously dark-blue eyes laughed up at them all from under that disguising hat:

'Miss de Burgo!' exclaimed the others, with as surprised gladness.

'The misch—?' another voice seemed to mutter faintly, in still greater but horrified astonishment.

Before the two girls' embraces were ended, the mutual hand-shakings, questions and answers all round done—while Aileen was yet explaining that finding her aunt could spare her a fortnight she had come over unexpectedly to see Nannie and the dear old home again—they looked round, still laughing, for Mr. McCoy. His long coat-tails only were visible; making such a rapid retreat through the wicket-gate, that though Luke hallooed and took seven-leagued strides after him to give 'the poor fellow' some kindly re-assurance, he came back, reporting the fugitive as too far on the homeward road.

Then they learnt that Aileen had only arrived an hour before; had rushed down to the manse to surprise them all, entering like most of its household by the back door. There, in the kitchen, she had sprung as in her childish days upon Old Mary from behind, startling her; but no one else hardly, excepting Bonnibel, had ever been such a favourite with the old woman. And, hearing they had a stranger at dinner, she had not cared to go in among them just then, but had been patiently waiting till the meal should be finished.

'And where is Bonnibel?' she now asked.

'Why, she has gone yachting with Mr. de Burgo,' cried the old minister.

'With grandpapa!—really?' said Aileen, beginning in a tone of astonishment, changed at the last word into careless lightness.

For, the little harum-scarum hoyden of Black Abbey woods had been living in the great world since, and had learnt to conceal her private feelings discreetly when that was wisest, like any of its oldest inhabitants.

CHAPTER 30

A DRAGON-FLY

Aileen de Burgo had come back a delightful puzzle to the manse inmates. She had travelled in classic lands, to the envy of two of them at least; seen with her own deep-blue eyes pictures, statues, buildings, which they still longed to see; wandered by the castled Rhine, through the historical cities and legendary forests of Germany; knew every foot of that fair Riviera where traces of its successive masters in many a ruin, of Gaul and Roman, Frank and Saracen, mingled their associations in its southern beauty. How Nannie, living afar in cold fog, had wished to feel the delightful charm of that warmth-blessed winter refuge of the northern nations! Aileen, too, had bared her dark head under the very Italian sky, standing among vine-trellises, seeing the dark-blue tideless waves, dotted with white lateen sails, drinking in the air, the sights, scents, sounds, the wholly inexpressible spell with which Italy has for centuries enchained, and still enchains artist-natures. Nannie yearned with artist-hunger to feel it too.

And yet Aileen was so little changed!

Her face kept its childish promise; the small dark-crowned head, blue eyes, like deep love-lamps, somewhat brown skin, just tinged with red—all was beautiful.

'Oh yes, I am well enough, as to my head and shoulders; and artists have asked to paint me till I am tired of refusing them,' she would laugh, turning her long graceful neck that had still the antelope curve. 'But otherwise there is nothing of me; no figure!—only an insignificant little body.'

Miss de Burgo's person was thin and small, no doubt; but

she could never be insignificant, while in her brain, and out through her eyes, burned so bright, active a flame. The sense of her presence seemed to pervade all things and beings at the manse during the next fortnight, when from morning to night she spent her time there. For Nannie felt that she could never again go through the Black Abbey gate—till she went at its owner's request, as Hector's wife. So, as Aileen and she were now more than ever sisters (Aileen's delight at Nannie's engagement to Hector being unspeakable) and that the old minister and Luke were only too pleased and proud to have her company. Miss de Burgo gladly gratified them.

'She has poked that impudent little nose of hers into every pot in my scullery, and every clover-blossom in the far field.'

Thus Old Mary pretended to grumble whilst conscious of a smile in her eye, and a warmth reviving in her chill heart.

'There's not much escapes *her*, mind ye.'

And, indeed, in two days, Aileen seemed to know the affairs of every one as well as, or, on the principle of lookers-on seeing most, better than themselves. An out-of-doors, Bohemian spirit now seized on the ductile minds of the rest. At tea-time, the white cloth of the table was seen, to Old Mary's despair and her master's delighted surprise, to flutter under the apple branches of the orchard, where Luke in huge glee had bodily transplanted it; and there every evening now they sat out; Nannie, as the gentle genius of the teapot, seemed to preside over them all; her face as bright now as the September moon, that was rising seawards in the dusky blue sky and would soon illumine the mist-wreathed lowlands in front, and deep-hearted woods behind. Since Hector had been with her, she had never felt so happy. Meanwhile, Aileen cooked them foreign dishes and salads, flitting backwards and forwards between Old Mary's kitchen and the tea-table; whilst Luke, who felt quite awkward at being thus waited on, was always jumping up to help, and upsetting something in his eager awkwardness, or following her with long strides and arriving just too late. He found a new and incomprehensible experience in the independent self-helpfulness of Aileen's spirit that wanted no one to aid her, or even to take up her time by asking leave to do her bidding. Bonnibel, during his visits, was always alternating between paroxysms of treating him as her victim, or behaving as his self-devoted slave. Nannie looked on him as a wise true friend, who encouraged, criticized or comforted her. Honest Luke knew these two among women best; thought he understood them. Others he did not very well understand.

'Stop, Mr. Luke,' now cried Aileen. 'Carry out my dish of curds? No, no … no one must touch it but myself. You don't know me. Where my cookery is concerned I am a perfect dragon.'

'A dragon-fly, you mean,' laughed Nannie, as the other darted towards the house, and returned with a quickness reminding one of those blue, living arrowlets.

'Ah now, Luke, ye may just sit down,' laughed Mr. Cosby, his rosy face beaming, as with his hands on his knees, he himself remained in blissful composure, proud of being waited on, he said, by two such peerless handmaidens. Luke was standing in a waiting attitude, with his tall head caught Absalom-like among the apple branches; a chivalrous, puzzled expression of belief on his face that he ought to be helping some one *somehow*.

'You may just content yourself, my dear boy, *like me*, that Miss de Burgo wouldn't be bothered with you to help her,' went on the old minister. 'Miss Aileen is above any assistance, or if she wants it, she'll ask, quick enough. She's one of those tight little women that rule the world—begging her pardon.'

This was on the very first evening of Aileen's arrival. Then they all laughed and settled down round the table, and voted tea in the orchard delightful.

It was a pleasant and pretty scene in the orchard, on which Diana, 'the Hunter's moon' of September looked luminously down. Around the table spread with good cheer two fair maids, an old man and young one, making wisely merry; while overhead—

> 'There hung the apples growing red;'

and around—

> 'Windless the ripe fruit down did fall.
> The shadows of the large grey leaves
> Lay grey upon the oaten sheaves,
> By the garth wall …
> The startled ousel-cock did cry,
> As from the yew-tree by the gate he flew.'

'The only one we want, now, is Bonnibel, to make us perfectly happy,' exclaimed Mr. Cosby, looking around benevolently, and speaking from his full heart.

'But of course she is coming back to see you, before you start for America on your lecturing tour. When do you go?' asked Aileen, looking at the younger Cosby. She noticed with passing surprise that he seemed confused; the old minister troubled.

'I must start very soon,' replied Luke, with some slight effort to speak unconcernedly. 'But I should be very vexed if she curtailed her pleasure on my account. We *did* expect her back by now; but we got a hasty note this morning, putting off her return for the second time, for a few days more.'

'She was too hurried to explain, that one could see; but you may be sure she had good reasons—Bonnibel always has,' nervously added the old grandfather, so anxious in his darling's cause, that he looked about him with almost a challenging air. Aileen, at that, eyed him quite lovingly; scrutinized Luke with one swift glance unperceived; and gliding airily to other topics, described her own late wanderings. With surprise, the simple others listened to names of world-famed painters, musicians, sculptors, whom Aileen said she and her eccentric spinster aunt had 'stumbled against' in travelling, and apparently afterwards made their fast friends.

'You must have had a mutual affinity for each other,' observed Luke, surprised.

'So we had, as Bohemians all,' laughed Aileen, who saw little remarkable in the fact that almost all their acquaintance was with individuals well-known or even celebrated for their gifts. They were as easy to know as any others, once you knew one or two, she now affirmed. 'As I always tell Aunt Harry' (the diminutive of Harriet), 'she once got into the circle of intellectual aristocracy by chance, and ever since she has been handed round amongst them as a sort of live curiosity.' Then she spoke of a French king of the academy, a profound savant.

'Did he tell you of his discoveries in astronomy?' asked Luke, eagerly.

'Pooh! not he. He taught me how to make *bouilla-baisse*.'

Again, of another, the prince of German painters.

'Now, now! I'll be bound *he* took an interest in you, because you had such a taste for drawing. You used to caricature me as the man-in-the-moon, when you were no higher than my knee; and later, your copies of the water-colours in the Black Abbey morning-room!—Dear, dear! they were quite as good in my eyes as the originals,' put in old Mr. Cosby, with growing excitement.

'I don't think so much of my copies now,' laughed Aileen. 'No; he, like the rest, came mostly to us to unbend his bow. Even the most warlike knights must have been glad to unharness themselves sometimes. And he liked to spend a quiet hour with us, and ask Aunt Harry to give him a cup of her English tea out of our travelling teapot. That is the one insular token we keep (and always some pounds of the most extravagant tea)—it is well to have *something* distinctive about one, eh, Nannie? … How the poor Fräulein used to try and impress that upon us! and to picture an ideal society in which each woman only cultivated her peculiar gift and was *thorough*. Well, you became a poetess, and satisfied her soul; but after all her toil, and trying every imaginable crop in the shallow soil of my mind, not a sign of a single especial ability could be produced. I am a living edition of *Love's Labour Lost*'.

'Far from that,' exclaimed Nannie, quickly. She did not like to hear even the self-depreciation of her heart's-sister. 'Far from that. Your mind is cultivated, and as you are not a field, but a human being (for if we ride similes too long they run away with us), you know how to admire and appreciate, though you cannot originate. What would the world of arts and letters be without dilettanteism? The players want a good audience. … Besides, you *have* a gift! Did not G— herself,' naming a queen of song, 'teach you to sing last winter, and the great J— too?'

'They amused themselves with my small voice,' parried Aileen, lightly; 'and in consequence I tinkle the slightest of ballads in a style that people are pleased to say is unlike that of other folk—"A poor thing, sir, but mine own." The Duchess of Sleepyshire (such a stout woman!) asked me one night at Rome, with some displeasure, how on earth *I* could afford to pay G— for my singing lessons? She said, "I wanted to have her for my daughter, but found her terms were quite too expensive!" So I dropped her a curtsey, and said, with malicious satisfaction, "Your Grace, G—'s lessons only cost me gratitude!"'

As Aileen thus chattered, Nannie looked at her in some surprise. For that very afternoon Aileen had confided to her—as women will—how that the duke's nephew and heir, a heavy young man, had implored her to share with him the future Sleepyshire glories.

'Hector was so angry with me for refusing him,' Aileen had told, gaily laughing at the recollection. '"A position that other women would think magnificent," he said. I told him that the very idea of spending all the beautiful days of my life in cold, gilded grandeur, society duties, and having fine, big houses, and not one home, would bore me to death! I should be like a swallow in a cage! Now, I am the happiest vagrant on earth. … No use! Hector could not understand—few people can—that others can be really happy in their own way. I should like to please dear old Hector certainly; but, as I have only one life, and that maybe a short one, I prefer pleasing myself.'

Nannie, naturally, could not believe that Hector—her Hector—had been altogether wrong; although Aileen might be almost quite right.

'And what was the ducal nephew like?' she asked.

Aileen yawned unconsciously at the recollection. 'Oh, excellent, most excellent! but dull as ditch water. He used to laugh solemnly at all our jokes, and ask me privately half an hour afterwards what they had been about.'

Nannie felt quite sorry for the 'excellent young man,' but not a shade of embarrassment was on Aileen's sparkling brown face as she recounted it, nor yet of vanity, or scorn, or sentiment; only a sort of Bohemian—and yet womanly—and yet common-sense air. She was not ordinary; she had violent likings and dislikes, and would show them prettily enough, but with vehemence of action; in fact, she was like a wild bird. She pitied society's cage-birds; they wondered at her.

> 'Dear heaven, how silly are the things that live
> In thickets and eat berries!'

The tea was ended; the gloaming deepened. But, luckily, it was then St. Martin's summer, so they could linger without much fear of colds or rheumatism yet awhile. They begged Aileen to sing for them, then. At once she said yes—as much as they liked; simply adding, she had already sent up to Black Abbey for her zither, thinking they would like to hear it.

'There now! that's what I call breeding,' whispered the old minister in vast delight to Nannie, who felt amused and pleased at his praise. 'Good manners are just copied from real Christianity; always being willing to oblige your neighbour. Dear, dear, and so many commonplace young women when they're asked to sing are as full of airs as an old piano, and as stiff at letting them out,' and the old man rubbed his hands, and chuckled over his innocent joke.

Aileen's voice was small indeed; it was rather a grace than a gift. But as they listened to her warbling ballads—simple ballads only—the feeling took possession of them that this was unique. Whether it was the exquisite expression, or the little sympathetic gestures helping out the voice, the speaking eyes set in that dark flower-face, none could say.

Was it the songs themselves come straight from the hearts of the people, and whatever language they were uttered in, finding their way to all human hearts—or other little unknown gems she had found amongst the music-rubbish of bygone years, and made her very own—that constituted the essence of her secret? They only knew, as they all watched her fascinated—long afterwards they still thought—that they had never heard anything before, or since, quite the same.

'I am glad you like it,' said Aileen simply, when the last low sound floated away among the dark privet hedges, and only a brown owl now, in the deep Black Abbey wood across the road, made melancholy music to the moon; 'but when age creeps on, and my voice goes, there will be no more profit in me—an empty fiddle-case!' (She spoke lightly, but as one does of a small private grief that must not be troublesome to others.) 'You,

Nan—you are an enviable mortal. Whether you are absent, or dead, or have a cold in your head, you can still give pleasure.'

> '"Peace, Chloris, peace! or singing die,"'

interrupted Nannie, laughing;

> '"For all we know
> Of what the blessed do above
> Is, that they sing and that they love."'

Then Aileen said she must go homewards. Before leaving, Nannie and she went upstairs for a few moments' more private talk; the pleasure of being together being more than what was said.

'We are real sisters now,' they had said to each other that day; more than are many sisters they already had been to one another.

'Tell me,' said Aileen, with a keen, quick voice and glance that made one feel pleasantly dissected, for she knew what *not* to search into, 'is Bonnibel being brought up as Mr. Luke's future property, and is he afraid—as he well may be—that she is bowing down before those golden calves, Mr. Brown-Jones and Ludovic Mudson? I have seen them both; fast young men, loud, and common-place, but both of them rich.'

'Oh, Aileen, no. Indeed you misjudge her,' said Nannie, distressed. Then she explained what she might, without betraying any special confidence. 'She has been brought up, as it were, for her cousin; and knows he has never thought in such a way of anyone else, and that it would be a terrible blow to him.'

'First loves do not mean with men only loves, nor yet a *grande passion!* said Aileen, the little cynic; then added:

'People must expect blows on life's forge, and many a man would do no good without them. Every male individual I have as yet known intimately, that was worth anything, had an unhappy first love. Well, they talk of non-marrying men. I have made up my mind, I am not a marrying woman! I like men well enough to talk to for an hour; a day of any one of them bores me; and I love my liberty.' And so downstairs she flitted, where Luke, waiting in the entry, with coat and hat on, since a quarter of an hour, only asked, 'Are you ready so soon. Miss Aileen—would you not have liked to talk longer with poor Miss Nannie, who will feel deserted when you are gone?'

'Why—perhaps you are not ready?' asked Aileen, with such a charming unconsciousness of her own sins against his patience, that Luke gave a great guffaw of kindly laughter, and Nannie and the old minister, standing in the doorway to see them go, laughed too. So out they two went into the dewy darkness of the manse-shadowed garden; along the moon-lit road under the high Black Abbey wall; into the hushed heart of the woods, alone together. Every night afterwards they thus went; the sprite figure escorted to the old home of her ancestors by the gaunt Presbyterian minister who had now, strictly speaking, no home at all.

CHAPTER 31

IN THE MANSE GARDEN

It was a lovely morning late in September. An early shower had washed the autumn land clean; a warm sun was reviving it. The manse eight o'clock breakfast was over two hours ago, and now Luke, in his shirt-sleeves, was vigorously digging a flower-border under the last privet hedge. Digging at intervals, rather, and those but rare; since mostly he seemed leaning on his spade, looking, up at a little figure perched beside him on the meadow gate. This little person was having a hot skirmish in words with him, provoking the earnest man constantly into eager explanation of some pet hobby—(just now a particular salmon fly; a while back he was smashing the arguments of some particularly hateful ism-ending creed on which she demanded information—breaking it to pieces, while speaking tenderly, lovingly of the human souls that sought comfort in it). Then, as he paused, the adversary, who had picked up like a magpie queer scraps of knowledge with the notion they might some day be useful—and whose memory was as remarkable as, says Montaigne, are those of dunces—would slily flout his fly, remembering a former avowal that the nibbles thereat, save in certain weather, had been few, teasing him into self-convicted laughing; would flaunt in his face the one unanswerable tittle of dream in which the September morning's influences seemed to have steeped her, 'May it not be, that as our bodies are of the earth, earthy, they must have subtle affinities with the atoms of the universe around that are not enough taken into consideration in our self-balancing of accounts between mind and matter. … Air, sea, sun affecting our clay-cases; these the divine spark within—'

'A most disagreeable idea,' cried Aileen pettishly, 'and the worse for being too true of myself. I love my free-will and quarrel with my insignificant, hampering person. Why! it would make food influence my ideas most degradingly! … For instance, have I absorbed so much more of Black Abbey than of other earth in greens and milk and so-forth, that though my mind does *not* want to lead a quiet rooted existence here as Nannie's will be, still these last days among you all and in the old haunts—' (she stopped herself and laughed, a little confused). 'I am too lazy in this dying autumn weather, that is it; and could almost feel tempted to give up my dear changeful Bohemianism.'

'You lazy?' cried out Nannie, pointing to the grey sock at which, since a few minutes back (her apple finished), Aileen had been knitting with most marvellous quickness. 'Why! One never knows whether your tongue or your needles click fastest'

Aileen was so volatile, fitful, apt to accuse and defend herself in the same breath, that her friend (being self-engrossed that morning) would have thought no more of this utterance of the light, bright creature—but that she perceived Luke's grey eyes, under their shaggy brows, fixed upon the latter, as was indeed usual enough, but with unusual earnest piercingness of gaze.

Aileen perceived him too, and suddenly exclaiming, 'There is the postman!' sprang from her seat. For a wonder, there was one letter—from the neglectful Miss Hawthorn, too, and to Nannie. With the first page (there were several largely written) a sudden interest like a great light leaped up in Nannie's face, illumining its heretofore abstracted, gentle, far-off gaze. It was as if the soul, wandering abroad to meet its love, was suddenly recalled to the body to meet him in life. 'Oh! Hector is on board the yacht!' she said aloud, with fluttering voice. Her two hearers expressed their interest; then considerately turned to converse with each other.

Nannie slipped away with her precious letter to the arbour's seclusion.

Her heart was beating strongly; for weeks past it had never once so knocked for attention. A red flame burned in her now usually too delicately pale cheeks; her tenderly beaming eyes were so full of soft tears, she could hardly decipher the eager words—the almost illegible scrawl—that claimed welcome forgiveness, since it was the writer's gush of friendship, so the latter wrote, that hurried it.

Hector, it seemed, had at last thought fit to accept the constant and pressing invitations old Mr. de Burgo had sent his "dear boy" to join them. 'But lest you might be disappointed, I would not write to you before that he was, perhaps, coming,' said the letter. 'He seems to hate the society here; does not go on shore or to the other yachts with us; but stays fishing all the day by himself. It must be delightful to have a man so changed for love of one, for he used to be so fond of gaiety, you told me.' (Ay! but in a different class from that of the Brown-Joneses—and Mrs. Heavyside too, at whose flame, now lurid, but then sweetly shining, honest Hector had once apparently singed himself in days of yore.) 'He is so good-natured that he seems not to know how to be angry with his grandfather; for the old man plagues him with kindness, and would kiss his very shoes. But he bid me tell you he is very impatient for the next two years to be over! I am the only person on board he cares to talk to. I do believe he only came to get private news of you. Mrs. Heavyside is so jealous! But of course, dearest, *I* know he only likes poor little me for your sweet sake (though I don't tell her so), for he used quite to look down on me at the manse.' (Nannie could not forbear smiling; it was so true! She could fancy the writer's pretty pettish look as she penned that; and the underlying satisfaction yet of having gained his attention, nevertheless!—although for another's sake. She felt quite sorry for Bonnibel that Hector did not admire her more.) Then the letter described, how yesterday night, after dinner, Hector asked Miss Hawthorn to come out with him in the dingy, and tell him more of Nannie. The jubilant tone here changed. Plainly poor Bonnibel regretted the band on shore, and the chance of a moonlight stroll on the pier with her admirers. Only the chance, she truthfully added—for Hector was most anxious not to interfere with her pleasure, and knew it was the only time she cared to spare to him. So she had gone, and was rowed by Hector in the dark little bay till quite late—'talking, talking, talking to him,' as she wrote, of only their dear Nannie—plainly with warmest outpouring of loving enthusiasm. Yet her soul had hankered, as a word or two that seemed to have escaped her hasty pen, betrayed.

Nannie understood it all, and smiled. 'Poor Bonnibel! I must try to repay her sacrifice some day, in the manner that will best please her,' she thought. Other friends might do such a kindness without bargaining; but one must love Bella Hawthorn as she is. It was Nannie's creed that it must be the imperfect, fallible, tiresome folk among whom we are placed on earth whom it is our duty to befriend, and so better—not evermore waiting for ideal kindred spirits. And she practised her high belief, as, alas! too many of us do not. How well Nan could imagine the little boat, with the two figures in it, heaving softly on the dark palpitating water; while overhead a few stars had lit their lamps; and, fringing the bay, the lights of the town were brilliantly reflected below. Ah! had she but been there too!

Meanwhile, Luke still leant on his spade, and furtively watched Aileen, or now much more slowly turned a sod or two. The carts still rumbled along the road, the calves still gambolled in the clover: only these two seemed changed with Nannie's absence. They hardly spoke, yet neither was offended with the other. Aileen was again knitting, with still more intent and intense haste.

'How good it is of you to make those for me!' said Luke softly, after a while. 'I do not believe anyone else would have taken the trouble.'

'Then it is a great shame for everyone else; and it is no trouble,' said the lively little lady.

'I have asked Bonnibel, sometimes, to do them for me, but she says she never could turn the heels,' said the grateful man, gazing with admiration at the deft way in which Miss de Burgo was rounding that corner of difficulty to beginners and dunces; innocently unaware that he thereby lowered his pet cousin a good deal in his hearer's good opinion, who somewhat scornfully glued together her pretty lips.

Just then Nannie joined them. No wonder she had lingered so long: her eyes looked quite dilated, and softly dazed with pleasure. She told the other two little scraps of her letter with smiles. 'Bonnibel says that Hector has been working hard' (at what?) 'ever since June,' she ended, with engaging slight confusion. 'He told her there was nothing else he cared to do, and is glad to be adjutant now.'

'Does he so? Then you may be sure he has,' cried Luke cheerfully, with decision. 'Mr. Hector is not a man to do things by halves.'

For a few minutes the others wondered, and supposed this and that as to Nannie's news, till she, listening, gently observed, 'Well, we shall know better soon, when Bonnibel comes back, in a week.'

'In a week!' exclaimed Luke, startled; then, recovering himself, added, with attempted playful reproach, 'Miss Nannie!—Miss Nannie! You said there was no other news.'

'I am so sorry … I don't know how I could forget it,' said the shame-stricken culprit; at which both the others laughed. Luke began to dig again, but his heart was no longer in the work. By-and-by he shouldered his spade and left them, on some poor pretext.

'Why should he be so discomposed? Did he expect her back sooner? That must be it,' wondered Nannie softly, with a puzzled, still dreamy expression.

'I don't believe—if you are asking me—that he has been pining for her return at all,' responded Aileen, with an abrupt downrightness that, quick though her tone generally was, surprised the other into a reproachful:

'Oh, Aileen! He is so fond of her! And now he will have barely three days to be with her. It must be terribly disappointing.'

'Humph! Well, it may be so! Some people have a wonderful gift certainly of disguising their feelings,' rather murmured than said Miss de Burgo. 'I am really impatient to see this Bonnibel. She was a bouncing schoolgirl, with a mane of hair flying loose, when last I saw her.' Then she looked at Nannie, whose soul seemed as if absent in a happy flight, while in departing it had left her eyes gazing after it into space, a faint sweet smile playing round her mouth. Looking at her thus—or listening to Luke Cosby, when he talked seriously—Aileen would lose the air of raillery and lightness that had at first always characterised her when she came to the manse—and now she drew Nan's arm through hers, and said quite softly and persuasively, 'Come, dear! tell me all about it.'

So Nannie did tell her all that was passing in her mind, as to another self.

Throughout the week after this, while they awaited Bonnibel's return, Luke seemed changed—unlike the former heartsome, cheery-laughing, toughly-arguing man. Averring that these were his last days, he devoted them now from morning to night to his old uncle; going dutifully with him through the parish, showing him all the gentle attentions in his power. With the fair guests, towards evening, when he again perforce joined them, he apparently tried to be as kind and pleasant as before; but *then* no effort, it had been as plain, had been needed.

At times, Nannie by sweetness, Aileen by her brightness, beguiled him out of his constrained, serious, somewhat silent mood; but he would soon seem to recollect himself, like a man who has his private reasons for feeling stern, though wishful that no others should thereby suffer. They felt free to guess at the why, and pitied him much. Even Nannie—who was no longer quite sure that Bonnibel had stayed solely in self-sacrifice to give Hector news from the manse, as she wrote—felt that the girl, who had grown up as Luke's promised wife, was treating him ill by having so delayed her return time after time. Now, at most, she could only see him for three days, and he must be away during a year.

Even old Mr. Cosby seemed troubled. His eyes were sometimes turned on Luke quite apologetically, with dumb humility; and when his pet's return was spoken of, he would mop his head nervously with his red handkerchief, as if feeling that she had not acted quite rightly *this* time.

CHAPTER 32

A PRETTY PRODIGAL

Bonnibel had just come home.

Luke drove to meet her; and now the old gig stopped at the yard-gate, as it had stopped a good many years ago, when bringing her first to the manse as a child. Softly—lightly for such a large girl—she ran up the garden-walk to meet old Mr. Cosby with outstretched arms, embraced Nannie next fervently, then paused a moment, asking leave for 'Auld lang syne's sake,' before touching with her lips Aileen's cool cheek, to the infinite surprise of that proud little lady, despite of her declared Bohemian liking for easy manners. Bonnibel seemed in too good humour to dream that her advances could be ill-received, so turned again to her grandfather and drew him, laughing, by his sleeve, into the parlour; there she pushed him into his great chair, and seating herself on its ample arm, embraced his neck lovingly, showering kisses on his bald head, and repeating 'Here is your prodigal again, you see; you foolish, darling old grand-papa! Did you think I was never coming back?'

Luke had come in, now, from the stable, and was watching her with a curious sort of grave comicality. She began eagerly explaining to them all, then, why she had dallied so long about returning, appealing to her cousin every now and then with a—'You know, Luke; I have told you already,' as to an ally. She gave them all to understand—in a meaning subdued tone—that her first delay had been caused solely by the belief that Mr. Hector would—would like to see her. It was well said; even Nannie hardly felt embarrassed. The second time, both Mr. de Burgo and Mrs, Heavyside had urged her to wait, in order to travel back with the latter, since she would otherwise be alone, and the journey was long. No one could say a word against this. Plainly Bonnibel had—or believed she had—herein sacrificed her own wishes; and Aileen noticed, with a sort of doubtful amusement, that Luke looked at the pretty pleader with quite a calm convinced expression of the propriety of her actions, now they were made plain.

The elements of the manse group had all at once shifted, and unconsciously ranged themselves round Bonnibel as a new centre. They all found themselves regarding her with a curious analytical interest, as cultured mind, soul, and the active bodily members that work for common human good, might look on a simply living heart pulsing with red blood; conscious of existence and of passions, without being troubled about their cause. The talk, too, changed, as if their ideas were lured down from the breezy uplands and higher levels of thought to the warm fat valleys, where dwell the contented ones of the earth at ease. Nannie, when aroused as now to every-day life, could see keenly, and noted many small alterations—several improvements in the girl. Bonnibel's thick chestnut hair was now arranged elaborately, her dress neater in all details (somewhat extravagant for her means it always had been), and she mimicked unconsciously Mrs. Heavyside's low laugh and pretty accent. Handsomer, lazier than ever—or tired, as she softly averred—she reclined in their midst with her hands lying idly in her lap; her ox-eyes seeing, with apparently approving satisfaction, Miss de Burgo's nimble movements in making tea, cutting bread, knitting Luke now a winter muffler, while Nannie following, gave all the needed after-touches to her friend's rapid work—both doing Bonniber's duties.

'She is a useless goddess,' was Aileen's secret, sharply-delivered verdict on their hostess of the manse. It put her out of patience that they, the two guests, should be really minding the dear old minister's present and Luke's future wants, whilst both foolish men were in humble attendance on the household sovereign, whose fatigue Aileen plainly did not believe in.

If Bonnibel suffered her guests to exert themselves for her, at first, when tea was over, however, and both her grand-father and Luke had retired to smoke in the arbour, she did try with all her heart to make herself agreeable to her own sex. Always unable to restrain herself in talk, she was now brimming over with all she had done and seen; and made them most amusing, irrepressible confidences on the subject of her various admirers, which she could not well have told before old Mr. Cosby or her cousin. It was all in questionable taste. She told of her many little plots and plans for bewitching her victims; how, once, she put up all her hair with a single hair-pin, so that it fell accidentally; how, once, Mr. de Burgo wanted her to go for a walk, when she was just dying to stay and see Mr. Brown-Jones, so she tried to pretend feeling faint, and the terrible old man told her, chuckling, that 'she had too high a colour.'

Aileen listened, at first, too much astonished to speak. She did not understand the tone of mind, nor that fashion of making sudden friendships by boundless confidences, that had been prevalent at Miss Hawthorn's boarding school. Nannie, though somewhat used before to the same kind of thing, still, after their late separation, was almost as much struck with the absence of self-restraint or refinement; but Bonnibel told it all with such utter honesty, her eyes brimming with fun, as she made most naive admissions against herself, that putting away all other considerations of vexed friendship, even Nannie had to laugh heartily; while Aileen was soon divided between amazement and convulsions of satirical mirth, unchecked by much softer feeling. The girl was lying back, meanwhile, as luxuriously as she well could on the old horsehair sofa; looking so handsome and good humoured, that, thought little Miss de Burgo, it 'made one quite angry to see such gifts wasted on a person who did not understand how to use them.'

At last—when all her stock of personal adventures and treasured compliments was almost exhausted, Bonnibel looked up to Nannie with her melting brown eyes, and in her lazy, gurgling voice, uttered with a heartfelt sigh recalling late happiness, 'Oh, dear, you don't know—for of course you never felt it—*how delicious it is to know one is pretty!!*'

Nannie's grey eyes slowly opened, as the sublime simplicity and truthfulness of her friend's sentence slowly dawned upon her. Her sensitively formed lips quivered and curled with such an expression of entertainment and humour that Aileen could no longer restrain herself—and answered with so sharp a little scream of laughter that Miss Hawthorn, raising herself, asked her in sudden surprise, 'What is it?' Said that pleasant little sinner, with a cheerful disregard of the example of utter veracity that Bonnibel had so lately set her, 'It was only that I have been taught to read characters by seeing the hand. And just at that moment I could see that you are plainly a person very much admired in society; but that, perhaps—forgive me for saying so—you could also be jealous by the way your fingers turn back.'

'No!' cried Bonnibel, delightedly, extending her plump, rosy-tinged palm for further inspection. 'Where do you see it? But mine don't turn half so much as yours, dear Miss de Burgo. Still—I am afraid I am jealous … there was such a delightful Colonel Fitzadam that Mrs. Heavyside wanted to keep all to herself. One day, she persuaded me to go off and amuse myself, pretending she had a headache—and would you believe it! just afterwards he came on board. I could have cried.'

'Colonel Fitzadam? … I remember meeting that—person,' observed Aileen.

'No, did you? Don't you think him charming?'

'He may be charming, but I did not think him nice' said

Miss de Burgo, with conciseness.

'Oh, don't you really?—but he is so amusing. Not handsome, certainly, but one of those fascinating ugly men like Talleyrand, as Mr. de Burgo said when teasing me about him, who boasted he only asked half-an-hour's start to outdo the handsomest man in Europe. Mrs. Heavyside says that Colonel Fitzadam has been the dream of her life.'

'What a bad dream!' just murmured Miss Aileen with scornful, faint voice.

Nannie quietly sat by and listened to them both, with a world of fun lighting her grey eyes; to use Rebecca's favourite expression, these two 'were as good as a play to her.'

All that evening, Bonnibel overflowed with mirth and sweetness towards them all, especially endeavouring to ingratiate herself with Miss de Burgo, of whom alone she was not sure. She smiled on her to the last, when Luke, still grave and pre-occupied, came as usual to escort his nightly charge back to the old house in the woods. Then she praised their departed guest to Nannie most warmly, remarking on her piquancy, the sweetness of her deep blue eyes, and the sharpness of her tongue; 'the air of pride with which she carries that little patrician head, you know, dear; and yet no more conceit about her than a dairymaid. What a pity she is such a thin little thing.'

'Well, no one can accuse you of being that, anyway, my stout lassie. You will soon be a dear grand-daughter to me, for the gig will not hold the two of us if you go on at this rate. It's a jaunting-car I'll have to buy,' laughed her grandfather, trying to speak with a disparaging air of his child's robust proportions; yet all the evening his eyes had been devouring her in delight, and even now were shining with loving pride.

'Good-night, you teasing, unkind old man,' said the pouting beauty. 'Look how late you have kept poor Miss Nannie up.'

'Good-night, my pretty prodigal—and may God bless you,'

said the old man, gazing after her with truest affection, as she shaded her candle going up the stairs. The two girls did not go to bed then, however; for till far late in the night they sat together, Bonnibel expatiating on Hector's looks, and words, and ways, with really most good-humoured warmth and prolixity, considering she was tired; whilst Nannie could have listened untired for hours, but was at last ashamed of her own selfishness.

CHAPTER 33

A JEALOUS WOMAN

BUT next morning Bonnibel was changed; and all in the manse were made to feel that a fog clouded their sun. Nothing seemed right with her, but—'Oh, nothing was wrong!' She had a slight headache, as she bitterly confessed; but begged no one should trouble themselves or pretend that they cared for that … excepting, indeed, Nannie, whom (as she apologetically turned to assure her) she always found sympathetic and *truly* friendly. However, she thought she would be better if left alone, to-day, in the garden.

So Nannie left her. Aileen de Burgo had resolved not to come down to the manse, except for half an hour in the evening, having privately agreed with Nannie, she might be in the way of Luke and his cousin, who, as they had so little time left to be together, might feel her entertainment a tax on their politeness. Therefore all day Nannie wrote alone in her room, or looked out longingly through the narrow window at the dear Black Abbey woods so near.

Only after the red sun had tinged with sinking fire the topmost leaves of those umbrageous masses of tree-tops which seemed all the darker by contrast with that glow behind—when the light had faded, and the shadows had grown long—she at last ventured downstairs. But, on the threshold of the parlour, she stopped dead short.

Bonnibel was flung in one comer of the sofa, in an attitude of sullen anger, Luke, with his face averted, and his arms sternly folded, stood gazing out of the furthest window. Plainly there had been a bad quarrel. Nannie, seizing on a book, and murmuring some pretext about it, would have at once slipped out, but that Luke hastily stopped her.

'Do not go, pray. Miss Nannie—*I* am going,' he said firmly, though appealing to her with a sad look in his light grey eyes; his kindly face wearing a most weary expression, as if fretted by troubles, yet steadfast with the inward resolve to bear up against them, Nannie, however unwilling, was obliged to stay. 'You seem the only person who has a good influence over my cousin to-day. Will you use it to convince her of the truth, that since she came home to us my one wish has been to please her. Unfortunately—all I can do or say to make her happy seems only to confirm her in the contrary opinion.'

He would have gone quietly out of the room, but up sprang Bonnibel with flashing eyes, and stamped her foot on the ground.

'No, Luke! you shall not go! Not till I tell all to Miss Nannie before your face! … I have not said it all out even to *you*, yet; but I will now.'

Luke started, almost recoiled, as if before some hitherto unfeared danger.

'Bonnibel!—hush! child, what would you think of saying?' then tried to look at her reassuringly, both for herself and him, with a pale noble smile.

'I will—!'

The girl's cheeks burned now in a passionate flame. She would not be silenced.

'You have only eyes for Miss Aileen de Burgo, now; ears for Aileen de Burgo! Everything *she* does is perfection. You have been walking home alone with her every night, and you are so much in love with her that I am nothing to you—'

'*Bella!*'

With that one exclamation, all Luke's passionate, excitable temper of past youth seemed to blaze out again. His honest face grew dark red, then again white with shame. But—with a great effort—he controlled that wild surge, and said to Nannie with trembling lips, but calmly and sorrowfully, 'Miss White, I am more bitterly ashamed and grieved than I can say. I do not know how my cousin could have so far forgotten herself as even to speak Miss de Burgo's name in connexion with mine. … Forgive her! … The utterances of a jealous woman are not worthy of your consideration.'

'Oh, *are* they not! Bonnibel almost shrieked in infuriated bitterness. 'Would she bear it in my place, do you think? Would she endure it in my place, do you think? Would she endure it, if Mr. Hec—'

Under Luke's quiet, penetrating eye, the girl broke off short—hard-breathing; the storm paused in mid-fury. Then, in that strange lull, his voice asked, 'Bella, what right have I ever given you to consider the cases alike?'

There was a silence terrible to all three.

The girl stood transfixed. The shadows in the parlour almost concealed the man's expression, but the little light there was fell on her beautiful, wrathful, bewildered face. Dumbstruck, she pressed her hands unconsciously on her bosom; then the tears rose up in her eyes still passion-blazing, slowly overflowed, but did not yet altogether quench that fire, the effect being like moonshine now in two dark welling fountains. Bonnibel was a woman in a thousand in this, that she looked her loveliest when in tears.

Between the man and girl, Nannie stood like a silent saint's statue, to which both had appealed. The trust both felt in her sympathy at the beginning must have been very strong.

Then, with a little beseeching cry, Bonnibel covered her face; her voluptuous figure swayed; she dropped in a heap on the ground at Luke's feet, like a crushed creature awaiting its doom.

Nannie White, at that, seeing she had not fainted, softly

quitted the room, leaving them alone together.

After almost an hour came a knock at Nannie's door.

'Tea is ready, please. And you are all alone and in the dark!' said Bonnibel, coming in with humility; yet nevertheless, a restored cheerfulness of manner, as if purified by her late storm of tears. Then she drew nearer, going softly, like penitent Ahab, and supplicated low with very real affection in her voice, 'You will forgive me, won't you? You are so good to me always' (Nannie looked her through and through searchingly, then, as if satisfied, made a silent yet slow, and almost severe gesture of assent.) 'It is all right now. May I tell you all about it?' went on the girl, reassured but still subdued, sinking down as usual on the bed, as if comfort was unconsciously always a first, prime want with her.

'Surely, my dear,' said Nannie with grave gentleness; and rising, came and stood beside her, leaning by the bed-head like a guardian-angel to the grateful gaze of the exhausted late fury.

'I am engaged to Luke now; so it is … all right,' murmured the girl rather shamefacedly. Then after a pause added, with recovered volubility and excitement that banished embarrassment, 'But it was *dreadful* that minute! wasn't it? He did not know that I had ever overheard him and grandpapa settling that he was to marry me.'

She gave a little laugh of real amusement that as verily startled Nannie; who, however, forgave her, supposing it hysterical, since the next moment she was nervously interlacing her fingers. 'To tell you the whole truth, dear'—she half-weeping blurted out—no other word would so well express her manner—'I did think that either Mr. Brown-Jones, or that other man would have proposed to me. … And they were so rich! … It would have been such a different life!'

'Oh, Bonnibel!'

Nannie looked aghast at the unsought confession; and after such a scene!

'Why not? Don't look like that. Luke would not have minded one bit after a time, for he has only thought of me as his wife as a matter of habit. Then, with terrible candour, she would go on disclosing her mind. 'But was it not horrid of them (after all they said, too!)—they never did! And Mrs. Heavyside kept on sneering and laughing in her low, hateful way, and, "warning me," she said, that they were only amusing themselves. And the old man pretended to scold me for hooking my fish, he said, and not landing them properly; and I hated them all for pitying me, and it was so lonely and miserable, though I tried to pretend it only amused me. … Then, when it was of no use, and I did get home, it seemed such a comfort to have Luke after all. He has always kept to me. I don't like being poor, but it would be worse not to be married. … You can imagine it all, can't you, dear?' she ended, her brown fervid eyes burning appealingly up at Nannie, and her lips framing a quivering, apologetic smile. 'You understand, it did seem so hard, then, that Miss Aileen should step in and—'

'Hush, Bonnibel!' and Nannie haughtily rose. 'Let it be understood that that foolish, wild idea of yours is never again to be spoken of between us.'

'Very well, dear; I beg your pardon. Yes, dear; it is dreadfully stupid of me, of course, to annoy you. She is come, and we will go down to tea,' glibly answered the young hostess in tones of soothing, subdued apology; putting her warm, comfortably-rounded arm very affectionately through that of her guest. Yet her gaze, in spite of that denial, scrutinised Nannie's expression inquisitively; and she gave her head a little victorious nod, unseen, as Nannie passed before her into the now lamp-lit parlour.

When Aileen's time came for going home that night, Luke, with a sort of hesitating gravity, asked Bonnibel would she accompany them. And Bonnibel, with a quiet unembarrassed cheerful air at once said, 'Yes.'

CHAPTER 34

LUKE'S LEAVE-TAKING

It was the last day of Luke's stay at the manse—a fine September day. The swallows were all sitting in rows along the house-roofs, chattering together over the course to be taken in their southward flight; or else the younger ones were exercising their powers by dashing in airy circles round the tops of the ash-trees. The sound of the flail* was heard in the barn, the folk at the manse being old-fashioned as to farm utensils.

Most of that day Nannie and Aileen had spent at the shore, wandering between the land's edge and the waves' edge, by sandy nook or by shingle bar. They. had much to say to each other, for soon Aileen would be obliged to go; being, as usual, bound to spend the winter with her old aunt in sunnier climes in the South; and so poor Nannie, like Mariana, would be left 'aweary.' She tried not to show how she drooped at the thought, but secretly just longed to go too. She felt somewhat like, as when—

'A stork which idle boys have trapp'd
And tied him in a yard, at autumn sees
Flocks of his kind pass flying o'er his head
To warmer lands, and coasts that keep the sun.
He strains to join their flight, and from his shed
Follows them with a long complaining cry.'

---

* The hand-flail for threshing chaff from the corn (oats) was by this time a thing of the past, except for the poorest and smallest of holdings.

But the strong wind roused both girls, mind and body, to feel cheerful; and again there was many a cranny under the lee of the rocks where, warm and sheltered, they could sit or eat the lunch they had brought with them—milk and fruit from Black Abbey, and some griddle and oatmeal cake baked by the hard-handed country girl who acted as caretaker up at the lonely big house. Aileen had indeed rough fare there, but was as merry over it as a migratory bird, fore-seeing sunny climes in winter. Both girls had wished to leave the cousins at the manse alone together this last day. The Rev. Joseph Cosby himself had been sorrowfully obliged to leave his 'boy,' and drive alone in the gig to a meeting of his brethren, his honest red face looking like a signboard of sadness.

Nevertheless he had been as happy as a child the day before, when told by Luke and Bonnibel of their engagement. He had laughed and cried, dear old man, and blessed them both; only regretting that he might not claim other congratulations, since Luke had decided, and Bonnibel had doubtfully acquiesced, that it was best to have no gossip. Old Mr. Cosby, in his own excitement, wondered at the one for taking the matter so lightly, the other so gravely. Then, secretly sighing—supposed to himself—'those were lover's ways nowadays!' and tried to calm his evidently old-fashioned enthusiasm, or keep it private,—

> 'Till one by one the fresh-stirred memories,
> So bitter-sweet, flicker'd and died away.'

For he, too, remembered such a time when he had been engaged to Bonnibel's grandmother. Ah, dear!—

When the two wanderers by the sea returned to the manse in the gloaming, the light was low and golden; the minister's cow was lowing as she was driven in for milking, and the sparrows were noisily quarrelling and gathering among the sheltering ricks and stacks before the night. The engaged couple called out eagerly from the orchard to the new-comers, 'Where have you been all day? We are so glad to see you!'

'We have been hard at work shaking down the apples and gathering them, ever since you went away—and now I am so tired!' went on Bonnibel, throwing up her arms with a great yawn. 'I must go to the byre and have some fresh milk.'

It seemed as if these lovers, who were bidding good-bye with to-morrow's sunrise for a year, had been spending their last hours together in a most marvellously useful manner; but they seemed surely somewhat phlegmatic. Still, true, they had been used to each others' society since childhood. Luke was still busy searching in the grass, gathering a last barrow-load of apples; and Aileen, looking at him, doubtfully suggested that some one might offer to help him; then, when Nannie said 'I will,' herself readily went away with Bonnibel. Either she had seen a momentary dissatisfied glance on the latter's pretty face at the preference of Luke's possible wishes to those of their young hostess, or had her quick, subtle mind divined something, however slight, of Bonnibel's late jealousy? although certainly not a syllable thereof had ever been breathed by Nannie's loyal lips.

Luke looked after them both, but silently kept on picking up stray apples with diligence. Some few minutes passed, during which Nannie quietly helped him; then, straightening his back suddenly, he stopped, and meeting her eyes with his straightforward gaze, said, as if shaking off his late gravity with a determined effort, 'I am so glad you have stayed with me, Miss Nannie, for I have been wanting to have a talk with you before I go. … And first I must tell you, how thankful I am that you have been so much with Bonnibel this summer. The good such a friend must do—has done—my poor girl is immense … deepening, refining.' He broke off as if having said perhaps rather much, and began stooping in an apple-quest again; adding, however, in a full-toned voice, 'I trust you may be much with her next year also.'

Nannie, deftly spying out all the while more spoil than he did among the rank late grass, discreetly answered him; gratified by his good opinion. Then she took the opportunity to explain that she had heard from her old governess a few days back, who would shortly be installed in a modest home in London, with her brother, the professor. The poor lonely soul yearned for Nannie to join her there soon, she said.

'Ah! well,' said Luke, as if unable to urge any personal plea against a plan that seemed to her benefit. Then, after a pause, 'Still, if you could promise me that, so far as in you lies, you would watch over my cousin, as it were, even by letter? If I could ask you, would you be her friend through life?'

'That I will. It is a poor friendship that cannot last for a life,' said the girl earnestly; and, indeed, this was her creed, as also that one's friend sinning, possibly against one's self, was a sinner, but none the less to be beloved. She added, 'I do not make friends readily, like others; I can but *keep* them.'

Luke gave a comically rueful sigh, for he was always, in his stumbling, headlong, very kindliness of heart, offending a score of Calvinistic, time-stiffened Cosby kinsfolk, who, on the score of relationship, called themselves his friends, assuming all privileges, but conveniently overlooking any taxes attached to the title. They were folk mostly in trade, who looked sourly on him as a setter-forth of dangerously easy 'new' views, almost capable of preaching that hell-fire was not material, and none predestined to it. A scholar-like, eloquent, nay, even sometimes powerful and burning speaker they owned, but who would willingly welcome many to heaven at whom themselves, the elect, would put on their spectacles, and stare in offended surprise. And Luke went as far as they feared, and perhaps might yet go further—having dim hopes he dared not utter, unless in his own mind they grew to seem living truths, but then would surely do so like an honest man!—Luke for this cause was glad to go to America, and said, laughing, 'I wonder which is easier—to keep up good relations with your friends, or to be good friends with your relations?' Then, striding up and down the cabbage path, diving every now and then for a last russet pippin, he told Nan something of these private difficulties of his just mentioned, of his hopes and doubts. Confidence begets confidence. So Nannie took courage to speak to him for the first time of his engagement to Bonnibel, wishing him all happiness. Luke thanked her curtly with a sober air. It had always been a wish of the dear old minister's, he said. He himself had grown up with the thought; still, he would own, he had feared hitherto that his cousin might not yet have seen enough of the world to know her own wishes; but these, she had assured him, were now irrevocably fixed.

He did not say whether he also rested assured; but Nannie believed that, in spite of that passionate scene, he yet felt uncertain of the warm-hearted but wilful and too impressionable girl, whom they both, in spite of her faults, really loved. This had been cause enough surely for his unsettled manner at first, and even now for his gravity, if not depression. A shower came unawares on them as they talked, driving from behind the covert of the thick woods across the road.

'You are wetted now, and must be tired after your walk from the sea. How thoughtless I was!' exclaimed Luke, self-reproachfully, as Nannie hurried laughing into the kitchen. 'You had better dry yourself.'

There was a bright fire, beside which he placed her a chair. Old Mary was out in the byre milking, so they had her pleasant enough small day-den, with its red-tiled floor, thickly-furnished dresser, and ceiling hung with herbs, hams, and bacon-flitches, without its sour inhabitant's company. On the well-scoured table beside Nannie was a bowl of apples left for peeling, and on these she began to employ herself while enjoying the warmth and rest; while Luke, nearer the open door, with her leave, smoked one of his many daily pipes, and likewise seemed soothed by the pleasure of toil-earned repose, having been digging since early dawn to leave Uncle Joe's garden in good order. The white rain drove wildly across the yard outside, keeping all the others presumably storm-bound in byre or dairy; so these two talked on without selfishness of their own private small ambitions or vague hopes, as at other times and in more company they would not.

'I am glad you do not think of ceasing from your poet's work, even when you will have many other duties, and ease from the prick of necessity,' Luke suddenly began saying, impressively. 'Whoever has received the divine gift is bound to use it for human delight.'

'Ah, *if* one has received it! If I could only know myself to be a true poet, however small; therefore my labour rightful, however unnoticed.' And Nannie's tender eyes became fixed on Luke's truthfully expressive, rugged face, with a sudden earnestness, betraying close, hidden doubt. She had so long, so often, kept its pain quietly unspoken in her soul. This once she felt impelled to seek an honest opinion and know the truth. 'But we women are so intensely appreciative, so receptive, rather than original, I think, that the thoughts of others sinking into our minds and mused over become absorbed, and coloured by our own individuality till they seem our very own. Is not that useless reproduction if I give such to the world—even worse, a sham, and self-deceit? Ah, you men should be happy; you are creative. What woman was ever a great poet, musician, painter, compared with those of your sex?' And in her heart poor Nannie longed to be one of that godlike choir—as she herself once wrote,—

Who through all ages sing, because inspired.
... So, all genius,
Working with colours or in marble, brings
The divine, the beautiful, down to earth;
Though music still and thought spoken or sung,
As least material, are highest means.
She blessed the chosen souls who are
Priests to mankind to show some higher life,
Some gleams of heaven.

Then she went on, apologetically, 'Our half of human kind, perhaps, feels more keenly the utterances of others; but is it not pardonable to envy such a godlike power of giving the best gifts to our fellow-men?'

'Be content,' said Luke softly; 'contentment is also an excellence; and remember, if we fully believe in the teaching of the simple triad of words, "God is love!" women may—nay, I hold, do—possess more of the essence of that Divine spirit, and bless our poor human race with the highest and holiest of gifts.'

Nannie still peeled, and Luke puffed on in silence. She, with quick change of mind, bethought herself that he had not answered her troubled query—could not. Indeed, who could! until she did what she dreaded—appealed mutely to the world to judge whether her work was real or false? She musingly went on, 'Yet may one not be a true poet, even in reproduction? How often have I not made some small supposed discovery, and then been startled to come suddenly on what I thought my very own thought, or fresh-found grain of truth, found out or said by another, years ago. It comforted me, however, to read what Locke says on this very point: "That invention, or not invention" lieth "not in thinking first, or not first, but in borrowing or not borrowing your thoughts from another."'

'Yes, you,' said Luke—

'"Are pent,
Who sing to-day, by all the garner'd wealth
Of ages of past-song. We have no more
The world to choose from, who, where'er we turn,
Tread through old thoughts and fair."'

Then, being anxious to talk out her trouble, and help her from describing his point of view to see its true size better, he went on heartily, 'Any way, if it be a blame in a poet to sing what others have sung, you sin in good company. Why, Meleager, the Greek, chanted harmoniously of the sweet daffodils that he would weave with white violets for his sun-maiden, how many hundred years before Herrick? And Agathias prays his mistress to leave "a kiss within the cup," in almost the selfsame words of rare Ben Jonson's song.'

'And then, too,' uttered Nannie, half-consoled, how many English poets have borrowed from "the rich pages of Bocaccio." And Shakspeare, in "Measure for Measure," took from Whetstone what Whetstone took from Cintio. But then he changed dross to gold, when such as I would turn gold to dross.'

'Come, come,' Luke interposed; 'not so. Good metal will bear beating into many shapes; and it is well that truth should be said in different ways, to make it accepted by different minds. Many good thoughts might be lost to humankind, if others did not take them up and hand them on to fresh generations; just as in our material world all things change, but nothing perishes. The dead beast nourishes the grass of the field; the grass, living cattle; they, us—all a death-birth! Part of your finger-nail may have come from the highest peak of Slieve Donard yonder, which wind and rain have been crumbling through long centuries. And as to mind, men's thoughts of to-day are not much more different, I fancy, from the thoughts of mankind a thousand years ago, than our gilded cornfields are to those of Boaz; or, if new, mean not fresh elements of thought, but combinations unmade before.'

'Fresh combinations! Yes, as Tickell put it—

> '"For mortals ne'er shall know.
> More than contained of old the Christ-cross row."'

'Nevertheless,' cried Luke, knocking out the ashes from his pipe, 'I believe in the words, "*Let us go on unto perfection*," not only as we are doing, in studying what Kingsley calls "Nature's great green-book," of which all the phenomena equally existed around our forefathers thousands of years ago, but in the higher spiritual knowledge of which Paul more expressly spoke. I believe there are hitherto disregarded hints in our great Revealed Book also, as Butler says, which are yet to be investigated as natural knowledge is come at, with learning, liberty, patience—if ever the scheme of Scripture "comes to be understood before the *restitution of all things*."'

The rain had slackened its fury, and just now the rest entered with quick talking and laughter.

'Whom have we here, do you think?' cried Aileen, and pointed to old Rebecca smiling demurely in the midst of the group. 'The doctor brought her in his gig, and dropped her at the gate; and we waylaid her from the dairy, where I was skimming the cream—'

'And I was drinking it,' laughed greedy Bonnibel, not at all ashamed, her bright brown eyes looking boldly round to gain a smile from Luke.

'As I heard tell you were starting for America to-morrow, sir, I made free to come over and say good-bye,' the old woman explained, shaking hands with Luke Cosby heartily, in the independent spirit of her race and sect. She could only stay half an hour, till the doctor should call for her again; so Bonnibel graciously bid old Mary give her a cup of tea, and herself went singing to the parlour. Thence, she soon called to Luke to follow her.

Nannie solicitously went upstairs to search for a warm shawl to lend Rebecca, who was a little wet, and looked worn, the apple-face being sadly withered.

Left alone. Miss de Burgo, although knowing Rebecca's weakness for gossip, was somewhat surprised when the old woman promptly informed her she had 'heard tell' of the late engagement in the manse. 'Old Mary let it out to me. No, no! don't be feared; I'll not vex Mr. Luke, poor young man, by spreading it further. *Yon one* (Mary) is so bitter, she wanted to vex me with saying her young lady was engaged before my second one—that's you, dear. Oh, well; humph! my—I *hope* he'll have got a good bargain.' And Rebecca nodded her head significantly, as if she *could* say more.

'Why? What do you think of it?' asked Aileen, with quick, curious desire for her opinion. 'Is she not handsome enough?'

'Oh, *handsome* enough!' assented the old woman. 'Ay, a handsome, black-hearted poppy!'

'Oh, nurse; she is not as bad as that,' said Aileen, in a low voice, rather shocked; for such a word seemed treason to the young hostess under whose roof both were, and whose bread Rebecca was even now eating.

But the old nurse hastily set her right. 'Child, dear! you don't take me up rightly. All I mean is, that I never conceited much myself flowers with black hearts—poppies and tulips and an-enemies. They're gay and showy, like herself; but still, the gold-hearted flowers for me, if it was only a daisy! They're simpler, and sweet, and that's Miss Nannie, to my mind. Not that I'm evening* that other one to the likes of *her*.'

* evening = comparing

'But still you don't much care for Miss Hawthorn. Curious! ... You were the only one, I remember now, who never much did.'

'Never! though, *in her place*, I always took her for a fine lump of a girl—and that she is still,' decided Rebecca with dignity. 'No; I disapproved of your all colloguing* together when you were little ones, but I never had my own way. I said once to Mr. de Burgo, "Sir," said I, "it grieves me to the heart to have my children *adulterated* by going with that one from the manse." But there! ... my master only saw fit to laugh at me. He allowed her; and his word was a law of Nebuchadnezzar.'

Rebecca hazily thought she alluded hereby to the Medes and Persians; and she never spoke of the Redbay doctor as her master now, but just as 'the Doctor.'

Aileen thought herself a wicked sinner, because it did give her a certain pleasurable sensation to hear another person's dis-favourable opinion of Bonnibel, although she herself would never have uttered such.

Then the old woman had to go, and Luke came to wish her farewell. She grasped his hand, but lingered, and cleared her throat. 'Maybe,' she said, in an almost ashamed way, fixing her age-dimmed eyes on his face with a yearning look, more touching than she was aware of, and lowering her voice so that old Mary, her sharp-eared rival, should not hear, and be able afterwards to gibe at her weakness, 'maybe, Mr. Luke, if you were down anyway near Ohio, you might hear something of my husband, John Steenson.'

'If I can get there, I will inquire after him most assuredly, Mrs. Rebecca,' answered Luke, giving her a hearty parting hand-grip.

'The folk here give me Steenson, for shortness, but Stevenson

---

* colloguing = conspiring

was the right name,' said the poor soul, using the old formula they all knew since childhood.

And so, with the morrow's fresh, and, as yet, low-shining sun, Luke Cosby left home on his way to America.

PART III

'Nay surely, she is well enow
As her wont is to be, for, sooth to say,
She for herself is ever wont to pray,
And heedeth nothing other grief and wrong
And be thou sure, my son, that such live long
And lead sweet lives; but those who ever think
How he and she may fare, and still must shrink
From sweeping any foe from out the way,
These—living other people's lives, I say,
Besides their own and most of them forlorn—
May hap to find their lives of comfort shorn
And short enow—'

The Earthly Paradise.

CHAPTER 35

WHAT THE SUN AND MOON SEE

A YEAR, a whole year has passed by; it is once more late September.

Up in a poorly-furnished room, in a very quiet London street, Nannie White is sitting in the evening. The window is open to admit some cooler air, for it is close, oppressive here in the low-ceilinged attic—and even more so down in the dull, unfrequented street below, where the small, sadly-genteel brick houses are grimy-brown in hue, and before the doors that look never opened are small, sad-looking flower-plots; some of black earth without the flowers; others surrounded by little doll-paths, and in which the flower-plants seem neither striving to blow nor grow, but only to keep alive.

Nannie was grown pale and thin; hollow-cheeked, hollow-eyed. The greatest change these twelve circling months had brought her, was in this of her appearance; otherwise little. Since she had come here from the homely Northern-Irish manse, among its green if somewhat bare fields, to this sleeping, unlovely street, as of a forgotten city, here she had been existing—it seemed only half living.

A pile of manuscript lay on a writing-table; a pen had dropped from her fingers; but her heavy head leaned on her hand. 'If I could but get out, the evening air might revive me,' she was thinking; then, making an effort to rise, felt that she could not drag her weary limbs. 'No use!—I might faint if I tried it.'

She pushed the window down further and leaned out, hoping to cool her feverish head. The view was only over hundreds of roofs, of soot-topped chimneys, but still west-ward, so that at least she could feast her dawn-starved eyes now on some golden flames and rosy streamers from the evening court of the great God of Day. Being captious, poor girl, the air seemed smoke-tainted up there; came heavy to her, she imagined, full of the breaths and even thoughts of all the other living millions in great Babylon. She had not often felt it so, before; but to-day hers seemed unable to come and go from her in the overcharged atmosphere, as with their old freedom, when green-smiling mother earth meeting the senses refreshed them.

Seeing her face reflected in the glass on the poor dressing-table, cleanly but scantily draped with muslin, Nannie suddenly bent forward and examined it with a gaze of newly attentive surprise. 'I look as if I had not eaten enough lately—and that may be true,' she murmured; 'and as if I had not slept enough—that is true.'

For, in the spring of that year, Fräulein Schmidt had met with an awkward accident, having slipped on the stairs and hurt her knee. The hurt had aggravated and brought on a long and painful complaint, through which for weary months Nannie had faithfully nursed her night and day. And now the good governess was again about and well; but her devoted young nurse—was not what she had been.

'Weak! silly! I dare not fall ill to be burdensome to her, in turn. And she, too, who never could nurse any one,' thought the girl. (Alas! poor Nannie; and yet it must be so.)

'If only my mind could settle to my poem again; but it has got out of its old grooves; it has been too long idle.'

... Only a few hues, written with difficulty before the Fräulein's last relapse!—scarcely a few pages since spring, when this burden had been laid on the poor little household.

Sighing, Nannie sank on her chair again; then scanning with weary gaze the last unfinished sentence on a half-written page before her, tried to complete it. Tried—tried, with heavy head, that the spirit, though itself weak, longed to rouse. All in vain; useless! Her ideas seemed broken loose from control; some tired, some teasing; all in dulled confusion. If one poor thought came, the next condemned it. She could not think to any purpose, and yet could not stop thinking. At nights, of late, how she longed for dream-less slumber, for any repose—but for hours lay wakeful, while her ideas, like overwilling horses, rushed round and round as at a mill-wheel—grinding nothing! She could have cried in her mind-weakness and despair; could have exclaimed with poor Clough—

> '*Hang* this thinking, at last! What good is it? oh, and what evil!
> Oh, what mischief and pain! like a clock in a sick man's chamber,
> Ticking and ticking, and still through each covert of slumber pursuing.'

If only—our possible lives are all founded on ifs—if only she could have gone a week ago to the dear old Black Abbey manse, whither she had been invited. She had been strong enough to go then; the journey, fresh air, country scenes would have restored her; and good Fräulein Schmidt have been left free to visit a kind compatriot schoolmistress at Margate, who had offered her change of air.

But then, a few days ago, had come another letter. Bonnibel had again been asked by old Mr. de Burgo to go for a trip in his yacht, had gaily accepted, writing with glad sincerity that she knew her own dearest, truly-beloved friend would forgive this, and postpone coming to Ireland.

Bonnibel had advised her grandfather to go meanwhile for a holiday to some relations of the sour Cosby clan, whom he ought to visit; and some painting could be done most conveniently then to the manse windows. It had been a severe disappointment to poor town-tired Nannie; but no! she could blame no one. Of course, she was glad Bonnibel should leave the dull manse for a few days' more changeful scenes; and she had never written that she needed change herself. They had all acted aright, quite aright.

Still!—no one *knew* how home-sick she felt to see the dear Black Abbey woods! their great, rolling, green outlines now, doubtless, tinged warmly by the dying sun; and in their heart the dear old house, with every western window flaming fire-smitten, a beacon to the country round that the sun was bidding it good-night. Good-night, good-night, dear old Black Abbey!

The girl was home-sick, yearning for her childhood's home; mind-sick, body-sick. Ah! how happy she had been in those days of freedom in heart and brain, roving unchecked under the green and golden network made of sunlight and shadowing branches. She had not known how happy! had not loved it all enough.

> 'But now, but now—when one of all those days
> Like Lazarus' finger on my heart should be,
> Breaking the fiery fix'd eternity,
> But for one moment—'

That was how she thought.

Could she see once more—

> 'The brown boats standing in from sea,
> . . . . .
> Or in the beech-woods watch the screaming jay
> Shoot up betwixt the tall trunks, smooth and grey—'

There is no need to describe more of the sad thoughts of a sick, low-spirited, lonely girl; there is sadness enough in all our lives, which, remembered, will help imagination to fill up any blank. Let it only be added that most of Nannie's little money had already gone in buying necessaries for the sick-room, unknown to her invalid governess, who trusted their common household purse and cares to her; that the professor, a quiet, shambling old student, who spent all his days in the British Museum, investigating manuscripts in Sanskrit, and left his thoughts apparently there at night, was of no help, but rather an additional burden—and that want and winter were approaching.

Nannie laid down her head and cried bitterly.

Then she felt the ring touch her cheek that Hector had sent her after the first days of their separation, and looked at it. A sapphire, the colour of hope, set in pearls, symbolic of tears. Hope set in tears. She smiled at the conceit, and her brave spirit rose and overcame the body's weakness. *Sufficient—sufficient for the day was the evil thereof!* She would not weep faithlessly, and care and fret uselessly for the morrow, saying, 'What shall we eat, and what shall we drink, and wherewithal shall we be clothed?' She trusted the promise that the All-fatherly care, which had never yet forgotten her, knew she had 'need of these things.' She had done her best in works, and, though a poet, done it practically: now, she as practically strengthened herself with faith.

But how glad she felt, weary of mind though she was, *that Hector did not know* how ill things now were with her. Since many weeks she had heard nothing of him, as Aileen was gone abroad, and so could send but old news, and even that seldom. But poor Nannie wrote him daily such long letters—in imagination! telling to his kind ears all her troubles, and so—got rid of them in a manner very often. Where was he this evening? enjoying himself she fondly trusted, and, with the thought, blessed him.

. . . . .

At the same hour, that evening, where indeed is Hector? The sinking sun is sending a parting ruddy glance over the hills that stand round a still, Highland loch. Those hills, such ages old, are topped with great, brown, heather stretches where the grouse lie snug and safe from gun to-night; brooks travel clearly down their sides; the cattle linger knee-deep crossing the ford. And here the water is so limped that, looking over a boat's edge, you shall see clearly the pebbles deep, deep down; the strand is silver; the reeds seem to grow double.

A young man and maiden are sitting in a boat that they leave to drift idly with the current.

'How cool the water is. Put in your hand, too, as I am doing ... Yes, *do* try it, Mr. Hector,' says Bonnibel Hawthorn (for she is the maid), with pretty, engaging persistence, making the water ripple, sparkling through her own fingers, as she speaks. The young man lazily laughs, and leaning over a little does as he is bid; looking idly in the burning brown eyes that are always so ready to meet and gaze so long into his. The current imperceptibly drifts her hand towards—into that of Hector, where caught it is as idly held. The girl turns her head and looks over the boat's side, saying, doing nothing till after a few moments Hector releases his hold, speaking lightly:

'There! your fingers are quite frozen with the cold.'

Some hours later, the moon looks down on a yacht anchored in the sleeping lough, under the hill-shadows. It is so late that only two figures are to be descried on the deck, for the sailor on watch discreetly keeps aloof.

'It is very late ... I really must go now, Mr. Hector,' murmurs the girl's voice in a whisper, not to disturb old Mr. de Burgo down below; yet she makes no movement of departure.

'No, don't; stay a little while yet, Bonnibel. I hate turning in so early, and I hate my own company,' he answered, in like undertones.

'It is so cold, Please put my shawl round me; it has dropped; and I am too lazy to move. … No, wrong! Now, it has dropped again. You don't put it on rightly.'

'Or rather you don't *keep* it on; I suppose I shall have to do that for you,' and Hector, still in the same spirit of teasing idleness, put the offending shawl for the third time round the girl's shoulders, and kept his arm there in as idle a caress. Bonnibel upturned her face to him in the darkness in tender reproach, and, mindful of her schoolgirl traditions, just murmured, while her breath mingled with his, '*Don't!*'

It was a fair challenge, and—Hector was but human—it was accepted.

He kissed her . … .

What he meant, he did not know; or rather, he meant nothing. Whether Bonnibel meant anything, she hardly knew herself. Whether any thought of Luke flashed to her brain at that meeting of the lips—who can say? Only this she may have felt:

> 'Womankind more joy discovers,
> Making fools than keeping lovers.'

. . . . .

About that same time of evening, in the little house, in the quiet London street, Fräulein Schmidt, holding a candle, was bending over Nannie, who lay motionless—almost as if dead—on the outside of her bed. The old governess's parchment face had grown yellow in the past weeks, and was now livid with alarm.

'Child of my heart!' she was saying, 'I thought you were sleeping, and would not awaken you. But now—Ach! good heaven help us—I fear me, you were in a faint.'

Too weak to answer, the sick poet-girl feebly smiled once in the other's face, and stroked the wrinkled hand.

Then Nannie knew no more, but lay ill in low fever for many weeks, and would have died, but that Aileen de Burgo—her more than sister—came back from the coast of Normandy and nursed her day and night.

The sun and moon see many different scenes, verily! when they look down on earth.

CHAPTER 36

CHRISTMAS EVE

'News, news of the Trinity,
The snow in the street, and the wind on the door.
And Mary and Joseph from over the sea!
Minstrels and maids, stand forth on the floor'

It was Christmas Eve at Black Abbey manse, but yet there was neither snow nor wind. Rather, in the garden-strip between the house and the low road-wall, some pale roses bloomed; enough for quite a fair-sized nosegay the old minister had pleasurably thought to give to sick Miss Nannie to-morrow.

Outside, the roads were pleasantly hard with moderate frost; the village children's voices came audibly ringing across the bared fields; the sunset seen beyond the stack-yard was all of a soft yellow, under a tenderly grey sky.

Just such a day as poor Miss Nannie would have enjoyed, but she is lying very quiet inside the parlour on the horse-hair sofa. Old Joseph Cosby, thus thinking to himself, as he drove in his ancient gig, sighed and shook his reverend head. But the brisk air was pleasant; the old mare's hoofs rang quite gaily, though unhastened; and, in another few moments, the old minister astonished himself by a sudden chuckle and a grin illumining the whole ruddy disc of his face, since all day his mind had been oscillating between mild regret for Nannie's low health, and secret mirth on his own private account. In spite of his reiterated efforts to think sympathetically only of the weak state of his dear guest, and be of a sorrowful countenance—this last secret amusement yet always reingrossed the old man's mind, and tickled his fancy into continual outbursts of such glee, that he peered across the bare hedges with quite an ashamed air, lest any chance labourer might have overheard him.

'Ha, ha! Oh dear, the fun of it!' he laughed to himself, wiping his eyes, since the air was sharp, with his red handkerchief. 'Not either of them to guess a single thing; except, indeed, that my Bonnibel—ah, the clever one! was so persistent to come and drive with me—and now she thinks because I was hard-hearted, that it must be a Christmas present for herself I am off to get. And so it is, my dearie.'

Meanwhile, as he supposed, Nannie White lay very still in the parlour, having only come downstairs late that afternoon. Her face showed signs of a long and severe illness since last September. More than one illness, indeed; since, after recovering with difficulty from the weary typhoid fever which had first attacked her, and being taken by Aileen and her eccentric aunt for a change to their own lodgings, she had fallen an easy prey to another form of sickness—brought on by the first—and gave them through the dreary November month much anxiety. The day before this, however, she had been able to cross from England, on the good minister's pressing invitation. She felt already the better for the change, although not allowed by her friends to exert herself as yet. What rest it was! Just to lie and look out at the Black Abbey wall and woods across the road. Such utter blessed rest to one who felt as if completely tired out—exhausted with the preceding months! The little manse had thus, for the second time, become a haven of refuge to her.

'Let me give you another cushion, dear. … Are you *sure* there is not something you would like for tea; if you would only just think about it, and then tell me?' Bella Hawthorn had said, repeatedly, with over-sweet, though real solicitude, ever since her guest came into the parlour. Nannie blamed herself for being worried, at last, by these affectionate repetitions, feeling smothered in feather-beds of kindness; and for wishing that her care-taker would devise any obnoxious dish for tea, rather than bring the necessity for that meal before her invalid mind, depriving her, beforehand, of appetite. She conquered herself, and turned her eyes—her face seemed all eyes now—with a faint but sweet smile on the handsome, healthy 'Dowsabel' (not 'tidied-up' this day), who was fussing with a new-humbled lovingness, a restless eagerness to do something for her friend—anything, apparently, rather than be still.

'Come and sit down, you good, uneasy spirit. I don't care what I eat, I only feel hungry for a long talk with you. You have so much to tell me, remember. Since last year and a half, you have been so gay, so gad-about, so admired, compared with your old country-mouse life. And then' (with a faint blush) 'you have seen so much of Hector. Yesterday you would tell me nothing.'

'The doctor gave orders you were to be kept quiet,' replied Bonnibel, with some secret discomposure. (After all, *what harm had she done?*—young men will be young men! And if even poor dear Nannie knew anything of it, she need not be so silly as to be vexed about a little harmless nonsense between Mr. Hector and her true friend. But still—Bonnibel tried to escape from the net she had woven round herself by putting forth a plea of friendly concern.) 'Are you sure that talking will not excite you too much to-day, even?'

'Quite sure; a thousand thanks! … First, you were all September on board the yacht with him—'

'No; he was not on board *all* the month. It was several days less.'

'Thanks, for telling me so exactly. And then, when you went down to stay with Mrs. Heavyside, lately—for three weeks, was it not?—how long was he there, too?'

'Oh, bless me! Let me think! … Not all the time; I am sure. A good part of it. … Not very long. You see, you poor thing,' cried Bonnibel, reddening at her short-comings, and extricating herself with an embarrassed laugh, 'I did not think so much of his coming and going as you would. … There were—other gentlemen there, too.'

'Ah, yes! It was nothing to you, of course,' murmured Nannie, gazing—but with eyes hungering for news—through the narrow window at the wintry woods yonder, and trying to conceal disappointment at her friend's deadening want of interest. 'Well, why should I grumble at such a common thing as that you had, and did not care for, what I should have given so much to have?' … And silently she said to herself:

> 'What makes thee struggle and rave?
>   Why are men ill at ease?
> 'Tis that the lot they have
>   Fails their own will to please.'

Hector's regiment had been moved to Ireland, and was now quartered in a Midland county town, among bogs, as Bonnibel described it, a few miles from the home of the Heavysides, with whom the formerly unknown minister's granddaughter had actually been invited to stay; 'changed times for her!' as old Rebecca remarked, with a sarcasm that may have done herself good, and did Bonnibel no harm.

'Now, don't get low, dear, or I shall have to shake you into good spirits. Come, now! I mean to recount you every little tittle I can about your Mr. Hector,' cried Bonnibel, assuming an air of light banter, yet willingness to fulfil her offer. 'Well, first, he used to be out all day shooting with Captain Heavyside, and that dear *delightful* Colonel Fitzadam; so, of course, I can't tell you much about what he did *then*. In the evenings they were always too tired to come into the drawing-room, and Captain Heavyside always fell asleep and snored; so the others played billiards and smoked, and we used to go in and watch them. They only smoked a little dear, you know; it was quite nice and quiet, I assure you.' (Bonnibel having, as a simple, country nymph, been rather surprised at the freedom and easiness of behaviour in her friend's household, was eager to assure Nannie, who she knew was as unsophisticated as herself, that, as to smoking, anyhow, Grandisonian manners were out of fashion.) 'Well, we did go out sometimes to walk with them while they shot, and lunch with them; but Mrs. Heavyside didn't always. She said it would look so bad to see us always trotting after the gentlemen; and so it would,' added Bonnibel, pursing up her rosy lips with quite a pious air. 'Why are you laughing to yourself?'

'Only,' said Nannie, with quiet humour, 'that I don't think either of you would carry such stern discipline to a foolish extent.'

'You darling poetess!' laughed Bonnibel, vastly amused, and with a sudden air of reassured joyousness. 'Now that is so like what I always say of you, when Mrs. Heavyside calls you a prude. Not a bit, I say; it is only that she has a nice quiet nature herself; but she never maligns us poor souls who were made differently, and *must* have a little fun in life!'

Nannie checked the quick, satirical repartee that leapt to her lips on the 'must' of some in life, and the placidity attributed to those who with the same flesh and blood, and human passions, tell themselves they 'must NOT;' but she could not check the slightly scornful light of her eyes accompanying the question, 'And pray, what else does Mrs. Heavyside accuse me of, when you both talk me over?'

'Oh, well, she says you are so dreadfully clever. And I always say, "Well, she is—but still, she is really very nice, too; if you only knew her as well as I do." Indeed, dear, she never said anything worse. You don't suppose I would allow her.'

As the speaker drew herself up with an air of strict righteous dealing and aggrieved feeling, Nannie again laughed within herself heartily. There was no good in being angry; and there was much good she believed in laughing in life.

'Yes, I say; you are not a bit prim really, you patient dear. Isn't it too silly to be prim when life is so short, as Colonel Fitzadam says,' exclaimed Miss Hawthorn, gaily pursuing her fresh track, escaping with secret relief from the subject of young De Burgo, and entering into a flowing description of the gallant Fitzadam's charms. In vain! She was gently reminded, at her first pause, of the principal object of their conversation.

Unhappy flirt! Her inner perplexity was laughable but almost pitiable. For, as she said to herself, 'the worst of it was,' she did love Nannie sincerely; revered her as a woman whose mind daily lived on such far heights as made Bonnibel feel a shivering disembodied spirit only to imagine.

She thought she

'Could not breathe in that fine air.'

And now further evasion was not to be dared under the glance of those clear though truthful eyes, whose very lovingness of gaze, and pure grey depths of tenderness frightened the conscious culprit, as, says Milton, 'extreme frost *burns*! What would that inexperienced heart of but one love, that nunlike mind as regarded earthlier matters than those belonging to the spiritual life of poetry and high-souled imagination in which hers had grown up apart, think—if Nannie knew that the friend in whom she put all faith had beguiled her lover! though into never so slight a flirtation; tried to thieve some of his love, though, only such a little piece—and for fun!'

Miss Hawthorn did not like to consider this; the question had verily loomed unpleasantly over her before, but always been repulsed: 'Time enough to bother about things when one *must!*

Now she *must*; and could have cried over the ridiculous

embarrassment of it all, but have laughed too, and felt almost injured.

After all, she was only what?—a pretty little sinner! quite shame-stricken about some really very tiny offences, thereby proving how good her heart was and the affection of her friendship.

(Miss Bonnibel liked calling herself little, though such a voluptuously proportioned 'brown Buxoma;' her pet sins seemed likewise thereby diminished.)

Care for Mr. Hector? Not a fig! Nor he for her, she lightly supposed, except that—well!—when she had tried her best to make him do so, he had behaved as a man might, a young man—and no St. Kevin.

So now, unwillingly, yet not daring to delay longer, Bonnibel plunged into a flood of speech about Hector; yet fluency without body; words, not spirit. At first, poor love-starved Nannie listened with avidity, eking out bare outlines with fond imagination, investing the insignificant details, which her friend could only apparently give, with meaning. Then, as hope deferred maketh the heart sick, Nannie grew secretly disappointed, miserable, absolutely faint Bonnibel's pleasant gurgling tones sounded to her no better than 'sounding brass.' And at last, the poor soul, unable to restrain herself, cried out, almost with passion, 'But did he say *nothing* more—send no message ever to me?'

Bella Hawthorn reddened.

'My poor dear, remember from the first you never would give me any very sentimental messages to him; so it was not likely a man would make love through me. I did ask him once—last September—and he said he hated men who, when in love, talked drivel to the world.'

'True, true. But still you might surely both have spoken of me.'

'So we did. Especially when first I went on board,' cried

Bonnibel eagerly. 'Then—don't you know—we had neither of us anything new to say, and I hadn't seen you for ages; and when I went to stay with Mrs. Heavyside, you had been so ill, you hadn't written me news for ever so long.'

'Yes ... yes. ... But did Hector say nothing of my illness?' asked Nannie slowly, two red spots burning in her white cheeks.

'Indeed, he did. He said that he had never known of it till you were better, for his sister would not distress him, knowing he might not go to you. And twice he said earnestly, when something caused you to be mentioned, that he was very thankful you were well again. I really think,' and Bonnibel glanced with compunction but sincerity at her friend, 'that he did feel too much about that to speak much, don't you know.'

'Yes; Hector is frank and talkative enough about his horses and his dogs; but he does not care to talk gabble, as he calls it, about what touches him more nearly. ... I like him all the better for it ... I am too impatient.'

Something in the real, great patience of the speaker's low voice touched Bonnibel unusually.

'How fond of him you are, to be sure! ... Well, he ought to be very happy, and you deserve to be so,' she exclaimed in a curious, subdued tone; humiliated in her heart, inclined to be regretful. Yet again asking herself with a sort of soft impudence, that she called 'innocence,' 'What harm have I really done? What nonsense to feel guilty about such little trifles! I am too conscientious!—that is it'

'Are not you just as fond of your cousin?' said Nannie, with brighter playfulness, in answer, putting out her weak hand to caress that of her friend. Bonnibel soon withdrew hers from the loving touch softly, and then forced an apologizing, self-ridiculing laugh.

'I! ... Oh dear no, I never could break my heart about any man, as you would. Of course, he is very fond of me, dear old

Luke; not that I deserve it. He is a goose! … all men are, I think, where a pretty face is concerned.'

Then she rose with the new, soft-footed, low-voiced restlessness that seemed quite strange to the big, healthy girl herself, fearing it was more apparent than in truth it was to others. She felt soul-disquiet, yet dared not utter it; must meet her friend's loving smile and yet not blush. It seemed to her as if she must go softly with the penitent all the days of her life. She turned to the window.

'What a delightful afternoon it is! It is really not a bit cold (for I was out all the morning), and there is just enough frost to make the air nice. *Do* you think, dear, it would do you any harm just to come out for ever so little a walk? It seems such a sin to stay in on such a day.'

'It is indeed a sin for you,' answered Nannie, smiling, but resisting the honeyed persuasion of tone, feeling truly too weak to stir. 'You must go out, Bonnibel.'

She would take no denial; so by-and-by her friend reappeared, warmly wrapped, to say good-bye with many expressions of regret, but some secret relief.

'Oh,' observed Bonnibel lightly, turning back a moment, 'did you hear, by the way, that Mr. de Burgo they say came home yesterday evening? Old Mary told me; is it true, I wonder?'

'He often used to have business here at Christmas. It is to be hoped he won't stay long, anyway,' replied Nannie, in a very tired accent; and saw smiling, rosy-cheeked Bonnibel gaily depart down the high road, an incarnation, it seemed to the invalid behind, of good luck, good looks, and good health and spirits—all herself had not!

Then the sick girl turned her face to the wall and cried a little. For she had been so hungering for some news of Hector; she had asked Bonnibel for bread, who had given her a stone.

But, outside, Bonnibel was gaily hastening with ringing

footsteps on the frosty road in the crisp keen air of that most delightful late afternoon. She could have danced, her heart was so relieved.

'You got well out of that scrape, my dear,' she thought joyfully to herself, with a triumphant chuckle; then, solemnly added, shaking her head, 'but you must never, never get into such another. Or, at least—leave your friends' goods alone, you naughty girl. Oh:

> '"What a tangled web we weave,
> When first we practise to deceive!"

I wish that old thing had never been written; it rhymes so in my brain. Heigho!'

Thinking more quietly then, the culprit quite pitied herself, remembering the terrible load her conscience had borne since Nannie had come to the manse—when she had imagined beforehand the late interview with her friend as so much more difficult, even dreadful, than it had been. Now it was happily over; and by those two days of black penance and fear her treason seemed fully atoned for.

'After all, it is hard to be boxed up for days in the same yacht or country-house with a man who you know would talk nonsense fast enough about another girl if one were to draw him out—and not like better to hear a little nonsense on one's own account. Still, poor dear, she is as poor as myself, and not so pretty; and she has his heart, though I might turn his head. … Bah! he is not half such a man as good old Luke, whom I can trust anywhere. … Luke, dear, you had better come and look after me; for, if I'm left to myself, I'm a perfect naughty child. I can't help it. As Dr. Watts says, "it is my nature to."'

Whereupon, with a look of mischief sparkling in her bright brown eyes, the comely maid glanced at the Black Abbey gate near—the quiet farm-gate among wintry trees, which one might enter unquestioned, unperceived; hesitated—then, with a little self-reliant laugh, went through.

CHAPTER 37

A STRANGE CHRISTMAS GIFT

THE mellow afternoon clearness had faded into brown twilight; out of doors the frost grew crisper and keener; indoors it was almost dark. Nannie White had fallen asleep some little time ago, being left alone, and still so weak that sleep seemed almost as natural a state of existence to her as waking, when Old Mary cautiously introduced the stout figure of an old woman into the parlour. This person approached Nannie with caution—bent over her lovingly—and seeing her asleep, with a tear still undried on the now sharper outline of her pale cheek, could no longer restrain an impulse of affection, and hastily kissed her.

'Rebecca!' cried out the late sleeper, roused from her light slumber by the touch, and slowly opening her bewildered eyes.

'Och, yes, it's me, my lamb! my own child!' ejaculated her old nurse, between laughing and crying.

To her foster-child's gladly welcoming questions, she explained that the worthy Redbay doctor (in whose service she still was), having known Nannie since a child, when he dosed her with 'salts and senna,' and hearing from the Black Abbey minister of the weak state of the invalid after travelling, declared the best medicine for Miss White would be the loan for a few days of her old nurse's care, with home air.

'So he and the minister just made up between them, to bring me over for a little surprise to ye.'

'But Bonnibel—Miss Hawthorn. Does she know? and will it not be any additional trouble to her?' asked Nannie, with most grateful eyes.

'Och, is it Miss Bella? She never would mind if the company

was tripping up each other's heels,' cried Old Mary jocularly, her usually so acrid tone having quite a flavour of pleasant bitters to-day. For, in her way, she too was fond of Nannie. 'Mrs. Rebecca has come any way; and—I hope she may do ye good.'

With which equivocal wish her small daily allowance of good humour having been, maybe, squandered in her previous sentence. Old Mary left them together. They were two happy hearts she left behind in the parlour, two that over-flowed with eager questionings upon their mutual welfare, and with a babble of confidences. For, it must always be remembered that Rebecca's was the nearest approach to parental solicitude that Nannie White had ever known.

How that fond sympathy now seemed to brighten all her troubles, as sunlight beautifies the gloomiest objects on earth! how the well-known northern accent warmed her chill heart again! She forgot, poor young soul, as one happy moment will often make each one of us forget, thank God! the whole thronging crowd of fears, doubts, and pangs that during the past painful year and a half her heart had silently endured, forgot—

'The thousand torments of divided love—
Children of absence and of loving well.'

Both were so engrossed that they never heard the gig-wheels stop in the yard. So the minister startled them when he slily opened the door, and stood chuckling on the threshold in the darkness, beyond reach of the illumining pleasant fire-glow.

'Bonnibel, my dear! … What! is she gone out—and not come home yet?' The old man's tone changed from one of great glee to as great disappointment. Then recovering himself, however, he rubbed his hands, and cried with returning cheerfulness, 'Well! well! well! … it can't be helped. But no matter; we'll play all the better a trick upon her, now—ha, ha! Miss Nannie, my dear, let me introduce a visitor from America.' And as Mr. Cosby, so saying, stepped aside, he burst out into a perfect grand explosion of laughing and delight; all the fountains of fun and gladness in the old man's soul being apparently broken up, and their overflow fairly carrying away his senses. From behind him now, came quietly forward, into the radius of the flickering firelight, a large, gaunt man.

'Mr. Luke!' cried out Nannie eagerly.

'Och! it's himself,' echoed Rebecca from behind, with varying intonations of surprise and heartfelt pleasure from both.

'Oh, ay; it's himself. No one else; just himself,' exclaimed the old minister, holding his sides with laughing, rubbing his-face with his handkerchief, and dancing round them on tiptoe, quite swelling like a pouter pigeon, as Luke Cosby, with all his old heartiness, but with considerate gentleness, was greeting Nannie, and inquiring as to her health.

'I never thought you could have been so deceptive,' said Nannie, after a few minutes' talk with Luke, turning to address her host with lively reproach.

"Deed, no more did I myself, Miss Nannie. But you see we never know what we can do till we try,' said the good man, with a slily excusing air; and then, after a few dying chuckles of ecstacy, he settled down into his usual state of cheerful serenity.

Rebecca, who hitherto had been so blocked up in the background behind Nannie's sofa by the group that she could not make her way out of the room, now came forward to do so; but at the same time respectfully offered to shake hands with Luke Cosby, bidding him heartily welcome home.

Becoming now first aware of her presence, the younger minister seemed strangely and suddenly taken aback; and with quite an embarrassed manner he ejaculated, 'Mrs. Steenson! I did not expect to see you here to-night,' and then shook hands in a very grave, though friendly way, with her.

'Why, no, no; I hardly thought she could have got leave to have come before to-morrow morning,' murmured the old minister, with as grave and very meaning inflection of voice; adding aloud cordially, 'But Mrs. Rebecca knows she is always welcome here; always has friends here, in her trouble as well as in her good days, in whatever affliction the Lord may send her to turn to her own blessing—I hope she knows that.'

'Thank you, sir; thank you, Mr. Cosby,' answered the old woman with a slightly puzzled look at this address, but curtseying her thanks in a series of undulations, as she moved towards the door—for Rebecca's manners were of the good old school, and at times, when she gave them an extra rub, quite superlative. But when the door-handle was in her grasp, she lingered—hesitated—half made a movement to go out, half drew back—then cleared her throat, and murmured, almost ashamed, 'Ye didn't, Mr. Luke, dear, I suppose ye didn't … ye didn't hear no word of my husband out in Ohio—John Steenson?'

There came no answer to her question. Luke's face was hidden in shadow; but Nannie could see him rubbing the thinning hair on his high forehead with such a suppressed vehemence that a strange foreboding seized her. Old Mr. Cosby, too, had turned away to the fire-place, in a manner she thought agitated.

Rebecca stood awaiting an answer. The silence still continued.

Then Luke made some inarticulate sounds in a kindly tone; but they were only interjections, since each time he stopped himself again, as if not knowing what to say. Many and many a pitying negative to this question Rebecca had heard in her past life; many and many a roughly-uttered, if kindly meant, piece of advice to give up all thoughts of the man who had so long deserted her, and who had been a bad husband at the best of times. Since many a long day, indeed, she expected to hear nothing else!—but what meant this? The silence, the significant constraint, alarmed the old woman; then, as Luke, unable to find a better means in his sudden surprise, turned and kindly patted her shoulder as if to prepare her for something, the poor old soul's knees trembled; her heart gave some great beats, and seemed then to go all wrong. With a choking voice she exclaimed, 'Och! ye *have* heard!—' and sank down into a chair, unable to stand. Nannie sprang to her side in consolation; Luke, while gently affirming it was indeed so, earnestly bid her take courage; the old minister, behind, kept murmuring, 'Oh, dear, dear!—but this is very sad!' while repeatedly pulling out his handkerchief and tenderly mopping his face, as if thereby vaguely trying to express his feelings.

'Mr. Luke, dear, ye may tell me now. I can bear it! The worst of it was over years ago,' gasped Rebecca. 'I suppose he's—he's took up with another woman?'

'No, no! Nothing of the sort,' eagerly but solemnly interposed Luke. 'His last messages—his last words—were full of kindness to you; for, my poor Mrs. Steenson, you will go to him, but he may not return to you.'

When the old nurse heard that, she took up the apron she always wore, and throwing it over her head, rocked herself to and fro, wailing low. The rest stood by, and looked on in quiet sympathy; almost curious wonder, too, as at any strange human spectacle. Did Rebecca forget, then, her ill-treatment during the short time of her married life with this man; her long desertion, and old age now? Did she imagine herself again the young woman of past years, regretting the husband of her youth; not seeing, as they did, how near she was to over-stepping that boundary beyond which human sorrows, something seems to whisper to our souls, do not pass? Or had she clung to the improbable idea of meeting him face to face in life as to a last earthly hope?

As Rebecca gradually became quieter, comforted mostly by Nannie's soothing and affectionate ministrations, Luke gently told her the outlines of his story. Indeed, nothing less would, naturally, now have satisfied her.

It seemed that he had gone out of his way to visit Ohio, purposely to gratify the longing wish of his good old friend, who seemed so convinced that her husband was living somewhere thereabouts. (Rebecca, with an effort, raised her voice sufficiently to bless him for that.) Luke continued that, to his astonishment, he had indeed discovered there, after some search, a John Stevenson, answering in every way to Rebecca's description; except that this was a man who had made so much money in business, and was still working on so steadily in his old age, that it seemed improbable he could be the poor nurse's runaway husband. On visiting him, however, and venturing some inquiries, the old man had made no attempt to disguise his identity; rather, he seemed morosely proud of the fact that he had thriven so well far from his native land and kin. It was difficult for Luke to guess how the news that his wife was still living, and always anxious for news of him, affected him. Rebecca inquired anxiously on this point; but all Luke Cosby could say was, that her husband's temper, if probably less violent by course of age, was all the more sullen and reserved; added to this, his health seemed failing, and his mind somewhat enfeebled. He listened without surprise—in utter silence—to the story Luke put before him with its touching details; only at the end he grimly observed, that his wife was always a good soul—one of the best, after all, he had ever known. When, however, Luke attempted to persuade him to make her some allowance now out of his fortune in her ageing years, he became at once obstinate and gloomily sullen, flatly declared that he did not need to be dictated to on a matter about which he had already made up his mind, and refused to hear another word upon the subject. Utterly disheartened, Luke was obliged to take leave of him; and, indeed, to take his departure from the town also immediately, in order to fulfil his lecturing engagements elsewhere. Hoping, however, to have one more chance of returning thither before finally leaving the States, he deferred writing to Rebecca, in the hope of then being able to send her better news. To Luke Cosby's surprise, however, a short while ago, and just when he was thinking over the possibility of again going to Ohio before returning to Ireland, he received a dying summons from Steenson, whom he had, apparently against the latter's inclination, furnished with his address. This message said that the old trader, finding himself at the point of death—and having long since determined to leave all he possessed to his wife in reparation for having deserted her—entreated Cosby, to come and receive his parting explanations as to his affairs, in order that there might be no hitch in the business. Luke obeyed the call at once, arriving in time to receive all the necessary directions from the old man, and a dying message to Rebecca. 'Tell her, she was as good a soul as ever I knew after all; tell her that.'

After a while of silence—when Rebecca's grief seemed to have given place to a dull vacancy, after the manner of her age—Luke gently said, thinking to rouse her, and also because it was right she should know the strangely different circumstances in which she would now find herself—'He has left you an ample fortune, Mrs. Steenson; your husband's prosperity, considering what he started from, was wonderful.'

Rebecca received this intelligence quite dully, as regarded herself; but then her thoughts seeming to become fixed on the dead man, replied with pride, 'Oh, ay! I can well believe it. John Stevenson, mind ye, was never a man to be sneezed at! for all folks used to be always casting up his unkind ways to me.'

'But, do you understand that you will be a rich woman, now—that you need never want any more; that you are rich?' repeated Luke, still more gently; hoping to make the sense of comfort and independence enter into the old nurse's mind, replacing the grief that surely, after more than half a lifetime of desertion and servitude, could hardly be poignant.

'Rich! what is rich? what d'ye mean by rich?' said Rebecca, with a puzzled air; as if riches were altogether a matter of comparison to her—which indeed is a truth.

'I mean that you need never go out among strangers again; that you will never want for anything money can get you. You are as rich now as any lady in the land—what even your old master, Mr. de Burgo, would call rich.'

'Ochone! My head is all of a bummle. Master Luke, dear! I thank ye most kindly for all you are saying; but still, if I could be my lone for a wee while, to think it all over' said the poor old woman, with bewilderment, beginning to sob again.

And Nannie gently led her away.

The latter returned soon to the parlour, since even her presence could not then be well borne by the aged mourner, who felt it was better to be alone with her God. She found Luke and the old minister already discussing the matter with a cheerful air; and marvelled at the greater practicalness of men above women; she herself feeling still deeply impressed with the sight of her old nurse's grief.

'There could hardly have been a greater blessing for Nurse Steenson,' said Luke, 'since, if you think of it, even if I could have procured her a reconciliation with old John Stevenson, she could never, at her age, have survived such a transplantation as that of going to America—of such a different income, and a husband who after the change of years would be a stranger to her. And neither would she have believed herself happy apart from him, her heart's yearning having survived so long. Death solves many a difficulty.'

Nannie acknowledged it was all true—that even Rebecca's sorrow might be rather one of sentiment than reality. Still, she had an idea that some grief, or want, however slight or imagined, seems necessary to what we call earthly happiness, since were the cup filled to the brim it would kill. Whether she was right or not as to other organizations than her own, it seemed likely enough now that Rebecca, having no other equipoise to her sense of riches and comfort, would lament her dead husband, as she had regretted him living.

The old minister had now bustled into the dark porch, where he peered out anxiously, watching for Bonnibel's return; occasionally taking little runs down the garden-plot to the wicket to listen; then more slowly returning, unmindful of the cold and the starlight, half disappointed, yet still somewhat elated.

'But what is this I see of you in the English papers. Miss Nannie? said Luke, eagerly. 'Your great work—that one I saw begun—has not yet appeared; but this tiny volume of poems that has just come out has taken the world by storm, has stolen the heart of the public. So little, yet such a success! I congratulate you—with all my heart I congratulate you.'

Poor Nannie flushed crimson in the semi-darkness, and answered with unsteady voice: 'I never meant to publish them. They were written in—in the June of the summer before last; and I never meant them to be seen by any other eyes than my own.'

'Ah! said Luke, drawing in his breath.

(That was the June of her engagement to Hector; and these songs were a mere few but passionate rhymes, or tenderly-sweet love-sonnets, each with a living fire burning in its heart; songs so true, singing of love, youth, spring—the three harmonies in life—that no wonder the great worlds that has silently felt love and youth too, should take up the words and echo them.) The girl went on in haste.

'No; I did not think I could have borne that others, the cold outside public that I fear so much, and know so little of, should see them. But it was last spring—and the Fräulein fell ill, and we ... were badly off—so I sent first one to a magazine. It seemed as if I was sending a piece out of my heart! Then she grew worse, and the little money I had got for that was gone, so I sent another; and then another. Oh, Mr. Luke, it was like a traveller flinging one by one his loaves to the wolves that are on his sleigh-track; and still they came on, poverty, sickness, even *hunger*'—(her voice dropped). 'At the last, when I was recovering from my own illness, but still so weak that I could not be consulted on the matter, Aileen—who is a sister to me, as you know—collected them together, and sent them to be published of her own accord. I was so utterly astonished when I grew a little better, and she brought me the reviews and the book, exulting over them, that I could hardly believe my senses. Only I fear that—that it may not please others as it does her; and so my triumph, as you call it, is more pain than pleasure.'

'Trammelled!' thought Luke; but said aloud, 'Do you remember a simile in some modern poet I have read, that as only a storm brings the sea-shells and weedy treasures of the deep to shore, so is it with the poet' thoughts? Do not be afraid; all those who really love you will be only glad that you should show the best that is in you, and so fulfil the destiny that is surely appointed to each one of us, whether brickmaker or ruler. I told you of your first little songs that you sang well because you felt; I say the same now. As Poe wrote:

> '"None sing so wildly well
> As the angel Israfel."

And why? Because his—

> '"Heartstrings are a lute."'

At that instant the old minister hurried in on tiptoe, whispering, with his finger on his lip, 'Hush, hush! Bonnibel is coming! Luke, my dear boy, get back a little more into the dark. Oh my! but this will be a glad surprise!' and he rubbed his hands. Nannie rose, and would have slipped quietly and quickly out, but that Luke Cosby exclaimed, in a tone of such genuine surprise, 'Why are you going away? You are surely not going just when she is coming? Oh, stay!'

So Nannie stayed a moment. In a few seconds, Bonnibel, being a little breathless, it seemed, as if she had been running, and bringing in with her some of the keen outer air, stood framed in the doorway.

'Well, grandad, so you are back,' she carelessly said, untying her hat-strings. 'Oh, who do you think I should meet this evening but old Mr. de Burgo; and he was so over-civil that he kept me out too late. Why are you laughing so to yourself? … Gracious! what!—who is that sitting in the corner?' And then, with betraying ejaculations on the old minister's part, who could no longer rest himself, and an outcry and quick reproachful exclamations from Bonnibel, Luke was discovered, and came forward and embraced his cousin with all his old brotherly affection for her, yet with gravity subduing his gladness to be once more with those he loved, and under the dear old manse-roof; as was surely natural for a man of his age and thoughtfulness, and one thankful that in the past year they had all been kept alive to meet together once again. What seemed less natural to Nannie was Bonnibel's own sudden quietness. That the girl was glad, you could see, now the candles were lit, by the excited and eager glow on her cheeks, and although her eyelids were lowered, by the happy light shining in her brown eyes; but a hush seemed fallen upon her. She looked at Luke certainly, and looked again, but it was by stealth; she seemed constrained, and spoke very low and quietly, at least, for her. Seeing that, Nannie now did slip away, and was not opposed certainly by Bonnibel. Rather the girl reminded her grandfather of certain household changes which must now be made on Luke's arrival, and with a caress bade him go and see after these things himself, since he had already had so much more of Luke's company than she had. And Nannie, on leaving the room, heard her remark in a satisfied undertone to her cousin, as he soberly, with a strange smile, drew up to the fire at her bidding, 'Ah! now this is pleasant; now we can be for a little while by ourselves.'

Going back to her old nurse, Nannie found her sitting still as she had left her—too still. The stout-figure was terribly bowed, the withered face—ah! it had not been withered before she went into strange service—wet with the dull-flowing rheum of old age. Kneeling softly down beside her, the girl put her arms about her neck.

'Oh my dear, my own dear! is it you? I bless God for the comfort you have been to me, since your mother left you with me in this weary world,' said the old woman, waking from her lethargy. 'Well, it's an ill wind blows nobody luck, they say; and so I bless him, too, that now no living soul dare stop your wedding. No, not Mr. de Burgo himself; Mr. Luke said it, that even he would call you rich! … Ah! dear, if I've lost my old husband, it will get you your young one, so why need I be crying?'

'Nurse, nurse! What do you mean? It is not I to whom all this fortune is left; it is to you.'

'Child, I know that. But who else on earth would I leave it to? and I'm not long for this world. Every penny of it shall be yours. … Oh, darling, you'll be rich, and Mr. Hector may be proud of getting ye.'

Downstairs, at the same moment, Bonnibel was saying to her cousin, with deep and interested amazement, 'It is the most extraordinary story I ever heard. But is it *much* money, Luke?—really much, much money?'

'She could buy Black Abbey with it, and live there with ease,' answered Luke, with the nearest approach to a laugh he had yet made, but steadily resisting the pretty pleader's temptings to reveal more relating to the trust he had faithfully kept.

CHAPTER 38

MEETING AGAIN

Oh, money, money! the root of all evil. Yet, to whosoever holds that magical charm in their grasp, how the path of life smoothens and broadens! Little wonder that they that are rich shall so hardly enter into the kingdom of heaven! Why should they seek its strait gate and briery path, when the wider way before them is so pleasant? 'In the time of tribulation, in all time of our wealth ... *Good Lord, deliver us.*' So thought, even so in very reality prayed, Nannie White, in the white, keen January days succeeding that eventful Christmas-tide. This may seem foolish of her to some, but she had a simple faith, and found contentment and satisfaction in it. Can the followers of newer creeds, more vague, if wider, say more? It was the keynote of life to her. Without it the world and her own existence, pain, the evil that still struggles with the good, death, and the great question of hereafter, all seemed to her such a weariness, that when at times tempted to doubt her one hope, and put it away from her—to see if she could walk alone—life had seemed not worth the living. It was then but a dreary puzzle she could not solve.

Hers was, perhaps, as yet but a weak faith; she often feared it was such; but it existed.

What a strange month that of January seemed to be! After the almost changeless flow of the past year, when long weeks had only been marked by slight alterations in slow longer illnesses, which came at last to seem almost the natural state of the little household in the poor London home, Nannie was fairly dizzied with the sudden and many changes that three weeks brought. For here she was now again at Black Abbey; again in her old room, as if all the past year and a half had been an ugly dream; and Hector was here—Hector himself! Her marriage was being hurried on—was to take place so soon that her breath seemed to go with the rapidity of all this—and her, nay! *their* outlook into future years seemed quite dazzling with sun-shine.

To explain how all this came about, one must return to the Christmas-time after Luke had arrived home with his strange news. The story of Rebecca's fortune, as likewise of her resolve to bequeath it all to Nannie, having been told with discreet pride by the old nurse herself to Mary at the manse (that the latter might never again sniff at the mention of the deceased John Steenson), in a trice the whole village knew it. It was soon ringing through all the country-side, where Nannie's name had been long uttered with blessings in many a nightly prayer by the poorest, the sick, the aged; but, above all, it flew like wildfire to Black Abbey itself, where the few servants in the big house, and all the Nethinims and labourers of every kind, from land-steward to garden-boy, were excited beyond measure thereat. The very next morning!—no less a person than Mr. de Burgo himself hobbled down in august haste to inquire of the minister as to the truth of the report; but in all carefulness managing to meet the latter at the Black Abbey lodge as by chance, and pretending to disbelieve the whole matter.

But once assured—and good Mr. Cosby spared no pains to make him so—then what a change had taken place in the demeanour of the master of Black Abbey. In half an hour afterwards he was sitting in the manse parlour on a visit to Nannie; blandly congratulating her on her good fortune, and making most solicitous inquiries after her health, with earnest assurances that if he had only rightly understood before how ill she had been, he would, waiving all other considerations, have come to inquire immediately for the daughter of his dear dead friend. Then rising, and pressing Nannie's reluctant hand, he observed, with fine effect, that he trusted to her good sense and good feelings to understand by his prompt visit that no dislike of herself had ever actuated him in the past to withhold his consent to her union with his grandson. Far, far from that! It had been her want of suitable fortune alone to which he had been sorrowfully forced to object. Now that they were alone (Bonnibel having reluctantly felt it necessary to retire) he would tell her, in strict confidence, that his property was a little dipped—pooh! not much; a mere trifle. He had himself been, perhaps, a little too extravagant in his youth; so was his dear boy Hector. Could Nannie wonder, therefore, at his conduct? Nannie did not wonder; she even believed him, remembering the sales of outlying parts of the estates—of timber; and for the first time in her life felt almost inclined to justify his conduct, so thoroughly was she imbued with unselfish pride in Hector's future position as De Burgo of Black Abbey. Herself, the old man said, he had always most highly valued; and as she might remember, would, but for that one point of misunderstanding, which might now happily be cleared away, have wished her indeed to remain under his roof.

Following this, little presents of a few bottles of rare old wine were sent down that very afternoon for the invalid's use—game, grapes. And, behold! next morning came a letter, earnestly requesting Nannie to return to the home of her childhood, asking Rebecca, her ' foster mother,' with many flattering expressions, to accompany her also, knowing, wrote the old gentleman, they would not wish to be parted. It was a long letter, and excellently well written. Mr. de Burgo, indeed, could write like a Chesterfield; and composition came more easily to him, who belonged to the generation that paid half-a-crown for their letters, so liked to feel they sent the value of their money. He reiterated vaguely the reason he had already given her for his former opposition to her match; with repeated assurances that the encumbrances on his property were, however, not serious; appealing to her on this account to forget the past, and come back to show she 'forgave an old man soon to step into his grave!' He could not doubt her love for Hector; would she blame him for his, that had caused his seeming harshness to herself? he could not believe it!—Nay, it would be a bond of union between them, he trusted, henceforth.

That last sentence, it must be owned, touched earnestly Nannie's heart; otherwise she felt inclined to harden herself (with a touch of the evil old nature that is so hard to get rid of). Laying the message, however, before Rebecca, she found the latter, to her surprise, not only most anxious to accept the summons to Black Abbey, but in a stolid manner seemingly to have expected it The old woman's heart was set upon returning in triumph to the roof-tree that had been so long her home, and whence she had been thrust forth, after having lived there in long years of faithful, but despised servitude. What sweet revenge to have De Burgo of Black Abbey himself bowing down and asking her to return in honour! Yes, yes; for her three children's sakes, too, she would go back. No doubt everything had gone wrong in her absence, and Master Hector's future property been nigh ruined by carelessness. Both the old minister and Luke, too, also reminded Nannie of the beauty and duty of Christian meekness. Bonnibel alone declared, with pretty poutishness, that it was hard that Nannie should come to their poor little manse in evil days, and desert them in her prosperity. Finding that every one at first assumed this to be a jest, and that it had no effect, she said no more, indeed; but her disappointment became so evident in her manner, that poor Nannie (who was so delicate-minded she was always ready to suppose herself possibly in the wrong) began in distress to apologise; thinking that perhaps her conduct might seem ungrateful. Upon this the minister, however, stopped her, and spoke to his granddaughter with more reproof than he had almost ever before been heard to use towards her:

'It is wrong to damp Miss Nannie's natural joy, my child, by our selfishness; and worse to try and withhold her from doing her duty. Blessed are the peace-makers!'

And so Nannie had gone back, being self-installed again in all her old duties, with this change—that whereas she had always received unreasonable blame before, Mr. de Burgo now besmeared his words to her with as unreasonable, unseasonable praise.

As for Rebecca, she was an honoured guest; she might have had the great bedroom in which King William once slept. But, at her own request, she only re-occupied her own former chamber, and a little sunny south room, high up under the roof, and overlooking the garden, that she owned she 'had always been consaity* of' as a sitting-room. Mr. de Burgo's laboured politeness to the old nurse, and the difficulties in which her position involved him, were quite laughable. He even consulted Nannie beforehand, with grave anxiety, as to whether Rebecca would like to dine in state with them or not; and though relieved by the assurance that she would drink tea instead, and preferred her meals in her own room, he was evidently prepared, if necessary, to act Sir Charles Grandison to her Juliet's nurse. The question as to whether Rebecca would crave to enjoy the delights of her former tyrant's society also in the old saloon might, no doubt, have been distressingly delicate; since, in his opinion, riches must at once make her scorn the pleasant housekeeper's room where, in olden days, she had been so happy. But the poor old woman laid it to rest unconsciously; for the shock of her husband's death so affected her that she had a slight stroke, and could not leave her own rooms.

* consaity = proud

And now Hector had come! At first hasty letters, astonished answers, full of mutual wonder and congratulations on the strange course of events, had been exchanged. Then he had got a few days' leave—with a little difficulty, since he had been away from his regiment before Christmas—and had come northwards with all haste; with such haste, indeed, that his first meeting with Nannie was strangely different from what she had so often pictured to herself, in a thousand ways, it might be. How she had looked forward to this moment, each day of the past long year and a half! They would meet thus, or thus; at this hour of the day, or at eve—by some most fortunate and happy chance, or by glad design! Her heart had beat, as her excited loving fancy imagined it all with such intense vividness, that many a time she could have believed she heard Hector's voice in the distance—his very foot on the stair. Hector's brain had been troubled by no such silly womanish phantasms, sure (as he would have said himself) to be utterly different from the reality, whenever it came. And he was right!

It was afternoon; and by evening Nannie meant to go down to the lodge-gate to meet him coming home, feeling dizzy with delight at the thought. She was now in Rebecca's room, bending over her with solicitude, for the old woman was faint and unwell that day, when there was a hasty step on the stairs outside—a joyful sound of a voice she knew—a tall form in the doorway, bringing the sunshine into the darkened room. And so, when Hector and Nannie clasped hands closely once more, it was beside their old nurse's chair. But the first words Nannie found herself uttering, after all those she had spoken so differently in thought, were, 'Hush, dear Hector!—Pray be very quiet for Rebecca's sake; she is far from well.'

'I thought you would have come to meet me,' was Hector's reproachful answer, with injured affection; being utterly unmindful of the fact that he had come two hours before his time. It was strange on both sides, and both laughed over it, afterwards, together.

But Hector, once he understood how matters were, made ample atonement; waiting most patiently while the old nurse, who had now roused up, held his hands in her withered ones, and stroked them long. Then looking in his face, while welcoming tears ran down her cheeks, she murmured with affectionate but alas! maundering repetition, 'Och, ye've heard tell about it? ye've heard tell? It will all be yours. Master Hector, darlin', some day soon; at least it will be hers. My! but it's a wicked world, and money makes things easy. Your grandfather won't hinder your marriage, now!'

Afterwards, when at last Hector had Nannie to himself, he said hotly, with a sort of excited irritability in manner she remarked in him as new, although he tried to smother it, 'You will not mind my telling you the truth, dear—that it vexes me almost that Rebecca should be leaving you this fortune, and that everyone speaks to me about it. It is enough to make one fancy one's self a fortune-hunter.'

'Oh, Hector! how can you be so foolish?' the girl softly replied, half-laughing at him. 'What change has it made in our marriage, except in your grandfather? And surely we need not mind what strangers think?'

'No,' assented Hector, yet somewhat gloomily, as if he did mind, nevertheless; 'only I was congratulated even on the journey here by several people who had heard of my engagement to an heiress; but who had never heard I was engaged to you before. Well! let them say what they please! ... Still, oh, Nan! my dear little Nan! I would much rather give you everything myself.'

A very little while ago, and Nannie would have agreed with her whole heart; now there was still a soft demur in her mind, although she strove to console him. For though for herself, being as we know countrified and inexperienced in world-wisdom, she was ready to exclaim with Hugo—

'Vivre ensemble, d'abord! c'est le bien nécessaire
Et réel;
Après on peut choisir au hasard, ou la terre
Ou le ciel!'

Yet—since old Mr. de Burgo had told her that this future fortune would perfectly restore all those trifling nibblings (as he expressed it) he had been forced to make at the Black Abbey estate—she had been glad in her soul. What a delight that Hector should get his beautiful estate in all its old glory by her means! She was so proud for his sake of the history of the De Burgos of Black Abbey, who had lived there in pride for generations; proud of the beautiful old estate; proud of Hector, with his handsome head and tall broad figure and easy carriage—the manliest man in all the little circle of her life she had ever seen. For Hector's sake, for his only, she was glad to have this fortune; and yet it all, laid in mind at his feet, was not worthy of his acceptance as the smallest return for his great goodness in choosing such a poor, pale creature as herself. So she thought; and yet was proud of herself, since he had chosen her. But as for having this money for herself—for her own private use—for that she cared indeed as little as anyone could, who yet had common sense.

And now, Hector urgently declared, they must be married at once. No one resisted him; but yet he seemed to take matters with a high hand, and spoke with a sort of excitable defiance to all but Nannie, as if his thoughts still ran on the opposition and temptings he had met with during his engagement. Nannie, indeed, was at times aware that in his too great pride Hector was still sore and ready to take offence on the subject of her fortune; and thought it Quixotic on his part—foolish—but yet loved the fault that was an excessive virtue, for his sake. But she was so happy, that she could not be vexed about any such trifling matter!—so happy, that, when with her, Hector could not be vexed.

On the very first afternoon after his arrival, Nannie begged Hector to come and walk down with her to the manse. She was afraid lest, after all their kindness to her, her good friends there should think themselves neglected. She urged this wish so prettily—when Hector exclaimed with laughing, but very real reluctance, 'What!—so soon?'—that he was obliged to grant she was right, adding a hope, however, that Luke and the old minister would be in the manse; he always liked the dear old man, and Luke was a capital fellow—as good a fisherman, he thought, very likely, as were any of the Apostles.

Hector had his wish. Both old Mr. Cosby and Luke were at home; and he talked to them, indeed, all the time of his visit, seeming quite engrossed in the old man's account of Black Abbey parish, and in Luke's description of his travels.

As for Bonnibel, she received them both with an expectant air and discreet demureness. Hardly ever raising her eyes to Hector, she talked all the time to her rich and fortunate friend; in a tone full, indeed, of suppressed warmth and affection, but so subdued, that to the others present it seemed a graceful propriety of manner; as if she only wished to show gladness, but no adulation, to the princess whose sun shone again with such tenfold splendour.

Just as they left, however, when Hector was bidding her good-bye and the attention of the others was diverted, the girl murmured to him, 'I wish you all joy!' She looked up, with one full-fraught, earnest, almost bewildering glance of her brown orbs into the young man's eyes—let her warm hand rest in his just one second or so longer than need be, with ever so slight a lingering pressure—then hurriedly added, 'I am sure you are … and she is … worthy of it.'

Hector only said, 'Thank you,' and seemed relieved to gain the door.

On their homeward way Nannie talked, as was natural, much of the manse inmates—praised them all. Her companion agreed warmly about old Mr. Cosby and Luke; but as regarded Miss Hawthorn his assent seemed forced, and given with some hidden reluctance.

Nannie taxed him with it, in half-laughing reproach: 'You never did do poor Bonnibel justice,' she said.

'Excuse me,' replied Hector carelessly, 'I admire her immensely, on the contrary. I only think she is sometimes—well—rather *too* much of a good thing.'

'Why, what do you mean?' and the gentle damsel beside him raised her wondrously-tender grey eyes—whose limpid look reminded one of a child's innocence of expression—in amused wonder.

Hector laughed, but then looked away: her gaze was too clear. Ah! how he wished he could meet it likewise. 'I only mean, dear, that she has too much colour for my taste; and too much height; and too much of personal charms altogether. Just now my idea of perfection in womanhood is very different. It is—'

But Nannie would not hear him say more; indeed, the fond look he had given, admiring her slim figure's pliant grace, the sweet face, with its pale, softly-rounded cheeks and poet-eyes, had said enough.

And now, how the happy days flew! Past and future mornings and eves all seemed merged together for Nannie in one blissful consciousness that yesterday she had been—as to-morrow she would be—happy! Again, she and Hector rode together down the wintry turf of the rides between the noble, bared woods; or over the hard, wide strand, listening to the solemn sea-psalm of the sounding waves, and watching in the clear afternoon some ray of sunshine light up the far Scotch coast across the heaving channel. It was true, Hector had soon to go back again; but he was returning so shortly for their wedding, that his absence seemed but a necessary breathing-time in the midst of too great gladness.

And Aileen had come, too. She was stronger now, and able to bear the winter, but was to go abroad with her aunt before the cold winds of early spring; so also on her account the marriage was being hurried. She brightened them all in the house; the keen, sharp-spoken little creature, with her clear laugh, would sit amusing Rebecca for hours—who, to their gladness, seemed regaining strength.

'What a change it really is for her!' Aileen exclaimed to Nannie and some of the manse party; 'and yet she does not seem to feel any pride—rather bewilderment.'

'The only change she does seem proud of is old Mary's new civility to her,' laughed Nannie. 'They were such bitter enemies before, but the manse dragon is all sweetness to Rebecca, now.'

'No—is she?' exclaimed Aileen, with quick ingenuous disapprobation of such sycophancy. 'Well, I really had a better opinion of old Mary!'

'Oh, Miss Aileen! Miss Aileen! How like you that is,' said Luke, who, standing silently by, had overheard them; and he gave the first, great hearty laugh Nannie had heard from his lips since he returned. She was glad of it.

The manse party were asked up almost daily to dinner in those days by old Mr. de Burgo; and treated with a suavity and condescension by him that secretly incensed poor Luke almost past bearing, and set the minister wondering at such a marvellous change. Bonnibel, alone, liked, nay! insisted on going up to Black Abbey.

'Has it ever struck you that she might become our grand-mamma?' Aileen suddenly one night asked Nannie.

'Oh, nonsense!' ejaculated the other, in indignant amazement 'She would do nothing so base to Luke—so outrageous! if even

Mr. de Burgo so far lost his wits. She is only so eager to have a little more pleasure than in the dull manse-life, that she would make herself agreeable to Caliban for the sake of getting it. You are really not quite fair to her.'

'Perhaps not,' said Aileen penitently; 'I have distrusted her. But since you are fond of her, I will try to think better of her for your sake.' And she, indeed, after that tried to keep her word, to all outward seeming.

And then—then, in the midst of all their happiness, all was blighted one dark night—as the frost that same night blighted many a tender bud. Rebecca had another and more severe stroke, and by morning her life was almost despaired of.

CHAPTER 39

LIKE SNOW-WREATHS IN JUNE

Old Rebecca's illness had come so closely before the wedding-day at Black Abbey, so suddenly and terribly, that to Nannie's sorrowful imagination it seemed as if the death knell was mingling with the merry marriage chimes. Ah! the same bell rings for both, but few of us remember that.

Then, thanks in great part to her foster-daughter's devoted nursing, so the doctors said, the old woman slowly rallied, though a long illness seemed in store for her. Of course the wedding was postponed. Nannie would not have listened to any other suggestion; but even Hector could not but regretfully own that her place was by the bedside of the only mother she had ever known. Aileen went abroad, hoping sincerely to return with the warm weather and the swallows; Luke went to London; the little party was broken up.

Old Mr. de Burgo stayed on, however, at Black Abbey—a longer visit than he had paid his home for the last quarter of a century; protesting affectionately that so long as Hector's leave lasted he would not break up their little party, but would remain to play the guardian. No, no; he had been young himself, and could now sacrifice some of his own pleasures to the happiness of his grandson and dear ward. As it seemed, indeed, a sacrifice for Hector's sake, Nannie did verily think better of the old man for preserving this one affection still in his otherwise selfish, frozen heart. And yet, watching him with her clear, impartial gaze, she was soon obliged to come to the different, secret conviction that no liking for herself, and but little affection for his grandson as an individual, actuated him; only intense anxiety lest old Rebecca's business affairs should not be satisfactorily settled, and any of her money thus be lost to the heir of his name and estate. Extravagant though he had been, the wish bred of the usage of generations, to leave Black Abbey unimpaired to his next of kin when leave it he must, was still strong within the old man's breast. Perhaps he had a dim thought that, lying in his vault down under the ruins of the old chapel, he would know that other generations of De Burgos moved over the green sward above him; and he might seem to retain some hold, thereby, on his place that would know him no more. As it was, he stayed, torturing himself to control his temper within doors; but reaping a rich harvest outside by making the lives of all the souls in his pay a hideous torment to them by constant alarms, which he gaily termed making them 'bustle a bit!' or 'brisking them up!'

Meanwhile, Hector lingered out the leave that he had got in anticipation of his marriage drearily enough. There was no hunting to be had in the neighbourhood—but little shooting, since Black Abbey demesne had been very ill-preserved of late years, and under the circumstances he did not care to go often to the neighbours, who knew him indeed, but not Nannie—nor, nowadays, his grandfather. Being as kindly-hearted a young man as ever lived, honest Hector, though naturally disappointed, was anxious not to let poor old Rebecca see this. It grew to be trying, however, that, each time he went to visit the old woman his joyous prophecies to her of speedy recovery were falsified; and she seemed only feebler than before. He could see hardly anything of Nannie, either; for though the old nurse was most uncomplaining, it was evident that no one else so well understood her difficultly-uttered wants; that no other hands could so tend her to her liking. Good-natured though he was, handsome human Lancelot was imperfect; he at last grew impatient, being young, accustomed to his own way, and in love. Instead of wooing an earthly-passioned bride, with feelings like his own, he only saw at intervals a saint—sweet indeed, but whose best thoughts, as most of whose time, were given to nursing the sick. Once or twice he even reproached poor Nannie with neglect of his own feelings in her devotion to Rebecca, and wrung her heart for the first time in his life. Then, seeing what he had done, Hector was full of remorse, and—refusing to accede to Nannie's urgings to leave her, and spend the rest of his time in some place where he could have more amusement, resolved to pass his loneliness as best he might. He avoided his grandfather's company, since the old gentleman busied himself out of doors in planning, with much gusto, new drives to be made and new stables to be built (after Rebecca's approaching decease!) with Nannie's money, as he confided to his grandson. Hector was so incensed, that they very nearly quarrelled outright; and afterwards apparently tacitly agreed to keep apart; one thinking his grand-father grasping and a fortune-hunter, the other considering his grandson a romantic young fool.

There was no one else to visit, except the inmates of the manse. Hector, however, would not go there for some while; although Nannie frequently suggested it as a means of passing time, and a pleasure to those in it. But after meeting Miss Hawthorn—accidentally on his part—several times rambling through the woods, since the girl took ample advantage of old Mr. de Burgo's invitation to her to do so, Hector's reluctance, whether of shyness or dislike, gradually vanished, as Nannie perceived. In her Christian unselfishness she was glad of it; wishing most heartily to see Hector good friends with all his neighbours, humble as well as rich. And now, when she encouraged him again to go to the manse at times, knowing how his visits gratified the dear old minister—he went.

Nevertheless, there was a change, when one day Nannie came to him smiling, and said, 'Dear Hector, Bonnibel Hawthorn has just been with me. She has heard that you must go back to your regiment next week, and wants me to beg that you will be an escort to her—since, to leave me still more deserted, Mrs. Heavyside has invited her for some time. So you are both bound for within a few miles of the same town.'

The young man's face darkened, and to the gentle suppliant's surprise he answered quite roughly:

'What does she want with an escort? She might travel alone well enough! … And what on earth made her get you to ask me?'

'Because she was afraid of asking you herself—why, I cannot think! but she was plainly right,' returned Nannie in amazement, laughing outright; then went on pleadingly, 'Come, Hector, do be good-natured. As she hinted herself, it is true that plainer people might travel unmolested, but such a pretty girl may be plagued with unwelcome attentions from strangers.'

'Unwelcome! She is such a flirt, it would be strange if any attentions were unwelcome to her,' muttered Nannie's lover, under cover of his moustache.

'I will not believe she is a flirt!' cried Nannie, firing up in defence of the absent, who had so long befriended herself, with a flash in her eyes and a flush on her cheeks that were most becoming, although she did not understand why Hector looked at her in such sudden admiration; it was of her innocence of mind, as well as of her face. Then she went on in a tone of real distress, 'I cannot bear to hear you misjudge anyone; as I really think you do her now. Hector. If you, as I do, knew all about Bonnibel' (thinking of the latter's engagement to Luke, and Nannie's conviction that the girl really cared for her cousin more than she herself knew, and above all others), 'if you had been as intimate with her for months, you would be as fond of her as I am. She does like admiration, perhaps, but she is so pretty that is little wonder; and she may be a little giddy and impulsive, but which of us has not our faults? and I am sure she is good and true at heart!'

'I think I know one person, at least, who has almost no faults, and who thinks well of everyone. Well, perhaps, Nan, as *you* say so, I will believe she is not a flirt,' said Hector, with a strange smile.

'And you will take her, for my sake?'

'For your sake—yes. Remember, it is only because you ask me,' was the reluctant answer.

And so it was settled; and those two went away, leaving Nannie to keep house for only old Mr. de Burgo, and to continue her painful watch. Weeks passed, however, and as the aged nurse grew no better, though but little worse, and as her will had been made entirely in Nannie's favour—Rebecca with some pride having requested her former master to witness it—old Mr. de Burgo began to think he, too, would go away. He made many excuses to Nannie, left many promises behind to return on the very first occasion that he might be needed; and so, with inward relief, the girl watched him go also, and found herself alone with her sick charge in the old echoing house, whose environing woods separated it from near neighbourhood. She had not even her good German governess's companionship; for one of poor Rebecca's first acts of charity after she got her fortune had been, at Nannie's suggestion, to 'send the cratur' an offering of goodwill, that enabled the Fräulein to revisit her Fatherland—a wish long deferred. She would, of course, in time return to Ireland, being, as Hector said, an heirloom among the De Burgos; but Nannie thought her best away, with sickness in the house.

This was in March, when the roads were hard, and white with dust, and the clear evenings longer, and the gorse in yellow bloom. Two more months passed in loneliness for Nannie, in lovingly anxious care by day and vigils by night—two months of ever warmer days, brightening skies, of tender green unfolding over the whole landscape, of bursting flower-buds; but two months of only failing strength to the old nurse, gently sinking to sleep in her darkened room; and then, seeming most softly slipping away from earth, one evening old Rebecca was gone. She too, as the great Roman wrote, submitted to her dissolution, 'like a ripe olive, which, when it falls, seems to bless the earth which nourished it'

. . . . .

And now came warm, sweet-scented June again; and once more, as two years ago, Nannie White leant upon the grey stone balustrade above the quaint curved steps, awaiting (as she then had unconsciously) her lover, whose horse's hoofs would soon be heard coming up the wooded drive. She was dressed in deep black, since Rebecca had two days ago been laid to rest under the daisied sod of the ancient burying-place beside the ruined chapel that was nestled in the woods. Few of late were buried there, as Mr. de Burgo wished to discontinue the practice; but Nannie had now influence enough to manage that it should be so; so they laid her old nurse, like Deborah, under a tree. Although there was still a sweet paleness in Nannie's cheeks, dark shadows under her large grey eyes (signs she had gazed into the valley of death!), yet in her eyes themselves beamed only peace, and the reflection of a great trust in the future of the old woman she had, nay, still! loved; that comforted her—of the courage that, when alone in the sick chamber with death, had upheld her.

And so this afternoon, when Hector arrived, and, after his first greetings—greetings that seemed embarrassed—exclaimed, with his handsome face, much troubled, 'I am utterly ashamed to look you in the face, poor little Nan! Fancy your being left all alone here to undertake Rebecca's funeral! ... terrible! I *could* not come myself, for the truth is, your letter followed me out to the Heavysides', where I was staying; and even then, by some dreadful mistake or other—Mrs. Heavyside said she could not understand how it was—it was not given me till next morning, and so the only train that could have brought me was missed. But still I made certain that my grandfather would have come over. Bonnibel (I mean Miss Hawthorn), too, said she was sure he would; and so, counting on that, I felt more consoled. But otherwise, you do believe that I would have come if I could, don't you? … *Say* you believe me, Nannie!'

Believe him! of course Nannie believed him; and said so, with a look in her grey eyes that made them seem like wells out of whose depths shone sweetest truth; in her heart believing he could and would only do everything that was good, and true-hearted, and kind. But when he reiterated his regrets and commiseration on her being left alone with *death* in the house, she answered him with steadfastness, and a pale, heroic smile, 'If that is the worst I may ever be called on to undergo, dear Hector, I can bear it. It is not painful to see a Christian die; there must be far more terrible things! Besides, good old Mr. Cosby came up, and helped me in everything.'

'Ah! yes, Bonnibel Hawthorn said she was sure he would; and besides' (looking at her with a sort of distant admiration not unmixed with wonder), 'you certainly have, as she said too, so much self-control and—well! command over your feelings, and that sort of thing, that other women would envy you.'

Nannie said never a word; but a faint, almost satirical smile, flickered one instant about her lips. Did he and she—did Hector and her friend—forget then how she had learnt that lesson? by what dreadful experience during the past year of illness, loneliness and want, almost of starvation, in London? If Hector, however, did not remember it, she would not recall it to him, to vex his mind.

'When is Bonnibel coming home?' she only asked.

'Home! I don't know; how should I? I have not escorted her back, if you mean that. … I should hope not for ever so long—for her own sake. It must be deadly dull here; and she gets on capitally with the Heavysides. What on earth *should* bring her back?'

As he spoke with quite an irritable air, Nannie said to herself, very stilly and sorrowfully in her heart, 'I see! Bonnibel has found her conscience pricking her for leaving the poor old man so much alone; and so she has been justifying herself to Hector and the Heavysides by saying how dull it is here, till they pity her.'

Aloud, she only softly answered, 'I have missed her, dear, that is all; and, no doubt, her grandfather must have missed her more.'

To this Hector answered nothing; but after a few minutes stopping short, as they slowly wandered along the flower-terraces between the clipped yew hedges near the house, he exclaimed with energy: 'But now, we must have no more delays! we must be married at once, Nannie; we will have no more delays!' And then he went on, eagerly, feverishly, urging and pleading, and arguing with her, till she, who had wished to delay longer, out of reverence to Rebecca's memory, gave way at last—so promised that the wedding should be as early as could well be after the late funeral; stipulating only that it should be as quiet as possible.

'It seems so soon after her death,' she murmured. 'And your grandfather appears anxious, from his letters, that all the business affairs should be settled first. He is seeing about some of them, now, in London.'

'Was that what prevented him from coming over to the funeral, as he had promised. *He* had no difficulties about leave, as I had.'

'No, no; I think he has a horror of death, and that, at the

last moment, he shrank back. Don't speak so bitterly of him for that, dear Hector.'

'It is not for that! It is because I hate—I hate to know that he is so mercenary—that he is glad of our marriage for your money's sake! Don't think me utterly foolish, Nannie, but I cannot endure the feeling.'

This thought, indeed, always set Hector afire. His face was agitated now with a kind of defiance against the whole world—a confliction of inward thoughts, that Nannie could not understand. There were only sweet calm and anticipative gladness shining in her eyes, as she softly said, trying to console him, 'I should be glad to be a beggar-maid, if that would make you happier.'

'I wish you were—only that is impossible,' said her future husband, half lovingly, half gloomily. 'Well, there is no use in talking about it!—but you will have no more delays. Nan; promise me that!' Then, as she smiled softly but sadly (remembering that the delays had been none of her making), he, not understanding rightly, but misjudging her manner to be a mere modish shyness, a prudery of reserve, exclaimed hotly, almost irritably, 'Surely we have known each other long and well enough to do away with all little pretences of proprieties! ... You are good, Nannie, as good a woman as lives, I do believe! but—you *are* so cold!'

Cold! Poor Nannie! He did not know how white her face had been until he came, although now it was tinged with the flush of a half-opened rose. He did not realise fully how grim and lonely had been the past long weeks for her, though her heart was now beating with a gentle gladness which, by contrast with the past, was most delicious.

But the shadow of death was upon her yet, still chilled her being; she sometimes shivered. It seemed strange to her that he could not see that—though the house and lawns were flooded with evening sunshine—yet all, still, seemed dark!

And even had it not been so, perhaps she could not have done violence to her deep, still nature by showing even him, as yet, the whole secrets of her heart, and how his image was shrined in its inmost recesses—an image veiled in clouds of love's incense, and beautified by her imagination, till it seemed not ordinary human clay, but almost perfect.

Perhaps it came of their natures, and was unalterable, that to honest, foolish Hector, she seemed set far, far above him like his 'moon of poets;' so far above him, in an atmosphere of utter serenity, and goodness, and purity, that it maddened him to feel dimly, although he would not have had her brought down to his level, yet that, strain upward as he might, he never yet had attained to that height—nay! of late had fallen far below it.

And yet she only lived for her God first, and then for him; and after him—too much after, it may be—for her fellow-beings.

So that evening it was finally settled, that, within a month, they two should be quietly married by special license. Hector rode back to the inn at Redbay, where he was putting up for two days. He might, indeed, have perhaps contrived to stay longer, but that Nannie thought it was best not; she being a solitary girl there, and somewhat fearful of the tongues of the surrounding Veres, and Hares, and Desboroughs; who, indeed, had been so long used to connect impropriety with Black Abbey, during the present Mr. de Burgo's life, that the habit had very likely grown fixed in them.

So Hector left, and Nannie took out her wedding-gown that had been folded away since January, and kept solitary rule over the Nethinims.

By-and-by, before the wedding, Hector returned, and again went to the Redbay inn, although the old minister with hospitable humility offered him a room in the manse; but, as he told Nannie, he preferred being free. Bonnibel, too, came back on the same day as Hector. She had written a pretty note, begging Nannie to let her act as bridesmaid, although the only one, 'for sake of old times,' to which the latter gladly consented. Unfortunately, Aileen de Burgo could not get back in time from Germany, whence she wrote that her aunt, though the sparest little woman imaginable, was laid up with a twinge of the family gout.

'How glad I am to see you, dear! I suppose—I am afraid—you think me very wicked for staying away so long from grand-papa,' exclaimed Bonnibel, somewhat nervously, in deprecating tones, when she met Nannie. 'But I do assure you, he wrote to me every single day what he was doing, good old dear! and said you were such an interest to him while poor Rebecca was ill, and that he had to be such a constant companion to you, and tried to be of use and consolation too, that—that in fact I was as well away. Forgive me, dear; *say* you don't think badly of me!—although I am a foolish creature.'

Nannie, accustomed to be appealed to as a gentle judge by Bonnibel, smiled a little doubtfully on the sinner who, however often she cried '*mea culpa!*' never restrained herself from indulging again, with fresh enjoyment, in the old forbidden pleasure. But she did of course give the required absolution; the more readily that Miss Bella Hawthorn for once did seem really penitent, and said, heavily sighing, that now she must roam no more away from home, since there would soon be no kind angel to look after her grandfather, as Nannie had done. And then the latter asked in her turn—with an anxious look that was for a moment suffered to overspread her face, since they two were sitting alone together in the manse parlour; and she, though used to bearing her burdens in silence and alone, for once felt the human need of confidence:

'Tell me, Bonnibel, did you remark any change in Hector when you saw him at the Heavysides'? When first we met again, after Rebecca's death, it seemed to me as if something had happened to distress him whilst away. It was not that he seemed less fond of me—oh, no; not that!—but, now, he seems even more troubled at times, since he has come home this second time.'

'They play rather high at the Heavysides'; and I think—he—lost some money,' said Bonnibel in a low voice, hesitating. 'I suppose, that, when he went back there lately to get his revenge, he lost more. Still, I would advise you—I do advise you' (speaking very earnestly) 'not to say anything to him about that. For, though he is easily led, and is so kind and good-humoured that he is ready to join in anything just to please other people, still, I heard them all laughing at him for being no real gambler—and not really caring to play in his heart.'

The advice was extremely unnecessary. Nannie was too reserved and delicate-minded to be likely to speak lightly to Hector on such a matter, when he had not mentioned it to her himself. She listened to Bonnibel's repeated assurances that, for certain, whatever he had lost was not much!—nothing to torment herself about—indeed, should be nothing to him!—with a grave smile which puzzled the other as to whether it hid sadness or meant doubt. But in her heart she proudly wished that she had not been weak and troubled enough to have been betrayed into questioning even her friend about Hector; and loved him all the more for thus brooding over the fault that Bonnibel thought 'need not vex him.'

And then, for some days, the two girls saw little of each other. The one was busied up at the great house with the affairs of many beside herself—of indeed all Black Abbey. The other, down at the manse, was either finding the hours unutterably dull, hating home occupations after her late life, or sometimes stitching at her bridesmaid's gown with slow, strangely unwilling fingers, that seemed loth for once to deck out her body in its new bravery.

CHAPTER 40

A THUNDERBOLT OUT OF A CLEAR SKY

THEN came one sunny June evening; how well Nannie remembered it afterwards!

She was strolling down the long drive, and smelt the hay sweet in the air, and watched the herd of red cows coming homewards through the low meadows at milking-time. Yonder before her, through the dark vista of a wood, she saw the lodge like a little arch of light far away, with here and there a few beams of golden light smiling athwart the thick branches; so she saw it all many a day again.

Hector was not coming this day. He had sent her word in the morning that he was going fishing, up the little river that ran into Redbay.

Nannie had been spending the day, therefore, looking after the thousand small matters, from the household wants of the poor in the village to the fowl in the home farmyard, that had so long come under her government; reproaching herself a little for having seemed to neglect them because her mind had been so taken up with her marriage, that was now to be in three days. And then she would be going away with Hector for good, and only returning here for holidays; so it behoved her to see to the welfare of all those who had grown to depend so greatly on her care. She had been working hard all this day from dewy dawn; and now only felt at leisure to stroll a while, and be careless, and at rest; feeling tired, but glad of the sweetness and warmth of this blooming evening, and to hear the occasional notes of the birds in the woods.

How strange to leave all this and go away with Hector into a new existence, an almost unknown world! She had only known him all their joint lives, hitherto, as the heir of Black Abbey, as a country gentleman. His soldier life was for the greater part to her like the closed leaves of a book that otherwise she knew by heart; he and Black Abbey were so intimately associated in her mind, that she could hardly realise him as away from home—but soon she must learn to do so.

Nannie's white summer gown was easily visible from some distance, as she sauntered along the sunny drive that sloped straight down to the lodge. It must have attracted the attention of a passer-by, on the dusty road outside the great iron gates; for by-and-by she noticed a figure shambling towards her up the hill between the noble, shadowy trees; and a sing-song voice greeted her from some way off with the well-known refrain, 'Ye are my darlin'-deary; ye are so! Och! *ye* are so.' Nannie smiled kindly as the old beggarman, the bogey of her childhood, shuffled eagerly towards her, almost running; but looked surprised, when placing his hand mysteriously over his pocket, Darlin'-deary nodded significantly, looked eagerly in her eyes, and with his own staring wildly, whispered, 'A letter—ay! I have it here, safe—Mr. Hector giv' it me, and ye'd best read it. Ay! my darlin-deary, read it at wanst—wanst/ And the poor soul smiled and gibbered, producing a folded scrap of paper; yet, nevertheless, again holding it back with so knowing an air that Nannie was half provoked, and the moment he let her have it quickly opened it, to show that it could be no very important a love-message after all, entrusted to so strange a carrier.

It was a mere scrap torn out of Hector's pocket-book, as she easily guessed; and on it was written in pencil,

'To-night at half-past nine, Chapel Wood; for the last time, as you wish it.

'H.'

Nannie looked up bewildered. She never had met Hector before at the Chapel Wood; she had not wished it—and for the *last time*, too!

'Did Mr. Hector say nothing more when he gave you this? where did you see him?' she asked.

The idiot again nodded mysteriously with a cunning look, as if they two had a secret understanding, and affectionately whispered, 'Och, up the river, fishing … sure, it was there I found him at twelve this day … after running all the way this morning with a letter from the minister's lass,' and glancing first pitifully at his own bare feet, he nodded in the direction of the manse.

'The minister's lass!—whom do you mean? Not—not Miss Hawthorn?' faltered Nannie, utterly at a loss, startled—no, not frightened; not that!—but still afraid of seeming so, even before this daft beggar, 'Not Miss Hawthorn?'

'Ay, *her*; the minister's Bella … that same. She bid me find him, wherever he be'd to be*; and gave me a sax-pence. And he runshled† up his brows whenever he set his eyes on the writing, and scrabbled this down on a bit paper and gave me half-a-crown, and bid me go back with it and give it to no living sowl but Miss Bella Hawthorn, at the manse—intill her own hands,' went on old Darlin'-dearie, pouring out his words close to Nannie's ear in a sort of frightened, muttered gabble, looking furtively round him as he ended, while the girl who heard him seemed not to hear him, so still she stood. 'But he's courting *ye*,

* be'd to be = had to be

† runshle = crunch, wrinkle

my darlin'-deary, *so I brought it till ye!* Och! for God's sake, don't tell upon me, or he'll kill me—for ye are my darlin'-deary—ye were always good till me!—ye are so! ye are so!'

And Nannie, never answering him, shivered as if frozen in the sunlight; and stood still with the note in her listless hands, each written letter of which seemed to burn into her brain like fire.

CHAPTER 41

THE CRISIS OF LIFE

WHEN Nannie had read the note old Darlin'-dearie brought her, after a few long seconds the colour dyed her pale face with a sluggish tide of crimson; but there was no other sign. She softly put the note in her pocket with such slow, lingering fingers, that the idiot, believing she loved it, grinned kindly at her. But her eyes were fixed on the westering sun that was now burning in a hot blaze through the fringe of the shelving wood.

Then a sudden thought darted through her, and starting in pain she hastily drew out the note again, having just remembered—*it was not hers!*

'Can you read, Darling-dearie? she quietly asked—in a voice, however, that did not sound in her ears like her own.

The old beggarman emphatically shook his crazy head, as if it would be shaken off. 'Na; niver a worrd.'

'Then you had best take this on to Miss Hawthorn, as Mr. Hector desired you. You should not … not … have given it to me. Never mind, now! give it only to herself, and say nothing about it'

Rubbing his torn sleeve across his eyes, the faithful daft creature whimpered, as fearing he had maybe done wrong with all his cunning, but muttered, 'A sup of milk? All the way to the river and back this morn on my two bare feet and come in here, all for you. Och! ye are my darlin'-dearie!' This last was uttered with a jubilant cry, as Nannie made a gesture of assent.

'Go to the kitchen, and say I sent you,' she just said, waving her hand kindly, and walked back towards the house, while the idiot shambled hastily off by a cart-lane through the trees leading to the back premises.

Nannie remembered afterwards wondering to herself how she could be so quiet; she even spoke to two of the labourers making hay beside the drive, when they greeted her. There was a dull thought in her mind, in the very air that seemed pressing down upon her—'It has come at last!—it has come at last!'

What? The ill-fate, the loneliness, the forsakenness that since a little orphan child, she had had a dim foreboding was apportioned to her in life; and had cried out and struggled against, in soul.

By-and-by, like one walking in a dream that yet seemed most real, Nannie found she had gained her own room; quietly locked the door; sat down—and dully wondered why she did not swoon as other people might; wondered why this seemed to hurt her so very little.

Some minutes thus passed. On a sudden, stifling a great and exceeding bitter cry, the girl sprang up straight, then dropped upon her knees beside the low bed, hiding her face in it and writhing bodily in anguish, while whispering repeatedly in agony to herself, 'It is too much! … Oh, how *could he? how could he?* … And how could she?' Deceived, shamed by the lover whom she had believed in with her whole heart and soul, who had seemed to surpass all other men in honesty and goodness—by the friend whom she so utterly trusted. There was no doubt possible. A hundred trifles that of late had a moment puzzled her, and been no more thought of, started back in remembrance, clear as noon-day. There was no doubt, no doubt, no doubt—none!

Ah! if any were but possible!

Love had blinded her to what she might have otherwise guessed. Her idol had fallen with a crash, and she—the foolish worshipper—seemed to stand stupefied and lonely looking at its ruins, with no devotion possible to her any more.

'Oh! how could he?' she still moaned in her heart, but utterly voicelessly. Lonely as was the old house, she could not in her pride and quivering pain have borne to think that any living soul should overhear her lips even murmuring aloud.

Then, 'Lord have mercy on me! ... have mercy on me!' (with a little cry of intensest agony) 'for I can *not* bear it.' And yet she knew she must bear it. For long she lay there, heavily; crouched on the ground like some poor animal that when stricken only asks to creep out of sight to die. Two thoughts alone beat back and forward in her brain, ever and ever recurring, changing—but only felt dully, dully!—the one that maddening wail of reproach, the other that dumb, hopeless outcry for help. Sometimes she restlessly hid her face a little more, as if in pain, but with no violence of movement; she felt too spent for that; her head was sick and her heart faint.

At last the loud clanging of a bell in the trees near that belted the stable-yard roused her; it was the workmen's bell, six o'clock, and she had been on the ground there an hour and a half. She rose up mechanically, feeling older by years since afternoon, and moved to the open window that looked on a sea of fresh tree-tops, and the garden far below, and the distant mere. The sweet evening air came in and revived her a little.

She could think now, as with haggard face and burning eyeballs she stared out, seeing all, but noticing nothing; she could think more indeed, but thinking only meant 'madness in the brain.' How *could* Hector be so cruel to her? was still the stupefied heart-cry. How could God be so cruel as to suffer her to go on praying, morning and night, for the man she loved these two long years, while He knew all the time her lover had ceased to care for her and loved Bonnibel? Were the wicked alone to have happiness on earth, and she be denied who had struggled and prayed that her love might be blessed as was that of others; as holy women had prayed, and been answered. She was mocked!

mocked by her God whom she served, by the man she loved, who—Ah! no, not that; she must not be unjust. He was meeting Bonnibel this night *'for the last time;'* and doubtless they two, who loved each other, would bewail together the hard fate that bound him in honour to be married to herself in three days.

And somehow, at thought of their passion, which no doubt seemed hopeless to themselves, and their misery that now she must take upon herself, the band that had seemed to press round her brain like iron—forbidding weeping—burst; and while her tears fell down like rain, in spite of that last outcry of almost blasphemous, wild feeling, Nannie found herself ejaculating brokenly, 'Lord, I will forgive them, utterly and entirely … yes, both! Have mercy upon them, and forgive them. It was not their fault.' And sinking down upon her knees, she murmured through her tears, 'Yes; I can say Thy will be done, O my dear Lord! … I have prayed for so many years that I might be made strong to bear my cross, whatever it might be; and I can bear it! … I will!' And still and again the outcry of Job, the grandest utterance of faith ever writ by poet, rhymed in her brain—a living-voiced consolation sounding across hoary hundreds of years, from that unknown time when the world was young, but already the mysterious struggle between good and evil, and the seeming strange haphazard of sorrow and joy bewildered man's soul: 'Though He slay me, yet will I trust in Him.'

So three more hours passed. The sun had sunk. Shadows came, and the sky grew cool and clear; darkness deepened, and some little stars began to peep. Then, with a set purpose in her mind, Nannie White went out of the house, outwardly calm again, and strong for the time being in soul. Courage seemed lent her to pass through the coming ordeal, that whilst her faith lasted would not fail; unless, feeling weak and human, she were to look earthwards, at her shattered hopes and blasted life.

Fearing to delay, she flitted rapidly like a ghost through the dark woods. It would have been quicker to cross the dim lawns and low-lying meadows, before the house, to gain the Chapel Wood. But she dreaded being recognised by anyone, any figure being distinctly seen down on those flats, and so went a long way round among the trees. The summer night-wind blew softly round her hot head and aching temples; the dusk was grateful. On she slipped through the wood paths with curious quietness, not daring to think much of what was coming; looking continually into the shadowy leafy recesses to right and left as if afraid, her fancy oddly endeavouring thus to divert her attention, as it were, and relieve her brain from the madness of one sole possessing thought. The hares loped softly before her down the dim, dewy wood-paths, or sat up sometimes with wondering eyes and drooping forepaws to gaze at her before taking to easy flight. Rabbits that were out by scores, nibbling the juicy greensward, scudded into the brushwood on either hand; then, little alarmed by such a spiritual vision stealing by, pertly peeped back again.

A holy hush was on all things around in earth. God grant, she prayed, as now she neared the Chapel Wood, that the same blessed calm might be given her also in heart; a word of anger, or even reproach, would seem desecration in the present still resignation of her soul to the all-wise inevitable Will.

Nannie did not wish to steal unawares upon the two who must be there; but it was very dark in the Chapel Wood; and even when she drew quite near to the ruins, she stopped, hesitating, wondering where they really were.

Listening, in the silence, then, she heard some one sobbing.

CHAPTER 42

IN THE CHAPEL WOOD

It is above all timid, but highly-strung and sensitive persons who can do wonders in excitement, that themselves would be the first to shrink from as too painful or impossible when the blood runs colder; so not daring to pause or think, Nannie went swiftly forward through some intervening bushes. Before her was the old chapel wall pierced by one window, through which the moon was shining. Behind this, almost surrounded by the ruins, was a little court of green sward, where those other two must be.

How the stars shone out just above here, in a perfect galaxy of glory; how clearly the moonlight lit everything! Oh, a dark sky would have been better, poor Nannie thought, as she stole out of the grateful shadow of the wood, reluctantly; would have seemed to hide her misery better.

So she crept round the corner of the ruins, guided by that sobbing, and found herself so close, that in two steps more she could have touched those there. At the suddenness of this, and the terrible feeling of being now brought face to face with her trial, and that there was no going back, she shrank. For a few moments her strength failed, and, even at the risk of being thought an eavesdropper, she could neither have spoken nor moved, but stood still, being by chance in the shadow of the wall; a ghost-like figure—for she wore a white summer dress—trembling like an aspen leaf.

Bonnibel was sitting on an ancient stone bench (when children they had used to call it the king's seat, and think whoever sat on it happy!), and was weeping loudly with no restraint

Hector was standing beside her against the wall, his arms folded, his head bent; and something in his whole outline that seemed to suggest dull wretchedness, but yet a dogged resignation under it, and a stolid endurance of fate.

'I am so miserable! … I am the most miserable woman alive,' cried Bonnibel, wringing her hands, and rocking her large, finely-wrought figure to and fro.

At those accents, uttered in exaggerated despair, Nannie violently started—then silently contradicted them in her heart. No, not the most miserable; far from that!

'Miserable!' Hector's deeper voice echoed very bitterly, 'And what do you think I am? Disgraced, dishonoured in my own eyes; for if I have not broken my word to poor Nannie in the letter, yet how have I kept it in spirit? Miserable! yes;—that is what I am too, in a way a woman like *you* could never understand.'

'Why not?' and with a slow movement of voluptuously expressed grief the weeping girl slid to the ground at Hector's feet, as if she would have kissed them, and there stayed. Yet still, as she crouched, she was not so utterly self-abandoned to sorrow but that she could keep her grace of posture through its every phase.

Hector stooped and stroked her head with a sort of well-nigh contemptuous fondness, that made Nannie quiver all through her; and answered, with a sound in his voice of very bitter mirthfulness against themselves, that had yet no mirth for him:

'Never mind, pretty one, and don't be taking this so much to heart; you will console yourself very soon; I know you well enough for that'

'And will you not have your consolations far more? You will have your rich wife, and all that money can give you both; while I am poor and have nothing. *You* are not to be pitied!' came in wrathful vehemence from the woman at his feet.

An exclamation, at that, from Hector made Nannie recoil;

he never had—never would so have spoken with an oath to her, she felt.

'You have galled and worried me about getting a rich wife—you, and you only!—as if you did not know far better than anyone else in the world, that I am not marrying her for that, that it is an additional torment to feel people may think so; you know I would keep my word to her, if she had not a farthing!'

Bonnibel gave a cry, and softly clasping his knees, shook back her cloud of dark hair, till the moonlight showed her face gazing up at him, and—refined in that radiance—seeming beautiful.

'But, still, you love me?' she murmured with tenderest beseeching.

'Why could you not have left me alone?' answered Hector gloomily; although by the change in his voice, plainly his honest, soft soul was all moved within him. 'Why did you set yourself to *make* me care for you; otherwise, we might all have been happy enough. Nannie is a better woman than you.'

'But still you love me?—say you love me! reiterated the girl, as if beside herself. She rose; she put out her hands towards him, with a little imploring gesture. Then, though Hector stood motionless, mutely asking her to tempt him no more, she drew closer and closer; until, as if unable to restrain herself, she fell upon his breast, with her arms clinging round his neck, in a passionate, unsought embrace. For one brief moment, Nannie felt mad; she stared in a sort of frenzy, with bursting eyeballs, waiting to see! Then Hector, flinging away his last feeble self-restraint, and giving way to his new passion, caught the girl to him and kissed her repeatedly. No; he had not repulsed her, as to the foolish watching heart, it had seemed for that sickening second that he must—because he *should!*

Hitherto Nannie had been a listener, only because, feeling like a stone figure, she had been entirely powerless to speak, move, or go. But now she was choked; the ground seemed reeling under her, the trees rushing this way and that; while there seemed to be ice in her veins, not blood—her heart was so faint, and her brain sick with what seemed to her the horror, the cruelty of it. Why did no voice sound from above out of those dark brass heavens, in which the gold stars seemed all whirling, that should come like a lightning flash, denouncing the treachery of these two—her lover and her friend—who had no *right—no right!*—to stand thus there before her very eyes? *Ah!*—

Unconsciously, in her great agony, Nannie's overcharged heart relieved itself of its bursting feelings by a cry not great indeed, but that startled the other two, who were still locked together in their embraces.

They turned, saw the pale creature, who now with effort crept forward into the moonlight, and stood conscious-stricken.

For a few terrible moments, none of them spoke. But then Bonnibel, who first partly recovered herself, affected a little scream, and with hysterical gaspings clung to Hector's arm for support; reiterating in beseeching accents, as if utterly terrified, 'Keep her away! … Don't let her speak to me—don't let her come near me! … Oh, I am too miserable already; I shall *die* if she comes near me.'

From her shuddering gestures one might have thought Nannie was a murderess, and herself the innocent victim; or that her shrinking rival would smite her with the plague. This so took Nannie aback in her wretchedness that she stood ashamed, as if guilty, looking at both imploringly in her turn, with wandering, distracted gaze.

'Forgive me,' she faltered, her too-sensitive brain being all confused, so that with difficulty she could separate right from wrong, and know herself blameless. 'I followed you here, when I found out by accident you had this meeting-place; because—because it is best to speak soon, and have it over, for us all.'

'So you tracked us here; you have been playing the spy! Is that your high-breeding? Is that what you think the conduct of a lady?' shrieked Bonnibel, now starting forward, her brown eyes aflame, her beautiful features working in convulsive excitement.

Hector at that drew her back, almost roughly, ejaculating with impressive sternness, 'Be quiet—.' And she was quiet; perhaps because he kept his arm round her waist, as if to restrain her violence.

'You might know me better, Bonnibel. You might have trusted me, both of you,' came from Nannie's pale, faltering lips. Then turning her eyes on Hector, with a far-off, unearthly look—as if he and she were dead to each other, and like disembodied spirits could feel no more human love—she added, 'How could you dream I would wish you to keep to your engagement, if I had only known—Ah! you should have had more confidence in me, and we might all have been spared much misery. … But I came here because we can talk so quietly together. And what I to say came was—that I set you quite free from your word, Hector, and I hope you and Bonnibel will soon be married.'

'WHAT—?' came from both the others. She had been speaking in such a dull, apparently quiet way, that until her last word, neither of the listeners seemed to apprehend the drift of her meaning. Hector's exclamation was more like a stifled groan; for he knew well that his relief was bought with the pain of another. But Bonnibel, clasping her hands, uttered it as the jubilant outcry, of a bliss too extravagant for further speech. Then the girl sprang forward, as if she would have hugged Nannie in her senseless delight. But the other, grief-stricken, put her hands up, warning her off; for the sight of that transport of gladness in a friend, (unrelieved by one expression of sympathy!) made all seem worse—almost too hard to bear. At that, and the nearer sight of Nannie's face, Bonnibel stopped short, slowly drew back, and by-and-by faltered in a whisper so low that Hector could not hear (he still stood inert indeed and apparently stupefied, like a strongman shorn of his strength by Delilah), 'I do beg your pardon—I would on my knees if you wished it! I know you think me a wretch, selfish and unfeeling towards you—but O, remember, you are so rich, now, and can have everything else you like. It cannot matter so much to you, now! Otherwise, when you were poor, believe me, I never would! *Don't* look at me like that: I cannot bear it' Whereupon Bonnibel covered her face with her hands and burst into very real crying, as if Nannie's clear gaze had hurt her like the evil eye. Then, still trying to justify herself, and being in a passion with the impossibility of that, she sobbed:

'You never loved Hector as much as I do. You cannot!—or you would never give him up so quietly as this! No, indeed; you would never give him up at all'

At those words, a rush of anger such as she had never known, or should know again in all her pure life, shook Nannie like a reed, and the white moonlight seemed all a sea of red flame before her eyes; the awful dark abyss of wickedness over which each one of our souls seems to hang, while yet our bodies walk the solid earth, and heaven's brightness bids us strain upward to God, was visible to her in that brief instant. She had just power left to steady herself by taking hold of the low, ruined wall beside her; self-command enough not to speak a word. Some ancient carved stones had been piled on this wall, and her fingers grasped one unconsciously; then groping over it, in that strange way the body has of acting when our minds are at too great a tension, found it was roughly outlined as a cross, having been an ornament of the chapel wall. As her right senses slowly returned she took knowledge of it; ever more and more as still she held her peace—until the other two had begun to wonder at her silence, though not daring to interrupt it. At last, she very stilly answered:

'Some day you will both learn that the highest love means sacrifice, not selfishness.' Then moving a little, as if longing to be away and at rest, though all impatience seemed think you owe me any reparation, the best and only way you can show it gone out of her: 'And now, if either of you think you owe me any reparation, the best and only way you can show it is to hurry your marriage, as I said before. Why need you wait? Everything was ready for mine; let it be for yours instead! Bonnibel, you are welcome to my wedding-dress and all my things; we will change places, and I will be your bridesmaid.'

'Nannie, you are mad. You are speaking like an angel of goodness, but we are not so utterly lost to all consideration—not quite so heartless as you think,' interrupted Hector, flushing crimson, the veins in his forehead swelling, his voice thick with emotion.

Bonnibel had only been able to utter an astonished outcry.

'It is the only, the last kindness you can do for me. Hush! listen! The greatest pain to me, the unpleasantness to you, will be the gossip about it all beforehand; once done, the worst is over,' returned Nannie, with such new eagerness, like a dying fire flaming up, that both knew she was in great earnest. 'Besides, Hector, your grandfather will never give his consent; you must forestall it. Oh, I have thought over it all this evening, and there is nothing else possible for either of you!—and nothing better remaining for me.' Then, while the others listened in confused amazement, or with conscience-touched, feeble hesitation, Nannie, with the same painful quietness, went on explaining all that had been in her thoughts. She spoke of their future prospects with such reasonableness, though sadness and sweetness that they could only listen as to one whose spirit was now straining above earthly things. She seemed so much above them neither could speak, feeling more grossly human in their selfishness; nor offer ashamed, half-hearted objections, that must pain her anew. Only misery could come of Hector's fresh engagement to a penniless girl, and his grandfather's anger might be briefer under the more violent shock of knowing him absolutely married; lessened it could not be, either way.

'Talk it over together now,' ended Nannie, raising her hand. 'And when you have decided, come and tell me. I shall be there.' She pointed to the ancient graveyard that lay behind the ruins, almost enclosed by the chapel wood, and went thither. There, a good while later, in the chill of the night and the white mist that crept up in that low ground, Hector found her, standing under a tree beside her old nurse's grave. A motionless, white figure, she was leaning on the headstone, and thinking—he dared not guess of what.

'We have decided; we have agreed you are right,' said the young man, drawing near with slow, heavy steps, and a voice utterly humbled. Then, with an impulse of sorrow and repentance, 'Oh, Nan, can you forgive me?' he burst out. 'We have known each other since we were such little children, and this is the first time I ever deceived you. Indeed! indeed! I never meant to do so. Will you not believe me? … Will you not hear how it all happened—although indeed I hardly know myself.'

'Better not,' she replied, in a voice that seemed to come from far away, between herself and him a great gulf being fixed. 'What can it matter now?'

'Still speak to me … Say you forgive me.'

'Forgive you—yes. I can even say, God bless you—*both*.' At that her voice trembled very greatly; she could not have borne to say, nor he to hear, more. As she ended, Bonnibel, who had followed Hector with a lingering foot-step, approached with jealousy in her heart, not even then trusting those two together.

'Good-bye now till to-morrow,' said Nannie, in the same soundless voice, moving away. 'And Hector, remember, I take the blame of breaking off all between us on myself, when your grandfather comes. You need not thank me ... we have been good enough friends for me to do that. What can his anger matter to me now?'

'Stay one moment—dear Nannie, stay,' cried Bonnibel, in a pitiable tone. 'Only think, how am I to face my grandfather? I cannot tell him to-morrow. He will kill me, he will be so angry; and he never was angry with me before! ... Will you—Oh, like the dear, good angel you are this night to both of us—will you not break it to him?'

'Even this!' thought Nannie bitterly in her heart; then answered aloud: 'As you wish it, then, I will tell him, too.' And so she left them.

CHAPTER 43

AFTER THE BATTLE

But it is after the battle that wounds begin to pain worst. When the heat and excitement of the struggle is over, then is the time for the faintness of reaction, disgust and weariness of life, and the wonder whether it is worth dragging on, maimed and sick as we are—without hope, so it seems, of any better days in store.

And so Nannie White felt, when that night, somehow—for she neither knew nor much cared how—she dragged herself homewards, and found herself upstairs in her own, old-fashioned room. Home! No, dear old Black Abbey was no home for her now; this room, in which she had lived so much of every day since she was a little child, would soon never know her again. She strained her memory, trying to imagine rather than recall the dim time when a little orphan child had been brought to that old house in the woods; then all later days seemed at once spread out before her; how she had grown up happy there and careless, if solitary and shy; how the hope of never leaving the old roof-tree had gladdened her (she hardly dared remember the wild joy of having been loved)—and now, and now—all was over!

The woman's heart felt utterly shamed and despised. She was too crushed for pride or anger.

No one wanted her; those whom she had so loved and trusted would only be relieved in their inmost hearts to be rid of her. She would go away in three or four days at most, not caring whither, only longing to hide from all eyes.

Rebecca was dead, and not another human soul cared to have her presence, except, indeed, poor Fräulein Schmidt. Nannie would join her old governess, and take her with her away; it was something to know she could be of use to one living being, although that but a withered-hearted woman, to whom study was more than all the joy or pain in real life. There was still Aileen—but, in the bitterness of her soul, Nannie unjustly thought: 'She is a De Burgo! After the first natural sympathy for me, blood will assert itself, and little by little her brother and his wife will be all to her, and I, ever growing by degrees a stranger … I am different from these De Burgos; I gave them my whole heart and life, and they will only give me hold of a little part of theirs. I love them too much to bear this slow sundering of affection; better break with Aileen, as with her brother, at once.'

Nannie crept softly into bed and lay down, numb and cold. She dully hoped to sleep; because otherwise how was she to go through the morrow and the next day, and the next, and show no sign of pain to all the prying eyes whose pity or coarse gossip would drive her mad? But in purgatory sleep surely comes not; and she tasted its worst torment, memory, if it be indeed:

> 'A fire of soul in which they burn,
> And by which they are purified from sin—
> Rid of the grossness which had gathered round them.'

Past scenes, loving looks, kind manly words, leapt up in her brain like tongues of flame in hell, persistently, unceasingly.

Under an uncontrollable impulse, Nannie hastily rose, struck a light, and resolving to force sleep and forgetfulness, poured out some drops of laudanum. With the bottle of poison in her hand, a sudden terrible thought struck her! A few drops to dull pain was no harm!—a few more only, where began the supposed evil?—and all the lifelong pain, hopelessness, wretchedness she foresaw, would be stopped.

What was the use of thinking of God, if indeed there *was* a God?—for He had mocked all the prayers for herself and Hector she had so long offered up, and blessed Bonnibel, who thought so little about Him. What said Epictetus: 'The door is always open when the play palls on the senses.' She remembered reading that so long ago with her old governess, and had not the dead philosopher that said it surely known pain, too? Quick leapt up another answering memory; the saying of Pythagoras, which she herself, whilst still untried, had loved to quote, 'No man has a right to desert his post, without the orders from the great Commander.'

Nannie dropped the bottle and turned away trembling; not a drop tasted. The awful temptation surely came not out of her own heart, she trusted; some demon had sat on her shoulder and whispered it into her ear. The Fräulein had moved her, though not brought her to doubt that there was a devil, a real Spirit of Evil; but that night and thenceforth Nannie verily believed in his existence—knew she had almost fallen under the sudden, insidious attack on that side she would in calmer moments have contemptuously thought impregnable, fortified by custom, philosophy, religion.

It was not a night for sleep, but for prayer and watching; and thus Nannie White, in terrified humility, passed it.

Grasping again her old faith, that all things in her life were ordered beforehand, and must turn to her good, because she did love the mighty unseen Father who, as she believed, had in return promised her this, she became by-and-by calmed by weeping; comforted by that spiritual consolation she asked for and believingly received. Brokenly came thoughts of those who, like herself, had chosen the thorny path, yet thought it 'not strange concerning their tribulations, but rejoiced … who had felt purged to bring forth more fruit … had passed through a baptism of fire' … had gladly repeated, 'Nearer to Thee, e'en though it be a cross that raiseth me.'

And so, towards the still, grey dawn, Nannie did indeed find that peace of soul she had striven for through the night; and her over-wearied body was even plunged in sleep, as in a bath of rest.

Too soon came morning, with all its accustomed noises, and the bustle of day. Nannie awoke slowly, with a sense of a terrible weight burdening her mind. For a few moments she actually sleepily supposed it was some dim nightmare, and could have laughed, being so relieved that the unknown horror was gone. Next followed sickening doubt … remembrance … certainty!

That was a gray summer day, all overcast. To the end of her life Nannie never afterwards lived through such another day of heavy, sunless warmth, without living again through some part of the pain of that long-past one. But of that day and the following, only two scenes stood out with distinctness in her memory; other details seemed all as if merged in a sky of grey, dull pain.

The first was, she remembered going down in the morning to the manse, to fulfil her promise of the past night. At the small garden-gate the old minister met her, with his face all a broad blank as regarded knowledge of the trouble that yet flushed it, and was shown in his eyes and their surrounding additional wrinkles.

'Oh, Miss White, what is wrong—what has happened?' he cried, holding Nannie's hand and staring close into her face. 'My Bonnibel has eaten no breakfast; hardly a bite except what I coaxed her to, I assure you!—and only drank just her cup of tea. She began crying about I do not know what, and has kept on at it; and all she'll say is, that you are coming and you'll tell me.'

'Yes, Mr. Cosby, I'll tell you. Let us go into the house.'

'You haven't—you could never have fallen out with my girl, Miss Nannie? She may have offended you, but I'll venture to say beforehand it never was meant, for indeed, indeed, she is a good girl!'

'Come into the parlour, Mr. Cosby, and you shall hear all about it,' said Nannie softly, with a dull resignation that frightened the old man into looking at her with a presage of greater mischief done, than would her livelier emotion; than had even his grandchild's sobs.

How strangely familiar the little manse parlour seemed; reminding Nannie of all the days when she had looked on that small house as a kindly refuge. Old Mary was in the kitchen, washing up the breakfast-things, as distant noises of crockery told. Bonnibel was locked into her own room upstairs, doubtless. The old minister sat down, from habit, in his big arm-chair by the window, beside the little table that bore his few well-worn old books on theology. The blind was half drawn down; Nannie remembered even that later, and how she herself moved where least light would fall on her features.

Then, clearing her voice, she told what had passed. She told it gently, according to her nature; not one bitter breath of tone, or smallest severe word, passed her lips. But that great, sweet patience touched the heart of good old Cosby more intensely than could any other manner on her part. He covered his face in an agony of shame and vicarious remorse for his grandchild's treachery (such he felt it to be) towards her friend; towards this still, pale girl, who only raised her voice now to plead with him the cause of the transgressors.

'Oh, Bonnibel, Bonnibel! my little innocent lassie; how could you be so deceiving?' he groaned.

After that exclamation of righteous horror, for such indeed it was, Nannie dared not look at him nor guess how he took her further revelation. She only heard her own voice, and his laboured answering breathing.

But, when no more remained to be said, the unhappy grandfather laid down his shining bald head on the table, and wept with a strength of sorrow, that, at his age, was pitiful to witness.

'She cannot marry this man; she shall not—or I will never forgive her,' he groaned in abasement of spirit, through which flickered holy wrath.

'She will marry him now; it is best for them both. And you, as a Christian, must forgive her,' softly answered Nannie, like the voice of an angel in his ear.

The old minister solemnly raised his venerable head, looking to heaven with streaming eyes.

'Oh, what does it matter that my granddaughter has shamed me, and brought down my grey head with sorrow to the grave—my time, anyway, is almost spent. But you—you! she has ruined your life!'

Then what Nannie best remembered was the afternoon of the next day, when she stood above the horse-shoe steps at the door of Black Abbey House, awaiting its old master's arrival. She wore a white gown—so she often did—but her face was not always thus as white as her dress; nor did the old servants and even the labourers look at her with such curious glances, and hush their tongues, as if guessing something strange. But, although they had marvelled at seeing Nannie going down so very early to the manse in the dewy morning's freshness, how could they tell that the white summer dress, such as she usually wore, was indeed, this especial morning, a bridesmaid's gown?—and nothing was yet known of the hurried and strange ceremony (as it seemed to all concerned) in the manse parlour, that had followed. The secret was well kept. To Nannie the whole had seemed a distorted dream, even while she listened for the carriage-wheels bringing old Mr. de Burgo home for *her* wedding that was to have been—to-morrow! Throughout the long grey yesterday, she had helped to settle all things for the secret wedding, in a way that seemed quiet to indifference to any who were not close observers. She remembered afterwards how Bonnibel had congratulated her upon it, declaring, while weeping a little (not much!) in a shamefaced way, and carefully wiping her eyes lest their brightness should be dimmed for the morrow, that she could now feel quite relieved and thankful in mind, because Nannie 'minded it so little.'

Likewise, the new bride gratefully accepted Nannie's offered gifts of most of the wedding-clothes that had been made for the latter.

'I would almost like not to take them—but beggars must not be choosers, and I can't afford pride on an empty pocket,' had thought Miss Hawthorn, rapidly determining in her own mind to hide the origin of most of her new finery from Hector's knowledge. Luckily, he had come back so lately, and been fishing so much, to divert his troubled thoughts as she knew, that Nannie had not called on him to admire much of it; so Bonnibel could say with real fervour of thankfulness, 'Oh, you dear! you are far too good to me, indeed! Not that you would quite like to wear these yourself, oh, that I can understand, though you do mind about it so little! … And then you are so rich; and we shall be so poor, while the old gentleman is alive—but still it is inexpressibly good of you!'

'We have been—I mean, we are friends, so it is not very much to do this for you,' said Nannie; then went on with a dead smile, that was, yet, not without some latent satire, 'Will you not have the wedding-gown too? It seems a pity not to use it. You would hardly care to wear it to-morrow, as you will be married before eight o'clock; but it might do for balls and dinners afterwards.'

'Oh yes, dear; yes—even to be dyed later, it will be very useful,' Bonnibel answered, with glib, apparent gratitude, yet a touch of disappointment in her tone that Nannie did not understand. Did she want the wedding-veil too? That had belonged to Nannie's mother; and to give it would have seemed desecration. Otherwise, she gave the rest with a curious pleasure—glad to be rid of the sight of them; glad, too, in the secret feeling that it should be owing to herself that Hector's wife came to him in goodly raiment, and thus she would be heaping coals of fire, in forgiveness, on his head unknown. It was most sweet secret revenge.

On this very morning then—very early—Nannie went down alone to the manse, and met the few others. All stood silent and miserable, only awaiting Bonnibel, for the special marriage service to begin. Then the door opened, and lo, Bonnibel appeared; no downcast culprit, she, but a blooming, conscious beauty, all shimmering from head to foot in the gloss of a glorious white-satin wedding-gown!

Hector, who had stood like a stone, started and paled; the old minister looked aghast; but the bride knelt down with excruciating complacency, and arranged the folds of her gown. She thought, with inward glee and satisfaction, that Hector would remember afterwards how handsome she had looked on her wedding morning: not a mere dowdy in a travelling-gown.

Nannie, with inward amazement, wondered the dress did not scorch its wearer, like a Nessus' shirt. In a stony, stupid way, she found herself looking at its fit; thinking how late Bonnibel must have sat up last night to alter it, for she could see where the seams of the pretty bodice had been roughly unpicked and creased.

Then, with a start, she seemed to become conscious of what was *really* going on! There is no use in dwelling on the sacred agony of a noble soul, while the love that is dearer than life itself is being slowly burnt out, killed—passing for ever into the region of the impossible—hopeless! Such agony Nannie White felt then. Luckily, neither of the bridal pair could see her set expression. The old minister did so a moment, and covered his face in earnest prayer. But when they all rose, the bridesmaid's features were again calm and still as ever. It was Nannie, too, who first saluted the bride, with no Judas' touch of her lips;

then she took Hector's clay-cold hand with an earnest clasp, but seeing the conscience-stricken man could bear no more, left him in silence.

But at the door she turned again, and beckoned to Bonnibel, who stood gazing after her. The latter, with suddenly roused feeling, sprang with remorseful affection that pierced through all vanity and selfishness, to her side.

'Be good and true to Hector, my dear,' said poor Nannie, softly. 'Remember, he has a large, honest heart, but is easily led. Strive with him upward, and may God bless you both; but if not—you will murder all the best in him.' And she went out …

And now, all this past scene seeming as a dreadful dream—a sick horror—Nannie White heard the carriage-wheels that brought old Mr. de Burgo home turn in at the lodge. Old Robert drove him—that whilom* traitor and time-server, who now, according to his nature, was servilely ready to kiss the ground that Nannie trod. Only owing to her generosity, he was still coachman; for his master, when Nannie returned to Black Abbey in fortune and favour, had expressed his willingness to make a victim of the informer who had once betrayed Hector's and her courtship, if her revengeful feelings in the least desired it. But Nannie felt bound to forgive the man, because he had hurt herself alone, and, besides, was rather old and useless; for which reasons indeed he was allowed to stay at Black Abbey till he died.

On this day, too, Robert had surely hinted mysteriously to his master that something was amiss, although the cause was yet unknown; for old Mr. de Burgo looked quite anxiously into the face of the girl who met him.

'How pale you are, my white Nannie; too pale,' said the old gentleman, hobbling up the steps slowly with gouty legs,

* whilom = former

and touching her cheek with one finger, in a feeble attempt at pleasantry. And Nannie, seeing how shaky and life-worn the former snowy-haired old beau now looked, felt almost sorry for him; knowing how eager, even at this instant, were his fingers to clutch the money-bags of the orphan he had grudgingly reared, and how bitter must be his disappointment! Otherwise she had no pity for him in this matter. Why should she? knowing he had no real affection for herself. Seeing she did not answer, he croaked on with forced gaiety, 'Are we ready for the wedding to-morrow? and where is my young rascal—where is Hector?'

'There cannot well be any wedding to-morrow, Mr. de Burgo … not to-morrow. And Hector has gone off to amuse himself for some little time.'

'You have not quarrelled with him?' exclaimed the old man, with sharp (almost fierce) suspicion; though next moment he tried to qualify his feelings by dissembling an apologetic smile, that only made him resemble a toothless satyr to Nannie's sick mind.

The carriage had gone round into the courtyard; the servants had carried the luggage indoors; and these two remained alone before the door, on the stone terrace of the steps overlooking the rich prospect of lawns, wood, sea, and of the richly-cultivated champaign that the De Burgos had so long owned in pride.

'I have not quarrelled with Hector, Mr. de Burgo. Whatever has happened, we are still fast friends—yet! Would it disappoint you very much if I did not marry your grandson?'

Nannie spoke with a voice soft as the dropping of a summer shower; she even smiled with her white, weary face. But old Mr. de Burgo trembled as if palsy shook his bones, tried to speak, but made only a sound in his throat; while his dim eyes wandered feebly from her features over the landscape around with an expression of witless groping and anticipative despair. Then he murmured feebly—

'You could not throw him over! ... Why, I have watched you often, and he is the one man on earth that you cared for, or ever will care for in the same way! ... Other women may be fickle fools; but I have seen some like you in the world in my day, and know what I say is true. Child! make this up again with him.'

Nannie trembled at that, and then she told him all. It was she who had broken off the engagement, she even said; Hector had tried his best to keep his word. But as by degrees the whole truth dawned upon old Mr. de Burgo, he passed through stages of ever-increasing astonishment and rage, till at last, in a paroxysm of frenzy, he screamed—

'Married! ... married this morning! Then all is lost, lost, lost; and this house may be sold over my head to-morrow, and the whole Black Abbey estate is gone!'

'What do you mean?' ejaculated the terrified girl. 'Are you so much in debt?'

'Debt, girl! I am ruined. And now Hector is married—fool! jade! Curse them both! Your money would just have saved us in the nick of time; now it is too late.'

'Not too late. Take it still!—take all I have, and save Black Abbey for Hector!'

But Mr. de Burgo did not hear, having fallen down unconscious in a fit, and was carried by the affrighted servants, who came running to Nannie's terrified call, into the house he might never more call his own. Nannie's generous out-cry came too late to give comfort to the miserable spirit of the old man, who had always sought his own before others' good, and had broken hearts rather than forego any gratification of his own pleasure. After many days her former guardian somewhat recovered; but his bodily senses, those servants of the busy brain, could impress no more messages from the outer world distinctly on his mind. The man had existed for self alone, and in that shock his intellect found its mainspring broken.

But what Nannie had uttered in the excited impulse of the moment, to that she immediately steadfastly kept, and redeemed her word. She was not too late to save Black Abbey from alien possession. Before gossip could be spread about the matter, before even Hector de Burgo knew more than that the old estate of his ancestors was hopelessly in the grip of strangers, and his prospects ruined, it had passed into her friendly hands. And although in doing this she sacrificed all the fortune her old nurse had left to her, Nannie thought it well spent.

PART IV

'But she was one of those wrought by the Gods
To be to foolish men as sharpest rods
To scourge their folly.
… And her great eyes
Truthful to show her to the cold and wise
E'en as she was, would make some cast aside
Whatever wisdom in their hearts might hide.'

W. MORRIS.

'For though her smile was sad and faint,
    And though her voice was low,
She never murmured a complaint,
    Nor hinted at her woe.
Nor harboured in her gentle breast
    The lightest thought of ill,
Giving all, forgiving all,
    Pure and perfect still.'

WHYTE MELVILLE.

CHAPTER 44

THE MISTRESS OF BLACK ABBEY

Five years have glided away; five times the sea of green-wood around Black Abbey has broken into bud, and been covered with glorious leafage, that has as often passed through russet and yellow tints into winter bareness. By such dates, one quiet woman dwelling in the house reckons time.

Beyond the prospects of the woods, on the blue sea of waters, the far ships sail, coming and going as of yore. Nothing outside Black Abbey is changed; nature only changes to renew itself.

Within the gabled, gray old house, there was still as much silence as had been of old for many a year. The blinds in the side wings were still always drawn down, since no one ever inhabited the deserted guest-chambers there; the ivy mantled as thickly as ever on the walls; the pigeons cooed and strutted on the steep-sloping roofs. Nevertheless, there was an air of renovation everywhere; the care of a loving mistress was once more visible after a generation of neglect. The fountains played again in the garden, the flower-borders were gay, the yew-hedges trimmed, the walks and smooth greensward marvels of exquisite tidiness. There was not a single alteration to be found in all the grounds, except, indeed, these pleasing small ones, that were only carefully loving restorations. Otherwise, closing one's eyes and forgetting time, one who knew the place might easily fancy that out of the oak hall and down the horse-shoe steps three laughing children—Hector, Aileen, and Nannie—might come running any minute; or remembering later times that the latter, alone, like a second sleeping princess, might be seen leaning on the stone balustrade before the door, awaiting unconsciously some fair young prince.

But no merry madcaps, nor slim, gracious maiden, fancy-free, came out now. Instead, steps forth only a woman still young, whose figure has indeed lost little of its former slim pliancy, whose face is still gracious, and sweetly rounded as five years ago. Yet, looking at her, one seems to become aware as by a sixth sense, to perceive as with eyes of the mind, that a change is there which bodily vision cannot descry nor words quite describe; except that imagination may say vaguely: She has passed through some refining fire, she has come forth purified out of some furnace of affliction. It was not that she seemed unhappy; far, far from that! Rather there was a new wonderful contentment in her expression, but it seemed one not drawn from this earth, of the spirit essentially; that strange, bright satisfaction which the things of the world cannot give.

Every day that was warm and sunshiny, she might be seen walking at the same hour down the wooded drive beside a bath-chair that held old Mr. de Burgo; if that shrunken, decrepit figure could be he, that was utterly doting, toothless, bald, a ghastly wreck of the former keen-witted and spruce old beau, so proud of his snowy hair and still vigorous health. His constitution in youth must have been marvellous, for although, after all his life of excess, the popular verdict of Black Abbey declared he 'ought to have died three or four year ago,' there he was still, like a lamp flickering on long after it is expected to go out, and at this rate bid almost to become a centenarian. At moments, too, he had flashes of reviving intellect, mostly shown unhappily in fits of weak rage, when he would attempt to strike Nannie as she sought to soothe him, threaten to turn her out of doors for a beggar on his charity, or to dismiss all the servants at a moment's notice. Often he would point with a shaking finger at the trees, and desire Nannie, in a mumbled whisper, to have them all felled, for he was a poor man, very poor—ruined! and then he would feebly weep.

Nannie did her duty nobly by the old man, even those people granted (and they were many), who believed that she had been entirely dependent on his bounty since her baby-hood. The world outside her woods was not even generally aware that she had veritably bought Black Abbey. Many supposed it was 'some mere temporary arrangement,' or she would not have kept her counsel so close, lived such a retired life for an heiress (although to be sure she had been jilted!); and it was even credibly declared, she had been heard to say several times when questioned by curious peasant-folk, anxious to know if the ould family was really turned out—that, for her part, she trusted Mr. Hector, or 'the captain,' as he had now come to be called, would yet 'come into his own' again. Thus, at least, the spirit of her perhaps differently worded answer was rendered in the popular dialect.

Meanwhile, after these five years, there was not another estate so improved in all the country round; few now to match it. So said any of the neighbours, the Veres, and Hares, and Desboroughs, that ever chanced to ride or drive past that now little-visited part of the country. Some few match-making matrons, admiring, they declared. Miss White's beautiful conduct to her old guardian, and struck by her strange history, even made their adventurous way through the great, rusty iron gates and came to call; admiring still more the view inside the gates of woods, park, old house and gardens that for twenty-five years and more none of the 'county' people had deigned, as they declared, or had been asked, as old Mr. de Burgo contemptuously used to answer, to behold. But these few visitors were so stilly received by the gentle recluse of Black Abbey, whom no temptations could lure into accepting their invitations, or persuasions to appear at this or the other small country gathering under their matronly wing, that she was by-and-by left again in the utter peace she alone desired of them. The affair of Hector's marriage had been a nine days' wonder in the county; was now almost forgotten, except as a story to recount to any new-comers or strangers, who, happening to see the noble woods from afar, inquired who lived at Black Abbey. The Veres, and Hares, and Desboroughs all repeated, that of course it was strange that young De Burgo should lose his property, and give up an heiress to make a runaway match with a Presbyterian minister's granddaughter: but they unfailingly added, that there were so many strange stories about the De Burgos of late times, that really one had grown to expect nothing better of them.

And thus Nannie, who had longed all her life with a poet's longing to travel and see all the beauty of nature and art denied to her northern home, still lived on here, as she had lived since childhood; in the old home, among the old haunts. The associations might have been full of daily pain to her; but none could guess it from her behaviour. In former days she had used to cry, in rare complaining moments to her old governess, that she often felt like a caged migratory bird in autumn. The Fräulein lived again at Black Abbey, just as if she had never left it, but Nannie never complained to her, now. Rather, when the latter, bewailing that such gifts of mind and a young life should be self-devoted to the care of a doting aged man, declared wonderingly that her pupil practised a virtue she herself would have found impossible, Nannie would smile, reminding her old preceptress that the latter, and no one else, had first taught, her 'the beauty of self-abnegation for the good of the human race. The Fräulein applied her philosophy vaguely indeed; thought the few should be glad to suffer, that the many might be blessed; and so would have had Nannie leave the care of one imbecile invalid to gladden with her gifts more of mankind, by being only a poet and less a woman.

And Nannie—she held the doctrine a little differently, that was all.

But still, with all her cares of the Black Abbey estate and the feeble old man, a little book of song stole into the world silently once a year (or even less often), and was welcomed with ever increasing pleasure and praise by the jostling crowds in that great arena of which she knew so little, as the work of an almost unknown, nameless woman-poet. This was the only relaxation of her otherwise austere life. In these, denied many of the material gladnesses of other women, her imagination revelled, singing the ever-new sweet unities of love, and youth, and spring, so that those who never saw or knew her believed the writer was indeed a happy woman.

Well, and so now, thank God! she could say low to herself she was. She had learned the lesson of life; she had learned the lesson of love; she had learned the lesson of all true poets, which a living one has sung so well, that—

> 'Only suffering draws
> The inner heart of song and can elicit
> The perfumes of the soul …
> … therefore it comes
> That suffering weds with song.'

'She is a true poet now; but she never could have written thus, perhaps never would have gained a place among those who live on earth after their death, had she married Hector de Burgo,' thought Luke Cosby often gravely to himself. 'She tried to believe him her master, or at least a fitting mate. And while love blinded her, and riches smoothed everything it may be—she would have been contented. But if sorrow or sickness came, she alone would have been the care-carrier, the brain, the soul of their union. Even prosperous, he would not have appreciated her one gift, would have thought his wife left her rightful home-sphere and catered too much for the public by being a poetess, to please him altogether. It would have choked her soul; it would have veritably shortened her life, to have been so torn asunder between her art and her duty to him.'

Duty! the praise of devotion to duty, its laud above fame, above learning, above genius, above all gifts of the gods! the beauty of common everyday duty, that indeed was the one theme Nannie now hymned most musically in many a different song. She never forced her lesson upon those who read; but, like an impalpable, sweet essence, it pervaded all her thoughts and breathed melodiously through all her verse.

Her teaching was all of comfort, too; of comfort and hope both for here and hereafter. Some thought she was almost a heretic in her largeness of mind and brightness of hope, but her words stole comfortingly into the hearts of the sad and life-weary, reviving them like soft spring rain after the bleakness of winter. She would have said herself had she known it, 'Life is worth living, with all its pain, if only to feel one has given one drop of gladness to another.'

Five springs had been; and with each one Aileen came back, with the swallows, sunshine, and south winds, to Black Abbey, to stay and lighten Nannie's cares as long as she dared—only regretting that the latter could not come abroad with herself and her aunt, in autumn and winter. But Nan did not like to leave old Mr. de Burgo in the care of servants alone; none of whom naturally were attached to him either.

'You always seem to be doing what *ought* to be the work of some of us others,' said Aileen with loving commiseration. 'You are a true poet, and do not naturally care for everyday work, yet here you are improving Black Abbey like a dream, because I verily believe we De Burgos were not good enough to have it any longer. No; I will not hush! And you have longed, far more than ever I did, to travel and see the world, and still here you have been fated to stay. And when we were children you were always far more afraid of grandpapa than even I was, and disliked him more; but now you have nursed him all these years, as no one else would, and I go abroad and amuse myself.'

'You have your aunt to live with and care for—and I have no one, remember,' said Nannie; and then at a certain sharp look of regret in Aileen's face, quickly smiled cheerfully and asked the lately-come spring visitor to saunter out in the pale evening and see the garden, and how all the vineries were restored, and the old stables improved, since the mistress of Black Abbey could afford this expense lately, having in the bygone four years thought far more of the estate outside the demesne walls.

Aileen's words will serve to show her feeling now towards the companion of her childhood. On the same day she heard that Hector had deserted the latter and married Bonnibel, the bright, energetic little creature started home-wards (having been abroad), and travelled without resting, to bring her friend what loving consolation she could. Since then the two women had been knit together in heart and soul, even as never before in their lives, with a love passing that of sisters which would endure to their lives' end.

It was the fifth spring now, since the crisis of Nannie's life had been played in the dark of one summer's night down in the chapel wood. Aileen had but just arrived back from foreign warmer shores, with a heart full of love as ever for her adopted sister, who waited for her always with great patience, but even greater yearning. They had much to tell each other; and, as usual, talked often of Luke Cosby. Aileen had gone to hear him preach on the Sunday before. She always waited in London to do that before coming over to Black Abbey, in order, she said, 'to tell Nannie about it;' nothing else would have delayed her return 'home' as she called it. She was still a Bohemian, but not to the former extent by any means; despised society, so-called, more than ever, but sometimes wished as she had never used for a home life. She did indeed go back to London later to spend some weeks of the season with her aunt; but this was from a sense of duty. Then both aunt and niece came again to stay the rest of the summer, till autumn, with Nannie; each year went round alike.

'I never saw such crowds before of fashionable people, as those who went to hear him preach this last Sunday, although he is not of their church' (him meant Luke Cosby), Aileen this time said, with a tone of subdued pride that the gifts of their friend in childhood were at last recognized, as she had long felt they deserved. 'It was a splendid sermon, and all those listening hundreds seemed almost as deeply interested as I was; and yet he said to me afterwards, that he would rather have preached to a congregation of the very poor, who so seldom hear the Gospel. He is a truly good and great man; he does not care for his fame—does not even seem to understand how widely he is known and revered. It has almost made me angry to hear him talk so humbly of himself and his position as he has done, the few times during these past years that I have met him.' For though Luke had now gained his soul's wish, and since some four years had a chapel in London, that great heart of England, where his breadth of views and fiery eloquence, far from being found unorthodox, as by his Cosby kinsfolk and former congregations, were blessed by hundreds of thinking listeners, who would not have hearkened to present-day Scribes and Pharisees, nor even to the many good men who preach platitudes—still, he remained out of his pulpit gaunt unassuming Luke Cosby, with the same simple hearty laugh as of old for his intimate friends. He had been greatly shocked by his cousin Bonnibel's treacherousness, when her strange marriage news reached him; but, as regarded himself alone, more shocked than grieved, as after a while those who knew him well perceived. So he lived in London; and Aileen de Burgo, as we know, was in London each year for a short time in spring; yet they very seldom met, although such fast friends. Aileen was shy of asking him to come and see her; Luke, without encouragement, too shy to come. She used at rare times to slip in a corner of his church to hear him preach unperceived; that was all. He ventured to pay her a formal visit each year, and was once or so asked back by her old aunt. His holiday-time, too, he took towards winter out of kindness to a friend who relieved him in his duties, and spent it quietly in the Black Abbey manse trying to cheer up his old uncle; and at that time Aileen was always gone abroad!

But now, as these two talked together over Luke, his writings and his success (and it was wonderful how Aileen, who generally led the conversation, seemed always to come round again, by the most unlikely paths, to the same attractive starting point), Nannie observed, 'I wonder if he would have risen in the same way, if he had married Bonnibel.' She never would allow herself to shrink from speaking of Hector's wife, when it was natural in the course of talk to mention her; and yet she often felt a slight, inward hesitation before pronouncing that name.

'Risen—not he! Or, if he had, it would have been with a weight round his neck. Look at poor Hector,' said her companion with low scornfulness. Nannie winced. It was by no means the first time she had heard similar hints from Aileen's lips; for that hot-hearted little woman would forgive her own enemies, after a blaze of resentment, but she had never yet forgiven her brother's wife for supplanting her best friend. From the first time that—some months after their marriage—Nannie had forced herself to ask cheerfully after Hector and his wife, trusting (and that from her heart) it was well with them, she had heard no blissful auguries from Aileen. Happy?—perhaps! As happy as they deserved, under the circumstances. The truth was, Aileen knew the details she could give would only grieve Nannie; and yet she herself could not altogether keep silence. But the tidings of old Mr. de Burgo's ruin, that Black Abbey must be sold, had been a terrible blow to Hector; had been a bitter disappointment to Bonnibel—who indeed made as much outcry to strangers, although she dared not to her husband, as if Nannie had somehow cheated them out of their lawful inheritance. She had realised her childhood's wild ambition, and married Hector de Burgo, but not the heir of Black Abbey! she was aghast at the discovery of their poverty, then furiously indignant. Hector took his change of prospects after the first shock in silence, manfully; changed out of his cavalry regiment that was an extravagant one, into the line; and was quartered for a long time in dismal parts of the South and West of Ireland. At first, so Aileen very vaguely hinted, Bonnibel felt obliged to put a good face on the matter that she should not seem to have married Hector for money. Afterwards—pretences at being satisfied were a bore! She hated the bogs around them; the society was dull, dull as ditchwater. A man's desire is his paradise; but she, thinking she had gained hers, found herself outside in the wilderness instead. It was not in her spoilt-child nature to conceal her ever-growing discontent.

So much Aileen had gathered from her brother's own curt observations, on the rare occasions when they had met since. She knew no more; only that Bonnibel, longing for more amusement, managed at times to get it here or there, leaving him meanwhile alone. He never said a word to his sister against this; merely observed, with a heavy air, that perhaps it was hard on his wife to lose the prospect of all she had expected, and so he let her take what pleasure she could. Poor Hector! Of late they had moved to England and were in gayer quarters, consequently Bonnibel was in higher spirits. But all Aileen now said of this was, 'They came to see me in London, and Bella was looking—well, very handsome; and was expecting to enjoy herself. As for Hector, he does not seem to care to stir about much, except for fishing and yachting. He seems entirely devoted to his profession now, and to have given up all thoughts of a country life—so much the better for him! And I saw the two little children, my namesake the eldest, and the boy. Hector seems very fond of them—fonder than their mother, who thinks children plagues.' (She never called her brother's wife by the old pretty name now.) 'But his looks are certainly changed for the worse, he is grown so much stouter, much quieter.'

'Oh! what do looks matter in a man?' said Nannie, with a deprecating smile: she always took the part of these absent ones as far as she could.

'Oh! nothing, of course,' answered Aileen quietly, 'except—some persons' good-looks seem to come from the soul, and to conquer the plainness of the features.'

'You make me think of Luke Cosby,' said Nannie; indeed, she said it to change the subject. 'How much I should like to see him here now.'

'And so you may, if he keeps his word. He told me last Sunday that he would try to come over and see his uncle for two days, soon.'

'No, really? And you never told me until now!' cried Nannie, changing from a tone of jubilee to one of lively reproach.

'I—we have had so much to talk about,' said Aileen with a most embarrassed air. 'But very likely he won't come at all. It was only that I regretted never meeting him now at Black Abbey, as in old days; and he said if he had known that, he would have managed to come somehow—only he thought I did not really mean it. So I—Oh, I suppose I said I did—but here were a good many people about; so I am not quite sure what it was. Only when we shook hands he said he hoped to be over shortly—that was all.'

'Ah!' said Nannie; no more. But she said and thought a good deal more in her heart.

CHAPTER 45

LOVE AND DEATH

A FEW days later came a soft May evening. The whole land was now fresh-washed with late April showers, scented from hawthorn-brakes, decked with fresh green, and the birds were jubilant in the woods and every hedgerow.

In the long, sweet twilight, the two young women went down from the house at Black Abbey to pay the old minister at the manse a visit. Hardly a day passed, indeed, that Nannie did not visit him, and that mostly for a good time; but on this especial one, old Mr. de Burgo had been too ailing all day for her to leave him until now; her daily life indeed was spent between these two aged men, who both needed her gentle care so much, yet so differently.

They had reached the manse orchard, that was all snowy-sweet with masses of blossom in the tender evening light; then, just as they were about to pass through the garden-wicket, Aileen started back. 'He is here—he has come! Oh, do not let us go in.'

'He—who?' demanded Nannie, surprised.

'Mr. Luke. Don't you see a long clay pipe on the bench there—the old minister only smokes short ones. Come, quick; let us turn back. It would look so strange, as if we were coming to call on him.'

While Nannie, loth to disappoint the poor old minister inside there of his expected visit, still hesitated—preparing a laughing expostulation against Aileen's new extreme concern—what should rise above the hedge but the tall figure of Luke Cosby himself! Had he overheard them? for even as he uttered his greetings, repeating how glad he was to see them both, he looked awkward and confused; then, striding to open the wicket, said to Nannie, with an appealing look, 'You are surely not going away? Are you not coming in; my uncle has been so looking forward to your coming all the afternoon.'

Nannie felt Aileen plucking her sleeve, with another appealing look to do nothing of the sort, but come away. Still, it was only a half-hearted plucking; and so she, hardening her heart against her own sex, granted Luke's petition with a sweet smile, not daring to meet Aileen's reproaching eyes.

They found Mr. Cosby sitting in the little parlour after his tea. His large arm-chair had been wheeled by Luke to the window, that the dear old man might sit there and enjoy the view of the orchard in its beauty, since he was grown feeble in these last years, and not able to go out in the evenings. Nevertheless, by day he still went, though very slowly, all about his parish, and did its whole work by himself! Work kept him from thinking so much, he confided to Nannie, and it was thinking, not work, that had grieved and aged him; he hoped to die in harness. The old man's kindly face was no longer broad and rubicund as it had been; his mouth was sunken now, his hue greying. His bald head that had shone like red-gold above its ring of silver hair, was covered with a black silk cap to keep out the cold. Indeed, he was altogether greatly changed; he had never held up his head since the day his granddaughter married, so all the folks who knew him best said under their breath. But however his body might have grown decrepit, old Mr. Cosby's mind was as bright and peaceful as ever, his heart as fresh and loving with all his years; and as he stroked Aileen's hand and welcomed her, she thought somehow of the Apostle John, who, as St. Jerome tells, when too aged and feeble to preach, used to be led to church that he might say to the people, 'Little children, love one another.' But though he was delighted to see Aileen, and talked to her gladly, telling with pride how Luke, 'his boy Luke,' had come that very day to the old home, gladdening and surprising every one in the parlour beyond measure, and what a great scholar Luke was now and well-known and sought after, dear, dear! only to think of it, while as a lad he had been so wild after his rod and gun, and so forth—while yet he thus prattled to her, yet soon the good old man's thoughts and attention strayed to Nannie, and there plainly stayed. She was his daily comfort and consolation now—she brought him his inner sunshine; and this day it had seemed long of coming. More than that, since the morning on which he said that his grandchild had ruined her life, all the old man's love and pity had gone forth to Nannie, without let or hindrance. To try and share with sympathy her small daily troubles, to even feel, that by his own loneliness and feebleness he gave her an interest in life, was some satisfaction to the poor aged minister; but when he succeeded in doing something that gave her even the smallest pleasure—that indeed was the brightest moment of the day to him! She was so rich now, and still young, and a woman, whilst he was only a poor and infirm old man, whose granddaughter had robbed her of the one thing she truly prized. Still, he could daily give her words of pity and blessing; carefully guarded for her the earliest as the latest flower-buds in his garden-plot, trusting that there might be none such in the big Black Abbey garden; insisted on bestowing upon her each year his finest swarm of bees—and prayed for her.

Now—so soon as he had unconsciously turned his whole mind and attention to Nannie, who had set herself down, as usual, beside his chair—the other two, naturally, had begun to talk together. And, as after a little while Aileen admired some flower in the garden-plot, Luke bashfully asked her to come outside and see it nearer; and she hesitatingly thereto agreed. After which, with half-reluctant steps, they might have been seen to stray towards the orchard—after which last they were lost to view. Meanwhile, Nannie was stoutly endeavouring not to indulge at all her inner curiosity as to their movements, but to devote her whole mind to the conversation of the dear old minister. Anything more sad than his aged, utter loneliness, now, her mind could not conceive, remembering 'what had been;' nothing more beautiful than his gentle Christian resignation could be seen. Even now, while rejoicing with him over Luke's visit, she said something of the sort.

'We must all pass through the refining fire, sooner or later, my dear; sooner or later,' said the old man softly. 'For such a long time in my life the Lord had given me only good things; and now should I grumble because since five years a cross is laid upon me, to try how I will bear that? I am old and not capable of much enjoyment, anyway, so why should such as I mind loneliness? And this world is only a probation place, Miss Nannie, in which we are encompassed, remember, with a great cloud of witnesses. When I have been tried sufficiently, then will come the blessed end, and it will be beautiful to lie down leaving my body under the green grass yonder … and to rest' Then, after they were both silent a few moments, he said again: 'Ah! it does not matter for me! It is far sorer, far sharper for those whose time of trial is appointed in youth: for so, humanly speaking, they lose what would otherwise be their season of joy. It is all for the best, we know; no doubt of that, thank God! Still, it makes me very sad when young persons must suffer, and to see them not happy.'

'I *am* happy,' replied Nannie bravely, though with a little choke in her voice, knowing he meant herself. 'When trials come early, one should be all the stronger to bear them. You yourself are always reminding me, we are given no more than we can bear, and I know *that* to be true; and saying it is good for us to have known sorrow, and *that* I feel to be true ! … How often am to tell you that I am contented; believe me, now, once and for all. Nay more; how could I be otherwise, believing fully as I do that my life is ordered all beforehand as the best for me? therefore it seems utterly idle to speculate as to whether any other would not have suited me as well or better, according to our finite ideas. Besides, how many women that are married are unhappy: how many unmarried are happy, though the world only with difficulty believes it!'

'True! true! "the unmarried woman careth for the things of the Lord,"' murmured the old man, raising himself and sitting up straight, with brightening eyes. 'My dear child, it makes me very happy to hear you say that.' Nannie felt much moved. The old minister had never before ventured to address her by such a term of familiar affection; and from that and the expression of his whole gladdened face, she knew he did indeed know for a moment again what it was to feel, in an earthly sense, happy.

They two sat on then in that silence which is full of speech, and gazed out. The pure evening sky was tender, though pale in hue as the old man's peacefully closing life, from which the warmth and colour of day had ebbed; the rush and passion of life had gone past him, too, as from this still eve in which all was hushed. Beyond the green close, hedged with privet, the low orchard-trees made a little alley; all embowered and roofed in sweetly with rosy white blossoms, and beneath the new-sprung grass was thick-strewn with daisies. What a bridal path, for a bridal pair to pass down! But see! what two figures are coming, stepping hither side by side, with a sort of slow, glad lingering in their motion, that may be guessed at rather than discerned from afar? And surely, though so near, they are shy of each other; and surely though shy they are loving; and why Nannie thought all this in a few brief seconds, and held her breath in pure gladness and gazed at them as if thrilled even at that distance by some sympathy of foreseeing knowledge, she could not have told. Yet she did so look, and putting her hand on the old minister's arm in silence, made him see, and he gazed out silently too; seeming to have become aware by that touch of what was passing in her mind. Two happy faces came towards the manse-window; two other faces looked out in welcoming: the old minister's indeed, being full of mild, benignant wonder, but Nannie's seeming with a discreetly unobtrusive gladness to say, 'I foresaw it all; I have been sure it would be so, for a long time; but now I am so glad it is so.' When they came in through the low window, Luke just said, in the expectant silence that reigned unbidden among them, his strong voice trembling with the deep flood-tide of emotion that surged all through him, 'Uncle Joe, I bring you my promised wife.' The old man tried to rise to meet Aileen, but being stiff with rheumatism, and besides trembling very much, remembering such another time when he had thought he blessed Luke's future wife, he was so slow that, before he knew or could hinder it, Aileen had dropped down instead on her knees beside his chair. She could not say one word, although ordinarily so glib of tongue. The old minister laid his hands reverently on that dark, delicate head, while he seemed collecting his bewildered thoughts, and all waited in the solemn hush. Then he raised his eyes to the evening sky, and said with faltering thankfulness, 'I bless the Lord for this great gladness to me, even at the latter end; and may He bless you both … "Lord, now lettest Thou Thy servant depart in peace!"'

That was pleasant weather in the May land, and those were happy eves. But a few days later came a sudden change. A wild wet wind from the west blew the apple-blossoms in the manse-orchard down in showers on the dripping ground; the young leaves in the Black Abbey woods bent shivering before its blast.

It did damage to more than this young existence of nature, for one human one, aged and almost extinct already, that of the former master of Black Abbey, quivered between life and death, as might a feeble flame under its breath. So one morning when the grey dawn brindled coldly up the eastern sky, the watchers in one room of Black Abbey saw only before them a stiff figure of clay, in which they had just watched the last vital spark depart, like a candle snuffed out when the morning light arises.

Thus old Mr. de Burgo was gone at last—whither? Remembering his life, who yet can even dimly surmise where and what like is the dim shadow-land to which wend after death such as he; thought being checked by conscience with that dread warning, 'O man, who art thou that judgest?' And so, as once before at Black Abbey, marrying and burying clashed together; and thoughts of both were strangely mingled, as happens so often in life.

CHAPTER 46

'TAKE IT BACK AGAIN!'

No answer, strangely, came from Hector to his sister's urgent summons that he should come to their grandfather's funeral, and see the last of the De Burgos who had owned Black Abbey laid beside the bones of his ancestors. Nannie had written too, asking him to stay under 'the old rooftree;' thus she phrased it, neither implying that it had been his, nor that it was hers. She had likewise added a loving message to Bonnibel, his wife.

But the two women wondered and waited alone in vain; and the day of the funeral came. Yet no one but the old Presbyterian minister was there to give them any help, or to join them as a mourner; for Luke had perforce returned to London. But just as the dark procession was winding slowly down the approach towards the family burying-place in the Chapel wood—the coffin carried by some of the former De Burgo tenants, for Nannie hated hired mutes and mourning coaches, and she and Aileen thought this simple form of burial the truest and best reverence to the dead—just then they were joined by Hector de Burgo, who arrived travelworn, dusty, and in haste. He took his place in silence, and it was only when the vault was closed, the last ceremony ended, after the knot of farmers from around, and the Black Abbey servants and peasants had begun to disperse, that Nannie and he found themselves touching each other's hands again, over the dead man's grave. Then they two and Aileen quietly walked together towards the old home which had nursed them.

'You are coming to stay with us to-night, and for a little time longer, I hope, Hector?' Nannie asked falteringly, yet with sweet dignity.

'I cannot, indeed! … thank you a thousand times, all the same. Nan; I must catch the afternoon train. But if you will allow me, I should like to go up now for an hour or two and take a last look at the dear old place,' replied the last De Burgo of his race heavily, but wishing, it was evident, to answer with all kindliness.

Nannie understood, remembering it was the first time he had been there since Black Abbey had passed from his family into her own hands. So she only said, 'I hope you can spare me a little time, however, since there is a matter of business connected with your grandfather's death I wish to speak about to you.'

Aileen looked up in amazement; she had heard nothing of this. 'Well—I, too, have something to say to you before you go, Hector,' added his sister, with a vivid blush dyeing her cheek. He nodded, not looking at either of the women, nor thinking much apparently of what they wanted of him; but gazing about him at the trees, his soft, honest soul taking grieved farewell of each that was an old friend since childhood, as Nannie could see. And what a different Hector this was who trode heavily beside her, from the one that the woman who had loved him best in the world had last seen! Nannie's eyes, even at the burial, in one quick grey gleam, had perceived the whole change as others might not. The brave upright air of the former young man had passed away. Hector's bearing seemed now as if—but for the discipline of habit—his broad shoulders would gladly be downbent under burdens before unknown. His body was much stouter; his gait slow beyond his years; his expression dulled. The thought that he must be seeking forgetfulness of some trouble (perhaps of his altered fortune) in too much eating and drinking, without due exercise, passed pitifully through Nannie's mind; for all the man's features, though handsome still, were altered, thickened—and she remembered with touched feelings, yet as if these two were different beings, the chubby, merry boy she had played with in childhood. For if we be like sparks of divine spirit enclosed in clay lanthorns, through some of us (as with Nannie White for one) the light shines ever clearer, brightening towards the end. But with others (as now with poor Hector de Burgo) the spirit-flame burns lower, when, instead of living and striving, we exist and strive not; till the clay case coarsens and becomes the most apparent part of us.

'I am glad I was in time for the funeral,' said Hector at last, breaking the silence as they went back. 'Your letter never reached me till the last moment; for Heavyside and I were off for some days roughing it together in a small cutter of his, and our two wives, during our absence, took it into their heads to go up for a little amusement to London … that is how it came about.' (Yachting, now, in such a friendly way with the man he had used to laugh at and despise for being conjugally befooled and kept under slipper rule. Poor Hector!)

They came out of the deep woods close to Black Abbey itself now; and, looking round, all three who had played there since childhood could not but note how all about the old home, with its ivied gables and weathercocks flashing in the sunlight, was brightened, restored as by a charm, yet unaltered. As of old, pigeons clustered on the steep roofs; a noble peacock strutted in welcoming down the grey horse-shoe steps. They entered the old saloon, where the windows were set wide open as of yore, and all the pleasant scents and sunlight from the flowery, steep garden terraces below stole sweetly in. Looking out to the front of the house, all three keeping mutual silence. Hector gazed fondly on the close-shaven lawns, the clumps of shrubbery and noble standard trees, and further, the low, green, moist meadows, in which the red cows grazed as if they were the very same that fed there twenty years ago. The brook still babbled between its level edges, down from the shining broad mere to the sea of green woodland; beyond which, on the dark-blue sea of waters were many motionless specks afar of ships with idle sails, that warm windless day. All seemed unchanged since they three, as little children, held their solitary kingdom here, and thought there was no such House Beautiful on earth as their own old one among Black Abbey woods. Ah! would they were such little children, happy and innocent, again—thought the disappointed man.

Nannie, anxious again as ever for Hector's wants, offered him refreshment. But saying his time was too short to waste it in eating, he refused everything except some wine; because, seeing how jaded he was, she brought it him with her own hands. Then, first, he took courage to look at her firmly, and see again the sweet face with its somewhat pale cheeks and large grey eyes, and the soft hair meekly brushed back; all so little changed since he had seen it five years ago—except for its great present calm. 'I want to thank you, Nannie, for all you have done for the poor old man, and that with my whole heart,' he faltered with much feeling; 'I could never express what I feel about it; but you have indeed returned good for evil—to us all!'

She made a little gesture of deprecation, but was mute.

'I am glad to have had the opportunity of saying this,' went on Hector in a great heavy voice, 'because I may never have the chance of doing so, or of seeing you and dear old Black Abbey again. For we must be going to India this autumn.'

'Not see Black Abbey again!' cried Nannie, starting, and losing her presence of mind. *'But—oh! Hector—I wanted to ask you now to come back to it—for always!'*

She had uttered the whole wish of her heart. This was the business about which she had wished to speak; this the secret end for which she had been working and hoping these five years back. In the moment's impulse she lost self-possession; forgot all the calm discretion with which she had resolved to lead up to the matter, the long train of grave, well-thought arguments that were to support it; the ingenious colouring by which this offer was to seem not dictated by pure generosity, but as a merely formal affair of sale and barter, of common giving and taking. Then she saw two faces gazing at her in utter amazement, as she breathlessly hurried out her words, 'What do I want with a country place like this? It is a great burden upon me! I only took it to save it for you, hoping you would take back your rightful place some day again. … . And now that your grandfather is dead, there is nothing to keep me here; and I would—I would *like* to go away.' She said that last with brave effort, loving the dear old place as she did, surely, as well as any De Burgo of them all.

But Hector hoarsely answered, 'My dear Nan, what can you mean? Do you not know that I am a very poor man, and could no more buy back my former home than I could fly; if even you are so utterly generous as to give me the chance of doing so.'

'You could pay me by degrees! … It does not matter when! It is in better order now, the whole estate, and you could save off it, instead of spending on it. Oh, Hector! I have in sacred truth always considered I only held it for you till now. For your children's sake! … Let them grow up, as they ought, as De Burgos of Black Abbey. Think of how long your ancestors have held it; of the old associations.'

Nannie's voice failed. Her heart was beating violently with generous agitation; but all her courage died away as she read too truly in the man's face opposite her the signs of gathering determination that presaged the death-knell of her hope. For Hector's face, though stern-set, was alight now; all through his heavy features an inner fire worked. But still as yet—there was so weighty, so solemn a silence that each felt the words coming must be an irrevocable answer, when thus laboured over in thought with a strong man's hard-drawn breathing and swelling of veins. Then it was said—as a doom.

'Nannie, *never* speak of this again! You have been to me like an angel from heaven. Oh, I feel—choked with your generosity! … but you have already heaped enough coals of fire on my head. Don't you understand that I could not accept this from you in honour? Let me suffer the just punishment I deserve—*but never say this again!*' He caught Nannie's hand, pressed it warmly; then hastened out through the open glass door into the solitude of the garden, there to hide his over-mastering emotion unseen.

The two women left behind wept.

Nannie felt utterly bewildered. Was her whole life, then, to be the building of one castle of happiness after another in fancy—each of which must be ruthlessly shattered?

And she had so lived in anticipative delight these past five years, secretly looking forward to restoring Hector to what she called his own again. Not a jot of morbid wish to make him repent his desertion the more by contrast with her own magnanimity had been in it. In pure nobleness of soul, with the old affection she had felt for Hector from childhood, the offer was made; she had not needed to be afraid of loving him too well, knowing she loved in a right way. And therefore she had looked at him this day, as if the period when they had been young man and maiden was dead; or the Hector and Nannie of the glad passionate THEN, were utterly different beings from these of NOW. After all that had been, she felt still the sisterly affection for him of their former new-born innocent lives—only mingled with pity. And now, Black Abbey she loved so dearly was henceforth all her own—hers only! yet bitter tears washed her face There was no earthly point beyond to strive for, no goal of good to others.

'He could not take it from you, dear; he could not in honour,' Aileen consolingly murmured, while crying greatly herself in womanly sympathy. Then, with eyes sparkling through their tears: 'I would disown him for my brother if he did! Although

I feel altogether with you—although I think it is just what you would do, and I might have guessed it all along—still, he never could take it. Content your-self! Black Abbey is in the best hands, and so Providence willed it.'

But Nannie could not as yet receive consolation.

Almost an hour had elapsed before Hector, for whom they sat and waited, returned with very slow footsteps, heavily crunching the gravel upon the terrace. When he came in, Nannie raised her head quickly; then she knew at a glance that the man's heart was hardened. He must have been gazing with deep sorrow at all the well-known nooks, the dear remembered haunts, associated with careless youth; at the cradle of his own glad childhood, and the home of his race that he had always believed in proud confidence must be his own too, till he suddenly knew it was lost to him for ever. And now Hector de Burgo was taking his affliction, as if sent him from below, not from above; as we too often do.

'It is time for me to go, now,' he briefly said, and holding out his strong hand with determination, gave Nannie a farewell grasp that almost hurt her. But his mind must have been struggling with evil thoughts in spite of that show of gratitude in gesture, since he added, 'Thank you again for your offer—but *you must have known* I could not accept it!' That was a stab to the heart of the gentle woman who heard him, and whose sweet dove's-eyes that had been looking up in his face were hastily covered by their meek lids, dropped to hide welling tears. But the man with his stern averted glance saw nothing of this. Poor Nannie almost ejaculated one, '*O Hector—!*' which if uttered in its touching intensity must have melted a heart of stone.

But a choking lump rose in her throat; her sensitive mind, already over-strung, felt cruelly hurt by his unexpected injustice; there was a real pain in her fluttering heart, and so—she was silent.

Hector gloomily prepared to take his leave. But Aileen sprang forward with quick nervousness. 'Stay a few moments, Hector. As my only relation left, I have something to say to you.' The words first hung hesitating a moment on her tongue, then rushed out in a hurry on the top of each other; the vivid impetuous creature could hardly control herself, even now, much more than had the childish mad-cap long ago, who always blurted out everything with directness.

'You—you know Luke Cosby very well—and have always been fond of him; and indeed now he is your own cousin.'

'He is my wife's second cousin, I believe; but I do not acknowledge that that gives him any claim upon me,' replied Hector, gruffly enough. He was annoyed at being stopped short when he wished to go; made hot always at the recollection of Bonnibel's engagement to Luke, of which he had gained knowledge. 'You will make me miss my train, Aileen, with chattering about this Presbyterian fellow, who may be very worthy in his own way, but for whom I don't care two straws. What in the name of goodness have you to say about him to me?'

'This—that I am going to marry him!' flashed back Aileen, quick as lightning. She was annoyed, too, knowing that Hector had ample time to catch his train; while the slighting words about Luke were as a lighted match setting her ready wrath, pride and affection ablaze. Once the words were said, Aileen stood with her head thrown proudly, defiantly back, watching a dark cloud of great displeasure gather slowly on her brother's brow (his mind being always tardy to grasp a new idea in all its bearings); become more lowering and sullen each moment, as he remained in indignant silence. 'Well!' she quickly breathed, 'what have you to say against it? Of course, I am my own mistress; but still, as you are my brother, I should like you to be pleased with him.'

'You!—YOU—Aileen de Burgo—actually mean to marry

Luke—Cosby? slowly ejaculated Hector, bringing all the contemptuous emphasis of which he was capable to bear on each word.

'I do! You married Bella Hawthorn, his cousin; so why should not I marry *him?*'

Her brother stood grasping the back of a chair with his powerful hand, and at that moment resembled somewhat in massive frame and dogged expression, the middle-aged Hercules, represented leaning heavily on his club after troublous toil; the man of action, not thought—life-weary; no longer the youthful hero full of animation, going forth to conquer in his might. He seemed struggling with old passions aroused in his breast, family pride, ambition for his sister at least!—and heaven knows what feelings as regarded his own marriage! Then he thundered, 'I raised my wife to my rank of life, remember. But your husband must debase you to his level'

Aileen satirically began to laugh, uncertain whether not to cry. Debase her! As if Luke Cosby, the good, gifted divine—the great preacher who had won affluence and fame, which he only prized so far as they could be used in his Master's service—was not in a much higher position now than poor dear Hector, whose name and prospects had sunk sadly indeed. Nannie, too (whose nobler spirit despised the small earthly considerations to which Hector still clung, although he had found their vanity) felt at that moment: This is the man to whom I sacrificed the best of my life, thoughts, and love! whom I thought to honour and obey. Twice that day Hector had shown himself unworthy. But with a strong intuition of how, while her mind had gone forward untrammelled, his had been kept at a standstill, or rather dragged down by domestic trouble, and a not ennobling yet most familiar companionship—a great wave of pity washed out her contempt. Meanwhile, Hector bitterly groaned, 'Good heavens! A Presbyterian minister's wife! . . . And if you had only played your cards properly, you might now have been a duchess, and—'

'The wife of a Fool of Quality,' interposed his sister with vivacity, whilst her lovely blue eyes gleamed, and a damask crimson flooded in anger the delicate brown tinge of her cheeks. 'And so I might, but that I made up my mind five years ago to marry no one else but Luke Cosby—*if he would kindly take me*.' With that, as Hector stood dumbfounded, she flashed out of the room in high anger.

Nannie had hitherto stood by like a waiting angel of mediation. She knew the man's soft heart; that he would groan, indeed, but make no more opposition. Now, seeing that Hector still remained in the middle of the saloon lost in heavy thought, but that by the relaxing lines of his face dejection had succeeded anger, she softly asked leave to walk with him down to the lodge, where he must meet the mail-car that went to Redbay. It was a welcome offer to poor Hector, made soothingly as it was; sympathy and the great human relief of talking over this new trouble with a friendly listener being now grateful to the cast-down man, who had passed through such a variety of unusual emotions that day. And, indeed, it was as successful as it was seasonable. For, before they parted, Nannie's sweet reasonableness and powers of persuasion had worked a wonderful reconcilement to the inevitable in Hector's grieved mind.

'Yes!—she was always a bit of a Bohemian at heart; it might have been worse. She might have taken a fancy to some musician of the future, or unappreciated artist,' said the poor man, as they stood together under the last trees that stretched over the highroad outside the demesne. 'But, oh, Nannie, you, who know how proud I was of her, can understand how vexed I am. And I had hoped that she, at least, would not have gone down in worldly position like the rest of us De Burgos. … But worldly ambition and I have now parted company!'

'You still have your profession, remember,' murmured Nannie, knowing he was now singly devoted to it; all outlooks of a country life, that had divided his allegiance being evermore self-closed. 'And so you are going to India this autumn! But why did we never hear of this before? You did not even tell Aileen!'

'Because it is a sudden resolution, and I am exchanging into another regiment to do so. To tell you a little of the truth, Nannie,' said her former lover, dropping his voice, and feeling an irresistible impulse to confide again in the dear companion who had kept most of his secrets since boyhood, 'it has become a necessity to do so. We shall be ruined if we go on living at our present rate; not that Bonnibel' (bitterly) 'seems much to care.'

'But she will like India. I have always heard it is a paradise for women; that it is so—'

'So gay, I suppose. Yes; but we shall be going to one of the dullest of stations, so she is miserable at the idea, for that and—other reasons. But she *must* come.'

Nannie said nothing; feeling what little Hector had said was almost too much, understood as it was by their mutual sympathy that did not need speech. But just as the mail-car came in sight round the far bend of the dusty road under the park wall, she suddenly exclaimed, 'But your two children!! What *is* to be done with them? … You cannot take them abroad?'

Hector looked grieved. 'I can't tell yet. There is no one in my family to whom I can exactly send them; unless poor Aileen will undertake the bother of them. Their mother says they can be sent to the manse—and be brought up like herself.'

'No, no; the good minister is too old. Give them to me!—*do give them to me*,' Nannie begged and prayed, and then finally urged again, after every rapid additional plea she could think of, 'You must!'

Hector dared not give a decided yea or nay; but still, as the post-car, with its reeking* horses, now came rapidly up, he wrung her hand, saying in a moved manner, with most real gratefulness, 'Well, well; we will see about it'

When Nannie went back she found Aileen, after the latter's quickly mutable fashion of mind, already regretting her own sharpness and anger towards Hector. 'I should have been more patient with him. Poor fellow! he sometimes is quite heart-broken. I never told you before, Nannie—but Bella does not care in the least for him! She only wanted his position at first; and now she wants the horrid admiration of other men. She is terribly talked of with that old Colonel Fitzadam, whom you used to admire as a girl, you remember. He is a rich grey-bearded Lovelace; with the face of a satyr and the manners of a saint.'

* reeking = 'steaming' as if giving off smoke

CHAPTER 47

ANOTHER LITTLE NANNIE

One wild autumn night in that same year, Nannie was sitting alone, but pleasurably enough, in the Black Abbey saloon, with the old tapestry curtains closely drawn, a great fire of ash logs leaping in sputtering flame up the old-fashioned chimney, and reflected back in glows of brightness from brazen dogs and fire-irons, while tall wax candles softly shone back double from the silver-framed Venetian mirrors hung against the walls. It was truly pleasant here, indoors; but a wild wet night for anyone to be outside in!

So thought Nan, listening to the wind soughing* through the woods, and then coming with an occasional greay vengeful blast against the window panes, as if it had taken a fickle spite against the thick-walled, comfortable old home. She listened dreamily, too, to distant sounds from the music-room, where the unchangeable old Fräulein was thundering forth classical symphonies in spacious solitude, as she loved, on the noblest of new grand-pianos. They were the self-same melodies resounding through the stillness that in childhood Nannie and Aileen, playing hide-and-seek at Hector's command through the affrighting darkness of the then desolate and unwarmed old house, had listened to before as yet little stealing footsteps made their hearts beat with the terror of a coming 'I spy—!' wondering as they held their breath, how any ten fingers could execute such marvellous music. How like!—yet how more unlike!—this night was to that past time.

* soughing = (of the wind) making a rushing, moaning sound

In Nannie's childhood, the beautifully inlaid wooden floor of the saloon had been dim from ill-polish; the many old-fashioned gildings of the walls tarnished, the ancient satin of the settees worn threadbare under their cotton coverings. Now all had been re-gilded, re-covered, polished, and that in such a spirit of lovingly delicate restoration, that had the De Burgo ancestress of two generations back stepped down from her portrait in the long gallery above, and appeared in the flesh, the room would have seemed to her as vastly handsome in its glowing colours and old-world bravery of adornment, as on her own wedding day. Nannie had dropped her book a little while ago on the Persian hearth-rug, and lulled by the warmth an stillness to laziness, was thinking of the past summer and of how happy she had been while travelling abroad with Aileen and the latter's aunt; thinking of how happy were Aileen and Luke Cosby, now taking their wedding holiday, a rest much needed by the hard-worked pastor … thinking how contented and satisfied with her lot in life she herself had now learned to be; how, asking little, she had yet received so much.

It was only three days since she had returned home to comparative solitude; but she was glad to be back, to get to her congenial task of preparing a book of poetry for the coming year, of which the germ had struck living root in her mind while abroad; and to see that all was set to rights in the demesne and on the whole estate against winter.

Yes; she felt on the whole very contented! The wild storms and passionate waves that had disturbed the summer sea of her youth were now lulled to rest, and she had found peace in a quiet haven. In her poetry she had a never failing occupation, and work that was a delight; work the divine law laid on human beings and the salt of life! She was removed far beyond all want, and her only anxiety was that while relieving the wants of many in a spirit of largest charity, she yet always feared net to be laying out her five talents to the best advantage of the Lord from whom she believed she had received them; and ever wished to do more and more good. So she felt contented and glad in heart of her life, after all that was past, this autumn night. One only thing troubled her, that she had received no answer to her lately-renewed offer of taking the little De Burgo children for some years under her care in the old home, while their parents were abroad. And yet Bonnibel had written during the summer warmly though sorrowfully thanking Nannie for the proposal 'of bringing up her unhappy babes, if their miserable mother was forced to go into exile!' And now it was within three weeks of the time when the latter must go to India with Hector; nevertheless, no appeals by letter were availing to extract any manner of reply from those two worst of correspondents.

It was strange! … but still, very likely some fine morning the children would be dropped at the gate by the mail-car. That would just be like Bonnibel's ways. Or Hector would bring them over suddenly himself, preferring the journey to the trouble of writing a letter. And so, musing dreamily, it grew towards midnight and Nannie grew sleepy, but was too much enthralled by the pervading warmth and comfort to move.

What was that? … a little noise against the window as of a groping hand. Nannie started and sat bolt upright, listening. The windows reached down to the ground, and this central one was made as a glass door, opening on the gravelled terrace. Then there came a subdued tapping on the glass, a footstep on the gravel as some one outside moved. Nannie started up, but hesitated. The circumstance was so unusual, and the hour so late; the servants were all in their beds already in the furthest parts of the house, the Fräulein beyond hearing of a call and deafened by her music. A voice now spoke gently through the window; though what it said Nannie could not tell. Still, gathering bravery from the thought that no midnight robber would be likely to act thus, and having plenty of moral courage (though as to nervousness an utter bodily coward), she went forward, trembling, as have done many heroes, and drew back the curtains.

An old face, on a lower level than her own, was peering into the room, with locks of white hair surrounding it that the wind blew hither and thither. Affrighted, Nannie started back, not recognising who it was in the least, till she heard a well-known aged voice say imploringly, 'Miss Nannie, please let me in. It's only Joseph Cosby—only Mr. Cosby.'

'Oh, come in,' cried Nannie, quickly unbarring the door, and bringing in the poor minister, whose coat was streaming with rain, while a gust of wind entering after him blew out some of the candles, and seemed almost to shake his feeble frame. 'What a terrible night for you to be out in! But—but—what is wrong?' For old Cosby's agitated expression, yet apparent anxiety to collect his well-nigh spent energies, was evident.

'Hush, Miss Nannie, my dear; don't let the servants hear; that is why I came round to this window, instead of ringing at the door—to prevent gossip, you know,' maundered her midnight guest, as if she must know the cause of his caution; then, collecting his wits, added, 'for Bonnibel—my granddaughter—has come back to me to-night. She is down at the manse, now.'

'She has not quarrelled with Hector?—not left him?' ejaculated Nannie, in shocked sorrow, although even before the grandfather pitiably nodded that it was indeed so, she knew the truth by intuitive sympathy.

'Ay! I don't yet know what it was about. But an hour ago she came, and had just strength left to lift the latch; and then fell down in a dead faint on the threshold of the kitchen, where old Mary was. She had missed the last mail-car, and could only get some one to give her a lift to the cross-roads in the bog, and all the rest of the six miles she has walked.'

'What!—after her long journey?' ejaculated Nannie, horror-stricken, and knowing from Bonnibel's last letter that she was in no fit state of health for such an undertaking. Even by day, that road was drear, windy and desolate enough; but on such a pitch-dark night of cold and rain, she shuddered to think of the contrast between herself sitting these past hours so snug and sheltered here, and that poor outcast wanderer.

"Deed, yes; it will be the death of her, I fear, my poor girl! We roused up the boy, and sent him riding the old mare to Redbay for the doctor; and then, as I could do no more good in the house, I came to tell you,' answered the old minister, with quiet resignation, softly wiping the tears that ran as softly down his old face.

'I am coming with you at once.' Even while she spoke, Nannie was considering all that must be done, with a wonderful self-possession and constrained presence of mind that were most necessary at such a critical time for others; the instant message to the doubtless indignant or distracted husband, letting him know in what good keeping but state of danger, as she now learned by further particulars from the old minister, his wife was; the necessities and help that must be supplied from Black Abbey. Once these were done, and done quickly, she hastily put on a hat and thick cloak, and giving her arm to support the tottering steps of her old companion, they went down through the dark night and thick woods, the wailing wind, and driving rain showers. Two feelings were struggling together in Nannie's mind. She tried not to judge; and yet pity for the sick woman strove with still greater pity for the injured husband, raising indignation against his wife. No one who knew anything about the characters of the couple in question, even though having heard as few details of their married life as Nannie (who shrank from hearing of the hopelessly disappointed lives, and differences of these two), could reasonably doubt that the blame of this last rash and unhappy flight must be Bonnibel's mostly, if indeed not hers alone. Hector had truly been patient and longsuffering enough; having borne with her extravagance, petulance, and love of admiration under an honest, resigned idea that he ought to try and atone thus for his wife's terrible disappointment on discovering his want of fortune.

So the woman perforce thought, who had so faithfully befriended and tried to succour both, casting all memory of her own injuries far behind her; while yet endeavouring not to judge as she hastened on her errand of mercy through the woods.

But—when Nannie entered the little room upstairs in the manse, that had been given up to herself by its rightful owner for so many months, and saw by a solitary candle a figure lying death-like on the bed, while Old Mary moaned and rocked herself in useless woe beside it—she forgot all indignation, all the petty neglect and small daily injuries of husband and children laid to the charge of the stricken creature before her. 'Poor Bonnibel; my poor Bonnibel!' she softly said; was all she could think of, in a rush of great pity and affection, 'Do you know me, dear?—it is I, Nannie.' With a gleam of gratitude, the sufferer slowly unclosed those lustrous brown eyes that Nannie had not seen for five years.

'I have come back here to die, you see. … It is all over with me now, I feel … Stay by me, stay by me, Nannie, won't you?—to the last,' she murmured, too exhausted it seemed to have much dread of death or wish for life; only a yearning for rest, rest and peace—now she was in her own old home again at last. And Nannie faithfully promised to stay with her …

During the night, the angels of death and life seemed engaged in silent struggle about that couch; the messenger of death claiming the mother and the newborn infant too, which by the morning's dawn saw the light, that of life interceding for the latter and at last it seemed prevailing—although the issue hung doubtful. 'Take her, and bring her up yourself,' Bonnibel feebly said, when Nannie brought the dying woman this news, and asked what name she wished given to her child. 'Let her be another little Nannie. … You will teach her to be a better woman than I have been.'

Through most of next day, Bonnibel remained in lethargy, yet Nannie would never leave her side, to take even a few moments of needed rest; watching the dying with unceasing vigilance and tenderest, truest devotion. She feared lest by any unhappy chance, by only an instant's absence, she might break her promise of being with her departing friend at the last—even although the latter might still be unconscious.

Poor soul! poor handsome Bonnibel, what a sad end was this!

Thus, sitting for long hours since dawn, Nannie watched alone by the bedside of the woman who had most wronged her. The unhappy aged grandfather could not bear the sight long. He was on his knees in the study below, seeking strength in agonized prayer, the doors being left a little ajar that he might hear it the instant there was any stir in the sick-room. Old Mary, too, had to be banished; since she had broken out sobbing several times when she looked at the still figure of her former charge, whom she had reared so faithfully, if roughly, since that May evening when the merry little child was brought home in the old gig by Mr. Cosby.

So Nannie sat; often praying in her heart, thinking and silently praying again that autumn day; while not a sound was to be heard in the hushed manse, but occasionally a feeble cry from the babe in an adjoining room. Looking at the handsome head, with its rich and glossy brown hair, that she had not now seen for more than five years, Nannie remembered the little girl from the manse whom the Black Abbey children had petted, patronised, and admired; their games together in the woods; her eagerness to share in her companions' superior accomplishments, yet laziness to learn, ending in pretty, superficial mimicry. Later, how warmly loving she had shown herself when Nannie most sorely needed a friend and refuge! Although that feeling might have been shallow (according to her nature), yet it was genuine. She had yielded to inward tempting, to the lust of the eye and the pride of life; and carried away by these passions, had well-nigh ruined Nannie's happiness—thank God! only well-nigh—but wrecked her own. Five miserable years had seen her secret disappointment; her rage against ill-fortune, weariness, longings for distraction, and surely, surely!—hidden remorse for the evil she had done, secret cause of the petulance that had led to this last foolishly fatal step.

As Nannie so sat, she became aware of a slight flutter of the eyelids, a faint indefinable change like a languid setting in again of the tide of life in the comely, marble-white face at which she gazed. Then Bonnibel very slowly opened her eyes, those eyes once so scintillating, alas! now dulled and filming, but with more sensible recognition in them than Nannie had yet seen there since the previous night.

'Are you there, dearest Nan? I like to know you are beside me,' she faintly breathed, 'what o'clock is it?'

'It is three in the afternoon,' Nannie softly replied, bathing the sufferer's temples to revive her; and giving her some strengthening restoratives, with all the outward gentle calm of a faithful nurse, but a pang in her heart, thinking that this sudden revival was only the last upflaring of the lamp of life in its socket before going out.

'Raise the blind more, Nan; I want to see the sky above the Black Abbey trees The sun will soon be going down behind them, will it not? I always liked watching that … Dear old room, dear old home! rest, rest! no more worries, no whirl—peace!' The tears brimmed in Nannie's eyes at the weakness and weariness, the utter yearning for rest expressed in those accents;

but not daring to betray her emotion, for fear of exciting the dying woman, she looked out skywards, too; and only let her hand go out gently to cover the other's powerless fingers with a soft warm touch.

'But this should be your room! … I always liked you to have our best room when you came to us—our outcast princess, you were, you know,' went on Bonnibel, in a dreamy way, that showed the past and present were merged together in her mind. 'And when will—will Luke come?'

'You mean Hector, dear one; Hector, your husband, do you not?' said Nannie, in a very tremulous tone, dreading lest her correction should have dangerous consequences. For the slightest emotion might now be fatal, and a touch might shake out the life-sand that had run so low in its hour-glass, yet she longed with all the earnestness of her soul to heal the breach between this wife and husband. But the other only vaguely answered, as if nothing could now trouble her any more, she and life being ready to sunder soon softly from each other. 'Poor Hector! He was very angry with me about Colonel Fitzadam and those other men! . … but I never cared for anyone of them. Only in one's heart life seemed so wretched and disappointing, that I always longed to go out and amuse myself, and forget all about it; and it was so pleasant to be admired! … Poor Hector! he need not have minded, for I was always fond of him; he was so good and honest—*but*' (fixing her brown eyes with a sudden illuminating gleam full on Nannie's face, and dropping her voice to a low but earnest whisper that showed she was uttering the secret of her heart), 'the only man I ever truly loved in all my life was my cousin—Luke!'

The sweet face of the watcher beside her looked down on the poor speaker with ineffable pity, but showed no other sign; no pharisaical judgment, no memory of self-injury. If it were so, what a doubly-disappointing and miserable existence must

Bonnibel's late years indeed have been! Why had she said it now? Was it that her life, seeming a lie and illusion, it was a comfort to speak out the truth at last to one sympathetic human soul—since, while appearing to have been passionately in love with Hector, her fancy had been only an idle one, fanned by ambition; that while thinking to become mistress of Black Abbey, she had lost this and even the somewhat more affluent circumstances in which Luke could have placed her? And, as the latter's wife, she no doubt now thought, whether rightly or wrongly, she would have been happy.

'Come here, closer—so,' went on the dying woman, looking with real affection into Nannie's face, who still held her hand, quieting her with its warm pressure, by little soothing gestures, and murmurs of consolation. 'I always loved you, Nannie, as much as it was in me to love anyone; you believe me? I wish I had let Hector marry you! … but when I am gone I hope you will be his second wife, and a mother to my poor children. I was always jealous, Nan, but still, I would rather know you in my place than anyone else; besides, it seems yours by right.'

'Oh, Bonnibel, I dare not answer. I cannot tell what may be,' cried poor Nannie. 'I could have married Hector before, because we had grown up together, and he understood me as no one else ever could; and marriage otherwise would, perhaps, never do for me, because I have been brought up so far from the world, and wedded to my own thoughts and ways in solitude. But now, we have grown so much apart during these last five years that I do not know whether we can ever draw together again. … Only as to the children, I have always meant to leave Black Abbey, and all I have, to them; and if, while Hector is away in India, he will give them to me, I do promise you to try and be all to them you could have been.'

'More!' murmured the mother, with almost an amused smile playing on her handsome, voluptuously formed features; too weak to feel lively gratitude, too weak to feel self-reproach. 'Poor little wretches! I never cared for children much, you know, and it was a great plague to look after them; so I am glad you will do it. Perhaps I ought to make a fuss about them now, but there is no use in pretence, and I can't change suddenly—as one has lived, so must one die! The only three persons I feel sorry for are Luke, Hector, and you—for you all loved me, and I ruined your lives.'

'No, no; do not blame yourself,' earnestly expostulated Nannie. 'For myself, I know—perhaps because I accepted God's will—it has turned out best for me to be alone. I should have worshipped Hector too much if I had married him; and we have no right to hoard the love for one alone any more than for self, that God has given us to spend on all His creatures, even our enemies.'

A dreamy smile sweetened Bonnibel's face while she gazed on the speaker, as if comforted by the sound of those words, while yet her mind hardly took in their meaning. Then her glossy brown head turned once more close to its pillow, as if she had said her say, and nothing remained but to seek rest. The old minister now stole softly in. Nannie had not liked to call him before, till the dying woman had privately disburthened her mind of what she had apparently much wished to say; but now, bending over his granddaughter, who lay like a broken lily, he asked, his voice shaking with intense suppressed emotion, whether he might read some of the psalms he had selected as suitable to her state, and make a prayer.

'Yes,' she whispered back dreamily as before, 'only don't cry, gran'dad: let no one cry; I cannot bear that'

So in the solemn hush and sacred atmosphere of that chamber of death, both the living read and prayed with all their souls and strength while the afternoon waned; and the dying lay in stillness, with eyes sometimes unclosing to watch the red sun go down towards the west. Just as it became a fire-ball sinking behind the Black Abbey trees, there was a slight stir in the house, rather felt than heard by the watchers, and they knew Hector had come. Nannie slipped down to meet and warn him. Only thanks to her prompt message (so the poor man muttered, wringing her hand) he was in time. He had done his wife the injustice of supposing her fled with Colonel Fitzadam, and had returned baffled from his search; next, he thought she had surely taken refuge with Mrs. Heavyside, whom poor Bonnibel had declared in anger a few days before to be her only true friend, when Hector jealously accused her of abetting his wife in her flirtations.

Nannie led him grief-stricken upstairs, and left him alone with his wife, who seemed little moved by pleasure or pain at sight of him, yet dreamily satisfied as she murmured, 'Poor Hector—you are come?'

What passed between them none ever knew; but the others waited below with praying hearts, and sometimes quick-caught breath, and with anxiously listening ears—knowing the end was so near. At last they heard a low, alarmed call from Hector, who knew they were close by. They hurried in, and saw by the change in her face that the wayfarer had already almost reached that gate, black on this earthly side of ours, surely bright on that: it is called here the gate of Death; surely it is called yonder the gate of Life … that vast unknown life, wherein may be possibilities and depths of mercy and forgiveness not to be gauged by our poor finite minds, who yet may surely grasp, with all our strength of hope, that blessed divine saying, 'God is Love.'

Bonnibel feebly put out her hand, and taking Nannie's on one side of her, placed it in that of Hector. Then she smiled on her grandfather, who, with his silver hair falling on his shoulders, and his hands clasped in intense prayer, stood bowed forward on the rail at the foot of her bed. 'Give my love to—Luke,' she breathed; then with a gentle sigh, fell back in the arms of her husband and of Nannie.

And so she passed away from them, poor, pretty Bonnibel!

. . . . .

CHAPTER 48

THE END

WHAT yet remains to tell?

When seven more years have come and gone; when again the noble Black Abbey woods are fresh with brightest verdure under the temperate June sun and cool moisture-laden skies of Northern Ireland; while still the ships, like white specks, pass to and fro afar on the dark-blue gleaming sea beyond these tree-tops, and all nature, as ever is, seems unchanged since thirty years back outside the grey lichened walls of the ancient home of the De Burgos—anyone remembering that bygone time when this story opened, and now standing on the stone terrace, before the door, might well rub surprised eyes a moment, and wonder whether inside the inmates were not also still as unchanged! . . . whether these woods were not under the same spell as those which once enclosed the sleeping princess; and that time had stood still on its dial.

For down the well-worn horse-shoe steps leading to this terrace run three laughing children, just as when this tale began; a merry boy the leader, followed by two younger girls. But this is not a little Hector, but a young Hugh de Burgo, whose features, perhaps handsomer and more keenly marked than those of his father, revive the memory of his great-grandfather, who was buried some seven years ago in the monks' old graveyard behind the Chapel Wood. A bewildering likeness, since with all his promise of having inherited the personal beauty for which that snowy-haired ancient beau was well known in his fast, dandified youth, this little lad's clear resolute eyes have none of the cruel, hawk-like fixity that made his great-grandsire so often disliked and feared; while his broad brow has an expression of being honest as day that bids fair to outlive the innocence of mere childhood.

His next sister, too, whom they call Ailie, to distinguish her from an aunt Aileen, surely does not resemble the latter, but far more, with her chestnut hair and bright brown eyes, a certain small lass nicknamed Bonnibel, who used to come hither, to play, from the manse long ago. But the youngest of all, 'little Nan,' as every one fondly terms her, does sometimes indeed in her demure shy ways amusingly recall the former Nannie, no doubt owing to her training by the latter and the unconscious mimicry of infancy. A grave little maid she is, careful of the whiteness of her frocks, and with a chubby open face and flaxen hair curling at her neck, that almost ludicrously picture again her father Hector; and she is the best-beloved of the woman's heart who has reared her, and been a very mother in all but name to these three children whom seven years ago she received home under the roof of their ancestors.

Two women are standing now on the terrace, watching the boy and girls at play; one the Nannie of old, the other Aileen. Luke Cosby, too, gaunt and cheerful as ever, is smoking under the shady yew hedges of the garden close by, where the fountain is plashing* coolly, and a hundred birds are singing in and out the flowery pastures and shrubberies. He is thoroughly enjoying his rest, having been tramping since early dawn on a round of the parish, as is his first delight when he comes on a yearly holiday to Black Abbey; revisiting all the haunts of his youth, and remembering how the fish of the sea, and the birds of the air, and the beasts of the field (the latter, however, few thereabouts!) had cause to dread the young sportsman, whom the lord of the soil in those days called a poacher. But he no longer cares to

* plashing = splashing

go to the dear old manse; rather now stands at the bend of the road, near the farm-gate leading into the Black Abbey demesne, seeing thus from afar the little white-washed house nestling among its few elms and ashes, with the garden-strip at its feet and the orchard beyond. To go nearer, would be to destroy the associations that Luke loved to keep fresh and unspoiled in his memory; for a younger minister, with a commonplace wife and noisy children, lived now under that humble manse roof, and the place of the Reverend Joseph Cosby knew him no more. The good old man laid down his life gladly, not many weeks after his beloved granddaughter; he had but lived to see her again, he was once heard to murmur in his last days. He died, ready to exclaim like Cicero, 'Oh! the beautiful day when I shall journey to that heavenly assembly, that divine council of the souls, … dissevered from this heap of earthly clay.' And for many years afterwards old Mr. Cosby's name was still blessed and revered among the elder folk around; what more need he have wished?

'And so Hector will be back this summer? You hear from him much more often than I do, Nannie.'

'Yes; but then I write to him each mail, to keep him up in the knowledge of how the children are, and what they are like, and what doing,' answered the other, with a sweet gravity befitting her years.

Nannie's cheek, always softly pale, even in the tender bloom of youth, is as softly faded now. Her fair hair is already so much streaked with silver, that people say, with surprise, it will be snow-white by the time she is forty; and wonder whether it is being a poetess, or the sudden disappointment about her marriage in past youth, or the sole cares of a large estate—a heavy burden for a single woman's shoulders to bear—that have aged her so much before her time. But others, like the now matronly but vivacious Mrs. Cosby—whose beautiful eyes and high-bred face are still admired by strangers, whom the fame of her husband's preaching brings in crowds to his great London chapel—declare ardently that Nannie does not look really aged, and never can.

'White hair is lovely!' exclaims the sprightly little lady; she would like to wear her own dark locks powdered. And any one ought to see that Nannie's poet-eyes are still as deep and limpid as ever, and her brow wonderfully smooth, showing how clear and serene is the spirit dwelling beneath, unruffled by earthly storms; while the now irresistible grace of her manner and tender stateliness which have—some think strangely—only increased in attractiveness with her years, is the true sign of those who have most nearly approached that earthly realisation of the beautiful, the perfect union of noble mind with matter! What in comparison with such loveliness of spirit shining through the outer form, they say, is flesh and blood fairness, red and white colouring that is merely material; and that too often in its over-lusty youth dominates the spirit?

The people that said this were, perhaps, few; but they knew and loved Nannie greatly. The rest of the world looked upon her as a rich spinster, jilted in youth: an old maid, now the mistress of Black Abbey. They, too, might have admired, even loved her for her gift of poetry, but that to the end of her life she kept its secret close, feeling that women who step before the public must brave themselves to meet with and endure the rough jostling and neighbour's fare of life, while that she, owing to her lonely up-bringing, sensitive poet-nature, and perhaps past trials, was happiest unknown and in still seclusion.

Nannie went on, 'I think it is a matter of duty for me to write to Hector, giving full details of what some people might, without thinking, call too trivial matters relating to the children. For it is the little things in every-day life—the little gladnesses and sorrows, the little jokes and rubs, shared together—that link us by a thousand small fetters in families. And so, I trust. Hector will not have to meet his children feeling himself a stranger.'

'And, *I* trust,' interposed Mistress Aileen meaningly, with a keen glance, 'that he will get a different answer on another matter, from one that sent him back to India again four years ago.'

Nannie's face, that had worn a restful, dreaming expression, now was roused, and became suffused, in a moment, as with a wave of life, light, and brightness, that lingered a moment or two, then slowly receded; or it might be compared to the flooding of a summer night sky with soft lightning. Her friends loved to see her thus lit up with vivid, if passing emotion.

'I do not know; I cannot tell,' she replied, as she had answered Hector's dying wife seven years ago. 'At that time, as you might remember, I felt that we could best do our several work in the world singly. Hector had so thrown all his energies into his profession that he naturally wished to return to India and his regiment; besides, the times were stirring; and I was glad: he would not have borne to sit down tamely here, where there was no work requiring a man's help. But my duty was plainly at home. Little Nannie was ill, the other children required my care; and the estate could not at that time have been managed so well without me, for no one else quite understood all the improvements I wanted carried out. … Besides, we were past the first flush and passion of youth. I have never thought that the only aim, only meaning of a woman's life—though it is the Christian type of earthly happiness—must be marriage alone. Look! the noblest works are done in the land by the unmarried women, to whom all the orphans are as children, and who, while single, can best strive and toil for the wicked and sick and sorrow-laden.'

'True, true,' murmured Aileen in assent, but with a fine thread of disappointment running through her voice; then added rather weakly, 'Still, I always thought that—if you ever married any one, it must be Hector.'

'Yes, if—' smiled Nannie, as if while so using speech that might sound conceited and self-sufficient, she did not, in truth, consider herself as having ever been much worth the having. 'You know since your grandfather's death, since my recluse days, I have met other men in the world, some of whom liked me; and who perhaps were more clever, and as pleasant or pleasanter, and even better men then Hector! but he alone seemed my fate. It is so with some people, and they are not always the happiest'

'But now that Hector has done his work well, according to your creed—that the poor fellow has lost his right arm in this wretched African campaign, and has had illness enough if he has not had glory! He is poor, remember, and will not like to—what then?' asked Aileen, incoherently indeed, but with a breathlessness of earnest that conveyed more than ever she could have spoken.

'Hector knows that I consider I am only holding this estate for him; and if he *will* not take it from me, then I shall offer it to his boy, when little Hugh comes of age. They could hardly both submit me to the terrible disappointment never to have the one wish of my life realised—of seeing the De Burgos back at Black Abbey,' answered Nannie, with a steady voice, as if being in middle life, now some years past thirty, there could be no romance in so speaking. 'But—the estate has grown rather much for me since we bought back the land your grandfather sold. Hugh is outgrowing a woman's rule, and I have hardly time with other duties to educate little Ailie and Nan myself, as I would wish very much to do. … So it will be a great help to me if Hector cares now to come and sit down under his own vine and fig-tree.'

If! Aileen believed she knew the issue of that; and Hector de Burgo was on his way—*home!*

THE END.

GLOSSARY

ay, aye = yes

be'd to be = had to be

blathering = talking nonsense

bonny = pretty, attractive

bummle = turmoil

byre = cow-shed

certain sure = certain

childer = children

clever = completely

colloguing = conspiring

comp'ny = guests

consaity = proud

cratur = person

dandered = strolled

drim-and-dru = whining, sing-song tone

evening = comparing

feared = frightened, afraid

gimme =give me

gladiathering = attacking in unwarranted persecution

granda = grandfather

hauns = hands

hoke = dig, rummage

hunch = hunk or thick slice of bread

immejently = immediately

intill = into

is = are (plural subject) ("'My puppies is growing big,' uttered poor Hector, trying to be brave; but, in his flutter of mind, using the bad grammar he heard among the labourers. 'Is they?' mimicked his grandfather, with a withering expression. 'Those are no doubt the expressions you pick up from the low company you are so fond of; from that old brute Robert and the rest. I am thinking of giving those puppies a present to Lord William, and if you use such language again I shall.'")

lad = youth

lass, **lassie** = girl

lone (my lone) = alone (myself alone)

moily = hornless (breed of cow)

na = no

nawt = not

nawthing = nothing

niver = not (Na; niver a worrd.')

nor = than

oanee! = alas!

orphant = orphan

ould = old

owned = admitted

paple = people

parable = long-winded account of faults and misdeeds

peety = pity

plashing = splashing

purtect = protect

purtier = prettier

put upon = taken advantage of

reeking = smoking, steaming

rough-yun = ruffian

runshled = crunch

sax = six

scrabble = scribble

shandrydan = rickety converance

shuggar = sugar

soughing = rushing, moaning sound of the wind

sowl = soul

Steenson = Stevenson ('His name was John Stevenson, though the people here give me Steenson, for short.')('The folk here give me Steenson, for shortness, but Stevenson was the right name,' said the poor soul, using the old formula they all knew since childhood.)

tay = tea

thon, yon = that

till = to

took = taken

took up with = formed a new relationship with

twelvemonth = a year

wean = child

wee = small

weel = well

wet = brew (tea) (with the black kettle for 'Miss Bella to wet the tay')

whack = large quantity

whenever = when

whilom = former

whullabaloo = widespread rumour

word = news (ye didn't hear no word of my husband out in Ohio—John Steenson?')

wreath = snow-drift

wynd = horse command (to turn left)

ye = you

yon, thon = that

yun = one

Printed in Great Britain
by Amazon

64058804R00271